Death of a Mossad Man

"Stop them." Mikael was looking down at his chest in amazement, watching the blood flow out of three bullet holes. "Stop them," he repeated.

Thorpe started to poke his head up to take a look, but bullets tore up the edge of the road inches away and he ducked down. He heard a door slam on one of the vehicles. The firing from the front was dying down.

"Stop them!" Mikael was on his knees, staggering to his feet, bringing his weapon up. Thorpe reached for him when a line of bullets smashed into the Mossad man's chest, blasting him backward and causing Thorpe to dive for cover once more.

The Land Rover roared by, Akil spraying a full magazine out the window; then it was gone. Thorpe had his back against the side of the ditch nearest the road. Mikael was lying at his feet, empty eyes staring up into the dark sky . . .

THE OMEGA SANCTION

JOE DALTON

St. Martin's Paperbacks

THE OMEGA SANCTION

ISBN: 0-312-97188-5

Printed in the United States of America

St. Martin's Paperbacks edition/November 1999

St. Martin's Paperbacks are published by St. Martin's Press, 175 Fifth Avenue, New York, N.Y. 10010.

10 9 8 7 6 5 4 3 2 1

THE OMEGA SANCTION

Chapter One

The top of the castle wall looked like black teeth against the night sky, the space between the stone blocks where the soldiers of old had kept watch for approaching enemies. The castle was set on a small hill with a commanding view of the surrounding terrain for many miles. It had been built five centuries ago and rebuilt and added to many times over the intervening years.

The castle, around which the small German town of Bad Kinzen had grown, held a dark reputation. The people in the town rarely spoke of it openly. The SS had garrisoned a battalion in the castle during World War II, appreciating the high ground and the numerous stone rooms they could use to hold prisoners. In those rooms many Resistance fighters shipped from France had met their screaming deaths. In the rooms above the dungeon, young women had suffered their own shameful fate at the hands of the all-powerful SS. It was a subject rarely talked about among the elders in town except in whispers and after too much beer. The young didn't know the details, but they picked up the emotional drift and the castle held its own dark place in their minds.

Before the war, the Kinzen family had controlled the castle for generations and there had been whispers even then about what went on behind the massive stone walls. The Kinzen family had held a recessive gene that had come out every couple of generations and led to madness and perversion. Unfortunately, there was little that could be done about the madness, as the Kinzens were the wealthiest and most powerful family this side of Stuttgart. Before the rise of modern law, the Kinzens had held sway over the town and practiced their depredations against the citizenry inside the walls of the castle.

Going back even before the Kinzens, the castle, built in the late 1400s, had seen more than its share of death as the religious wars washed back and forth across Germany. A Protestant enclave had sought shelter behind its walls and held out for two years before Catholic forces under the emperor had starved them into surrendering. As they walked out under a white flag, every Protestant man, woman and child had been thrown into the moat and kept down there by spearpoint until all were dead. It was said at the end there was a pile of bodies with the strongest on top, above the foul water, and the last man to die took over a week, standing on top of an island of festering bodies, forced to drink the foul water even as his belly burst from hunger.

Such was the history of Bad Kinzen Castle until the Americans took it over at the end of World War II. It served first as the headquarters for the local military governor, then, as the Germans gained self-rule, it became the headquarters for various U.S. Army units, the last being a Pershing missile battalion. There were numerous other American units stationed around the town of Bad Kinzen, as the headquarters for the Seventh Corps and U.S. Army Europe were just down the road in Stuttgart.

With the collapse of the Berlin Wall in 1989 and the drawdown in forces, Bad Kinzen took its own share of cutbacks in American troops. The Pershing missile unit was withdrawn and the castle was empty once more. The Americans wanted to turn the castle over to the German government, but the debt-ridden federal government, still reeling from the negative economic attachment of East Germany, preferred the rent rather than the maintenance burden of the castle, so for the past eight years it had remained nominally rented to the Americans even though it was no longer utilized.

The castle had deteriorated over the years it was left abandoned. The massive stone wall surrounding it was still intact, as it had been for hundreds of years, but the buildings on the inside were dilapidated and falling apart. The moat, the death place of hundreds, was now dry, and the drawbridge had long ago been replaced by a permanent concrete bridge leading over the ditch. The road went through the wall and into the large open courtyard. A fence had been put across the bridge to prevent entry, but it had taken less than a week for a hole to be torn in it. The facilities engineers from Seventh Corps repaired the fence every few months, but by the end of the next weekend another hole always appeared.

Despite the removal of the Pershing unit, there were still Americans near Bad Kinzen. The Seventh Corps was headquartered at Stuttgart, although many of the soldiers were currently deployed on peacekeeping missions to Bosnia and the Belorussia. The castle, off limits to Germans because it was in American hands—and perhaps as much because of its dark past—was a draw to the teenage children of those American soldiers and it was they who tore holes in the fence as quickly as it was repaired.

Too young to drink legally, hassled by Military Police on post and German Polizie off, the American teenagers went to Bad Kinzen Castle, where MPs never visited and the Polizie were forbidden to go. The teenagers partied and hung close to each other, strangers in a distant land, with parents who were gone more often than they were home. They only had each other and they clung to that.

In a battered Camaro, two of those displaced youngsters were currently driving through the winding streets of Bad Kinzen, heading toward the hill on which the castle stood. Kirsten Welch was sixteen, a junior at the American high school in Stuttgart and she had been to Bad Kinzen Castle dozens of times in the past, the last four times with Tommy Pilchen, a senior at the same school. But she had never been there on a weeknight and just the two of them. Always before it had been the weekend and at least a dozen other dependent kids that had convoyed to the castle.

But Tommy had said tonight was special when he'd asked her to go during lunch break at school. Kirsten knew what that meant. Tommy's father was PCSing, army lingo for permanent change of station, back to the States in a week, and that meant Tommy would be gone soon.

They'd been going together for three months and things had progressed to the point where she had made sure that Tommy had condoms in his pocket before they left Pattonville Housing Area earlier in the evening.

It was late November and it got dark and cold early. Her contribution to the trip was several blankets piled in the back seat of the car. A six-pack of beer was on top of the blankets, another prerequisite Kirsten insisted upon.

They parked next to a construction site at the base of the hill on which the castle stood. Tommy threw the blankets over his shoulder and they walked the switchbacks up to the bridge. Tommy held the fence while Kirsten squeezed through.

They had spoken little on the ride down. Kirsten knew Tommy was thinking about going back to the States and she was thinking about how much she was going to miss him. Having been a military brat all her sixteen years, Kirsten knew it was the nature of things that friendships were brief, as each family moved every three or four years. But Tommy was more than a friendship. He was her first boyfriend, and considerable emotion and time had gone into this in the past three months. She'd given him a special part of herself and now he was going to be leaving with it.

They walked across the bridge, and Kirsten halted just before the tunnel through the outer wall. She didn't like Bad Kinzen. The tunnel opening looked like a gaping mouth to her, with two portals above it set like eyes in the black rock. The wind blew and she hugged Tommy closer to her.

"I wish my mom was working tonight," she said.

Then they could have used her house, as they had many times in the past. Her father was a squad leader in one of the infantry battalions and he had been gone now for three months to Bosnia-Herzegovina on the U.S.'s seemingly never-ending peacekeeping effort in the Balkans. Her mom worked in the housing area Burger King on a rotating shift, but tonight she was home, curled in front of the TV watching the Armed Forces Network and steadily drinking enough so that she could pass out in an empty bed. Her only comment to Kirsten on her way out was to be home before one.

"Me too," Tommy said. He tugged her forward toward the tunnel. "But at least I got the car so we could come here."

As they walked into the tunnel, their sneakers squeaked on the rock floor and echoed off the walls that closed over their heads. Water dripped from the stone, making slimy puddles. Their pace picked up and then they were into the courtyard. Tommy led her toward a low building built up against the stone wall to their right. It had been the headquarters for the Pershing unit and was now littered with empty bottles, needles and used condoms. Some enterprising soul had even hauled a stained mattress up here, but Kirsten didn't like it, thus the blankets.

Tommy pushed open the door, which protested loudly on its rusted hinges. Kirsten scuttled by him into the dark interior. She quickly took the blankets, putting half on the floor, and wrapping one over her shoulders as she sat down. She was small under the rough wool, just under five-foot-two, and weighing slightly over a hundred pounds. She had short hair that she bleached blond and combed straight back with plenty of gel to keep it in place. A long earring dangled from her right ear, while a small gold ring adorned her nose.

She could see out a broken window into the courtyard as Tommy settled down beside her, pulling the blanket over his shoulders and pressing his body against her side.

"Here," Tommy said, handing her a can from the six-pack he had carried up along with the blankets. She took it and popped the top. Despite the chill, she drank fast. If she'd ever stopped to think about it, she would have realized she'd never had sex with Tommy sober. But that was just one of many things that Kirsten and most other sixteen-year-olds had never stopped to think about.

Tommy pulled out a sandwich bag and waved it. "I got some good stuff off Pete."

He began rolling a joint, much to Kirsten's irritation. She didn't like drugs, even just grass. Too many kids at school were walking around wasted all the time, not even knowing what class they were in, and she knew every one of them had started with grass before moving on to heavier stuff. And the heavy stuff brought with it other problems, like AIDs. Heroin was big at school and readily available off post, but the needles scared Kirsten to death. Tommy hadn't done that yet, at least as far as she knew. She didn't ask, but she always covertly checked his arms for any sign that he might have used a needle. She loved him, but she wasn't willing to die for her love.

Tommy lit the joint and took a deep drag. He offered it to her, but she declined by taking another deep gulp of her beer. He didn't push. They'd talked about it before, and tonight, with his departure looming in a week, it just wasn't worth talking about anymore. She felt a rush of sadness and pulled Tommy closer.

A shadow passing by the window caught the corner of her eye and she stiffened.

"Hey!" Tommy exclaimed, trying to dig her fingers out of his shoulder.

"Someone's out there," Kirsten whispered.

Tommy looked out the window. The courtyard was empty, lit by the glow of a half-moon. "I don't see anyone."

"I did," she insisted.

"Well, someone could be up here. You know, someone from school."

Kirsten shook her head. "I don't want to be here. Let's leave. Please."

She felt Tommy stiffen. "We just got here. We've got more beer and . . ."

His voice trailed off, but she knew the rest of the sentence. The condom in his pocket wasn't going home unopened if he could help it.

Something moved outside again. This time she was positive it was a man. "There!" she pointed.

Tommy forgot about the condom momentarily. "I see him."

The figure was medium height, a dark shadow in the courtyard, standing about forty feet away. A brief glow—the person had lit a cigarette—then darkness. It was a man, not one of their friends, Kirsten knew that, but she could discern no details. Average height, slender build, dressed in dark clothes.

His hands had glittered strangely in the brief glow of the lighter.

"Let's get out of here," she whispered once more.

"He'll see us. Maybe he's an MP," Tommy said.

"He's not an MP."

"How do you know?"

"He'd have a helmet on. A uniform."

"Maybe he's Polizie."

"He's not Polizie." Kirsten was certain. "If he was Polizie he'd be in here already. Besides, they don't come up here."

Kirsten felt the man already knew that she and Tommy were in here and he was waiting on them. She couldn't see his eyes, but suddenly, staring at him, she felt colder than she'd been all evening.

"Shit," Tommy muttered, standing up, the blanket falling off his shoulders. He played defensive tackle on the school team and topped out at six feet and a hundred and ninety pounds. The figure in the courtyard didn't scare him. "I'll see who it is."

"Stay here," Kirsten said, grabbing his hand.

Her plea only served to irritate Tommy. "First you want to leave, now you want to stay. Shit, Kirsten, we can't do anything with this guy standing around."

"Let's just wait till he leaves," she said.

"We don't have all night. I need to have the car back by midnight," Tommy said. He pulled his hand free with more force than was necessary and walked to the door. He stepped out and the door swung shut behind him.

Kirsten was frozen. She knew she should follow, but she couldn't move. She heard muffled voices, then silence. Footsteps approached the door. It swung open and her eyes fixed on the figure that was silhouetted in the frame. Smaller than Tommy. The glint of eyes staring at her froze her breath.

"Where's Tommy?"

The man smiled, even white teeth showing in the shadowed face. "Busy."

"Busy doing what?" Kirsten found control of her muscles and slowly got to her feet. She still held the blanket tight, arms crossed in front of her chest.

"Drugs." The voice was odd, without an accent, definitely not a German who had learned English. Maybe American, but she couldn't place it, and she had met people from all over the States in her travels. There was a faint southern tint, but it didn't seem right. There was also a quality to it as if the man had a cold and his nose was stuffed up.

"What do you mean?"

"It seems," the man said, now stepping into the room, "that your boyfriend would rather do cocaine out there than be in here with a pretty young woman like yourself."

Kirsten looked out into the courtyard, past him. In the part she could see there was no sign of Tommy. He wouldn't just leave her like this. She took a step backward. "What do you want?"

The man's smile hadn't abated. He held out a hand. "Would you like some?"

There was small vial in his palm. It glittered in the light, made of some expensive metal. Kirsten could now see that there were rings on each finger, numerous jewels reflecting the scant light.

"I don't do drugs."

The man pointed at her beer can and sniffed the air, where the odor of the joint was still noticeable. "Come, now." His hand was still out.

"I don't do drugs," she repeated. "I'm going now."

She started for the door, but the man didn't move and she stopped before making contact.

"No."

Kirsten felt the single word hit her harder than if he'd struck her with a fist. She backed up.

"I highly recommend what is in here." The man held the vial out to her.

"What do you want?"

"Simply for you to party with me."

"What do you want?"

"Would you like to go to a very nice party?" the man asked. "I have transportation to take us there. We will be back before dawn. It is a party the likes of which I am sure you have never seen. Very rich people. Very powerful people. A beautiful girl such as yourself, you would do well to meet such people. You have a special look. I like that."

"I don't want to party," Kirsten said, her voice less strong than she would have liked. But she could feel reality starting to slip away, as if she were watching what was going on in this dirty room like a bystander. It was beyond the realm of her reality.

"You were partying in here with that young man. Surely you can do better." He pulled a ring off and held it out. "Here. Take this as a token. There will be much more if you come with me."

"Tommy!" Kirsten yelled. She slapped at him and the ring bounced into the darkness of one of the corners of the room.

The man's smile was gone, his lips now a dark slash. "Do not yell. It is very impolite."

"I want to go!" Kirsten insisted. But she didn't move, because he didn't move.

He put the vial in his shirt pocket. He pulled out a pair of thick gloves and slid them on, over the rings on his fingers. His hand went to his waist and pulled out a knife. A long, strangely curved knife.

"Would you like to go to my party?" he asked in the same even voice. "Make your decision now."

"No," Kirsten whispered.

"You are very stupid," the man said. "You could have a very nice time. Others have."

"I want to go home."

"Last chance."

"I want to go home. Please."

"Drop the blanket."

Kirsten's fingers tightened on the rough wool.

"Drop the blanket and we will go into the courtyard and talk with your friend."

Kirsten forced herself to let go of the blanket.

The smile was back on his face. "Very good. Now come with me."

"I'm not going anywhere with you."

"Last chance," the man said. "Come with me."

Kirsten backed up. "No."

"Then we will do this another way. Either way, it will be done." The man's voice was irritated. "Take your clothes off."

"No," she said in a low voice.

"To this you have no choice," he said. "You will either take them off and live or I will kill you with them on. Do as I say and you will not be hurt."

Kirsten believed him, at least that he would kill her if she didn't strip. She stared at the blade, trying to see if there was blood on it, Tommy's blood, but it seemed to be clean, the blade clearly reflecting a sliver of moonlight.

The man took one step forward. "Now."

She hesitated and the blade flashed in front of her and she gasped as a line of fire ran down the left side of her face. She reached a hand up and pulled it away. It was covered in blood.

"Nothing major," the man said. "It will heal. Do as I say and we won't have to do that again."

Kirsten pulled her sweater off. She watched her own fingers unbuttoning her blouse, surprised in a distant sort of way how steady they were. Why weren't they shaking? she wondered. She could feel dampness on her cheek but no pain.

She was wearing a black bra, a decision she had made knowing that Tommy and her would be coming up here and how much he liked it and also how he could handle unhooking it in the front. Tommy had gotten very frustrated and embarrassed when he couldn't unhook one of her other ones, and his resulting anger, trying to cover for his real feelings, had ruined the evening. So she'd worn this one so the evening wouldn't be ruined.

She unhooked it. The cloth fell away, exposing her small, pointy breasts. The man had not moved again once she started undressing and there was no sign that he took any interest in her nakedness as she pulled her jeans down. She unbuckled her belt and unzipped her jeans, then pushed them down before pausing. She'd forgotten to take her sneakers off and her jeans were bunched at her feet.

"Go to the window," the man said.

She bent over to pull her sneakers off, but the man repeated his order.

"Go the window. Now!"

She shuffled over, arms crossed on her chest, until she was facing the window. She could feel goose bumps on her naked skin. She could see the entire courtyard now and she saw a dark lump on the ground about thirty feet away. Tommy! He wasn't moving.

"Put your hands on the windowsill."

She could tell from the voice that he was right behind her. She put her palms on the grimy wood.

She flinched as she felt the point of the knife touch the outside of her left hip.

"Back with your feet."

She shuffled her feet back until the knifepoint on her left buttock stopped her. Now she couldn't move, half bent over, her weight caught between her feet and her hands on the sill. She didn't know it, but it was the way police and counter-terrorism experts were taught to search a suspect, putting them in a position where if they removed either hand from their forward support, they would fall over.

She heard some noises behind her. She knew she was going to be raped. Beyond that, her mind refused to go. She focused on Tommy's body lying on the stones. Was he dead?

Something looped over her head and she gasped. The man tightened her blouse down over her mouth. She felt the cloth with her tongue as he tied a knot on the back of her head. She panicked, sucking air in through her nose.

Then she felt a hand on her rear, holding her steady. She closed her eyes. Tommy and she had used this position before and she knew what to expect.

Or so she thought. She gasped with pain as the man's cock rammed up against her anus. Tears flowed as he vigorously pushed in. Tommy had never done this and she felt as if she'd been skewered. Through her pain, one thought flashed: Did this man have AIDS?

She opened her eyes and blinked out the tears. Her heart jumped. She saw Tommy move. An arm stretching out, then the body twitching and shaking.

The man behind her was slamming against her and she had to hold on with all her strength to avoid going down to her knees. She could feel the flat steel of his knife slapping against her right side with every stroke. The pain of his thrusts was terrible but also distant in a strange way.

Tommy was on his knees now, shaking his head. She could see darkness on his face. Blood. Tommy stood and peered about, getting his bearings. Kirsten tried to scream, but the sound was caught in her blouse and all that came forth was a mewling noise.

Tommy froze, his eyes locked into the window. Kirsten met his gaze and she knew he saw her. Saw what was happening to her and the blood on her own face. Tommy looked about, then picked up a piece of two-by-four and came striding forward.

Kirsten wanted to look over her shoulder and see if the man had spotted Tommy, but she dared not. There was no sign that he had, as his rhythm was getting faster, his breathing rough.

Tommy was ten feet away now. Five feet. She could see his face, the anger on it. The blood running down one side.

Then Tommy's head exploded, blood and brain bursting forth, splattering Kirsten with gore. Half of the head was gone as the body tumbled forward lifeless to lie right below her, outside the windowsill.

The man had begun coming as Tommy's body fell. The man slammed against Kirsten, pinning her against the windowsill, grunting in pleasure. She hardly noticed; what sanity she had left was focused entirely on Tommy's body. There had been no sound of a shot, but there was no doubt in her mind that that was what had happened. She looked up, across the courtyard, but could see nothing. It was like a movie, unreal. Tommy had fallen in slow motion. Even the pain in her rear was so far away now.

A voice—a man's voice—echoed in the courtyard, coming from the other side, calling out to the man behind her in a strange tongue, one she had never heard before.

She barely felt his hand reaching around her, his body pressed even more tightly against her back. The hand had the vial in it and the lid was off. He pressed it against her nostrils. With her mouth gagged, her next breath in sucked up the contents.

She felt the man step back from her, the cool evening air against her naked back. Then a spear of pain pierced her from the base of her skull to the small of her back. Her body snapped upright so quickly, bones cracked. She struggled for air, but her lungs wouldn't work. Her eyes bulged forward, blood seeping out around the edges. Her fingers grabbed at the dirty windowsill so hard her nails broke, leaving bloody streaks on the wood.

Kirsten's body convulsed forward, slamming her neck down onto the broken glass still in the window, her neck severed. She slumped forward, hanging over the sill. A small—unnaturally small—trickle of blood came out of the severed carotid artery, dripping down onto Tommy's body, the last thing her bulging eyes saw being the splintered bone and scrambled brains that had been part of her boyfriend's head.

The man had watched all this while zipping his pants up and putting his knife back in the sheath. He looked at the vial in his hand and carefully screwed the top on. Then he placed the vial back in his pocket. He removed the gloves and tossed them away. Reaching up, he pulled a set of filters out of his nostrils, placing them back in a case.

Using the jeans wadded between her legs, the man lifted Kirsten's legs and pushed her over the sill, her body falling onto Tommy's. He walked out the door.

He looked up into the shadows of the inner castle wall as the voice called out to him in the same foreign tongue. "It worked?"

The man pulled the zipper on his jacket tight against his throat, shivering from the chill German evening and the damp air. "Yes."

The owner of the voice appeared, a tall man, broad in the shoulders, a rifle in his hands, as he walked down the stone steps from the inside rampart. He twisted a screw just forward of the magazine well on the weapon and the barrel was released. He slipped the barrel inside his jacket, hanging it on a hook sewn into the material. The stock went on the other side.

He looked at the two bodies. "Not much blood," he noted.

"It acted quickly," the man with the rings said. "I think she was dead before she hit the glass."

"You're certain it worked?" the other man sounded irritated.

"It worked."

"You couldn't have just—" the other began, but the smaller man cut him off.

"It worked."

"All right." The second man glanced at an expensive watch. "The meet is scheduled in forty-five minutes. You cut it close."

"The meet," the first man spit. "I am tired of doing his dirty work. Why must we do his bidding?"

"Because he tells us to."

"One of these days . . ." The first man let the sentence trail off, incomplete.

The second man extracted a pistol from inside his large coat. He pulled the slide back, chambering a round, then handed it to the other.

"Why do I need this?"

"Because we are dealing with dangerous men now, not children." The man looked about. "I feel something." His eyes searched the dark ramparts. "Someone."

"Let us go, then."

Chapter Two

The Gulf breeze carried the faint scent of salt water and the distant thud of helicopter blades. The sound had been there for the past four hours, coming from all sides of the oil rig, although no aircraft could be sighted. Mike Thorpe, dressed in black combat fatigues and armed with an AK-74 automatic rifle, turned to Colonel Giles.

"What do you think, sir?"

The *sir* wasn't necessary as Giles had retired from the U.S. Army years previously; however, it wasn't from military formality that Thorpe used it, but rather personal respect. Giles was dressed the same, his stick-thin figure wrapped in a combat vest on top of the black fatigues.

"They'll hit soon. They have to."

"Why?" The third person on the platform was dressed in worn khaki and carried a small camcorder. Lisa Parker was in her mid-thirties, five and a half feet tall and slender. She had long brown hair that she wore tied up in a bun. Her face had high cheekbones and was creased with worry lines around the edge of her mouth and eyes.

Giles turned toward her. "They'd rather wait until dark, but we didn't give them that option with our demands. We've been photographed by satellite for the last couple of hours and they have a good idea what they're up against. Or so they think. Swimmers from SEAL Team Six are probably below us right now."

Parker looked over the edge of the metal platform they stood on, two hundred feet to the water below. The surface was calm and she could see nothing.

Thorpe shook his head. "You won't see them until they want you to." He pointed to the horizon. "The choppers are just over the horizon and their only job is to make noise. To cover up the sound the assault helicopters are going to make when Delta Force comes swooping in to take the oil rig back from us."

"You'll see them coming," Parker said. "What good does covering the noise do?"

"Yeah, we should see them," Thorpe agreed, "but covering up the sound gives them a few extra seconds before they're spotted, and seconds count. Deep down, they hope they'll catch us napping."

Thorpe, Giles and the other four men in their cell had been here for six hours. They'd come in broad daylight aboard the daily resupply helicopter that they'd taken over at the Louisiana airfield that was the rig's home base. A gun to the pilot's head had ensured a smooth flight to the rig and a perfect landing. And complete surprise.

The rig towered over three hundred feet above the smooth water of the Gulf of Mexico. The rig's crew of twenty-four men were now locked in a toolshed under the main deck, which was forty feet below where Thorpe and Giles stood. The main deck held a landing platform on which the Huey helicopter was parked, a barracks area, a control room and space for the various pipes and fittings that were required for the job the rig did. In the center, a tall derrick held the pipe that descended through the deck, through the water and into the bedrock four hundred feet under the surface of the water.

Giles had radioed their demands to the appropriate authorities less than an hour after they'd seized the rig. That was when the clock had started. A police negotiator from the town that held the rig's land headquarters had tried his best to keep them on the radio and talk. That was his job. Talk and win concessions and wear away at the minds of the terrorists. Distract them.

Giles had simply repeated his demands and told the cop

that he had only one word left in his vocabulary that he could use: yes, to all the demands. If the man said one other word, a prisoner would be executed. The only exception had been allowing a news chopper to fly Parker out to the rig. The radio had been silent for the last two hours. Thorpe imagined that the negotiator was not a very happy man at the present moment.

The problem for Giles, Thorpe and the rest of the team was that the yes to their demands hadn't come yet and there wasn't much time left before they would have to carry out their threats.

Of course, Thorpe knew, they—whoever *they* specifically were in this case—wouldn't give in to the demands. And because the rig was not just offshore but also outside the twelve-mile limit, it was a federal case and that meant that some very specialized people were coming to deal with this.

At the very least, Thorpe expected the navy's SEAL Team Six under the water and the army's Delta Force through the sky. Thorpe craned his neck and looked up, past the towering derrick into the clear Gulf sky, half expecting to see parachutes from a HALO (high altitude, low opening) parachute team floating down.

Giles's team hadn't spent the intervening four hours simply waiting. They had been busy placing charges all over the rig. If they blew the rig, the ecosystem of the Gulf of Mexico would take at least ten years to recover. The Exxon Valdez disaster would look like a fender bender compared to the head-on collision they were preparing here.

Which was the point of the demands. Publicizing the destruction of the Gulf's ecosystem that was already occurring because of the offshore drilling and the immense potential for an accident that would destroy the ecosystem. That was demand number one. Number two was eight million dollars.

Neither the publicity—other than having Parker film all this—nor the money had been forthcoming and the deadline would arrive in one hour.

Thorpe stretched his shoulders. He was a tall man, standing six-foot-two. He carried one hundred and eighty pounds tautly on his frame. The years carrying a gun for a profession had not been kind. His face was weathered deep brown. The skin already carried the deep lines and crevices that signaled middle age. He had deep blue eyes and dark hair, liberally sprinkled with gray. There were dark etchings under his eyes, and the skin over his cheekbones was stretched a little too tight.

"Maybe we ought to retire," Giles said, scanning the horizon with a pair of binoculars.

"We did," Thorpe said.

"No, from all of it," Giles said.

"You already retired once and I thought I had," Thorpe said. "Don't throw salt on the wound. Those dumb shits in the army . . ." He didn't want to go into that right now.

"Radar?" Giles called out.

One of the members of his team had a laptop computer resting on a plastic case. A wire ran from it to the rig's radar dish.

"Horizon is clear," the man reported.

"Let me give them one more jerk of the chain," Giles said. He flipped open his cellular phone. He dialed, then began speaking as soon as the other end was answered, not giving the negotiator a chance to start his own spiel.

"This is Colonel Lazarus of the Earth Army, First Battalion. I have not received a response to my demands. I am assuring you we will destroy this monstrosity of technology if we do not get the answer we want. There is no compromise. The earth demands no compromise."

The negotiator finally got a word in. "We're working on your demands, but it takes time to—"

"Time!" Giles yelled. "You've had time. You've had generations. You took the time to build this monstrosity. You can take it apart quicker. One hour. That is it. The people will know that this is your fault when they see what this reporter is taping. We want to end this peacefully. It is obvious you don't. Any blood will be on your hands."

Giles snapped the phone shut.

" 'The earth demands no compromise'?" Thorpe repeated.

"Hey, I'm making it up as I go," Giles said, which Thorpe knew to be far from the truth. Everything they had done today had been planned out to the tiniest detail.

"Do you think they'll give in?" Parker asked.

Giles didn't even have to think about it. "No. I'm going to check the west side."

As Giles wandered away, Parker had her first chance alone with Thorpe. "How have you been, Mike?"

Thorpe's eyes remained focused on the horizon. "Living."

"I heard—" Parker began, but she didn't get a chance to finish the statement as the radar man called out.

"Contacts, all directions."

Thorpe caught a glint of something on the horizon. "I've got a chopper low on the water," he called out, bringing Giles running.

Giles looked that way, then did a three-sixty. "Choppers on all horizons. Coming in. Game time." He put the glasses into a case. "Let's roll."

Parker swung her camera in that direction and zoomed in on one of the helicopters.

Giles and Thorpe started climbing down from the work platform to the deck. Parker hurriedly turned off the camcorder and followed. Giles was issuing orders as they descended. By the time they got to the main deck, the Huey's blades were turning, one of their men holding a gun on a less-than-happy pilot. The other men were pushing the crew out of the room they had been locked in, taping a toy gun in alternating hands of each pair. The other hands were handcuffed together. Soon they had twelve pairs of prisoners, with toy guns securely taped into their free hands.

"Forty seconds!" Giles called out, watching the approaching helicopters.

A man ran to each corner of the rig, dropped a timed satchel charge off and then sprinted back. Thorpe opened the cover on a remote detonator. He quickly punched in numbers.

"Set," Thorpe said.

"Another contact!" the radar man yelled. "Something real fast! From the east! Ten seconds out!"

"What the hell is that?" Giles was pointing to something low and fast to the east, heading toward the rig at tremendous velocity.

"Cruise missile?" was all Thorpe managed to guess as the

rocket gained altitude and skimmed across the main deck of the platform twenty feet above the steel.

The roar of the supersonic missile washed across the deck and small black objects tumbled out as the nose cone exploded into several small pieces. The bulk of the rocket kept going.

"Cover your eyes!" Giles yelled.

Thorpe closed his eyes and pressed his hands against his ears tightly. Flash-bang grenades exploded all over the rig in a cacophony of thunderous sound and bright light. Even with his eyes closed, Thorpe was half blinded as he opened them. His head rang with the echoes of the explosion.

He tapped Parker and pointed at the chopper as he screamed at her, "You want to stay or come?"

She stared at him blankly, indicating she didn't hear a word.

Thorpe pointed at the chopper, then simply grabbed her and pulled her with him. The team piled on board. As instructed, one of the pilots had been waiting with his dark visor down, so even though his copilot was blinded, he was able to still fly the aircraft. The mode of the delivery of the grenades had been a surprise, not their use. The chopper lifted.

As the members of SEAL Team Six surfaced next to each leg of the rig, they were greeted with the exploding satchel charges. Timers began ticking on the other charges placed all over the superstructure of the rig.

The Huey Thorpe was on headed straight to the west, where the rig's radar had told them a ship was hiding just over the horizon. They went past a Blackhawk full of Delta Force commandos, the men in each chopper staring at each other as they went by.

"They don't know what to do," Giles cheerfully said. "Their orders are to hit the rig."

"They'll hit the rig," Thorpe said. "They figure radar will keep us in sight."

"And it will," Giles agreed.

"They don't know if we have hostages on board, or even if there are any bad guys on board," Thorpe explained to Parker. It was something he and Giles had discussed when planning this operation. "For all they know, we could be good guys escaping."

Thorpe nodded to the front, where one of their men seated in the copilot seat was frantically radioing exactly that message to the ship they were flying toward. The man was doing a good job, sounding panicked and telling the ship they had some people on board who had been wounded in the escape.

Thorpe was watching the rig receding from them as Parker leaned out and filmed. Thorpe reached out a muscular arm and grabbed hold of her harness. She gave him a grateful glance as she learned farther out, trusting his strength to keep her from falling, and filmed what was happening on the rig.

The first helicopters were landing, disgorging commandos. Thorpe could well imagine the confusion as they faced twelve pairs of men with what looked like guns in their hands. It was going to be a mess. And as the number on the device in his hand flickered to zero, the confusion was greatly magnified as charges exploded. There were flashes on points all over the rig.

"There!" Giles said, pointing forward. A Coast Guard cutter was cruising through the water.

The Huey headed straight for the cutter, ignoring the radioed inquiries from the ship's bridge. Giles's man was acting hysterical, telling of wounded men and a desperate escape.

"See the back deck?" Thorpe asked Parker as he pulled her back in.

There were two vans tied down there, radio antennas bristling on the tops. They were just off the helipad on the rear part of the cutter.

"Yes," she replied.

"That's their C & C," Thorpe said. "They're airliftable vans that SEAL Team Six and Delta Force use for command and control."

"Goggles on!" Giles ordered.

Thorpe slipped a pair of clear plastic goggles over his eyes and pulled the charging handle back on the AK-74. He handed a set of goggles to Parker.

The Huey flared and then landed, the skids slamming into the metal grating. Four Coast Guardsmen with stretchers approached. Giles and his men leapt off and their superior fire-power and training made short work of the four men. The door to one of the vans opened and two Delta Force commandos jumped out firing. The battle was pitched for a few seconds.

Thorpe fired carefully with his AK-74. The familiar sound of gunfire rang in his ears, muffled somewhat by the earplugs he had put in during the flight. After eighteen years of this, he knew he had to take care of his hearing.

He zeroed in on one of the Delta men and fired. The man's expression told him he had scored a hit. For good measure, Thorpe fired twice more, earning him a curse from the commando as the hard plastic rounds smacked him in the chest. The rounds, designed to be used in training scenarios such as this, still hurt when they hit at over five hundred feet per second.

The other man was down and Giles ordered his men forward. They ran across the deck. While Giles took one van, Thorpe took the other. He kicked open the door and edged in, muzzle leading. He paused as he saw a burly figure seated at a radio console. The man held a pistol to his own head.

"Take another step and I kill the hostage."

Thorpe laughed, lowering his gun. "Long time no see, Dan."

Sergeant Major Dan Dublowski lowered his gun. "Damn, who'd have thought the bad guys would hit our C & C?" He pointed at the radio. "You should hear the shit going on at the rig. You got some pissed-off workers who got hit by plastic bullets from the rescuers after being hit by the flash-bangs. Then the SEALs are screaming about the simulators you dropped in the water. They got two guys with busted ear-drums."

"They'd be dead if we'd dropped full charges," Thorpe noted.

"Hey, I know that, you know that and now they know that," Dublowski said. "That's the purpose."

"What the hell was that missile?" Thorpe asked.

"Latest thing in special ops." Dublowski pointed at a console that had several TV screens mounted on it. "It's what you might call a pocket cruise missile. The technical dinks nicknamed it the Hummingbird. Not only can it carry a small payload, it also had cameras mounted, giving us a real-time close shot of the target just before we hit it."

"Not real time enough."

"True, but that was due more to a screwed-up plan than the equipment," Dublowski admitted. "The missile is retrievable. There's a chopper out there now tracking down its homing device somewhere to the west of the rig."

He walked to the door and stepped out, Thorpe following. Colonel Giles came walking out of the other van, a very upset navy captain with him, Parker filming it all. The captain had the distinctive gold insignia of the SEALs on his chest: an eagle clutching a trident with a muzzle-loader pistol and anchor superimposed; nicknamed a Budweiser, as it resembled that company's emblem.

"Goddamn it!" The captain's voice was loud. "This ship was outside the limits of the play of the problem. We thought we had real casualties being flown in here."

" 'Play of the problem'?" Giles repeated, giving a half-smile toward Parker and her lens.

"I knew you shitheads were going to do something like this," Dublowski said in a low voice as Giles and the captain continued their loud and angry discussion. At least angry on one side. To Giles this was a job, and he didn't get upset about a job.

"How'd you know?" Thorpe asked.

"When you insisted that no one, even those on this ship, have live ammo. At first I thought you were just being extra safe, but then I figured there was a purpose to your concern."

"How come you didn't tell him?" Thorpe asked, pointing at the irate navy officer.

"Because he's a jerk," Dublowski said. "We've been training with these SEALs for two weeks and they act like they shit ice cream. Since this operation was on water, he insisted that his people plan the mission. Our colonel didn't like the plan, but he had to bow to the CINC who agreed with dickhead there and gave OPCON to the navy. Plus," Dublowski added, "I don't like SEALs. Not after McKenzie and Omega Missile."

Thorpe knew the entire exercise had been set up three months previously to test Delta–Seal Team Six on joint operations. Obviously there was a lot of work to be done. But that was the purpose. Giles's civilian security consulting company had received the contract to play the terrorist force seizing the oil rig. They'd been given quite a bit of latitude to formulate their course of action, which was actually unusual, given the military's tendency to want to make every exercise into a dog and pony show, especially when the congressional SOCOM—Special Operations Command—counter terrorist liaison, Lieutenant Colonel Lisa Parker, was allowed to be part of the play of the problem to see firsthand how it went—and report back to the Select Committee on Terrorism.

"What was the plan?" Thorpe asked.

Dublowski snorted. "Plan? Hit the rig with everything all at once and use the Hummingbird dropping flash-bangs to shock you at the last second. That was the best he could come up with. You didn't give us much choice with your time limit. The SEALs were pissed because their real plan for an oil rig is to cut into one of the legs and come up the hollow inside and hit them by surprise. Except the oil company who supplied the rig and time for this didn't exactly want them to do that to their equipment. Plus two hours wasn't enough time to cut through. So they had to climb up the outside. They knew they'd get waxed, but they hoped the Hummingbird and Delta coming in from all directions with choppers would give them a chance."

"We were the bad guys. We weren't supposed to give you much choice or a chance," Thorpe said.

"Yeah." Dublowski sighed. "Well, we'll be hashing this one out for a while."

Thorpe looked at his old friend. He hadn't seen Dublowski in a couple of years—since the Omega Missile escapade in Louisiana. The two of them went back a long way. Long before that episode they'd served together in Desert Storm on a SCUD-buster team that had gone all over western Iraq searching for the elusive rocket launchers. Last Thorpe had heard, Dublowski had been overseas in Germany and everyone involved in Omega Missile had been scattered to the four corners. He hadn't known Dublowski had "gone behind the fence," working for Delta again, but Thorpe also knew that Delta tended to drag people with Dublowski's experience back in for more tours whether they wanted to or not. Once in the Force, always in. At least for everyone but himself, Thorpe conceded. He was the exception to the rule.

Dublowski looked older than his forty-seven years. There was a slight nervous tic under the skin near the sergeant major's left eye that Thorpe didn't remember seeing before; a certain lack of focus to the older man's eyes that Thorpe found strangely familiar.

"How have things been?" Thorpe asked.

"They've sucked."

"What's the matter?"

"Terri's gone."

Thorpe blinked. Terri was Dublowski's daughter. The last time Thorpe had seen her, she'd been fourteen years old with pigtails and dressed in coveralls, running around the backyard at the Dublowskis' house in Fayetteville, outside Fort Bragg. But almost four years had passed since then.

"What do you mean, gone?"

Dublowski walked over to the ship's railing. His eyes were focused on the sea. "After Louisiana, I was stationed with Special Operations Command Europe, in Stuttgart. Staff puke work while I recovered from some knee surgery and, as you know, getting me as far away from the States as they could. She was a senior at the high school there. One Friday night two months ago she went out with some friends and she never came back."

Thorpe didn't know what to say, so he remained silent, waiting for the rest of the story.

"Her friends said the last they saw her—as best they can remember, since most of them had been pretty drunk—was she said she was leaving, going home. They'd all been out in one of the preserves in the Black Forest, drinking and partying."

Dublowski looked at Thorpe. "She didn't like to drink and she didn't do drugs. She went out with those people because there were only so many kids in her class. But when she saw how bad it was getting, she must have left. We'd talked about it. I'd told her that her mom or I would always come and get her no matter where she was, no matter what had happened, if people were drinking or doing drugs. But she must have thought she could walk back to post. It was only about two miles to the gate.

"Shit, I don't know. That's guesswork on my part. We called the MPs, but they said the kids had gone off post and they'd have to check with the Polizie. The MPs didn't seem to believe me. The Polizie didn't really give a damn about some American kids.

"It's different over there now, Mike. Now that the Germans are no longer worried about the big red machine rolling through the Fulda Gap, they don't want us. The Polizie weren't too concerned about some American family member being missing. I made the MPs call in CID, Criminal Investigations Division, but there was no sign of foul play, so CID couldn't really do anything. As far as everyone was concerned, Terri just ran away. Hell, we even got investigated by Social Services to see if maybe we had been abusing her and that had caused her to leave."

"You haven't heard from her?" Thorpe asked.

Dublowski's voice was insistent. "She didn't run away, Mike."

Thorpe had known Dublowski a long time, but he also knew that even a parent couldn't tell what a kid would do.

"Something bad happened to her," Dublowski said in a low voice. "I know it and Marge knows it. I don't give a shit what anyone says, she wouldn't have run away. Everything was going right for her. She was accepted into college back here in the States, exactly the school she wanted. She was all excited about it and planning to come back in the fall. She was happy. We were happy."

Thorpe remained silent, dark, troubling images floating to the surface of his memory.

"Marge took it bad. Still is," Dublowski said. "She's been on medication ever since. Won't come out of the house."

Thorpe remembered Dublowski's wife. A small, quiet gray-haired lady who had suffered his long absences with grace and a smiling face. She'd lived through her husband's combat tours, but Thorpe could well imagine that something happening to Terri was a vulnerable area, one she had never been prepared for. He knew firsthand the devastation a career in Special Operations could have on a family and it was the biggest reason he had taken—tried to take—early retirement after Louisiana.

"Is anyone checking into it?" Thorpe asked. "Maybe she's back in the States. Maybe she got . . ." He paused as Dublowski gave him a look that froze his words, then the sergeant major's face crumpled and tears formed at the edges of his eyes. That startled Thorpe more than anything.

"I'm sorry, Mike, it's just that everyone always says, hey, she'll turn up one day. Everything's all right." His voice was harsh. "Well, it isn't. And it won't ever be. Something bad happened to her and nobody cares."

They both looked up as they heard a helicopter. The Huey was cranking up to head back to the rig. Giles was waving for Thorpe to come.

"Hey," Thorpe said, putting a hand on Dublowski' back. "I'll talk to you at the debrief."

Dublowski shook off the tears and got his voice under control. "I'm not staying for that. I have to go back to Bragg immediately. My commander will take the debrief."

"Well, then I'll see you at Bragg in a week," Thorpe said.

Dublowski wiped a sleeve across his eyes and straightened up, the professional soldier returning. "What are you coming to Bragg for?"

Thorpe reached out and touched the US ARMY sewn above Dublowski's right breast pocket. "I'll be back in uniform, doing my time."

"You're shitting me. I thought you retired."

"I thought I did too, but Department of the Army disagrees. I took the early out that was so graciously offered me, but it turns out that I wasn't eligible, even though the officer who signed the paperwork said I was."

"Hell, I think they just wanted to get rid of you after all the shit you've been involved in," Dublowski said.

"You got that right," Thorpe said. "I guess by the time the

papers hit some pencil-pusher's desk in the Pentagon, they decided I still owed Uncle Sam some time to get my money.

"Anyway, I've got to finish out a couple of tours in the reserves, which means I have to get what the reserves call a good retirement year. So for this year, I've got an ADSW tour for sixty days coming up at Bragg."

"ADSW?"

"A reserve term. Active duty, special work."

"What about Lisa?" Dublowski asked. "And Tommy?"

Thorpe looked at his watch. "They're gone."

"Gone?" Dublowski's face showed his confusion and growing outrage. "She left you after you got off active duty? I thought—"

"She didn't leave me," Thorpe said. "Listen, I'll talk to you when I get to Bragg."

"Where are you going to be?" Dublowski asked.

"That's up to the guy who handles reservists for SOCOM," Thorpe said. "Your guess is as good as mine."

Dublowski pulled a card out of his wallet and handed it to Thorpe. "Marge and I aren't listed, but here's my home and work numbers. Give me a call when you get in town."

"Will do," Thorpe said. He shook hands and walked to the chopper and got on board with Giles, Parker and the other men who worked for Giles. Thorpe looked out the side as they lifted. Dublowski was still standing at the railing, gazing out at some far point on the horizon.

"What's wrong with Dublowski?" Giles asked, ever the watchful commander, looking out for his men. He had saved Thorpe's ass on more than one occasion, including getting him this job to occupy his time. Giles also knew Dublowski from Desert Storm.

Thorpe kept his eyes on the figure at the railing. "His daughter disappeared in Germany."

"Disappeared?" Giles asked.

Thorpe shrugged, not from uncaring but from ignorance. "I don't know the exact story. I'll find out when I go to Bragg and talk to him."

"Tell Dan he needs anything, call me," Giles said.

"Right, sir."

"You need anything, call me," Giles said, poking Thorpe in the chest.

"Haven't I always?"

"No."

Thorpe forgot for a second about Dublowski. "Maybe you won't want to hear from me."

"You guys think you're indestructible. You're not. Call me if you need help. Tell Dan that too."

Thorpe looked past Giles and noted that Parker was watching them both, her forehead furrowed. Thorpe quickly looked away. He spent the rest of the flight in contemplative silence, which was immediately disrupted when they landed at the staging area on shore.

Parker walked next to Thorpe as he headed toward one of the rental vans Giles had hired for this operation.

"What's going on?"

"Nothing." Thorpe hadn't seen Major—now Lieutenant Colonel—Parker in over a year.

"How are things on the home front?" Parker asked.

"There is no home front." Thorpe changed the subject abruptly. "What are you going to report to Congress?"

"Don't change the subject." Parker folded her arms across her chest. "What happened to Lisa and Tommy?"

"Not here, not now," Thorpe's words were clipped. "What are you going to report?"

Parker regarded him for several seconds, then relented. "You know the Department of Defense people are going to be putting their own spin on what just happened. They're going to declare the joint Delta–SEAL Team Six operations a success no matter what really happened."

"Spin kills. If they aren't willing to admit they screwed up, then what are they going to do when the real thing happens?"

"That's why I filmed it," Parker said. "They can't deny the truth when it's on film."

"And then?"

"And then?" Parker shrugged. "Hopefully someone will do something."

" 'Someone will do something.' " Thorpe shook his head. "Right."

"I work for Congress," Parker said, "and the Pentagon does listen when the purse strings get tightened. This won't be swept under the rug."

"I think you're wrong about that. Maybe this whole thing wasn't to test the SEAL-Delta working relationship but rather the Hummingbird missile. Did you know it was going to be tested? You were in missiles, if I remember rightly."

Parker's eyes narrowed. "I knew the Hummingbird was an option available to the assault force."

"How much does one of those things cost?" Thorpe asked. "A million? Two?"

"Actually just under a million a pop," Parker answered, "but they're reusable—if they're not destroyed during the mission—with an estimated life of fifteen launches per. So that cuts down the cost considerably per launch."

"And you're telling me testing that wasn't the primary purpose of this exercise?" Thorpe asked once more. "Especially after they used the cruise missiles last year in the Sudan and Afghanistan?"

"Listen, Mike, there's not a—"

"I've heard it all," Thorpe said. "You think they assigned you to the slot you're in because they liked you? They did it to get you out of the way. We made some bad enemies—"

"Who were exposed," Parker noted.

Thorpe laughed. "Yeah, but how many of them are in jail? They're still all out there, doing their thing." He opened the door to the van. "I've got to go. Good luck with your report."

Chapter Three

Fadeyushka pulled his left leg out of the swampy mud and found his boot had not come up with his foot. He cursed and fell to his knees in the dank, cold water, his fingers frantically tearing into the ooze, searching for the boot.

He looked over his shoulder, through the dead trees and stunted growth, in the direction he had come. Nothing. He felt worn leather then and pulled. The boot came loose grudgingly, with a sucking noise, water pouring out of it. He took a moment to catch his breath.

He was on the north bank of the Sava, the river dividing Croatia from Bosnia-Herzegovina. The terrain was flat, wet, and crossed by innumerable streams coming from the hills to the north. Stunted pine trees covered the few dots of land that were above water. It was totally inhospitable terrain.

Most of the bridges over the Sava had been destroyed in the last five years of fighting. Fadeyushka had swum the river the previous evening under the cover of darkness, almost being swept away by the strong current. Once on the Croatian side he had stolen an old bike from a shack and ridden west, following the river.

Sarajevo lay a hundred and fifty kilometers to the south. It had taken Fadeyushka five days to walk the distance, hiding during the day, traveling only at night. Weaving his way through the hodgepodge of sectors controlled by warring factions and avoiding the UN IFOR—Implementation Force—

roadblocks that tried to keep those factions from each other's throats.

Fadeyushka's eyes darted about, searching as he remembered the history of the past few years that had brought him to this place, events that he had had nothing to do with, but which had swept him up in their own inexorable tide.

He had been a schoolteacher when it all began. April 1992. The sixth. Fadeyushka knew the date as everyone in this part of the world because it was the moment when his life changed even though he didn't know it at the time. On that date, Serb gunmen opened fire on peace demonstrators in Sarajevo, killing five and wounding over thirty. The once-proud city, host of the Winter Olympics in 1988, fell into a four-year-long siege. By the end of June 1992, the UN Protective Force, UNPROFOR, took over the Sarajevo Airport trying to keep the city alive via an airlift of essential supplies as the Serbs blockaded all ground routes in and out.

The Serbs—and the Croatians, Fadeyushka had to admit— had picked their time to act with shrewdness. The world had been focused on the Persian Gulf War and reaction was very slow. The UN had expanded its efforts in putting the force into the Middle East to counter Saddam Hussein. Ethnic fighting in the Balkans had been far from the headlines and thus the world's interest. It took years of atrocities for the UN and NATO to respond in ever-increasing increments, but never strong enough to achieve any sort of lasting peace.

Even the presence of UN peacekeepers did little to stop the mayhem. In January 1993 the deputy prime minister of Bosnia was pulled out of a UN car and shot to death by Serb militia. Fadeyushka knew these dates by heart, having watched his countrymen die. In 1994, a mortar attack on a marketplace in Sarajevo killed sixty-eight and wounded over two hundred. Footage of this attack briefly made the lead story around the world and NATO issued its strongest warning ever, demanding that the Serbs pull their heavy weapons back from Sarajevo.

While those highly publicized attacks were going on, a more insidious action was taking place. Ethnic cleansing, a rather neat term in Fadeyushka's opinion for murder on a large scale. Muslim versus Christian. Serb versus Croat. The borders in this part of the world had been drawn by outsiders after the First World War and then again after the Second World War, with little regard to culture or the people who actually lived there.

The Soviet Bloc had kept things under relative control until the fall of the Iron Curtain in 1989. For three years a tenuous peace had been maintained until 1992. For years, fierce fighting swept back and forth across the rough terrain of the Balkans. Even Fadeyushka had been sucked into the war, being drafted into a local militia unit and marched south to help protect his brethren in one of the many small, unprotected towns outside Sarajevo.

Finally, in 1995, even NATO had had enough and surgical air strikes against Serb sites were conducted. Force was what it took to bring the Serbs to the peace talks. On the fourteenth of December, 1995, the Dayton Peace Accords were signed. Over sixty thousand NATO troops under a UN mandate moved into the area to enforce the Accords. The IFOR, Implementation Force, separated the area into three regions and maintained a tenuous peace.

At least a couple of years. Four months ago, things had begun to unravel. As NATO and the UN went through a period of self-questioning about whether to keep the IFOR in place, Serbian Muslims infiltrated Croat Christian havens on hit-and-run strikes, trying to achieve through terror what they hadn't been able to by direct force of arms. Ethnic Albanians used the opportunity to try to break away in Kosovo to the east and the Serbs turned their wrath on them. The entire situation deteriorated rapidly.

Terror. Fadeyushka now knew the meaning of that word well. He emptied the water and mud out of his boot and tugged it on. What caused him to hurry was the person who had shot the front tire of his commandeered bicycle as he'd made his way down a winding dirt road a few miles to the east twenty minutes ago. The round had blown out the tire and knocked Fadeyushka off the bike. He'd grabbed his AK-47 and scrambled to his feet, only to have another round hit the stock of the gun, smashing it from his hands.

A strangely accented voice had called out in Russian, ordering him to run. He'd paused and a bullet had hit him in the left shoulder, spinning him completely about. Like the previous two, Fadeyushka never heard the shot. The voice again ordered him to run.

And he had. He hadn't stopped until now. He hoped whoever had shot at him had been left behind, but he couldn't count on it. He got the boot on and, breath regained, he once more began to run at a steady pace.

Before, every time he had tried to turn left or right, a bullet had hit a tree or splashed into the water in front of him, corralling him back in the direction his unseen pursuer wanted him to go in, following the swampy bank of the Sava River into even more desolate territory. As he'd run, he'd wrapped a makeshift bandage around his shoulder, but the cloth was soaked through now and Fadeyushka felt faint from the loss of blood.

Who could it be? And this far to the north? At first he thought one of the many snipers who prowled the country on each of the many sides of this conflict, but then why the order to run? Why not simply a bullet through the brain and be done with it? Why this game?

Fadeyushka had been on his way home, the war over for him. He was tired of the killing and the fighting. The IFOR sat and did nothing as men, women and children were killed in front of them. Their UN safe havens had in many cases turned into holding pens where Serbs attacked and scooped up large numbers of prisoners, the IFOR unwilling or unable— Fadeyushka knew not which—to put their own lives on the line to actually protect those they had promised to protect.

Old hatreds were boiling to the surface once more and exploding in orgies of killing, raping and maiming. But it wasn't just the Serbs. Everyone was descending into madness and Fadeyushka could not be part of it anymore.

After watching his militia unit kill twenty unarmed Serb prisoners in retaliation for the death of two of their own men to Serb snipers the day before, Fadeyushka had had enough. Several of the Serbs had been children, not even in their teens. Large enough to carry a rifle but not old enough to have a clue why they carried the gun or to understand why they were being gunned down. This was not the way war should be fought. But whoever was trailing him apparently hadn't had enough.

A small stream cut across his path. He splashed into it. Higher, dry ground beckoned on the far side and he scrambled up the slope, pushing through a line of bushes on the bank, then he froze in horror.

Six men were tied to wooden crosses in the clearing in front of him. Their feet were on the ground and their arms had been tied at the wrists to the cross-beams. A piece of chain went around each man's chest.

At least the arms had once been tied, Fadeyushka amended as he stared. Someone had ripped each man's hands off. Fadeyushka staggered to his feet and slowly walked over to examine the closest body. The wrist had been torn apart by some terrible force. Looking at the wood behind the limb, Fadeyushka knew what had done it. Someone had fired a large-caliber bullet and hit the wrist. He looked down and saw the severed hands lying on the pine-needle-covered forest floor like withered white spiders. Fadeyushka was surprised to see that the dirty camouflage fatigues the man in front of him wore were Polish army issue. One of the IFOR peacekeepers. Even the Serbs did not kill IFOR.

The man's eyes snapped open and Fadeyushka staggered back in shock.

"Please," the man begged in bad Russian, "kill me."

Fadeyushka spun as another voice spoke up behind him.

"Go ahead, kill him. I will give you five extra minutes if you do it with your bare hands."

A man was standing on the bank Fadeyushka had just crawled up, a large-caliber sniper rifle resting in his powerful hands. The man had sand-colored hair and he spoke fluent Russian, with that same strange accent that had told Fadeyushka to begin running. He was over six feet tall and very solidly built. Fadeyushka had no doubt the rifle in his hands was the one the man had used to keep him coming in this direction and to rip off these poor unfortunates' hands. The man wore unmarked green fatigues and a large revolver in a leather shoulder holster. There was no telling who he was or what country he was from. Of course, that meant little here, where each soldier outfitted himself with whatever he could scrape together and uniforms were few and far between.

Fadeyushka had fought for the past year and a half and faced death many ways. From artillery fire, to IFOR jets screaming overhead, to snipers picking off members of his unit one by one. He felt fear, but he could manage it now that he saw his pursuer. He stood straighter. "Five more minutes for what?"

The man gestured with the barrel of the rifle past the clearing, to the other side where the terrain sloped down and Fadeyushka could see stagnant water and dank vegetation as far his eyes could penetrate.

"As of now you get a two-minute head start into the swamp. For two miles due west there is nothing but swamp along the river. Then you will strike the railroad embankment. If you reach the embankment, you have won and you will live. If I catch you before the embankment . . ." the man pointed at the men tied to the crosses. "Those are the ones I wound and bring back. There are twice that number out there in the swamp who I killed outright. But some have managed to make it and escape." The man smiled. "Do you want the extra five minutes?"

"Who are you?"

"You have five seconds to decide."

Fadeyushka turned and looked at the dying man, blood slowly oozing from the stumps of his wrists. Fadeyushka wrapped his hands around the man's throat and squeezed, feeling the very slight pulse of the man's dying heart under his fingers.

"Very good," the man with the rifle said.

Forty minutes later, Fadeyushka was still running hard. He had been on the track team in secondary school, a distance runner. The man couldn't have known that, Fadeyushka exulted as he saw the railroad embankment ahead. He splashed through the water, ignoring the searing pain from blisters inside his boots and the scream of air out of his lungs. The bleeding in his shoulder had stopped awhile back. Whether the wound had sealed or he was simply so low on blood by now, he didn't know.

Fadeyushka scrambled up the side of the embankment, tearing fingers on the gravel until he was on top. He'd made it! Fadeyushka looked back. The man had never even gotten close enough to fire a shot this time. The extra five minutes, that was what had done it, Fadeyushka thought as he began walking. He knew that the rail bridge to the south over the Sava was most likely destroyed, which explained the rust on the rail lines. But there would be a town somewhere ahead to the north. Of that he was sure. He felt exultant and light-headed as the railroad ties and gravel crunched under his wet boots.

He raised his hand to wipe his brow and it was as if a giant beast had suddenly snatched hold of the wrist and jerked him backward. He spun and fell, pain exploding up his arm in torrents. He gasped when he looked down. There was no hand, just a stump, pulsing his blood out onto the gravel. He stared at the flow, realizing that the leakage from the severed appendage was so slow because he had little blood left in his system. He scrambled about in the gravel, searching, the fingers of his remaining hand closing on the severed appendage.

Fadeyushka knew he had to do something. He blinked, trying to remember what it was. His vision blurred and he had to blink several times. He slumped back, closing his eyes. Then he saw his wife and their baby. He forced himself back up with his good hand, dropping the dead flesh.

Using his remaining hand, Fadeyushka quickly pulled his belt off and tied a tourniquet onto his right forearm. He looked up when he was done. A long way down the tracks, a figure, rifle in hand, was walking toward him. The line was perfectly straight as far as he could see in either direction and the man had to be at least a half mile away. Fadeyushka could not believe such a shot. He didn't bother to waste any more time marveling over it, though, as he got to his feet and stumbled away along the tracks in the opposite direction. Even with the pain he knew he couldn't go into the swamp again. His only chance was to outrun this man and get to a doctor.

Fadeyushka began to run, churning his legs, aware even as he did it that the blood, forced by his straining heart, was seeping out past the tourniquet. He felt as if he were moving in slow motion. One leg, then the other, his breath coming in ragged gasps.

Fadeyushka's left leg flew out from under him. He wasn't surprised to rise up on his left elbow and see the torn muscle where the bullet had ripped through his thigh from back to front. Fadeyushka allowed his head to slump back on a railroad tie.

He thought of his wife and child, a hundred miles away, working the farm in his absence. They had not known he was coming home. His unit had not known he had left. No one would ever know that here, in the middle of this godforsaken swamp, it had all ended. He wondered how his wife would feel when he never came back. He wondered if his unit would wreak vengeance on his family for his desertion.

The stupid war. That was what made Fadeyushka the angriest. Not the man whose footsteps coming closer he could hear, but the damn politicians and radicals who'd screamed words that had made people take up guns against each other. Neighbor against neighbor. Fadeyushka didn't hate anymore. The last half a year had seen to that. He just wanted to go home and work the land.

A boot came down on either side of his head. Fadeyushka noted that neither had any mud on them. The man had not even tried to follow him through the swamp. He'd probably driven down a road around the swamp to the railroad tracks and waited.

The muzzle of the gun came from the top of Fadeyushka's vision and centered between his eyes.

"It was quite a shot, was it not?" The man asked. "The railroad line gives me the best long-range field of fire in this area. I tried getting the first couple of men to stay on the line, but they always ran into the swamp, so I turned it around. I started them into the swamp and made them think the rail line was their salvation. That way I could get the shot I wanted. Excellent."

Fadeyushka wasn't listening. He was praying, preparing to meet his God.

"You thought I told the truth when I said some had made it. That was necessary," the man continued. "Hope is fuel and you needed it to make it here. But none have ever escaped me. There would be no point to that."

The man heard the whispered prayer and strangely, given his actions so far today, waited until Fadeyushka had finished.

"Are you ready?" the man asked.

Fadeyushka nodded, his eyes still closed.

The man studied Fadeyushka's torn fatigues, looking for any marking. "Muslim or Christian?"

Fadeyushka opened his eyes, hope flickering. "Does it matter?"

The man smiled. "It might."

Fadeyushka figured he had a fifty-fifty chance, but that brief flicker of hope went out with the pain from his wounds. The man had already shot him several times. He had lost too much blood. It would not matter now if the man let him go. "Christian."

The man nodded. "Muslim would have been better, but Christian will work."

"For what?"

The flame from the tip of the suppressor singed the entry wound the bullet made as it went into Fadeyushka's skull. The back of the head made quite a mess on the tracks as the bullet exited.

The man pulled a small SATPhone out of his pocket, a most sophisticated and expensive device, and punched in memory 1. It was answered immediately and he could hear the whine of a turbine engine in the background and the stutter of helicopter blades.

"I am ready," he said in French, one of half a dozen languages he spoke. There was a very slight chance the satellite communication might get intercepted, and French would confuse anyone listening.

After getting an acknowledgment, he put the phone back in his pocket. He pulled two harnesses out of his backpack. One he buckled around the body, making sure it was secure.

The second he buckled around himself. Then he squatted, rifle across his thighs, and waited, motionless. He stared at the body, looking into the lifeless eyes. Soon the sound of the helicopter echoed across the countryside.

He looked up as a Bell Jet Ranger, painted with IFOR markings, came in low over the rails. He put his hand over his eyes as the chopper came to a hover overhead. He reached up, grabbing the rope that was hooked to the lift on the left skid. There was a plastic case attached to the end of the rope, along with a large snap link. He pushed the snap link through the snap on the front of his harness, then the one on the front of the harness on the body. Making sure both were secure, he grabbed the small controller attached to the rope just above the snap link. He pressed a button, notifying the pilot he was ready.

The helicopter lifted, the rope unreeling from the lift until fifty feet were played out, then the man hit the stop. He was jerked off the ground, the body of Fadeyushka slamming against him. They went straight up for thirty feet, then the chopper pulled them to the east.

The man didn't flinch as Fadeyushka's body pressed up against his. He stared into the dead eyes with mild interest, feeling the other man's blood soak into his own clothes. There was the smell of feces and urine that even the wind rushing by couldn't completely get rid of. The man had killed enough to know that the body voided itself upon death, the autonomic nervous system no longer functioning. The man not only had killed often, he had made a study of death, so that he knew about it not only from the practical side, but also the theoretical.

The helicopter came to a hover over the small hillock where the bodies tied to the tree were. Slowly the pilot descended until the man's feet touched the ground. He quickly unhooked himself, the plastic case and Fadeyushka's body from the rig, hitting the wind button. The rope quickly wound up onto the lift. The chopper moved to the east and landed in a small clearing, blades turning, waiting.

The man threw Fadeyushka over his shoulder. With his free hand he picked up the plastic case. He carried the body to the center of the clearing. Then he threw the body down, dead eyes staring up to the clear sky. He opened the plastic case and pulled out the sniper rifle inside. It was the one he had used on the bodies tied to the trees about the clearing, a twin to the one he had carried. He laid the rifle across Fadeyushka's chest.

The man stood there for several seconds, loath to leave the gun. It was a standard Soviet Bloc SVD sniper rifle, one of many thousands circulating around the area, but this one he had worked on for a long time, fine-tuning.

With one last glance, he walked away toward the sound of the waiting chopper.

Chapter Four

Despite the downsizing of the army, it appeared to Thorpe that Fort Bragg was growing as he drove onto post. There were sprawling new compounds for the Third and Seventh Special Forces Groups among the pine trees off Yadkin Road.

Located to the west of Interstate 95 and the town of Fayetteville in the south-central part of North Carolina, Fort Bragg was home to the army's Special Forces and the 82nd Airborne Division. Covering over 148,000 acres of North Carolina pine forest, the post was the tip of the spear for the army's rapid deployment forces. Nearby Pope Air Force Base was the point from which that tip was launched.

The post was founded in 1918 as the army geared up for World War I. Before the days of political correctness, it was named after the Confederate general Braxton Bragg. The first military parachute jump was made at Fort Bragg in 1923 from an artillery observation balloon, and ever since it had been the home of the Airborne.

As he drove onto the post using Bragg Boulevard, Thorpe was hit with an assortment of memories, some good, some bad. He'd been many places in his time in the army, but in many ways Bragg had been the start point.

It was where he and Lisa had first been together after getting married. Tommy had been born in the post hospital. Thorpe forced his mind away from those memories.

Thorpe knew that Delta Force had moved from its old

green-fenced compound near the ROTC summer camp area to a highly secure, modern facility specifically built for them a few miles out in the range area. He'd heard that they had various weapons ranges inside the fence that surrounded the compound, along with full-size aircraft fuselages, trains, buses and other training aids.

During his active duty time in Special Forces, Thorpe had served a tour of duty in the new ACFAC, Academic Facility for Special Forces, that had been built across the street from the old Puzzle Palace, the former headquarters for army Special Operations that now held the headquarters for the JFK School for Special Warfare.

Thorpe's destination was the army Special Operations Headquarters, a new addition since his last trip here. It was set on what used to be a virgin acre of North Carolina pine forest. Several stories high, it was all glass and brick, very modern. It was a long way from the beat-up World War II–era "temporary" buildings Thorpe had received his Special Forces classroom training in years ago.

There were no parking spaces available in the lot immediately outside, so Thorpe was forced to park a quarter mile away, near the Third Group area. Third Special Forces Group (Airborne) had not even existed when Thorpe first joined Special Forces. Its area of operations was Africa and it had been brought to life several years ago—despite the rest of the army getting smaller, Special Forces was actually getting larger due to the strong demand for those units. For the first time since its peak strength during the Vietnam War, Special Forces had a group devoted to each populated part of the world: Third to Africa, Fifth to the Middle East, Seventh to Central and South America, First to the Pacific and Orient, and Tenth to Europe.

The command he was going to, SOCOM, was the headquarters for all those groups and the other elements assigned to army Special Operations: the Ranger Regiment, which consisted of three highly trained ranger infantry battalions; the 160th Special Operations Aviation Regiment (SOAR) that flew all the army Special Operations helicopters; Civil Affair and PSYOPS—Psychological Operations—units; and the various units dedicated to supporting the special operations team.

As Thorpe stepped out of the car, he pulled his battered green beret out of his left cargo pocket and settled it on his head, a move that over a decade and a half wearing the beret had made a very practiced maneuver.

His spit-shined jungle boots silently padded over pavement as he walked toward the front of the SOCOM building. He noted that Bronze Bruce, the limp-wristed, eighteen-foot-high bronze statue of a Vietnam-era Special Forces soldier, had been moved to the plaza in front of the building from its original place next to the Special Forces museum. He'd heard about the uproar the move had caused among the old guard in Special Forces.

Thorpe detoured over to the statue and walked around. On bronze plaques bolted to the low concrete wall around the statue were listed the names of those Special Operations men who had died since Vietnam. It was a long list for a country that considered itself to have been primarily at peace since the end of that conflict.

The names only served to reinforce what Thorpe had learned by bitter lesson: Special Operations was always on the cutting edge and facing danger all the time, regardless of whether there was a declared war going on or not. Thorpe noted the names of the two Delta Force operators who'd been killed in Mogadishu trying to rescue a downed helicopter crew from Task Force 160. He wondered how many civilians even remembered that failed peacekeeping effort or the videos of the bodies being dragged through the streets. Thorpe remembered, most often when he wished he wouldn't.

He scanned the names, looking for those of other men he had known. Men who had died on missions with him. He spotted a few, the places and occasions of their deaths as listed in the bronze letters a blatant lie in some cases. At least the names were there, though, which was more than could be said about some of the men who had disappeared or died on classified missions during the Vietnam conflict. But there were other names, names Thorpe knew, that weren't on the list. Men who had died in places where the U.S. government would never acknowledge they sent American fighting men. Men whose families had been told had died during training accidents. A surprising number of Special Operations helicopters had "crashed at sea," the bodies never recovered.

Thorpe ran a finger inside the collar of his starched battle dress uniform shirt, uncomfortable in uniform after wearing civilian garb for the past year and a half. He felt awkward, out of place. It was a strange feeling for a person who had spent his entire adult life in the military. He had not expected this feeling, but standing in front of the names of the dead, he knew he no longer fit. He'd lost something and he wasn't quite sure what it was. He knew he'd lost it before the Omega Missile incident, even before the Lebanon affair, but he wasn't quite sure when or why he had changed.

Thorpe checked his watch. It after 1000. The NCO at the reserve in-processing center had not exactly seemed in a rush to do Thorpe's or the other incoming reservists' paperwork and it had taken over an hour to process onto active duty for the next sixty days. Then he had received instructions to report to the SOCOM G-1 section for work.

The military staff was broken down into four major sections, numbers 1 through 4: 1 was personnel; 2, intelligence; 3, operations; 4, logistics. At brigade or lower level, the letter designator was an S, so that a battalion or brigade personnel officer, the adjutant, was the S-1. At higher than brigade level, the designator was a G.

Thorpe strode up the walk, snapping a salute at a colonel who was coming the other way. He pushed open the door to the building and stepped into the lobby. Two turnstiles filled up the way to the left of the guard desk. An elderly black man in a contract security company uniform looked at Thorpe, noted that he didn't have a badge clipped to his pocket as everyone else in sight did, and motioned for him to come over.

"Are you on the access roster, sir?"

"I doubt it," Thorpe said, giving the man his ID card.

Noting that it was the red color indicating reservist, the guard flipped open a particular computer printout and checked Thorpe's name against the list.

"You're not on here," the guard said. "Who are you here to see?"

"I'm supposed to check in with the SOCOM G-1 for further assignment."

"We'll have to get someone down from there to escort you."

Thorpe waited while the guard called, then longer while someone from the office came down. Finally a master sergeant appeared, quickly walking up to the other side of the turnstiles. "Sign in the visitor's roster, Major," the sergeant instructed.

Thorpe did as he was told, the guard keeping his ID card to be returned when he left. Thorpe pinned a numbered pink visitor badge on his pocket. The bottom of the badge warned in large letters that he must be escorted at all times.

Obviously they were taking security seriously around here, Thorpe reflected as he followed the master sergeant to the elevator. Once they were on board, the other man turned to him and stuck out a hand.

"Sergeant Major Jim Christie."

"Major Mike Thorpe."

"I know. I've heard of you."

It was hard to tell from Christie's inflection whether that was good or not. Thorpe knew Special Operations was a small pond and he'd made more than a couple of splashes in his time, and if anyone was going to hear something about it, it would the G-1 section.

"This way," Christie said, leading him down a corridor.

"Where will I be working?" Thorpe asked. He hoped he got to go to a Special Forces Group; either Third or Seventh, both here on post, would be fine with him. His rank was O-4, major, and there were slots at both group and battalion level for that rank.

"That's up to Colonel Kinsley," Christie said.

"When do I get to meet him?" Thorpe asked.

Christie pointed to a door at the end of the corridor as he slid behind the desk to the left of the door. "Right now."

Thorpe knocked on the door. A woman's voice called out, "Enter."

Thorpe glanced at Christie, but the sergeant was studiously absorbed in paperwork. Thorpe opened the door and marched to a point two feet in front of the colonel's desk, all the while checking out her and the room.

Kinsley was in her late thirties with straight brown hair parted in the middle. Her face was well tanned and she had on heavily starched fatigues. She wore steel-rimmed glasses that gave her appearance a severe look, rather like the librarian who used to hush the kids at the library back home. On the wall behind her were several plaques and a large guidon. It was red and gold, from a quartermaster unit that matched the insignia on her collar. There was a combat patch on her right shoulder, which these days could mean anything from having served in the Gulf War to a peacekeeping mission in Bosnia-Herzegovina.

"Major Thorpe reporting, ma'am."

Kinsley had a file in her left hand and she kept it there as she returned his salute. "At ease," she said.

Thorpe spread his feet shoulder-width apart and put his hands together in the small of his back. He watched her, waiting, a little surprised at this overly official meeting. He wondered if this was the way the regular army operated. It had been over fourteen years since he'd last been in a regular army unit, in the infantry at Fort Hood, and it was hard to remember. Special Forces usually operated less formally, but more professionally than the regular army, an apparent contradiction that outsiders had a hard time understanding.

Kinsley shook the file. "Quite a record. At least the part that isn't classified."

Thorpe didn't say anything.

"I asked for your classified records. After all, most people who work for this organization have classified data in their personnel files and I do have a top-secret access. My request was denied."

Thorpe wasn't surprised at that. And he didn't see any reason why LTC Kinsley, SOCOM G-1, had a need to know, since he was just here to do two months of active duty to punch his reserve ticket so he could qualify for retirement pay.

"You people," Kinsley continued, "act like you have your own little private armies. I spend my time trying to make sure all the units manning rosters are filled, and then find out some commander decided to move people around the world wherever he feels like it."

Thorpe remained silent. He'd met people like Kinsley before who thought their support job was more important than the job done by the people they were supposed to support.

"Are you bothered to be back on active duty?" Kinsley asked, dropping the file and leaning back in her chair.

Thorpe was surprised at both the question and the tone. It sounded like a challenge. "I'm here to do my duty as ordered."

"You didn't have to," she said. "You could have turned the orders down."

"I'd like to get my retirement benefits, ma'am. I believe I've earned them."

She picked up a cup of coffee and took a sip. Thorpe felt very uncomfortable at his modified position of parade rest while she sat there drinking coffee. He was too old for this. She seemed to be sizing him up. He glanced at a chair to his right, but if she noticed the look, she gave no indication.

"There's a lot going on," Kinsley said. "Tenth Group is heavily involved in the IFOR in Bosnia-Herzegovina and it looks like Seventh Group might have to commit a battalion also to the peacekeeping effort due to recent developments. I've got tons of paperwork making sure the deployed units are up to strength."

Thorpe didn't say a word, waiting. Like I give a damn about your problems, he thought. Tell it to the guys who are on the teams executing those deployments where the bullets are flying. He'd always found that people far away from the firing lines tended to think they were as important as, if not more important than, the people on the cutting edge.

"See Master Sergeant Christie to get your security badge."

Thorpe blinked. Getting a badge meant that he was going to be working in this building. "Ma'am, I'd like to work in one of the groups if possible. My experience is—"

"I've read your file," Kinsley cut him off, "at least the parts they would give me. I know what your areas of expertise are. But I make the assignments here. You're only going to be around for a few months. I just lost my only eighteen-series officer to one of the groups and you're taking his place. There is plenty that can be done in this office. As a matter of fact, I have a major project that will take up most of your time." She reached into her in-box and pulled out another file. She glanced up. "That's all. Christie will brief you and get you set up."

Thorpe snapped a salute and turned on his heel. When he'd gotten his orders, he'd thought about calling some of his old acquaintances and lining up a job for the two months, but he'd decided against going through the trouble. Now he was regretting that decision. He shut the door behind him and Christie was waiting.

"This way, sir."

Thorpe followed him down the hall and to the left. Christie opened a door and a small, windowless room beckoned. There were two desks with computers on them. One of the desks was occupied by a young warrant officer.

"Chief Takamura, meet Major Thorpe. He's going to be working with you for the next two months."

Takamura stood and offered his hand. He was short and chubby. He wore thick-lensed, army-issue, black-rimmed glasses. "Major, good to meet you."

Thorpe shook his hand. Christie turned in the doorway. "Get him set up with a badge and tell him what the colonel wants done."

"Right top."

The door shut. Thorpe sank down at the desk facing Takamura's and waited.

Takamura pointed at the computer on Thorpe's desk. "Our job is to screen records for the next promotion board. Make sure the photos are up to date, awards, record of service, et cetera."

Thorpe stared at Takamura as if he were speaking a foreign language. He closed his eyes as Takamura went on.

"Per the commanding general's policy letter, 98-2-4, the SOCOM G-1 is responsible to make sure that all SOCOM personnel's records are in the best possible shape they can be when they go before a promotion board."

"Isn't that the individual's responsibility?" Thorpe asked. The army, perhaps the largest "corporation" in American, promoted on the basis of time in service and service records that held evaluation reports.

"Yes, sir, it is," Takamura agreed, "but the general felt that so many people were deployed that many soldiers won't have a chance to update their records or even check them, so he wants us to do it for them. He doesn't want any of his troops penalized for being deployed."

Thorpe hated to admit it, but that made sense. He just didn't want to be the person to have to do it.

Takamura smiled. "I was the only one doing it. Now, I guess, it's the two of us."

Thorpe looked at the computer. "Great."

∽⁀∾

Six hours later, two things were for certain. There were a large number of officers assigned to Special Forces that were facing promotion boards. And most of them had not updated their records. Thorpe wasn't surprised about that—most Special Operators were more concerned about doing their job than making sure their Department of the Army photo was up to date, or the record of their latest award or ribbon was placed in their records. Also, most of them were so rarely in the States that updating files was a low priority. Thorpe's first year in Special Forces he had spent eleven of twelve months deployed overseas.

There was another thing he realized as he stared at the computer screen. Whatever little Thorpe had learned about computers had been supplanted in his brain by other information. He wasn't sure what that other information was, but he spent half the afternoon patiently listening and learning as Takamura showed him how to bring up a personnel record, then review it against the master Department of Defense data file and then update the record. Thorpe's two-finger pecking style of typing didn't help much either.

Thorpe was glad to see the end of the workday come. That was probably the only advantage to this job that he could see. He wouldn't be going to the field, and come 1700 he could walk out of the building like the rest of the staff weenies he'd used to despise while he was on an operational team.

Which is exactly what he did at 1700. He'd called Dublowski during the day and arranged to meet him at the Green Beret Club. Dublowski was there waiting for him when Thorpe walked in the door. Thorpe slid in the opposite side of the booth.

"Beer?" Dublowski asked.

"No, soda," Thorpe replied. He noted that Dublowski wasn't drinking either. Maybe they were all getting too old for the business. At the bar, several young NCOs from the school were sharing a couple of pitchers and telling of their day's work in loud voices.

"So what do they have you doing?" Dublowski asked as he came back with the soda. Thorpe quickly explained.

Dublowski snorted. "Watch out for the stapler. I hear some of those people in SOCOM received Purple Hearts during Desert Storm when they got wounded by a stealth Iraqi attack stapler that was planted in the office. They had people fly in from the States with the mail and pick up a combat infantry badge and combat patch. Bunch of bullshit."

"I'm surprised the SOCOM commander thought of having someone check on his people's records," Thorpe said.

Dublowski nodded. "General Markham's good people. He looks after his soldiers. Others . . ." Dublowski's jaw set. "Others, they don't give a shit about us. We're just tools to be used. Put a Band-Aid of American soldiers on every damn little outbreak around the world. Don't fix it. Just shove us in there and—" Dublowski stopped in midsentence.

"No, go ahead," Thorpe said with a smile. "Tell me how you really feel."

Dublowski didn't smile in return. He averted his gaze toward the bar.

Thorpe glanced at the younger men drinking at the bar. Daylight through the window passed through the mugs of beer on the bar, highlighting the golden glow. He looked back at the older man. Dublowski was now staring out the window. A young girl was at the bank across the street, using the ATM. Her shiny dark hair reflected sunlight as she tossed her head, clearing a stray strand off her forehead.

"I don't want to bring up more bad thoughts," Thorpe began, but Dublowski shifted his attention back into the room and indicated for him to go on. "Our world of covert operations is a small one. You've got to have some contacts in the intelligence community. Did you check with any of them about Terri?"

Dublowski sighed. "Yeah, I called in every favor I could think of. Nothing. I had a buddy of mine in the FBI do a check here stateside just in case she had maybe come back. Nothing." Dublowski leaned forward. "But it was kind of strange, Mike."

When Dublowski didn't elaborate, Thorpe had to ask. "What was strange?"

"I called a guy I knew in the CIA. We aren't exactly buddies, but he owed me one. His son was in the Eighty-second and got in trouble a couple of years back downtown in Fayetteville and I pulled some strings and got the boy out of it. So I figured he'd be a good guy to get to check behind the scenes with the Germans, since the Agency has got to have connections with the German intelligence agencies.

"Anyway, this guy said he would see what he could find out. He was enthusiastic about it when I first asked. You know, like he was glad he could repay the debt. But a week later he called me back and he said he hadn't found out a thing."

"So? Maybe there was nothing," Thorpe said.

"It wasn't what he said," Dublowski said, "but rather how he said it."

"What do you mean?"

"He'd lost his enthusiasm. He didn't want anything to do with the situation. When I pushed him, he cut me off and said he was sorry. When's the last time you heard a CIA dink say he's sorry?"

Thorpe pondered that for a moment. "What do you think?"

"I don't know," Dublowski said. "It bothered me then and it still bothers me now."

There was only one thing Thorpe could come up with and he was loath to say it, but felt he had to. "Maybe he found out she's dead?"

"Maybe, but he would have told me. I was prepared for

that and he knew it. He wasn't that much of a nice guy that he would want to spare me the hard news. No, I just got the feeling there was something else bothering him."

"Like what?"

"I've been wondering that myself the past couple of weeks, but I can't think of anything."

"You check with anyone else?" Thorpe asked.

"Everyone I could," Dublowski said. "We get GSG-9 men through here quite a bit," he said, referring to the elite German counterterrorism police force. "I've buddied up to a few of them. I called a couple and asked them to make some inquiries for me in Duetschland."

"And?"

"And nothing. Nada. I tried following them up, but they're dodging me."

"That's strange," Thorpe said.

"That aint all of it," Dublowski said. "The Agency has a representative here at Bragg who's supposed to coordinate with SOCOM and Delta. A guy named Ferguson. He showed up one day and told me to keep my professional and personal life separated; that they'd gotten some complaints about me via the State Department from the Germans. That's bullshit." Dublowski pushed his glass around on the table.

"Is there anything I can do?" Thorpe asked.

"No, but thanks for asking." Dublowski was silent awhile. Then he spoke in a tone of voice Thorpe had never heard the sergeant major use before. "Sometimes, Mike . . . sometimes I question whether I did right."

"You've been checking into things as much as you—" Thorpe began, but Dublowski cut him off.

"I'm not talking about *after* she was gone, but before. Whether I was a good father. You know I was gone most of the time she grew up. We all were. Defending our country, or so we were told. But did I do enough to protect my family? Hell, I've never fought anyplace—be it Vietnam, El Salvador, Lebanon, Desert Storm—where I felt like I was really fighting for *my* country.

"None of those places were really threats to us, were they? Political bullshit. Games. That's all they were. And I went to all of those places they ordered me to and left my family alone." Dublowski looked up and Thorpe was disturbed by the confusion in the eyes of the older man. "Which was more important? Hell, even at the end, the last time, I left my family in Germany while I came back here to the States to get up to speed on that operation we ran in the Gulf. Left them alone in a foreign country."

Thorpe leaned forward in the booth. "Dan . . ." he began, but he found the words weren't there. Finally he spoke the truth, based on what he had learned with his own family. "I don't know."

"What's wrong with you?" Dublowski said. "We've been yacking about me all this time and you haven't said word one about your life. What happened with Lisa and Tommy?"

"They're dead." Thorpe said the two words flatly.

"Goddamn," Dublowski whispered. "What happened?"

"Last year. Just a month after I got off active duty. Car crash." Thorpe swallowed. "A truck driver fell asleep at the wheel. Sideswiped them on the interstate and rolled them eight times before they came to a stop. They were both dead at the scene."

"Jesus," Dublowski whispered. "I didn't hear anything about it. I'm sorry, Mike."

"I was at a job interview." Thorpe looked up. "Can you believe that? I'd put my papers in right after Louisiana. Retired. Finally did what it took for my marriage, my family, to be first. They were coming back from Lisa's mom's. And I was away. Not there for them once again when they needed me."

"There's nothing you could have done except died too," Dublowski said.

"Maybe that—"

"Don't go there," Dublowski said.

Thorpe spread his hands out on the table. "The thing is, Dan, we don't know. I don't think we control anything. Lisa and Tommy wouldn't have been on that road if I had stayed in service."

"But Lisa would have left you if you had stayed in," Dublowski said.

"I know that, but she and Tommy would be alive. I thought I did the right thing for her and Tommy by getting out. So I don't know, Dan. I can't tell you what's right and wrong, or good and bad." Thorpe stood. "You still have Marge. Go home."

Dublowski stood. "Who do you have, Mike?"

Chapter Five

The girls were brought in, connected by a long thin chain that was run through a loop on the cuffs that bound their wrists. The interiors of the cuffs were lined with padding, to prevent any marking or scarring.

The five girls were all young, under twenty. They were draped in baggy white pants and smocks. Their faces were covered with veils, leaving only their eyes exposed. They were all short, ranging from a tad under five feet, to two inches over. Except for the last one in line. She was several inches taller, a willowy form overshadowing the others.

Their heads were bowed, except for that last girl. Her eyes were green and they darted about, checking out the room, then settling on the two men reclining on couches at the other end, fixing them with her glare.

The others all had blue eyes, but these dared not challenge the men, rather remaining fixed on the floor in front of their feet. Their shoulders were drooped, the cant of their bodies indicating defeat.

One of the men waved a hand festooned with rings and the guard who had escorted the girls halted them, then went down the line, grabbing their shoulders and forcing them to face the two men, their backs against a white-painted stucco wall.

The two men spoke in French, a language of choice and one they knew none of the girls understood.

"We have wasted enough time on them," the larger of the

two men said. "They are expensive to keep and a security risk. We have much that needs to be done. We do not have time for this. We need to be going." He was without his sniper rifle but not a weapon, as a large-caliber revolver nestled in a shoulder holster.

"They are very valuable," the other man disagreed. In his right hand was the same vial he had had in Germany, made of titanium, the surface glittering in the light. His fingers rotated it from pinkie to thumb and then back, a habit he paid no conscious attention to, the titanium vial passing through the fingers and the rings that adorned them in an intricate dance.

"One is," the larger man said. "But the others . . . You are once more mixing business with personal—"

"I do what I do for us. It is the only way to gain our vengeance."

The larger man said nothing for a few seconds, then turned his attention back to the girls. "They are stubborn."

The vial stopped moving for a few seconds as the other man spoke. "They are stones plucked from the wild. We must find the jewel inside—if there is one. And then we must shape the stone. An unshaped diamond is not worth anywhere near as much as a finished one."

He nodded toward the girls. "They can be shaped. But it takes care and precision. And when they are done, they are perfect. You have to mine many rocks to find the perfect jewel. If we get the One from this batch, it will be worthwhile. It is not enough to bend them to your will, you have to bring out what is inside. The One must be willing on her own and that is very difficult to achieve."

"The One." The larger of the two men fidgeted. His hand caressed the butt of his pistol.

The first man sighed. "But you are right, my brother. They have been stubborn. We have wasted too much time on these. They are promising, but we must winnow out the unacceptable. Sometimes a hammer must be used to crack the stone to see if there is something valuable inside." He reached out a hand. "Give me your gun."

The larger man pulled his pistol out, but hesitated before offering it. "Remember not to damage the—"

"I know, I know." The smaller man took the pistol, then spoke in English. "Young ladies, your attention, please."

The girl at the end had been watching them the entire time, not understanding the words they spoke but trying to follow anyway. Now the other four lifted their faces.

"You know nothing right now. You don't know where you are. You don't why I have brought you here." His voice was low, so quiet the girls had to strain to hear him. It was as if he was speaking to himself. "You are to be a gift. The most valuable of gifts. One of you." His voice grew slightly louder. "One of you. Or maybe none of you. It will be up to you. One of you must accept her fate and become . . ."—he paused for a long second, then smiled at a memory—"the One."

The girl on the end started to say something, but his hand shot up and chopped down, stopping the first word before it exited her throat. "You will not speak. You are either the One already or you are not. Only time will tell. But we do not have forever."

He flipped open the chamber and emptied the bullets into his open palm. The gun was made of carbon steel, the handle of dark plastic. The barrel was four inches long and thick.

Once the gun was empty, he took one bullet and held it up. "This is a .45-caliber bullet." He slid it into one of the openings on the cylinder, then flipped it shut. "There are five of you. Six chambers in the gun. There is a good chance one of you will die. Then the others will be left to ponder their reluctance to accept your reality. Of course, there is a very slight chance all of you will live." He spun the cylinder.

He pointed the gun in the girls' general direction. "I am going to pull the trigger five times. Who wishes to be first?"

Confusion showed in the girls' eyes. The one on the end stepped forward. "Me."

"Very good." The man aimed down the long barrel and pulled back on the trigger. The double action pulled the hammer back until it was fully cocked. He kept pulling. The hammer slammed forward with a solid click, but no round went off. The girl's shoulders slumped in relief and she stepped back.

"The odds are now one in five," the man said. "Who is next?"

Another girl stepped forward. She thrust her chin forward, glaring at the man with the gun.

He pulled back on the trigger and the hammer crashed home on an empty cylinder. "One in four now."

Two girls stepped forward at the same time. The man swiveled the gun at the one on the left in one smooth motion and pulled the trigger. The sound of the hammer on the empty chamber was still echoing when he had it trained on the second girl. She involuntarily stepped back as the hammer cocked, then slammed forward. Again on an empty chamber.

"Fifty-fifty now."

"No!" the remaining girl protested. "Please."

"You must step forward," the man said.

"No." The girl was sobbing. She fell to her knees, hands covering her head.

The man leveled the gun and pulled back on the trigger. Everyone in the room was riveted as the hammer poised in the cocked position. It flew forward, striking home on an empty chamber.

"What luck," the man said. He stepped forward and shoved the pistol under the kneeling girl's chin, the long front sight digging into her skin.

"Leave her alone!" the first girl who had stepped forward yelled. The guard jerked her chain, pulling her back.

"You lied!" the first girl spit out. The guard jerked the chain harder, causing her to stumble to her knees.

The man pulled the trigger, the hammer cocking. He continued through the pull and the hammer went forward. With just a click. The man laughed. He held up his other hand. A bullet was pinched between ringed fingers. It made the same journey through his fingers the vial had, appearing and disappearing. A small pool of urine spread out on the ground beneath the cowering girl.

"You bastard!" the girl who had been staring at him hissed. "You lied."

"I never lie," the man said. He flipped open the chamber of the revolver and slid the bullet in. He rotated it with a practiced move, pointed it at the fifth girl, who was still on the floor, her hands held out in front of her face.

"No!" the first girl yelled.

The man took a step back, leaving six feet between the end of the barrel and the girl's head. The hammer clicked back. The sound of the gun going off was thunderous in the enclosed space. The round hit the cowering girl, going through her hand and hitting her between the eyes. The body pitched backward as the large-caliber bullet exited the back of her head, taking most of her skull with it. Brains and blood splattered the wall and floor.

"I never lie." The man handed the gun back to the larger man. "We will find the One. Use today as a lesson."

"What do you want from this One?" the girl on the end demanded.

The man had handed the revolver back to its owner. He seemed puzzled for a second by the question, whether by the fact she had asked it or by the question itself, it wasn't quite clear. "What do we want? Vengeance." He waved a hand at the guards. "Take them away."

The larger man stood once the girls were pulled out of the room. "We must leave. There is much to be done," he said in French.

The first man nodded, his mind elsewhere. "We must prepare them all now if the One is to be ready."

"Tell the doctor," the larger man said. "He's just been sitting around here anyway. Make him earn some of his money."

Chapter Six

Thorpe stared at the list of names whose service records he was supposed to peruse to make sure they were up to date, then he looked at the clock. It was only 1030 and he felt like he'd been locked in this room forever. The office had no windows, a gray-painted square, about twelve feet by twelve, with just the two issue desks in it. Takamura's area had a little bit of the personal touch in the form of a small pewter figure of the Starship *Enterprise* set on top of his monitor. The side of his computer was covered with various stickers with sayings from the same show. Takamura wasn't much for talking, the only sound the steady clack-clack of his keys, letting Thorpe know the other man was still alive.

Thorpe started to type the next name when a sudden thought stopped him. He went back to the main menu and entered the enlisted personnel database. He typed: *Dublowski, Daniel.*

In a few seconds, Sergeant Major Dublowski's personnel records came up on the screen. Thorpe scrolled through until he found Dublowski's evaluation report from the tour of duty in Stuttgart. There was no mention in it, nor should there be, about of his daughter. It was a glowing report that a commander would write for a soldier he'd want to serve with again.

Thorpe tapped a pen against the side of the computer monitor as he thought. The one thing that Dublowski had not mentioned was why he had been shipped back to the States so quickly. A normal tour of duty overseas was three years, yet Dublowski had been in Stuttgart less than a year. Thorpe knew that could be explained by his expertise being needed in Delta Force, which always had priority selection throughout the army, but it was still strange. Of course, everyone affiliated with the Omega Missile fiasco had had strange things happen to their lives.

Thorpe ran through the pages that had been scanned in, searching for a copy of the orders that had reassigned Dublowski. He found the order assigning the sergeant major to Germany, but no copy of the stateside reassignment. That was strange, although there was a possibility the file hadn't been updated yet.

"Hey, Takamura," Thorpe called out.

A head poked around the side of the large monitor. "Yes, sir?"

"Is there a way to check on family members?"

"Family members?" A frown creased Takamura's forehead. "Are you in the dependent personnel database?"

"No, I'm still in the active duty database."

"Sir, we're not supposed to go into areas for which we aren't authorized."

"Can you access family members?" Thorpe repeated.

Takamura reluctantly nodded. "If they have an ID card, they're in the computer. You have to access whoever the person is who has the primary ID card, then you can get to all dependents, or family members as they're now called, off the main page menu. In the lower right-hand corner there should be a small box labeled FM—family members."

Thorpe saw the box where Takamura had directed him. He clicked on it. There were two names listed. Marge, Dublowski's wife, and Terri, his daughter. Thorpe clicked on Terri's name.

He was surprised when a very pretty face appeared in the upper left part of the screen. Black hair framed piercingly green eyes. Terri had grown up in the past four years. The rest of the screen was filled with her basic data that was on the card: date of birth, blood type, expiration date, which was listed as her eighteenth birthday. That birthday was only a month away, Thorpe noted.

Thorpe noticed an asterisk in the lower right corner followed by a string of numbers. "Hey, what's this?"

Takamura walked around and looked. "CID case number."

"Can we access it?"

"Yes, sir, but we'll get a come-back tag."

"A what?" Thorpe asked.

"Someone will know we accessed it and they'll probably want to know why. You can't dig into CID records without authorization." He looked at Thorpe. "We don't have authorization, do we, sir?"

"No, we don't."

"What's happened," Takamura explained, "is that a new level of security has been added to the Department of Defense central database—indeed, every federal database—to prevent unauthorized access. The first, and old, level of security is a password. But since you and I have a password, along with tens of thousands of other people, there was seen a need for more security against unauthorized searches or against hackers breaking into the system illegally. So 'tag' programs were developed and installed. What they are . . ." Takamura paused, trying to decide how to explain it to the computer-illiterate Thorpe.

"The best way to visualize a tag is that it is sort of a mirror. It picks up someone doing an inquiry or search and bounces it back to find out who that someone is by noting their password and log-on location. Then the security personnel can track down whoever's making an unauthorized search. All the top-secret databases have them. I would assume CID has one due to the sensitive nature of their files."

Thorpe leaned back in his chair while Takamura returned to his computer. Thorpe thought for a while, then picked up the phone. He got an outside line and quickly dialed. It was picked up on the second ring.

"Anti-terrorism liaison, Colonel Parker."

"This is Mike Thorpe, SOCOM weenie here at Fort Bragg," Thorpe said.

"Mike," Parker said. "How's Bragg?"

"New buildings, same old shit."

"Where do they have you?"

"SOCOM G-1."

"You should have called me. I might have been able to get you some real work," Parker said.

"I should have called someone," Thorpe agreed.

"What's up?"

"I need your thoughts on something."

"Shoot."

Thorpe quickly sketched the story of Dublowski's daughter, then waited to see what Parker would say.

"No contact at all with the family, either by the daughter or somebody who might have taken her?" Parker asked.

"No."

"That's not good," Parker said.

"Dublowski didn't say it, but I know he thinks she's dead," Thorpe said. "I knew Terri and I agree with him that she wouldn't run away."

"If she's the victim of foul play," Parker said, "then it was either a random act or part of a pattern. A random act of violence usually involves someone she knows."

"Dublowski would have suspected something if someone she knew was involved."

"What about him?"

"What?"

"Police always look to the immediate family in cases of murder."

"Not no, but hell no," Thorpe said. "Dublowski would never have harmed his daughter."

"The mother?"

"Parker . . ." there was a warning edge to Thorpe's voice.

"Mike, sometimes you don't know people as well as you would like to think you do."

"Let's leave the family out of it for the moment," Thorpe said. "All right?"

"Okay," Parker agreed. "If it wasn't someone she knew, then it most likely wasn't random. If she'd been in an accident her body would have been found. That really only leaves one thing."

"What's that?"

"She's part of a pattern of killings. You're talking about a serial killer."

"How do you know so much about this?" Thorpe asked, surprised by her rapid deductions.

"Part of my job is to coordinate between various federal agencies' special operations forces on anti-terrorism—DOD isn't the only that has them. The FBI has its HRT, Hostage Rescue Team, and as an adjunct to that they have their Investigative Support Unit. The ones who get called into tough cases that the locals have trouble with. Used to be called Behavioral Sciences?"

"I've heard of them," Thorpe said.

"They do more than just serial killers, although that's the stuff that gets them headlines. I work with the guy who heads the unit on terrorist profiles. We talked about a lot of subjects—he wanted to know about Kilten and McKenzie."

Thorpe remembered the two men—the scientist who tried to destroy his own creation, the Omega Missile, and the former navy SEAL that Kilten had picked to help him who had an agenda of his own.

"They get their suspect profiles by doing a psychological study on people who have committed the same types of acts. Needless to say, McKenzie and Kilten weren't around to interview, so he's been tracking down those who knew them. He also said they were doing a profile of Hill—the NSA adviser who set up the Red Flyer missions—which I thought was kind of interesting."

Thorpe had tried to distance himself as much as possible from those events. He remembered getting a message on his machine from someone in the FBI—probably the same man—wanting to know about McKenzie who had been with Thorpe on the beach in Lebanon. For a moment, Thorpe was back there, being chased by an Israeli army tank, after gunning down several CIA guards while attempting to stop the transfer of weapons-grade plutonium.

Thorpe shivered. "Back to Dan's daughter," he prompted.

"Since he was asking me so much, I asked him a bunch of questions. It's pretty interesting. Like they can predict what sort of car a type of killer will be driving and that sort of stuff. They've made a real science of it.

"He told me that when someone disappears and foul play is suspected, it's one of three things. Someone the victim knew committing a murder, a kidnap where you'll hear from the kidnappers, or a serial murderer. From what you've said it's not the first or the second, so that leaves us the third. A serial killer in Germany."

It was an conclusion that Thorpe had considered but shied away from. "Why do you say serial killer? Why not an accident or someone who kills just once? A random act?"

"I'm just telling you what this guy told me and they are the best in the world at what they do. It's kind of scary how well they can profile those nutcases.

"If there's foul play involved then it's either someone she knows or someone she doesn't. If it was someone she knew, then it seems to me that Dan would have suspected that someone. Since he doesn't, it has to be a stranger. If it's a stranger, the FBI guy said the really dangerous thing is that then it's most likely not an isolated incident. It will happen again or it happened before."

"That's pretty pessimistic," Thorpe said.

"No, it's pretty realistic," Parker said. "And serial killers don't just stop. They go until they're caught or they die."

"Did this guy say anything about the victims? Would they be the same type of person or just whoever happened to be in the area?"

"Usually the victims fit a pattern. Same sex, usually same age, sometimes they even look alike."

"Okay, that gives me an idea."

"Glad I could help," Parker said. "If you need anything else, you'll let me know, right?"

"Right."

"Okay." There was a short, awkward pause. "Mike?"

"I've got to go now," Thorpe said.

"Okay. Call me—if you need anything, all right?"

"Right." The phone went dead.

Thorpe put the receiver down and stared at the computer. "Hey, Takamura."

"Yes, sir?"

"I want to find something out on the computer, but I don't know how to do it."

Takamura face broke into a smile. "What do you want the computer to do?"

"Can you get the computer to bring up all records that have a CID report tag on them?"

Takamura nodded. "All soldiers assigned to this command, yes. But that's outside our province of work, sir."

"Let me worry about what we're supposed to be working on."

"Sir—"

Thorpe tapped his collar where the yellow oak leaf of his rank was sewn. "I take responsibility. Can you bring up whether a family member has a CID file?"

"Yes, sir."

Thorpe stared at Takamura, who finally got the hint and began typing.

"That won't activate the CID tag program, will it?" Thorpe asked.

"Not if we restrict the search to the SOCOM personnel database and don't try to actually get into the files. Of course, the current total army database has well over a million people in it, including family members and—"

"Restrict it to Special Operations personnel assigned to Germany," Thorpe said.

"How far back do you want me to look?"

"Let's say two years."

Takamura got to work. After twenty minutes, he looked up. "I've got thirty-one hits on CID reports on Special Forces military personnel and family members in the past two years in Germany."

Thorpe frowned. Those reports could be anything from shoplifting at the PX, to a capital crime, to their quarters getting broken into. "Can you cross-reference those hits with those families that have been investigated by Social Services?"

Takamura's answer was to begin typing. A few minutes later he was done. "Eight."

Thorpe had been thinking while he was working. "Now can

you narrow it down to families that have daughters, aged fourteen to eighteen?"

Takamura was having fun. "That won't be too hard." Another couple of minutes and the field had further been reduced. "Four."

"Can you display those records?"

"The computer is set."

Thorpe reclaimed his seat. "Thanks."

As he expected, Dublowski's name was on the list. There were three other names. The first one was a staff sergeant who had been accused of molesting his daughter. There was no indication that the daughter had disappeared. The second one was a daughter who had been picked up for stealing an automobile off post.

Thorpe was beginning to think this was a dead end when the third name came up. A daughter, age seventeen, was reported missing. The family lived near Stuttgart, just as Dublowski had. CID had investigated and concluded she had run away. Thorpe jotted down the name of the soldier and his current assignment: Tenth Special Forces Group, Fort Carson, Colorado.

So perhaps there was another one, Thorpe thought as he leaned back in the seat. It was slim. But then again, there were a lot more American servicemen overseas than the Special Operations soldiers that Takamura had accessed.

"Hey, Takamura. Could you expand that search you just did to the entire army? All personnel assigned to Germany?"

Takamura tapped a pencil against the side of his glasses. "I suppose I could. I'd have to go on line with the main database in Washington though, sir."

"Will you get in trouble for that?" Thorpe asked.

"No. We do it all the time. It's just that it would take a while. If I do the past ten years with the variables you gave me, the computer will have to shift through a couple of million records looking for those specific variables."

"Will you do it?"

In answer, Takamura gestured for Thorpe to relinquish his seat. It only took Takamura ten minutes to set the search up, but the running took over an hour and a half. Thorpe grew impatient with the little clock on the face of the computer screen whose little hands going around in a circle indicated the computer was working.

At one point he asked Takamura why the computer couldn't just start showing personnel records as they fit the description, but Takamura responded with a ten-minute discourse on the inner workings of the machine and system that made Thorpe wish he had never asked.

Thorpe didn't understand computers and he didn't particularly care to. Nor did he particularly like them. He felt that people were overdependent on them. After what had happened with the Omega Missile in Louisiana, he would never completely trust a computer again. It had been Kilten's point that taking the human element out of the nuclear launch loop and letting computers make decisions was a dangerous course to embark on.

To hammer his point home, Kilten had recruited McKenzie and seized control of the Omega Missile, a command and control system designed to target and launch all the United States' nuclear weapons. He'd accomplished most of that by taking over the master computer that controlled the Omega Missile. After that traumatic experience, Thorpe was uneasy whenever people talked about the wonderful things computers could do.

Thorpe had noted during the Gulf War that every unit in the army now carried a small handheld GPR, global positioning receiver computer, that gave the bearer's location anywhere on the planet. He felt that soldiers were getting too dependent on the technology and wouldn't be able to find their way using the old map and compass. He'd just read that the Naval Academy was going to stop teaching celestial navigation to its student officers, making them completely dependent on satellite positioning systems. He wondered what those officers would do if the satellites were destroyed or electromagnetic pulse from a nuclear explosion disabled their electronic receiving systems.

Here, in this office, he was supposed to be checking files that would be used to determine whether a soldier was to be promoted or not, by a board that would never have met any of the personnel whose fate they were determining. The human touch seemed to have long ago disappeared and it made Thorpe feel like a dinosaur.

The clock finally stopped and the screen cleared. Four hundred and twenty-two hits. The large number made Thorpe reverse his earlier judgment of computers and wish it could narrow the field down a bit. He began going through each file, one by one, searching for missing daughters.

When he was finished, the workday was also almost done, but Thorpe had not noticed the clock on the wall. He had twenty-four possibles. He was surprised at the large number. He had the computer print him out a copy of the names and current assignments of each family.

Twenty-four. The number bothered Thorpe. There was no doubt some of those girls had run away and cut off all communication with their family. But twenty-four?

Thorpe knew it wouldn't be easy for a family member to run away while stationed in Germany. They couldn't simply fly back to the States because they'd traveled there on military orders with their parents, not on passports. They needed orders getting them back into the States and since they didn't have that, it ruled one avenue out. Thorpe supposed some of them could have run away and stayed in Europe, but the continent was so civilized now that someone without the proper papers would be picked up quickly, particularly in Germany, with its growing backlash against illegal immigrants.

"Hey, Major, you going to lock up?"

Thorpe was startled out of his dark reverie. "No, I'm leaving now too."

Takamura noted the printout. "I don't mean to be a jerk, Major, but you need to be careful around here. They check everything you take out down at the front desk. Plus, the colonel is real picky about people doing anything personal on the computer.

Thorpe folded the list up and shoved it inside his shirt. "They don't strip-search you, do they?"

"Not unless they have a reason to."

"All right, then. Let's go."

❧

Several hundred miles up Interstate 95 in Maryland, an analyst sitting at a desk in the bowels of the NSA, National Security Agency, responded as he was trained to do when his computer screen indicated a flag alert.

A flag alert meant that someone, somewhere in the massive federal computer network, was looking at material that someone else, somewhere else in the federal system, wanted to be alerted about if anyone looked. It could be anything from a congressman wanting to know about E-mail complaints coming from his district to someone digging into restricted weapons systems files.

The analyst worked to put a name and location to both sets of someones and somewheres. The first pairing was G-1 SOCOM at Fort Bragg. The second pairing, the ones who had put the flag alert in place, made him take notice. CIA operations at Langley.

As required, the analyst forwarded the alert information to Langley.

Chapter Seven

Dublowski studied the list for a long time. Thorpe and he were in the sergeant major's house, just off post in Fayetteville. Marge was nowhere to be seen and since Dublowski hadn't offered, Thorpe hadn't asked. The large two-story home felt empty and lifeless.

"There's eight disappearances around Stuttgart," Dublowski noted. "This is a lot of missing young women. How come no one's ever seen this pattern?"

"No one's ever looked," Thorpe said. "Also, that covers a time period of two years and every U.S. military family that was stationed in Germany. A lot of people. And it might not be a pattern," Thorpe added, picking up his friend's mood.

"Fucking CID," Dublowski said. "They should have checked."

"CID is limited in what it can do overseas," Thorpe said. "After all, Germany is a foreign country."

"They still could have checked."

"We're not sure we have a pattern," Thorpe repeated. "Look, CID has the same problem in Germany that every unit has. Turnover. There's no institutional knowledge there like regular community police forces have."

"Then why did you bring me this?" Dublowski said testily.

"We can go to CID," Thorpe said, "and give them that. They can get hold of the families and check. Maybe some of these girls did run away and have shown up. Maybe some have been accounted for in other ways. Maybe the German authorities have found some."

Dublowski stood. "Let's go."

Thorpe looked at his watch. It was almost six in the evening. "Why don't we wait until tomorrow during normal duty hours?"

Dublowski didn't answer. The screen door was already slamming shut behind him. Thorpe followed. He knew he was probably going to get in trouble for having used the computer to get the list, but he wasn't too worried about that. He'd broken bigger rules than unauthorized use of a computer during his time in service and now that he was a reservist there wasn't too much they could do to him except screw with his retirement benefits, and the army had already done that.

He hopped in the passenger seat of Dublowski's truck. The ride to the Fort Bragg CID headquarters didn't take long. It was located in a new building across the street from the post school. Dublowski led the way in and they walked up to a man in civilian clothes manning a desk right inside the door. He eyed Dublowski, with his big gray mustache and civilian clothes, warily.

"Can I help you?"

Dublowski pulled out his ID card and laid it on the man's desk. "I'm Sergeant Major Dublowski and this is Major Thorpe."

"Agent Martinez," the man replied. "What can I do for you?"

Dublowski slapped the computer printout on top of his ID card. "This is a list of teenage dependent girls who have disappeared without a trace in Germany in the past two years. There's twenty-four names on the list. My daughter's is one of them."

Martinez picked up the list and looked at it warily.

"I was told that there was nothing CID could do about my daughter disappearing," Dublowski continued as the agent read. "I was told she ran away. I know she didn't and the list backs me up."

"How does this list back that up?" Martinez asked with a frown as he scanned the list.

"There's a pattern," Dublowski said. "Someone is kidnapping young dependent girls in Germany."

Martinez cautiously put the list down and looked at the angry sergeant major. "I'm not really sure what I can do with this."

"Then get someone who knows," Dublowski growled.

"Hold on while I get the shift commander," Martinez said.

In the next hour, Dublowski told his story and showed the list to three CID personnel of increasing rank. Thorpe stayed in the background. He felt that they were getting somewhere as the rank went up. At eight he found out exactly how far. The full colonel who was the regional CID commander finally came in. He listened to Dublowski's story, then took the list with him into his office and shut the door. Twenty minutes later he came back out.

"Where did you get these names?" he asked.

Thorpe stepped forward and explained his part.

"Do you know what you did is illegal?" the colonel asked.

"Not exactly illegal, sir," Thorpe hedged. "I was just—"

"Exactly illegal!" the colonel snapped. "You're lucky I don't bring you up on charges, Major."

He turned to Dublowski. "Sergeant Major, I am sorry about your daughter, but the official file on your case shows that CID-Germany investigated and ruled that there was no foul play involved. The case agent's notes suggest that your daughter most likely ran away. It happens all the time." He shook the list. "In fact, I'm amazed there are only twenty-four names on this list for a time period as long as two years, given the numbers of soldiers who rotate through Germany. I would have guessed the number to be much higher.

"Do you know how many people disappear every day? And they aren't all victims of foul play. In fact, relatively few are. Even in our modern society, people can hide if they want."

"Wouldn't it be rather hard to do that overseas?" Thorpe asked, sensing the brewing volcano next to him and trying to avert an eruption.

"Not necessarily," the colonel said.

"My daughter didn't run away," Dublowski said.

"Sergeant Major, your friend here"—he pointed at Thorpe—

"committed an illegal act when he used the computer at SOCOM to get these names. Those personnel files are restricted and can be looked at only on an official need-to-know basis. How would you like it if someone was looking through your personnel record for some reason of their own whenever they felt like it?"

"Sir," Thorpe began, "I understand what I did was—"

A female voice cut him off. "No, Major Thorpe, I don't think you do." Lieutenant Colonel Kinsley was standing by the door. She looked very unhappy to be at CID headquarters at nine-thirty in the evening. Her battle-dress uniform wasn't as crisply starched as when Thorpe had seen it earlier in the day. She turned to the CID colonel. "Are you done with them, sir?"

The colonel walked over and handed the printout to Kinsley. "Yes, I am." He looked at Dublowski. "I'm sorry, Sergeant Major, but the case is closed."

Dublowski didn't budge. "What about all those missing girls?"

"Every one of those cases was investigated and closed," the colonel said. "Linking them together is not sufficient to cause us to reopen them. It's like saying every crime committed in North Carolina is linked. There's just no evidence. I hate to say it"—the colonel lowered his voice—"but the biggest problem with all of this is that of these twenty-four, not a single one has been recovered as a body. If your theory of a serial killer was true, then surely some bodies would have been found."

The colonel was warming to the subject. "The fact is that most serial killers want the bodies to be found. They want the world to know what they're doing. CID-Germany did as much as they could, given what was there in the case file and the limits of operating overseas in another government's jurisdiction.

"I'm sorry, but the case is closed. I will contact the CID office in Germany and check to see if anything new has turned up, but unless there is further evidence, there is nothing we can do here." With that, the colonel turned his back on them.

Thorpe put a hand across Dublowski's chest, restraining

him. "Let's go, Dan. We've done all we can here." He kept the physical pressure on Dublowski, herding him out of the CID building.

Lieutenant Colonel Kinsley walked with them to the parking lot. Her last words to Thorpe weren't very encouraging. "Major Thorpe, I will see you in front of my desk at exactly 0900 hours tomorrow morning." She was in her car driving away before Thorpe and Dublowski reached the older man's truck.

"I'm sorry I got you into this, Mike." Dublowski had calmed down.

"It's all right. I've had my butt chewed by experts. What's she going to do, send me to a team and make me carry a rucksack?"

Dublowski started the truck and they headed back toward the BOQ.

"What do you think of CID's reaction?" Dublowski asked.

"I hate to say it, Dan, but it's pretty reasonable," Thorpe said. "When I first saw the list, I thought twenty-four was a lot, but if you divide it by two years and the vast number of U.S. personnel going through Germany, then it's really a very low percentage. And the CID colonel was right: Most of those probably are runaways."

Thorpe could see the muscle on the side of Dublowski jaw clenched, but the sergeant major didn't say anything. Thorpe knew he was treading on thin ice, but he also knew what Dublowski was capable of and he felt he needed to defuse the situation right now.

"There was no evidence, no connection between the names," Thorpe continued. "Until we get that, we don't have anything. It was something I went off half cocked on, and we got caught on it."

"Yeah," Dublowski reluctantly said, "I guess so."

The truck pulled up to the front of Moon Hall and Thorpe got out. "Thanks anyway," Dublowski said.

"I'm not going to give up on this," Thorpe said.

"What can you do? That colonel you work for sounds like she'd love to have your ass for breakfast tomorrow."

Thorpe laughed, indicating what he thought of that fate.

"I'm going to call someone I know," Thorpe said, leaning back in the truck seat.

"What for?"

"We might not be able to do anything, but she might. She's got access to a lot of information and she's probably smarter than the two of us combined."

"Some smarts would help," Dublowski acknowledged.

The original CIA headquarters building was built in the mid-1950s by the same firm that had designed the UN building in New York. The then-director of Central Intelligence who oversaw the design directed that it be built like a college campus, perhaps a subconscious attempt to camouflage the mission of the organization even to those who worked there. The original building contained over 1.4 million square feet and was the hub of the nation's foreign intelligence gathering for the bulk of the Cold War.

A new addition of 1.1 million square feet was built in 1984, and consisted of two six-story modern office buildings attached to the original headquarters. Despite being less than eight miles from the center of Washington, CIA headquarters was set on 258 acres of rolling countryside in northern Virginia that made Washington seem much farther away.

The CIA was formerly founded by the National Security Act of 1947, which also established the National Security Council. Before that time, the organization traced its lineage through the Central Intelligence Group founded in 1946, and before that to the OSS, Office of Strategic Services, of World War II fame. The OSS had been led by Colonel "Wild" Bill Donovan, who had been awarded the medal of honor in World War I.

During the Second World War the OSS had been a bastard stepchild to the British's SOE, Special Operation Executive, which had far more experience at the nefarious art of espionage, but by the end of the war, under Donovan's guidance, the American OSS had earned its spurs. Not only did it give birth to the CIA, but it was also the same unit that army Special Forces traced its lineage to.

Despite being birthed from the same organization, over the years the CIA and Special Forces had more often been at each other's throats than allied in a common cause. This came to a head during the Vietnam War, when Special Forces felt it was being used by the Agency to fight its own dirty war. Many of the Agency's most controversial programs, such as Phoenix, were staffed by Green Berets. But when it came time for the Agency to support several Special Forces men accused of murdering a double agent at Nha Trang in 1969, the Agency refused to back up the military men, leaving them to dangle.

The CIA had many ups and downs in the first fifty years of its existence. On the darker side lay early events like the Bay of Pigs. Of more noteworthy mention during that time period was the Cuban Missile Crisis. Abuses during the Cold War led to the formation of the Select Committee on Intelligence, which was at first supposed to be temporary, but was changed into a permanent organization in 1976, allowing Congress oversight on intelligence matters.

In 1982, President Reagan signed a bill exempting the CIA from the requirements of the Freedom of Information Act, reversing a decade-long trend of more openness.

On the grounds at Langley, a piece of the Berlin Wall was set up as a memorial to what the CIA considered its greatest victory—the end of the Cold War and the collapse of the Soviet Union.

A solitary figure was now passing that memorial, the lights highlighting the cracked concrete piece of wall casting his long shadow along the walkway heading toward one of the new office towers.

The man noted the piece of the wall every time he passed it because it represented several things to him. One was indeed the fall of the Soviet Union, but Karl Hancock wasn't too sure how much the CIA had had to do with that; in fact, having worked in covert operations for over thirty years, he knew how much CIA distortion of Russian military capabilities had added to American paranoia for decades and maintained the

Western side of the Cold War at a footing far beyond what was truly necessary.

The reality of the unreality of covert operations was what the wall memorial represented to Hancock. And that reality could be manipulated by those who understand it to fit their own purposes.

Hancock pulled his ID out for the rent-a-cop security guards who manned the entrance to the building. The first layer of security. He again pulled it out as he passed through the second layer, this time showing it to guards who were actually CIA personnel. He boarded an elevator and descended below the surface to sublevel three. He exited into a small lobby, where he was required to get his retinas scanned before the steel door on the other side would open. A guard sitting in a booth enclosed in bulletproof glass watched him without expression as he performed the maneuver. Hancock walked down a black-marble-floored hallway, passing framed placards with the Agency's vision, mission and values engraved on them. He didn't waste any of his time reading them. Public relations devices to appease a country that wanted to be safe and free but didn't want to be dirtied by the processes necessary to ensure that in a world full of dirty players.

At the end of the hall a large CIA seal was bolted to the wall; double doors beckoned to either side. A fork in the road. To the left was the operations center. To the right, the Center for Direct Action.

The Operations Center had a large sign identifying it. CDA simply had a black falcon painted on the steel, one claw of the falcon holding a lightning bolt, the other the American flag. Hancock had had it put there when he took over CDA and he always paused to appreciate the art before pushing the doors open.

Hancock went down to the end of the hallway beyond the falcon painting to another steel door. He put his palm on the panel to the left of the door. It swung open with a hiss. He walked into his office, putting his coat on a hook just inside the armored door.

His desk was large and flat, without anything on it. To the left of the desk, eight chessboards were set on a marble pedestal. Each board had different motifs for the pieces, ranging from the traditional, through a Napleonic motif, Civil War motif, and a World War II one. Seven of the eight had games in progress on them, the pieces frozen in the midst of their combat. Hancock stopped and stared at the Civil War board for several moments. The game was in the early stages, only a few pieces moved.

With a sigh, Hancock turned. Just before he left his office he paused and looked at the cluster of framed pictures on the wall to the right of his door. There were several of him in the White House War Room with Presidents from Nixon through the current administration. Never the Oval Office, where publicity shots were taken—that was for the director and the chief of Operations. The chief of Direct Action only went to the White House through the underground tunnel from the Vice President's office building and only met with the administration officials in the secure War Room, three hundred feet under the White House. And the CDA only went to the White House when dirty work needed to be done.

Hancock's eyes paused on a particular photo—he was seated at the War Room conference table; standing behind him with a hand on Hancock's shoulder was former National Security Adviser Hill, now currently awaiting trial for his role in the Red Flyer teams and other purported abuses of power.

Hancock's gaze continued to another photo. A much younger Hancock was on a deep-sea fishing boat with another man. A muscle on the left side of Hancock's face jerked. The other man had the same angular face as Hancock, the major difference being the other man's hair wasn't yet burned white—nor would it ever be.

Hancock left his office, retracing his steps to the main corridor, the sounds of the taps on his highly polished shoes echoing off the walls. He crossed the main hallway and entered the other department that took up the third sublevel of the basement.

Night or day, the Operations Center at Langley functioned at the same level of intensity and manning. That was because the section was responsible for the entire globe, and while it was night over Washington it was daylight over half the world.

Also, despite all the advances in technology, night was still the preferred time for covert operations. Hancock kept walking while he took in the massive status board—an eighty-foot-long-by-thirty-high electronic map of the world. Anything of significance to the intelligence community was highlighted on the board with a briefly noted box.

Right now, the largest box, indicating its relative importance, and backed in red—indicating it was vital to U.S. interests—was hovering over Bosnia-Herzegovina. Hancock walked over to one of the terminals. He brought up a smaller image of the one on the screen, then clicked over the box. He read the summary, then closed the box.

Hancock pushed open the door to one of the sound- and bug-proofed conference rooms off the main action center. A younger man was seated at the end of the conference table.

"What do you have?" Hancock asked. He was in his late forties and he looked trim and fit in his three-piece suit. His voice held a tint of finishing school or perhaps a lot of practice in front of a mirror. As chief of Direct Action, CDA, a classified section answerable only to the director and the President, Hancock held the greatest nonvisible power inside the CIA. The CDA did what Operations used to do before Operations became subject to public scrutiny and congressional censure. The Oversight Committee didn't even know the CDA existed.

Welwood worked in Operations, the strongest visible part of the CIA. As such he was answerable to the chief of Operations. But the C/O was a new appointee, the first woman ever to hold such a high rank in the old-boy Agency, and there were many in operations who feared for their careers working for a woman who was going to be scrutinized for every decision she made or failed to make. If she went down, they'd all take a hit, and Hancock knew Welwood was smart enough to know he needed to cultivate friends elsewhere in the Agency's bureaucracy.

Welwood's voice was rich, developed in boarding schools and the Ivy League. "My desk received an electronic flag from the NSA referencing an unauthorized computer search that was conducted into the Department of Defense personnel database yesterday," Welwood said. "Normally, such a matter is no big deal. Some clerk checking something for a buddy. However, this one was a little different. This search triggered a flag instigated by our Agency."

Hancock had not taken a seat and was still standing, his posture indicating his impatience. "Why did you notify me?"

"A second, please, sir," Welwood said. He knew that information had to be presented in a certain order and he also knew Hancock's reputation. He had to impress Hancock the first time because there would be no second time. "The computer inquiry was a search for young women, military family members, who had disappeared in Germany over the past two years."

Hancock's face was an inscrutable mask. "And?"

"And," Welwood said, "the person making the inquiry was an army major named Mike Thorpe."

Hancock pulled out a leather chair and sat down, steepling his fingers together under his chin. "Mike Thorpe?"

Second hit, Welwood thought. "Yes. He's in the army reserves now, working an active duty tour for the Special Operations command at Fort Bragg."

"Why should that or this search interest me?" Hancock asked.

Welwood continued with the rehearsed presentation. "I checked on this Thorpe fellow. He was involved in both the Omega Missile incident and a covert operation off the coast of Lebanon involving nuclear materials."

Hancock leaned back in the seat and crossed his ankles. He was looking at Welwood with what might be described as mild interest. "So?"

Welwood knew Hancock's reputation too well to expect more than that on the surface.

"I checked the logs for the Lebanon operation. I believe it was called Operation Delilah. Something to do with keeping the balance of power in the Middle East by providing the Israelis with raw materials for nuclear weapons. An under-the-table deal that was an outgrowth of the original classified rider appended to the Camp David Accord. Updated when the Palestinians were given autonomy in the West Bank.

"According to what I could find, Operation Delilah was an operation run by Direct Action." Welwood was on thin ice now. He had guessed the objective of Delilah from the little information the computer had yielded and some discrete inquiries on his part from other personnel in the building.

"Seems our man Major Thorpe was working with a Special Operation Nuclear Emergency Search Team that picked up word of a transfer of fissionable material from Russia to an unknown group in southern Lebanon. Naturally it was assumed this transfer was to a terrorist organization. When he went in to check it out, turns out it was, shall we say, U.S.-supported elements, giving material to Israeli forces. Sounds like it was a bloody mess."

For the first time, Hancock showed emotion. "A bloody mess? Three of my men were killed by Thorpe. Killed while doing their duty to our country."

"Well, Thorpe thought he was also—" Welwood cut off what he was going to say when he saw the flash in Hancock's eyes. "Subsequently," Welwood continued, "another aspect of the classified rider became, shall we say, active? I believe it was called the Samson option?"

Hancock's mask was back on. He crossed his legs at the ankles and leaned back in the chair. "Do you know what the Samson option was?"

Welwood nodded. "A nuclear weapon emplaced by the Israelis in a house in Washington, D.C. With one of their agents baby-sitting the bomb with a direct Sat-link back to Tel Aviv. One call from Tel Aviv and he would fire the bomb."

Hancock nodded. "You know the what. Do you know why that was allowed?"

"A contingency to the classified rider to the Camp David Accord subsequently acted out during the Gulf War to keep the Israelis from responding to the SCUD attacks out of Iraq."

"Balance of power," Hancock said. "Everything is power. And it has to be balanced or else extreme action is taken. That is why my office exists. To take direct action if a balance is threatened. To maintain the balance. Do you understand that?"

Welwood nodded. "Yes, sir. But the Omega Missile terrorist strike upset many balances," Welwood concluded with more confidence than he felt. He had never been in the field and although he tried to appear casual about it, talking about such operations made his stomach churn, especially talking with someone like Hancock.

Hancock tapped a finger on the tabletop. "What was the result of the Omega Missile incident?"

"The terrorists who took over Omega Missile used it to launch two nuclear strikes. One against the Pentagon, one against Tel Aviv. Both were stopped. But before they could be stopped, the Israelis gave the go-ahead to their man in Washington to implement the Samson option."

"The Man Who Waits," Hancock said.

"Excuse me?"

"That's what we called him. The Man Who Waits. He was locked in a basement with that bomb for a year—no way out. His only mission in life was to activate it. My section had a team who waited on him."

"Yes, sir, and they stopped him before he could complete activation."

"Continue with the results," Hancock prodded.

"The head of the CDA, your predecessor, was retired early."

"Fired," Hancock corrected.

"Fired. Operation Delilah was exposed along with the Red Flyer teams, which were Special Operations teams designed to covertly insert a nuclear weapon overseas. Such an insertion was designed not to be traced back to the United States. Sort of our own Samson option. The National Security Adviser, Mr. Hill, was fired and is currently under indictment on an array of charges including attempted murder."

Welwood turned a page in his folder. "I also found it most interesting that the CIA liaison to the Special Operations NEST at the time this happened was a female agent. An agent named Kim Gereg. Who also happens to now be my boss, chief of Operations. It appears initially her career was damaged by the incidents, but it turns out she was never informed of any of this."

"So she got promoted for being ignorant," Hancock said.

"It appears so, sir. Actually I would say she was promoted for not being involved."

Hancock nodded. "Very astute. The best damage control sometimes is ignorance."

"You should have been the next chief of Operations." Welwood threw his cards on the table.

"But I wasn't ignorant," Hancock replied.

"Yes, sir. And now Ms. Gereg has a shot at becoming the director." Welwood also knew that Hill had been Hancock's mentor.

"And I don't?" Hancock asked.

"To go from CDA to director would require a review before a congressional panel. Since Congress is not aware of CDA's existence, they would wonder what you've been doing. Not getting the C/O's job cost you that."

"You have a good grasp of the politics of our organization," Hancock said. "Back to the computer search?" he asked. "Why's Major Thorpe doing it?"

Welwood had spent some time on that one. "Apparently one of the young women who has disappeared in Germany is named Dublowski. Terri Dublowski. She disappeared two months ago. Thorpe must be checking on it for his friend, now Sergeant Major Dublowski assigned to Delta Force at Bragg."

"Why was that search flagged for our attention?" Hancock asked.

"I don't know."

"What in the search specifically was flagged?"

Welwood looked at the file in Hancock's hand, then met the CDA man's eyes. "I don't know."

"Then—" Hancock began, but Welwood cut him off, playing his cards aggressively now.

"I don't know, but you should, sir. The flag was under a code name. Rather strange one, if you ask me: Romulus? Someone a *Star Trek* fan? I looked in the directory. There was no propagator listed, so that means the code name was propagated either by Direct Action, your office, or by Operations, my office."

"What makes you think it wasn't your office?"

"I've never heard of a file called Romulus," Welwood said,

"and I have clearance for all files in Operations."

Hancock raised an eyebrow. "Have you considered the possibility your boss may be keeping things from you? That you *don't* know everything in your department?"

Welwood looked worried. "Well, it was filed PF1. There's only one paper copy of the file under the title Romulus in existence. That means it's possible someone in Operations has the only copy and I don't know about it."

"If there's only one paper file, how could this have been tagged in the computer?" Hancock asked.

"I assumed someone tagged all file names and pertinent information."

"You assume a lot." Hancock leaned back in the chair and steepled his fingers. He considered the other man in silence for so long, Welwood began fidgeting. Finally he spoke. "What do you think is going on?"

"I don't know, sir."

"There's much you don't know," Hancock agreed, "but with the information you have, what is your best guess?"

"This Major Thorpe is digging into something connected with whatever is in the Romulus file," Welwood said.

"And you came to me with it, when it might well have originated here." Hancock abruptly stood, tucking the file under his arm. "Thank you. You are very thorough. I'll remember it."

Chapter Eight

Thorpe did exactly as Lieutenant Colonel Kinsley had ordered him. He knocked on her door at 0900, marched to a point two steps in front of her desk and reported as ordered. Then he got his first surprise of the day.

"Sit down, Major Thorpe," Colonel Kinsley said, her tone almost pleasant.

Thorpe carefully moved over to the chair in front of her desk and sat down, not quite sure how to take this departure from the previous time he had reported to her, especially in light of what had happened last night.

Kinsley pointed at a map of the world behind her desk. "SOCOM presently has troops deployed to forty-two countries around the world and I am responsible for filling every single personnel slot for every single assignment, from three men on a medical training mission in Belize to the deployment in Bosnia.

"The operational groups are stretched beyond their own personnel capabilities. Up to a month ago, Tenth Group could barely keep up with the operational demands of supporting the Bosnia peacekeeping mission while at the same time running Operation Provide Comfort to the Kurds in Turkey on the border with Iraq. First Battalion of Tenth Group, stationed out of Stuttgart, is one almost hundred percent deployed. Fourteen of fifteen A-teams, two of three B-teams, and the battalion headquarters are all currently deployed.

"Second and Third Battalions, out of Fort Carson, Colorado, are over eighty percent deployed. The peacekeeping mission has overwhelmed Tenth Group's resources. If you add in trying to make sure that soldiers get to their necessary schooling, such as O & I, and specialty training when required, such as scuba and HALO, there will always be some gaps. Plus there is the natural turnover of duty reassignments and soldiers who are finishing their time in service and getting out."

There wasn't much new here, Thorpe thought. When he'd been on a team it was standard to be deployed the majority of the year. It was hard on families and it was hard on the soldiers, but it was what Special Forces was all about. Special Forces wasn't a pure wartime asset, sitting around training, waiting for the big one. Its active missions crossed the spectrum from peacetime through all-out war. A Special Forces soldier expected to be away from home most of the time.

"As a stopgap measure," Kinsley continued, "we have brought in individuals such as yourself from the reserves to supplement the active duty forces. At best it's been a Band-Aid solution. At the recommendation of the Joint Chiefs of Staff, the President is considering activating parts of the Nineteenth Special Forces Group, which is National Guard, to supplement the Tenth Special Forces Group in its missions. Unfortunately, Nineteenth Group is behind the power curve in terms of personnel also. Instead of deploying the group intact, the SOCOM commander, General Markham, my boss, is considering using the members of Nineteenth Group to fill out the deployed Special Forces units. Allow them to give some of their people a break for a couple of months, before going back."

Thorpe was following this discourse with half his brain while the other half was wondering what had happened to her attitude from the previous evening.

"I have to travel to Europe to gather information for that activation to make sure, if it does occur, we can support it and how the deployed groups would like to rotate their personnel and use the reservists. Because you are in the reserves, I would like you to come with me to provide me with that perspective."

"With all due respect, ma'am, I've only been in the reserves a couple of months. I may have spent a long time on active duty, but this is my—"

"Major Thorpe," Kinsley said sharply. "Need I remind you that you conducted an unauthorized search into the Department of Defense database yesterday?"

"No, ma'am, but I don't see what one has—"

"Major Thorpe, I recommend you do whatever I tell you to do without the slightest question. You are going with me to Europe. That is all. Quite frankly, given your record, I don't particularly want you along, but on the other hand I'd rather have you where I can see you than leave you behind here to run amok. You can get our travel information from Sergeant Christie."

Thorpe knew when he was dismissed. He stood and saluted.

"By the way," Kinsley said, stopping him at the door. "Don't use the computer again. That's an order. Clear?"

"Clear, ma'am."

Thorpe exited her office. Christie didn't say a word; he simply held out a packet of papers. Thorpe took them back to his office. He checked the flight information. He would be departing in two days out of Pope Air Force Base.

"Heard you're leaving us for a while," Takamura said as Thorpe sat down.

"Small world."

"Heard also that you did something to piss the colonel off," Takamura said. "I hope it didn't have anything to do with our work on the computer yesterday."

"Actually, that's exactly what pissed her off," Thorpe said. "But don't worry, I didn't mention that you helped me."

Takamura looked concerned, but Thorpe wasn't in the mood to reassure him.

Thorpe stared at the computer on his desk. "Hey, Takamura, if you did what you did yesterday, that search, would Kinsley know?"

Takamura's worried look grew more severe. "Funny you should ask that. As I've been working this morning, I've noticed that someone's monitoring all the computers in the office. It's not easy to spot, but there are certain signs, if you know exactly what to look for. If whoever that is—and I assume it's the colonel—doesn't want us to run that search, we'd be shut down within a minute of getting started."

"Shit," Thorpe muttered. "I should have xeroxed a copy of that list."

"Actually," Takamura said, "I've got something better than that." He held up a 3.5-inch disk.

"What's that?"

"The list," Takamura said. "I downloaded it yesterday while it was printing."

"You're a genius," Thorpe said.

"There's some that might agree with you," Takamura said.

"Hold on to that," Thorpe said. "I have to make a call."

Thorpe put the travel packet on the corner of his desk and called Parker. He briefed her on what had happened so far and the meeting with the CID colonel the previous evening.

"He's got a point," Parker said when he was done. "Most serial killers do want the bodies to be found. You know, maybe Dublowski's daughter did just run away. Perhaps you're letting your emotions interfere with your rational thinking."

"I'll grant you that I'm emotionally involved," Thorpe said. "We're talking about a seventeen-year-old girl disappearing."

"They disappear every day," Parker said.

"That's pretty cold," Thorpe said.

"No, it's pretty realistic," Parker said.

"Listen," Thorpe said. "You were the one giving me lectures in Louisiana about family and how important it is."

"Point taken," Parker said. "Speaking of which, how are—"

"Could you do some checking for me on this?" Thorpe cut her off. "Maybe just call a few of the families of some of the missing girls and find out what they think? I'm leaving for Europe and I won't be able to do that."

"I thought your list was appropriated and you're not allowed in the computer anymore."

"True on both accounts, but I have a friend who backed up the list onto a disk. I can send it to you over modem; rather, the guy here in the office with me can send it. What do I need to be able to do that?"

"My E-mail address," Parker said. She rattled it off and

Thorpe copied it down. There was a short pause, then her voice came back. "I've been thinking about this since the last time we talked," Parker said as Thorpe slid the address over to Takamura. "Why did you limit your search to Germany?"

"Because that's where Terri Dublowski disappeared," Thorpe said. "I figured if something happened to her there, then the someone who did the something was there too."

"At that time, yes," Parker said. "But why was Terri in Germany?"

"Her dad was stationed there," Thorpe said. He immediately saw what she was getting at. "You think the killer might be in the army, or even be a family member."

"It's possible," Parker said. "If that's the case, there might be some disappearances here in the States around military posts. If the killer is military, then he's moving just like his victims. In fact, I think it's a pretty intriguing possibility," Parker said.

"Too bad I can't run the search again," Thorpe said, "and do it stateside."

"I'm sure you'll figure something out," Parker said. "I've got the list on my computer. I'll get back to you. Out here."

"Out." Thorpe put the phone down, then looked at Takamura, who was eyeing him with a mixture of unease and anticipation after sending the data to Parker.

Thorpe tapped his computer. "You said some people consider you a genius on these things, right?"

"I know computers," Takamura conceded.

"Can you beat whoever's put this thing in the system and do another search for me?"

Takamura pulled his glasses off and nervously cleaned them on his BDU shirt. "Oh, I don't know. I suppose, but I'd have to do it in a way that the system doesn't know it's getting beat, and that makes it harder than just simply bypassing the—"

Thorpe held up a hand. "Can you do it?"

"I might be able to."

"Will you?"

Takamura pursed his lips.

"I'll take responsibility," Thorpe said. "If Kinsley finds out, I'll tell her I did it."

"She won't believe that," Takamura said.

"Okay, then I'll tell her I threatened to kill you if you didn't do what I told you to. She would believe that," Thorpe said.

"You're not serious, are you?" Takamura asked, edging his seat back.

"No, I'm not serious. Geez, Takamura, why'd you join the army? I've never seen anyone who looks so out of place in a set of BDUs."

"For the college money," Takamura said. "I want to go back and get my Ph.D."

"Well, live a little," Thorpe said. "Take it to the edge, you might like it."

"It would be a challenge." Takamura was still playing with his glasses.

"That's the spirit!" Thorpe said. He tapped the other man on his chest, on the set of cloth wings sown there. "You're airborne, Takamura. I know you crave a little excitement now and then. You could have served in a leg unit, not airborne. You volunteered to be here. That tells me something."

"Well," Takamura said, "I suppose I could try."

Thorpe watched the door as Takamura worked. He had no idea what the other man was doing. He knew that everyone else—Kinsley, the CID colonel and Parker—thought he was chasing a ghost. But there was one thing that made Thorpe want to push this, and that was the sergeant major. Dublowski and he had been through a lot over the years and he owed the man to give it his best, even if it looked like there was nothing to pursue.

The bottom line as far as Thorpe was concerned was that Terri Dublowski was somewhere, whether living or dead, and he meant to find her. This was the best avenue he could explore right now.

He also wasn't satisfied with either the CID colonel's explanations or Kinsley's reaction this morning. Especially the latter. Why had she changed so abruptly? It was out of character. Thorpe didn't have any idea why he was feeling suspicious, but his experiences over the past two decades had taught him to trust those instincts.

After three hours, Takamura was still at work. Thorpe went out and got them both some food from the Burger King on post and brought it back. They went into the afternoon with Takamura still on the computer. The only thing Thorpe could compare it to was trying to sneak up on an enemy in the field. It took a long, slow, cautious approach.

The phone rang and Thorpe picked it up. "SOCOM G-1, this line unsecure."

"Thorpe?"

"Yes."

"It's Parker."

"Yes?"

"I think you might have something. I used a couple of my assistants to contact the families to do an initial screening. We managed to get hold of eighteen of the twenty-four. Six of the girls did run away and the families heard from them subsequent to the CID investigation.

"Of the other twelve, I think there are five that are worth a real hard look. I talked to one or both of the parents and their situation is just like Dublowski's. They insist their daughter wouldn't run away. They say she just went out one night, off post, and simply never came back. No packing of bags, no withdrawal of money. Just disappeared and there's been no sign since. What's also interesting is that all five, in addition to Terri, have disappeared in the last couple of months."

"Do you have the six's name? Date and location of disappearance?" Thorpe asked.

Parker rattled them off and Thorpe copied them down.

MARY GIBBONS, *Kelly Barracks, July 1999.*
LESLIE MARKER, *Panzer Kaserne, Aug. 1999.*
CATHERINE WALKER, *Kelley Barracks, Oct. 1999.*
TERRI DUBLOWSKI, *Patch Barracks, Nov. 1999.*
PATRICIA MAHONEY, *Ludwisberg-Kornwestheim Military Subcommunity, Sept. 1999.*
KIRSTEN WELCH, *Pattonville Housing Area, Sept. 1999.*

Thorpe stared at the list, running through his brain where each of those sites were. "Damn, Parker, do you realize all six of those are grouped around Stuttgart? Within fifty miles?"

"I know," Parker replied. "If they are all clustered together, that makes the possibility of one person being responsible for their disappearance much more likely. I think you've stumbled across something important."

"I've got to go to Europe day after tomorrow," Thorpe said. "I'll check these names out over there. There's a warrant officer working in the office here—named Takamura. He's going to do some more checking on the computer, looking over CONUS disappearances. I'll have him call you if he comes up with anything."

"He can tell me in person," Parker said. "I'm coming down from D.C. in two days. I think this is worth pursuing and I have other business to take care of there at Bragg."

"All right," Thorpe said. "I'll give you Sergeant Major Dublowski's phone number and you can link up with him. And Takamura's."

When he was done he walked around the desks to look over Takamura's shoulder. Thorpe didn't have a clue what was on the screen as Takamura scrolled through the program he had written. He told Takamura about Colonel Parker and that he should tell her everything when she arrived.

"I'm going to try the run now," Takamura said. "I think I've bypassed the security tag program and it won't notice that it's been bypassed."

"You think?" Thorpe repeated.

"We won't know until we try it," Takamura said.

"What's the worst that can happen?" Thorpe asked. "The computer explodes?"

"I don't know," Takamura said seriously. "I suppose the worst that can happen is the worst thing that whoever set up the security tag is capable of. This security program is very sophisticated."

"Well, let's go for it and see what happens," Thorpe said.

Takamura typed in a command and the screen cleared, replaced by the little clock with the hands winding. At the top of the screen, a green band also appeared, with the word CLEAR written across it in big black letters.

"What's that?" Thorpe asked.

"It means the program is running clean. No tracer or tag," Takamura explained.

They waited until the bar turned red and the word suddenly disappeared and was replaced by a new one flashing: TAGGING.

"It didn't work," Takamura exclaimed. He immediately began typing commands. "Someone's on to the program and trying to find out where it's coming from. I routed it through a bunch of systems, so it will take them a while to get back to us."

"How long?" Thorpe asked.

"A minute, maybe more."

"Well, then, get out of there."

"I'm trying to disengage right now."

Thorpe felt helpless and stupid as he watched Takamura's fingers flying over the keys.

"Shit!" Takamura exclaimed. "I can't disengage. This is a very good trap," he said. "They've got us and they're going to find out where we are." He sat back in his chair and looked at Thorpe helplessly.

Thorpe dropped to his knees and leaned under the desk. He pulled the telephone line that went to the computer and its power plug. The screen went dark.

"What did you do?" Takamura exclaimed.

Thorpe had the two cords dangling from his hand. "Will they find out we ran the program now?"

It was an option Takamura hadn't thought of and it took him a few second to collect himself. "No, I don't think so."

"Good," Thorpe said, dropping the cords. "We'll have to come up with a different way of checking this information."

"I'll work on it," Takamura said.

"Any idea who put the security program in place?" Thorpe asked.

"I initially thought it was Colonel Kinsley," Takamura said, "but once I got into it, I knew it was more sophisticated than anything we have here at Bragg. Probably someone in Washington. Maybe even the NSA—they have the best people there."

"You sound jealous," Thorpe said. "Now, why would someone in Washington be concerned about this?" he asked. He didn't expect an answer from Takamura, nor did he get one.

"What do you want me to do?" Takamura asked.

"Let's suppose there's someone who killed these six girls around Stuttgart in the past year. There's a chance that person is German, but there is also a possibility that the person is American. Most likely a soldier. I wanted you today to check military posts here in the States and see if there are any missing girls. If there are, then we have a pattern. We can then try and cross-reference to see how many military personnel fit the pattern. Which ones were in the right assignment at the right time."

"I might be able to access the personnel computer from a different location, now that I have an idea what the security program is like," Takamura said. "All I need is a phone line and I can use my laptop and cell phone in my car or, even better, work from my computer at home. It's a better machine than this crap."

"Great," Thorpe said. "Try to see if you can find anything stateside. Parker's coming here in two days and she'll link up with you. She has access to a lot of resources, so if you find anything, give it to her. If you run into any trouble, call Sergeant Major Dublowski." Thorpe gave Takamura the phone numbers.

"What do you think is going on?" Takamura asked.

"I don't have a clue," Thorpe said. "You need to be very careful. I appreciate what you've done so far. Don't take any chances. Push comes to shove, we'll let Parker do the digging. Using the Freedom of Information Act and some good congressional and media pressure, she can find out a lot. The main reason I'd like you to work it as soon as possible is that I want to be able to check on anything you might find out while I'm over in Germany. The last girl disappearing was only two weeks ago. The killer, if there is one, is probably still over there."

"I'll work the search again tonight from my apartment," Takamura said.

❧

"It was somewhere in North Carolina, sir," Welwood said. "They got off the net before the NSA could pinpoint it. We're still not sure how they escaped our hook. The program was designed to keep an intruder locked in until identified."

Hancock regarded the other man over steepled fingers. "Was it Thorpe out of Fort Bragg?"

"I would assume so, sir."

Welwood was on Hancock's side of the black marble hallway, deep in the heart of Direct Action. Hancock's office was dark, paneled with expensive wood. His desk was massive, over ten feet long by six wide, but there was still nothing on it. A computer was built into the desk itself, angled glass allowing him to read the screen from his seat. Recessed lighting in the ceiling above Hancock was angled forward to cause visitors to have to squint to see him.

Above each of the chess sets was a single halogen light hanging down from the high ceiling, highlighting each board.

"What were they searching for?" Hancock asked.

"A five-variable search in the Department of Defense personnel computer," Welwood said. "Military dependents, female, age sixteen to eighteen, with a CID file number, in the continental United States."

Hancock tapped well-manicured fingers on his desktop. His eyes drifted to the chessboards.

"Major Thorpe is turning into a problem again," Hancock mused out loud.

"I don't understand the significance of the searches," Welwood said. "First girls overseas disappearing and now in the States."

"I don't either," Hancock said, "but you can be sure if Thorpe is involved in it, there's trouble somewhere. Did you do as I asked and inquire about this Romulus file in Operations?"

"Yes, sir. I made some discreet inquiries but drew a blank."

"What else?"

"There might be some trouble." Welwood pulled out a sheet of paper. "I ran the records on the phone in the office where Thorpe is assigned. Thorpe made a couple of phone calls this morning to a number in Alexandria. I ran the number and it belongs to an office in the Pentagon. He talked to someone in the congressional anti-terrorist liaison office."

"Who authorized you to do such a thing?"

"I used my initiative, sir."

"Thorpe's going overseas," Hancock said. "I'm going to have some people in Europe keep an eye on him over there. As far as Fort Bragg, I'll also keep tabs on developments there. I want you to expand your coverage to the Pentagon and find out who he's talking to."

Welwood wasn't happy about that last part. "We need to be careful with the Pentagon. They're covered by the NSA also. We might run into some counterintelligence. The green and blue suiters over there can get pretty riled up if they think we're stepping on their turf."

"Then be careful," Hancock snapped.

After Welwood left his office, Hancock pulled two files from a drawer and laid them on his desk. One was labeled ROMULUS. The other REMUS.

The fact that the files were hard-copy paper and not loaded into the Agency's mainframe computer told Hancock that this was top-level stuff. No matter how good the hardware and software, computers could be compromised. There was only one copy of each file, the ones in his hands. The paper and photographs were coated with special chemicals that would react to any xeroxing or photographing.

Hancock flipped open the covers and placed them side by side on his desk. He stared at the pictures clipped to the left inside cover of each one. One was of a thin, dark-haired and slightly built man, wearing a flight suit with no markings. In the background, Hancock could make out helicopters and a control tower. Painted on the control tower were the words RUCKER AIRFIELD, ALABAMA, HOME OF ARMY AVIATION. The other showed a man who was larger, with sandy-colored hair, wearing camouflage fatigues with no rank or markings. His photo was taken with the jump towers of Fort Benning in the background.

"Gentlemen, gentlemen," Hancock said with a smile.

He added several other folders to the two on his desk, then leaned back and stared at the stack for a very long time. Then he rolled his chair over to the Civil War chessboard. He stared at the board for a long time, then his hands moved quickly, adjusting the pieces, moving those on both sides about until he was satisfied.

When both black and white were set at the stage he wanted, Hancock sat for a while with his chin in his hand, staring. Then he reached with his free hand and swiftly moved pieces on both sides of the board, deploying both colors further until suddenly he stopped. He stared at what had been done so far.

∽◌∾

On the other side of the corridor marking the line between Operations and Direct Action, Welwood was also deep in rumination. He was staring at his computer screen, looking at classified information. He was searching as much for what wasn't in the reports he was reading as for what was. One thing he had learned early in his career with the CIA was that lack of information was information.

Samson and Delilah. Welwood wondered who had come up with those code names. He looked up as the door to his office swung open. He quickly shifted programs on the screen.

"Yes, ma'am?"

The figure in his doorway commanded instant attention. Kim Gereg, the director of Operations, was tall for a woman, exactly six feet tall, and solid, weighing in just over a hundred and sixty pounds. She was fifty-five years old, having started in the CIA working as a secretary over thirty years ago.

She'd left to get an advanced degree in Russian studies and returned to the Agency as an analyst. She was one of the first women to go through field agent training when that became available to females. If ever there was an example of working one's way up through the ranks, it was Gereg. Despite those efforts though, she was still a woman in what was one of the last bastions of the old boys' club in bureaucratic Washington. Although the CIA didn't exclusively recruit off the Ivy League campuses as its predecessor, the OSS, had, there was still a prevailing attitude that spying was a man's job even though the closest most CIA employees had ever gotten to violence was when two of their number had been killed at the gate to Langley by a Pakistani terrorist.

"What's going on?" Gereg asked.

Welwood knew Gereg did this often—wandered the hallways, popping her head in offices, checking on her subordinates. He supposed she though it showed she cared about her people, but he just found it a pain in the ass.

"Following up on the satellite imagery from Bosnia," Welwood lied.

Gereg nodded. "Anything?"

"A lot of troop movement. The Serbs seem to have been resupplied with heavy weapons."

"Russia?"

"Some. There's a lot on the market right now from quite a few places."

"No surprise there," Gereg said. "Anything happening?"

"An IFOR patrol came across the bodies of those missing Polish soldiers. There was a dead Bosnian militiaman with them. It appears he killed the Poles—tied them to trees and tortured them first."

"That will throw some gas on the fire. Who killed the Bosnian?"

"We have no idea."

Gereg frowned and crossed her arms in front of her. "Where did this occur?"

"Just north of the Sava River."

"In Bosnia," Gereg said. "That's strange." She tapped a long finger on the bicep of the other arm. "Do you have the estimate for combat operations if IFOR acts against the Serbs?"

"The Balkan group is working on it with the military analysts."

"What's the initial readout?"

"I'll have it to your desk by noon." Welwood wanted her out of his office.

"Good," Gereg said, but she didn't leave. She stared at Welwood. He didn't exactly stare back, keeping his eyes from making direct contact with hers. After ten seconds she nodded slightly. "Keep up the good work."

The door swung shut behind her.

Chapter Nine

Takamura lived in a trailer on the west side of Fort Bragg. It was a long drive every day to and from the main post, but he enjoyed the solitude. His nearest neighbor was over a quarter mile away. The trailer was set in a small, secluded opening in the pine forest, accessible via a quarter mile of dirt road. Power lines ran about fifty feet behind the house, through a straight cut in the forest.

The thin walls of the trailer vibrated with the classical music every so often as the concert he was listening to went up in pitch, before sliding back down. He sat back in a battered leather recliner, a keyboard resting in his lap. His feet were up on the extended legrest. On his head, a headset held a pointer that maneuvered a small white arrow on the large-screen TV eight feet in front of him. A small boom mike wrapped around from the headset to in front of his lips. A voice-activated program that he had personally modified allowed him to point with headset and speak commands, removing the need for a mouse with a clicker.

Seventy-two inches allowed him to have several programs open on the screen. He was in four different chat rooms, under four different screen names, in each corner of the screen. Along the bottom an elongated box held the controls for every electrical device inside the trailer, including the stereo, lighting, and the heating/vibra pad on his recliner. Takamura could control everything from the deep comfort of the chair. It was the highest-tech low-rent trailer in North Carolina. What Takamura didn't spend on rent went into his computer system.

Right now, he was clearing the center of the screen, using the pointer and voice commands. He accessed the program he had used earlier in the day to try to penetrate the personnel database. He began scrolling through the program, his mind making sense of the letters and numbers, searching for a way to make it better.

The walls of the office displayed the accoutrements accumulated over eighteen years of service in the military. Plaques from units served in, certificates representing medals awarded, photographs of comrades, all dotted the wall.

What was more interesting and fresh in the memory of the person occupying this office in the first subbasement of the Pentagon were the units that weren't represented, the photos that weren't there.

Red Flyer and the Omega Missile.

Lieutenant Colonel Lisa Parker had served in both, and not only was there no sign of either unit in her office, records of each had been expunged from her official service record, leaving several years of her military service time unaccounted for.

Red Flyer had been a classified team selected from the various services whose mission was to covertly emplace a nuclear weapon anywhere in the world. Given that cruise missiles could target anyplace on the planet, the existence and potential use of Red Flyer had been more for political than practical reasons, a fact that had caused great consternation when the veil of secrecy surrounding it had been pierced.

Parker's last mission with Red Flyer had been to emplace what she had thought was a nuclear weapon inside of Israel, near their nuclear weapons storage facility in the Negev Desert. Although the bomb had been a dummy, the mission had had strong political overtones. She'd found out later that the mission had been run to counterbalance the Israeli Samson option—a nuclear weapon secreted in a house in Washington.

It had not made much sense at the time and as she'd had

more time to think about it, it made even less sense. A political shell game using nuclear weapons in a perverse balance of power in a new world order was the best she could fathom.

The man who had been the political force behind the Red Flyer missions, National Security Adviser Hill, was still awaiting trial, his lawyers slowing the process down due to the fact that almost all the material to be used in the trial was highly classified. The reality that Hill was still walking around Washington was another bitter pill for Parker to swallow. A petty thief would be thrown in jail quicker than a man who had misled his country and deceived the President.

And then Omega Missile, the other unit she had been assigned to after getting kicked out of Red Flyer. Housed in a silo in Louisiana, it was a doomsday weapon devised by Professor Kilten. She had been selected by him to serve on the launch crew after being banished from Red Flyer.

Omega was a missile whose payload consisted of the launch codes and targeting matrixes for all of America's nuclear forces—silo, submarine and airborne launched. Omega Missile had been taken over by Kilten and a band of mercenaries to hold the government hostage and demand changes in the nuclear infrastructure—most specifically to expose Hill and what he was doing with Red Flyer.

Kilten and McKenzie, the mercenary leader, had been stopped by Parker and Thorpe. She had hoped that some of Kilten's desperate message might have gotten through, but the status quo seemed to have returned. Her eyes shifted up to the TV screen on the other side of her desk. The VCR hummed as the tape played, but Colonel Parker's eyes were unfocused, not seeing what was being played out on the screen. She'd already completed her after-action report on the SEAL Team Six–Delta Force joint operation and watching the tape of the operation wasn't going to change anything. Her report told the truth and the tape backed it up, but the politics of interservice rivalry would ensure that not much of anything was done.

A turf battle had developed after the operation. The SEALs claimed that since the rig was on water, they were in charge. The Delta commander had claimed that since the rig was "dry," he was in charge. But given that it had turned out badly, he was willing to cede responsibility to the SEALs, who in turn were claiming that Delta had not handled their end of the operation. The joint commander sent to ensure this turf battle didn't occur had failed to take positive control and now everyone was pointing fingers.

After the Omega Missile incident, Parker had thought things would change. That she could make a difference. She laughed out loud, the sound bouncing off the narrow concrete walls of her office. She was in the first subbasement of the Pentagon. Buried. That was the word she would use for her office's location and for her job. She'd thought that with the power of the purse, Congress could control the military, but after being in the job several months she'd learned that it didn't quite work that way. The base closure list was one club the Pentagon waved over Congress's head. No senator or congressman wanted a base in his or her district shut down. After being in Washington for almost a year, she was amazed anything got done.

And then there were the weapons. The Seawolf submarine cost over one billion a pop and brought a ton of jobs to specific contractors. The Pentagon had learned long ago that it was as important, if not more so, to consider where the weapons systems were made as whether they really needed the weapons themselves. Thorpe's comments about the entire operation being staged to show off the Hummingbird missile bothered her more than she had allowed. When she had returned to the Pentagon, most of the questions directed to her during the debrief had revolved around the missile rather than the navy-army cooperation.

Parker glanced at the clock. It was after nine. She'd already scheduled her flight to Fort Bragg. She did have some business there, but Thorpe's phone call had intrigued her. She pushed a button on the remote, turning off the VCR and TV. She gathered her briefcase and coat and left her office, locking the door behind.

The walk to her car was a long one; she was parked in an outer ring of lots that surrounded the Pentagon. She slid behind the wheel and headed home. The men following her were good. During the ten miles to her townhouse in Springfield she never once suspected she was being tailed.

❧

Takamura moved the picture to the upper left corner of the large screen.

"One down," he whispered to himself as he typed on his keyboard. A steady green bar flashed across the length of the top of the screen, indicating his invasion into the DOD database had not been detected yet.

"Two." A photo flashed onto the screen. Takamura began moving it, then paused, staring at the image. Something bothered him, but he wasn't quite sure what it was. He focused back on the keyboard.

"Three." The photo of the third girl from the list appeared. This time Takamura knew what was disturbing him. He moved the girl to the left, under the other two. "Oh, man," he whispered seeing the three lined up. He quickly accessed the last three girls missing in the vicinity of Stuttgart over the past year.

When he was done, he stared at the screen for a minute, not quite believing what was there. Then he picked up the phone and dialed Moon Hall. He had the operator forward him to Major Thorpe's room.

"Thorpe."

"Sir, it's Takamura."

"What's up?"

"Sir, I've got something really strange that I found on the computer."

"Really strange?"

"It's about the girls."

"I'll be there in thirty minutes."

"I can download—"

"Thirty minutes."

❧

Hancock had rolled his chair over to the chess table holding the Civil War pieces. His chin was in his hand and he was thinking through moves.

Kilten had been a chess master. Hancock had never played the man before his unfortunate demise in Louisiana. But he had played Deep Blue, Kilten's computer alter ego. And lost. He had learned from that loss a simple truth. In any game, no matter what one's skill level was, there was always someone—or something, in the case of the computer Kilten had programmed—better than you. He had warned Hill about Kilten, but the national security adviser had ignored his advice and continued with his agenda.

The conclusion he had drawn from both Hill's action and Kilten's was that the only way to guarantee a win was to control both sides. Some might consider that cheating, but Hancock didn't. He considered it working twice as hard.

His hand reached out and hovered on top of the white queen. He slid it across the board and removed a black pawn. He kept his hand on the white queen as he considered the consequences of the move. Satisfied, he removed his hand, committing to a course of action.

When he was done, he went back to his desk and opened a drawer, taking out the secure phone. He had his secretary connect him to the NSA's computer monitoring office.

"What is it?" Thorpe was wearing a black windbreaker over a khaki shirt and pants. He filled up the doorway to the trailer.

Takamura had a glass in his hand and he took a deep swig. "Want a drink, Major?"

"What do you have?" Thorpe stepped in, declining the drink with a wave of his hand.

Takamura poured himself another one. "I was testing. To see if I could get in. I downloaded it. I didn't want to stay in the system too long."

"Downloaded what? Slow down and relax."

"This way." Takamura led Thorpe down the narrow corridor to his computer room.

Thorpe paused, seeing the large-screen TV, which now showed a swirling image that he couldn't quite make out. "That's hooked to your computer?"

"Yeah."

"You need to get a life," Thorpe stood behind Takamura as the younger man sat in front of his keyboard and put on the head pointer.

"That's my own screen saver. Designed it myself."

"Great."

"On screen," Takamura said into the boom mike.

The screensaver disappeared. The photos of the six young girls filled equal shares of the TV.

"Jesus," Thorpe whispered.

"That's what I thought," Takamura concurred.

Thorpe walked past Takamura to the screen. He put his hands out, running down each side, across the images.

"They could be sisters," he said, taking in the faces. Each girl had straight blond hair and blue eyes. Their faces were all thin and angular. All except one.

"Why is Terri Dublowski different from the other five?" Thorpe asked.

"I don't know. It's not only the hair and eyes," Takamura said. "They are all between five-foot and five-two. All weigh between ninety and one hundred and ten pounds. All except Dublowski's daughter. Those five can't be a coincidence."

"No," Thorpe agreed, "they can't."

Chapter Ten

"Hello?"

The girl's disembodied voice echoed down the hallway. There was no answer, so she called out again. Steel doors with small slits in them at eye level lined the hall. The voice was coming out of one of the slits, muffled, a whisper fearful of being heard by the wrong person.

"Hello?"

"Keep quiet!" another female voice hissed. "They told us not to speak! They'll hear!"

"I'm Terri. Terri Dublowski," the voice said. "Who are you?"

There was a long silence.

A third voice finally spoke. "I'm Leslie. Leslie Marker."

"Leslie," Terri said, drawing the name out.

"They told us not to talk," the second voice repeated.

"And we didn't," Terri replied. "Look what that got us. Does anyone know the name of the girl they shot?"

There was a long silence, then the second voice spoke. "Patricia."

"You knew her?" Terri asked.

"She was my friend."

"How did you end up here?" Terri asked.

The words tumbled out, as if a damn of silence had been broken. "We were together. In Germany. On the train. The man—the one who shot her—he offered us money. To go to a party. We got on his plane. He must have drugged us. We woke up here."

"That's what happened to me!" a new voice interjected excitedly.

"Does anyone know where we are?" Terri asked.

Silence answered that question.

"We can't give in," Terri finally said.

"If we don't, we'll end up like Patricia!"

"What's your name?" Lisa asked the second girl.

"Cathy. Cathy Walker."

Terri Dublowski pressed up against the steel door, her lips next to the slot. She didn't know how long she had been here. Her last memories before this cell were of walking in the forest outside Stuttgart, heading for home. Footsteps behind her in the dark. To her side. Then darkness. She awoke in this cell and she still didn't know how long she had been here. There was no way to tell day and night. Meals were shoved through a slot at the bottom of the door in no pattern that she could discern. She had not even known there were others until she was taken out of her cell earlier and marched in line to the room with the two men.

"There's one more," Terri hissed through the slot. "I saw you. Talk to us!"

There were a few seconds of silence, then Patty added her plea. "Talk to us!"

A tiny voice quavered, so low Terri had to press her ear against the slot to hear it. "I'm Mary."

"Hello, Mary," Terri said, then Cathy and Leslie also said hello.

"We're in this together," Terri said. "We have to stand together."

"What do they want?" Leslie asked.

"I don't know," Terri said.

"What did they mean by 'the One'?" Mary asked.

"I don't even know who they are," Terri said. "Do any of you know who the two men are?"

"The Jewel Man," Leslie said. "That's what I heard the small one called. The one with all the rings on his fingers. The one who shot Patricia. I was at a party. I met him in a disco in Stuttgart and he said he'd take me to this party. I went with him. He took me to a plane at the airport. A small jet. We flew for a while—I don't know how long. Then there was this party."

The words were tumbling down the hallway from Leslie in a rush. "They were rich. The people at the party. I could tell that. It was like he was showing me off or something. They were from all different countries. All different languages. When dawn came, I got scared. People at the party called him Jewel or something like that. The Jewel Man. All those rings.

"I told him I wanted to go home and he just laughed at me. I'd been drinking. And doing some coke. I knew it was bad, knew he was bad, but—I don't know."

"What happened next?" Terri prodded.

"I don't know," Leslie repeated. "I must have passed out. I woke here. That's all. No one's said anything to me. I don't even know how long I've been here. What do they want?"

"I don't know," Terri said. "They haven't said anything to me either." She proceeded to tell the story of how she had ended up here—as much as she knew.

"They got me at night too!" Mary said when Terri was done. She proceeded to tell her own story of abduction. She'd also been invited to a party by the Jewel Man. And when she awoke, found herself imprisoned in the cell.

"There's one thing we have to keep in mind," Terri said when the other girls were done. "If they are looking for one, that means the other three are expendable like Patricia. So no matter what the One is, none of us can become it, because by doing so, you condemn the rest of us."

Chapter Eleven

Sergeant Major Dublowski shuffled through the down-loaded pictures, lingering over each one, until his daughter's picture was back on top. He leaned back against the torn up-holstery in the cab of his battered pickup truck.

"We know it's not random, now," Thorpe said. "At least with the other five. There's a pattern."

Dublowski nodded ever so slightly. They were parked out-side of the Delta Force compound—the Ranch—several miles from the main post of Fort Bragg. Thorpe had called Dub-lowski as soon as he had arrived at work and arranged to meet him here. The sergeant major had driven out the main gate of the compound and parked behind Thorpe's rent-a-car.

"This isn't good," Dublowski finally said.

"I know," Thorpe concurred.

"This means there is a serial killer and she's dead," Dub-lowski continued.

"That's not necessarily true," Thorpe said. "She looks dif-ferent than the other five, Dan. Maybe something else hap-pened to her. These other five might be connected and something entirely differently happened to her. Hell, we don't even know what happened to the other five."

"Don't bullshit me," Dublowski said. He tapped the pic-tures against the steering wheel. "Any idea who's doing it?"

"I'm working on it," Thorpe said.

"I want the son-of-a-bitch. You get me a name. I don't care

where he is or who he is. I'm going to make sure he never gets another girl and he pays for what he's done."

Thorpe had expected that. "I've got someone doing some checking, seeing if they can find us some names. I'm going to Europe tomorrow. I'll be able to do some firsthand looking. I need some help, though."

Dublowski looked at Thorpe for the first time since getting the pictures. "What do you need?"

"I'm going to need some contacts in Europe. Someone on the German side of the house. Someone on the American. And maybe someone who knows both sides."

Dublowski nodded. "I'll call them for you. There's a guy in GSG-9, a Major Rotzinger. I'll have one my buddies in Europe Special Ops Command, Master Sergeant Joe King, arrange a meeting. You need anything, King's the man."

"What about someone outside the military?"

Dublowski thought for a few seconds. "Yeah, there's this guy. Retired E-8, lives over there, outside Stuttgart. His wife is German. He wasn't Special Forces qualified—a supply man assigned to Det-A for a while—but he's good people. He might be willing to help."

"Good. Do you know anybody high-ranking who can cut orders in Europe Special Ops Command?"

"Two-star general good enough?"

"Should be. I need someone to get me away from my boss."

"General Schaeffer, the Special Ops theater commander owes me a favor. He can do that."

"I'm going to call Colonel Giles also," Thorpe said, referring to his civilian boss. "He's got plenty of contacts."

Dublowski nodded. "He'll help."

"I also need some gear." Thorpe pulled a piece of paper out of his pocket and handed it to the sergeant major. Dublowski looked at it and nodded. "Come with me."

He put the truck in gear and turned it toward the gate for the Delta compound.

Takamura wove his way through the electronic hallways of the military's Internet, pausing before the database holding personnel records. Takamura's head was on a swivel—checking the door to his office, then back to his screen, back to the door, back to the screen. He was torn between excitement and fear. So far, his probe program had again accessed the DOD database without tripping any alarms.

He was checking the CONUS—Continental United States—database now, searching for reports of missing girls in the age range specified. The only problem with this check was that unless the family happened to be living on post, police authority would rest with the local authorities.

Despite that limitation, he came up with a rather long list. Now he worked on the hard part—pulling up the photos of the dependents.

After an hour, he had four girls who fit the profile.

He started as the door began opening, hitting the bar on the bottom of his screen, switching from the program to his word processing.

"You look guilty as hell," Thorpe said as he shut the door. He had a black satchel in his hand and he carefully put it down on his desk.

"You about gave me a heart attack," Takamura said.

"What have you found?" Thorpe came around behind Takamura's seat.

"Four girls in the States. Check 'em out." He switched back and the faces of the four appeared. "All missing in the last two years stateside."

"They look the same," Thorpe acknowledged. "When and where?"

Takamura had the data ready. "Two within six months of each other. Two years ago. Fort Rucker. Both from families on post. One from Fort Benning just after that. One from right here at Fort Bragg half a year ago."

Thorpe considered that. "Rucker, then Benning, then Bragg." He knew Fort Rucker in Alabama was the home of army aviation, where all the helicopter pilots were trained. Fort Benning was the home of the infantry and airborne schools. And then Bragg.

"A pilot, who goes to airborne school, then is assigned here, maybe for a short specialty course," Thorpe said. "Then is assigned to Germany a little over three months ago."

"Yeah," Takamura said. "That looks like it. But you have to remember these four hits stateside are only the ones from on post. Most families live off post, so there could be a lot more."

"Can you make a program that will check active duty soldiers for the assignment pattern of the girls we have? Rucker when those two girls disappeared there, then Benning, then Bragg, then Germany in the Stuttgart area?"

"That will take a while," Takamura said,

"Then take a while." Thorpe stood. "I've got to check on some stuff."

Thorpe left the SOCOM headquarters and drove across Bragg to the post library. He used the computer to find what he was looking for. There were several books on profiling serial killers and Thorpe grabbed them all. Then he sat at an unused desk and used the military phone to dial Parker's office as he thumbed through one of the books.

When she answered the phone he got straight to the point. "Do you think you can have your FBI contact do up a profile for this killer?"

"Whoa!" Parker said. "You're not even sure you have a killer."

"I'm surer now than I was yesterday," Thorpe said. He told her of the similar appearance of the five girls who had disappeared around Stuttgart.

"Okay, you're right," Parker agreed. "Sounds like you might have a serial killer. But it also sounds like your friend's daughter doesn't fit the pattern."

"Not in looks," Thorpe agreed, "but she's the same age as the others. She got taken at night. Maybe the killer couldn't see that well in the dark. Hell, I don't know a damn thing about this. Can your friend do a profile for me? Maybe he can explain why one girl looks different. I've got Takamura running through records, getting me a list of personnel who had the same assignments as the girls we've uncovered missing."

"He's not my friend," Parker said in a sharp voice. "And

they're backed up pretty bad at Behavioral Sciences."

"Tell it to the families of these missing girls," Thorpe said.

"Hey, don't get on my case." Parker said. "Why don't you let the people who are supposed to, handle this?"

"Because you know what happened when we went to CID. I think the killer is overseas now—so whose jurisdiction does that make it? It seems like these girls have fallen between the cracks."

"I understand, Mike, but—"

"If not you, who?" Thorpe threw at her. "You were the one after Omega Missile who was going to change the world. Or at least the military. How much has changed?"

"That's not fair," Parker said.

"Life's not fair," Thorpe said.

"Jesus," Parker said. "You've gotten worse."

"Are you going to check with the FBI?" Thorpe asked.

"I'll see what I can do."

"Thank you."

"Mike."

Thorpe paused. "Yes?"

"I heard what happened to Lisa and Tommy. I'm sorry. I'm sorry about what I said about you being worse."

"Yeah." Thorpe felt the hard plastic of the phone in his hand. His head was pounding and all he could think of was going to the Officers' Club and getting a beer.

"Mike?" Parker's voice was lower, concerned. "You there?"

"Yeah, still here. Listen, I've got to go. If you get anything, send it to me."

Thorpe put the phone down. He stared across the tables of the reading area. A young boy was whispering in his mother's ear. She laughed, picking up the pile of books they'd collected and heading for the checkout counter.

He blinked, took a deep breath, then focused on the open book on the desk in front of him. He tried reading, but he couldn't. After a few moments, he gave up. He checked the books out and drove back to the BOQ, taking a route that avoided passing the O-Club.

❧

Welwood shifted gears, feeling the vibration from the Corvette's engine through the leather seat. He punched the accelerator and roared out of the CIA parking lot, passing the site where two workers had been shot and killed by a Pakistani terrorist in 1993.

The killer had been caught, tried and convicted. Then, in 1997, four Americans in Pakistan had been gunned down on the street, in retaliation for the conviction. Welwood knew that in turn, Direct Action had sent a covert team into Pakistan and assassinated several of the killers. Tit for tat was much more a way of life in the covert world than the average citizen knew.

He took the turn onto the George Washington Memorial Highway. He headed southeast along the tree-lined road, the Potomac occasionally visible to the left. He turned right onto Kirby Road, heading toward his townhouse in Falls Church. His mind was on the information he had pulled together, trying to connect the dots.

He pulled up to a major intersection, waiting, the car in neutral, while his right foot gunned the gas every few seconds so that the entire car vibrated. The light turned green and he continued on his way.

He reached a stop sign at a busy intersection, awaiting his chance to cut into the fast-moving traffic. He spotted a gap, one only large enough for his powerful engine to propel him into, and he gunned the gas and let his foot off the clutch. The Corvette leapt forward. Welwood was shifting into second when the engine simply died.

The Corvette stuttered to a halt. Welwood's eyes flashed up to his rearview mirror. The grill of a large truck filled the glass. He watched with disbelieving eyes as the truck inexorably bore down on him, the shiny grill getting closer and closer. His foot hit the gas pedal impotently while the fingers of his right hand scrabbled at the keys, turning them, grinding the starter, but the engine wouldn't catch. Welwood heard the squeal of brakes, tires gripping asphalt, and then the truck hit.

Fiberglass cracked and shattered as the truck plowed over

the Corvette. Welwood was thrust forward onto the steering wheel, the entire seat, with belt strapped around him, being ripped from the floor. His chest was crushed, splintered ribs tearing into lungs. The pain was so great from those injuries, he didn't even feel both legs snap as they were jammed up under the console.

Then there was silence. Welwood blinked blood out of his eyes. He couldn't move. He tried to breath, and that only served to cause pain to jab through his chest.

"You all right?" a blurry face appeared in the smashed window next to him. The voice had an accent that Welwood momentarily tried to place, but pain was the entire center of his being.

Welwood could only moan. He faintly felt a pair of hands running across his chest.

"You're all broken up, my friend." The voice was very close to his ear. The hands were pressing against him.

Welwood tried to scream, but the sound was lost in the blood that was now beginning to fill his airway. The hand pressed harder, sliding a piece of broken rib against his heart.

"It's better this way," the voice whispered.

Irish? Welwood had time to wonder, when the bone lanced through the soft flesh of his heart, slicing it wide open.

Chapter Twelve

The noise woke Terri Dublowski out of a troubled sleep. The strip of lighting in the center of the ceiling was always on, giving her no idea of what time of day it was. She didn't move, but lay still trying to identify the noise. Her first thought was that it was a cat. Her neighbor at Patch Barracks had had one, a fat, hairy, ugly thing that had always been a nuisance.

She opened her eyes, still not moving. Her cubicle was ten by ten, with cinder-block walls painted off-white. A toilet and sink were in one corner. The bed was simply a mattress on a spring frame, with a rough wool blanket that she had wrapped tight around her.

Terri sat up, swinging her feet down to the smooth floor. The concrete was warm against her bare feet, a fact that had surprised her when she first felt it. How long ago that was now, she had no idea.

She didn't think her meals even came on a schedule, as there seemed to be long time periods where there was no food, then two or three closely delivered trays under her door. The man who delivered them wore khaki, was dark-skinned and spoke not a word. She had only seen him once. When she had opened the top slot to check when she heard him come one time, he had slammed her food tray against the slot, spraying her with food. She never opened the slot again when she heard someone out there.

Each time the sound of the steel door at the end of the

corridor echoed down the hallway she tensed, afraid that she would be taken out again, but as time passed she wished for something to happen.

The low mewling sound came again, muted by the steel door. Terri walked over to the door and knelt next to it. "Hello?"

"It's Mary," the voice she recognized as Leslie's reached her. "I think she's losing it."

"Mary?" Terri called. "Mary?"

The pitch of the cry went higher, the sound echoing down the corridor.

"Mary!" Terri pressed her mouth against the slot. "You have to get control of yourself."

The cry was now a scream, undulating. It went on for almost a minute, then stopped. Then it began again.

"Mary!" Terri pressed against the steel door. "Please, Mary. You have to stop."

"They did something to us," Leslie said.

"What do you mean?" Terri asked.

"Didn't they take you?" Leslie asked.

"Take me?" Terri said. "Where?"

"To the room. Like an operating room. That's all I remember, until I was back in here. They cut me. In my side. There's stitches there."

"What did they do?" Terri asked.

"I don't know. I'm sore and I hurt."

"Me too," Cathy Walker chimed in. "They cut me on my right side."

"Why?" Terri asked.

"I don't know," Leslie said. "Maybe they took something out. Maybe they stole a kidney! I don't know."

"There's something in there," Cathy said. "I can feel it. They put something in me. Something hard. Can't you feel it?"

"I don't want to open the scar," Leslie said. "I don't know."

"Mary," Terri called. "Mary, did they cut you? Did they put something in you?"

There was no answer, only the cries. This went on for almost five minutes, the other girls, Leslie and Cathy, joining in, exhorting Mary to stop, but to no avail.

"Mary!" Terri yelled. "Talk to us, please!"

Mary laughed, a wild echoing sound. "They did it! They put it in me! But I got it out. I got it out!"

"What was it?"

Mary's voice dropped. "But I'm bleeding." She laughed again. "I got it out! I got it out!" She began screeching incoherently.

The sound of the door opening at the end of the corridor cut off their voices abruptly. Terri listened to the footsteps—booted feet—moving down the corridor. A cell door swung open. Mary's keening grew louder.

A voice cursed in a language Terri couldn't recognize. The boots came back down the hallway, Mary's voice with them.

"Leave her alone!" Terri screamed.

Both sounds were cut off as the hallway door slammed shut. Terri slumped down onto the floor of her cell.

Chapter Thirteen

Large floodlights illuminated the interior of the hangarlike building. Thorpe estimated a C-141 cargo plane could fit inside. Instead, there were simply rows and rows of oversized wooden benches. At one end of the building about fifty men milled about. Closer by, there was only Lieutenant Colonel Kinsley and a handful of reservists destined for two-month assignments in Europe.

The building was called the Green Ramp and was the launching point for the rapid deployment forces from Fort Bragg. All parachute training jumps conducted by the paratroopers stationed at Bragg also originated in the large building. The benches were designed to hold jumpers with a parachute on their back and a hundred-pound rucksack dangling from straps between their legs. Early in his career, while attending the Special Forces Qualification Course, Thorpe had participated in a jump with the 82nd Airborne staging out of the Green Ramp. The one thing that had been impressed upon him was how early the 82nd prepared for a jump. In Special Forces, a team might show up at the airfield an hour before loading time. In the 82nd, because of the large numbers involved, it was not unusual for the jumpers to be there six to eight hours before the scheduled load time. And to rig four hours before loading, in order to make sure everyone was properly inspected in time.

In Thorpe's experience there were few things worse than

sitting around fully rigged for a jump. The weight of the parachute—main and reserve—along with rucksack, load-bearing
equipment, weapon, helmet—over a hundred and sixty
pounds—rested squarely on the jumper's shoulders. Even sitting, it was a most uncomfortable arrangement.

Thorpe had been visiting Bragg several years previously
when an air force jet had crashed into a C-141 cargo plane
waiting to take on a load of parachutists. The resulting fireball
had killed and maimed dozens of jumpers waiting outside the
Green Ramp. The price of training, something Thorpe was
familiar with.

"Major Thorpe." Kinsley's voice cut in on his meditations
on another reason he had been glad to "retire."

"Yes, ma'am?" Thorpe had just a rucksack with a couple
of spare uniforms and some gear at his feet. He had been
amused to see Kinsley make three trips in and out of the Green
Ramp, hauling a duffel bag, a suitcase, briefcase and a ruck.
He wondered how long she planned on being in Europe.

"I want to be very clear about something," Kinsley said.

Thorpe waited, not saying anything.

"You work for me," she continued.

The whine of jet engines pierced through the thin walls of
the Green Ramp. An air force enlisted man was walking toward them.

"I think our flight is ready," he noted.

"You work for me," Kinsley repeated.

"Yes, ma'am, I work for you." Thorpe shouldered his ruck
and headed for the airfield side door, leaving Kinsley standing
among her pile of bags. As he walked out the flightline door,
a small figure dashed out of the shadows.

Takamura thrust out a sheaf of papers. "Here. The names
of soldiers who were in all three places." He looked nervously
toward the interior, where Kinsley was picking up her duffel
bag, the air force NCO grabbing her ruck and briefcase. "I
was up all night doing that."

"Thanks." Thorpe shoved the papers inside his shirt. He
sniffed the air. The familiar smell of jet exhaust.

"There's a lot of names," Takamura said. "I'm going to go

back on the computer and see if I can't reduce the number for you."

"Good," Thorpe said. He took out his own set of papers. "This is a thumbnail sketch the FBI profiler gave Colonel Parker. Use it to narrow the list down. Then call Dublowski if anything else comes up. He'll know how to get hold of me."

"Yes, sir." Takamura scuttled away into the early morning dark.

∽✕∾

The countryside was wet and flat. A few roads and rail lines cut through it, on berms built above the stagnant water. Villages were few and far between. The north side of the Sava River was a no-man's-land and was now essentially worthless to the country's economy, but not to the people who used it to hide in.

Given that it was on the border between Croatia and Bosnia, the swamp was not only a place for people to hide in, it also allowed them to travel across the border. Since the UN peacekeepers had crossed the Sava and were centered around the towns to the south, more and more Serb forces had headed into the swamp.

Along one of the few rail lines that crossed the swamp, a group of twenty men, well armed, deployed themselves. Their motley collection of camouflage uniforms were covered in mud and worn. Their weapons, though, were clean and well oiled.

The leader of the band stood on the rail tracks, noting the rust. He knew the rail bridge over the Sava was down. He had supervised its destruction over a year ago, personally pulling the fuse ignitor that fired the arges that dropped the steel frame bridge into the river.

He looked in both directions, the embankment running as far as the eye could see both ways. Nothing. The sky was dark and overcast, with lightning rumbling to the south. He watched the lightning for a few seconds, wondering if perhaps it might be artillery or air strikes, but decided it was indeed the hand of God rather than man.

The leader wore mottled fatigues, the same style worn by the elite Spetsnatz, Russian Special Forces. He still had the subdued insignia of a major pinned to the epaulets, but where his name had been sewn there was only the less faded remains indicating the tag had been ripped off.

He cocked his head as his ears picked up a faint sound. He checked his watch. The timing was right, but one never knew.

He barked orders in Russian and his men faded into the swamp. He waited, alone on the embankment. The helicopter was very low, following the rail line from the west. The man turned and faced it. A Bell Jet Ranger, one of the most popular makes in the world. He noted the mini-gun bolted to the right skid. He didn't flinch as the chopper dipped even lower, the bottom passing less than two feet above his head, the rotor wash whipping him with air.

The chopper flew another fifty feet, then banked under the guidance of what must have been an expert hand. The marking hastily painted on the side indicated it was an IFOR aircraft. Even seeing that, the man didn't move, other than to continue to face the aircraft as it came closer, settling down on the rail bed, the skids on either side of the old tracks, the chain gun pointing down the rail line at him.

The man waited as the engine whine descended to a low hum and the blades slowed their rotation, gradually coming to a halt. A door on the right side opened and a tall man stepped out, submachine gun slung over his shoulder. The door on the pilot's side opened and a smaller man exited. He had no weapon in his hands, but the glittering rings that adorned each finger drew the man in camouflage's attention. He had a gas mask dangling from his neck, resting on his chin.

"You are Kiril?" the ringed man asked in accented Russian.

"You had best hope I am," Kiril responded. He gestured and his patrol materialized out of the surrounding swamp, weapons at the ready, all pointing at the two men and the helicopter. "And what is your name?"

"My name is not important." The man folded his arms across his chest and stared at Kiril. "What is important is what I can do for you, is it not?"

"Why should I trust you?" Kiril asked.

"You don't have to trust me," the man said.

"I have been thinking," Kiril said. "With NATO forces in-country, the situation has changed somewhat. It will be more difficult for us to do what you desire."

"What I desire?" The man laughed. "It is I who am helping you achieve your goal. To achieve your desires."

"For pay," Kiril spit.

"As good a reason as any. Speaking of which . . ." The man spread his hands.

"I have no proof you can deliver what you say you can," Kiril said.

"I am prepared for your doubts," the small man said. He turned back to the chopper and opened the back door. Kiril and his men brought up their weapons as the man pulled a third, previously unseen person out. The weapons went back down when they saw that the third person was a young girl, her arms bound behind her back. Her white smock had blood on the left side. A blindfold was over her eyes.

"What is this?" Kiril demanded.

"Proof," the small man said. The girl could not stand on her own, collapsing to the rail line, making a low whimpering sound. The small man barked something to his companion, who walked around the front of the helicopter. The larger man picked the girl up by the back of her smock and held her up.

Both men pulled their gas masks on. Kiril took a step back.

"You are safe at this distance." The smaller man's voice sounded distant, passing through the mask's filter.

The small man had something in his hands, a small vial. He screwed off the top and waved it once under the girl's nose, immediately screwing the top back on and putting it back in his pocket.

The girl immediately spasmed, her spine arching back. Her eyes bulged, an inarticulate sound escaping her lips. The larger man let go of her, stepping back. Her knees buckled and she collapsed onto the ground. After a minute, both men removed their masks.

"That fast?" Kiril whispered.

"Yes, that fast," the smaller man said. "I think a down payment is in order."

Kiril spoke into the small FM radio attached to his combat vest. A man came out of the swamp carrying a faded green backpack. He gave it to Kiril, who tossed it toward the chopper.

The smaller man retrieved the package and looked in. Precious stones glittered. The man folded the cloth and put it back in the backpack.

"My people took many risks to gather those," Kiril said. "It is everything we have. You have five days to deliver what you have promised. We will be waiting for you here. Do not think you can fly away beyond our reach."

"Do not waste your breath threatening us."

The two men got on the chopper without another word. The engine whined as power increased. The blades turned faster until finally it lifted and went back the way it had come. Still Kiril did not move. He watched the helicopter until it disappeared over the horizon.

He walked forward to the girl's body. With the toe of his boot, he turned her over. Her face was rigid, pain etched in the dead skin. He stared at it for a minute, imagining thousands of faces showing the same agony in death. A smile crossed his lips. He ordered the body thrown in the swamp.

Only then did he signal for his men to follow him.

❦

Hancock listened to the weekly intelligence summary briefers with mild interest. He had the seat to the left of the director, who sat at the end of a long mahogany conference table inlaid with the seal of the CIA. Directly across from Hancock was the chief of Operations, Kim Gereg, to the right of the director.

This briefing was always held the evening before the weekly National Security Agency briefing, where the director briefed the NSA—and the President, when an issue was particularly hot—on the highlights culled from this meeting.

Right now, Bosnia was the number one issue, with the discovery of the slain Polish peacekeepers, the movement of Serb heavy arms nearer to Sarajevo and the deterioration of conditions in Kosovo and the massacre of ethnic Albanians. After years of "maintaining" the peace, the situation was sliding back to the status of the early days when the IFOR first moved in.

"What are the Serbs' intentions?" the director asked. He turned to Gereg first.

"My sources indicate the Serbs want to end the stalemate. They want to make Sarajevo a repeat of Dien Bien Phu."

The director digested that blunt summary. Going first meant one was the favored person of the moment, but it also meant one had to define his or her position first. Hancock had always preferred having the black pieces in chess—the second to move. Some initiative was lost, true, but he had rarely encountered an opponent who could maintain initiative against him and he believed the advantage of seeing an opponent's opening move far outweighed the disadvantages.

The director turned slightly to the left. "Concur?"

"That they plan to fight?" Hancock said. "Yes, sir."

"And if they fight?" The director turned back to his right.

"IFOR will have air superiority but will be outgunned on the ground," Gereg said. "The Serbs are hoping the upcoming winter weather will assist them, but given the all-weather capability of NATO aircraft, even bad weather won't help them too much."

"So what do the Serbs hope to gain?" the director asked.

"Given the outrage over the loss of the six Polish peace-keepers, the Serbs are hoping that further bloodshed will cause NATO countries to pull out, rather than commit more force."

"Will it?"

"That's a political issue," Gereg said. "The State Department will have a better feel on—"

"What's *our* feel?" the director snapped. "Will NATO cut and run or will it fight?"

"I think NATO will fight," Gereg said.

"Think or hope?" the director asked. He didn't wait for an answer, turning to Hancock with a raised eyebrow, wanting his assessment.

"Does it matter, sir?" Hancock asked, then proceeded to elaborate. "Either way will end the quagmire."

"The President thinks it matters," the director said. "If IFOR pulls out of the Balkans, there will be a bloodbath the world hasn't seen since Cambodia and the killing fields."

"But it won't be *our* bloodbath," Hancock noted. "History is full of bloodbaths. This won't be the last one. We pulled out of Somalia and no one gave a damn what happened afterwards. All they cared about were the bodies of American soldiers being dragged through the streets.

"Most Americans don't have a clue who is who in the Balkans. Serbs, Bosnians, Muslims, Christians, Albanians. All are just words."

"You want me to go to the President with the recommendation we do nothing? He has to make a decision about *our* forces that are part of IFOR."

"Yes, sir," Hancock acknowledged. "But if the rest of NATO pulls out, we won't have much choice." He leaned forward. "The bottom line is the media. Given the current scandals in this country, coverage of the Balkans is down thirty-seven percent and I predict it will continue to go down. And no one can truly tell me that we have any sort of national security interest in that region."

"Ms. Gereg, what is your recommendation given the intelligence readouts?" the director asked.

"That IFOR enforce the Dayton Peace Accord. The President signed that accord."

"Mr. Hancock?"

Hancock spread his hands. "I agree theoretically that IFOR should do what it signed up to do. It is more a question of what the cost of that enforcement will be."

"The Serb heavy weaponry can be targeted by the NATO air forces," Gereg interjected. "The Serbs are hoping their campaign of terror can do what their force of arms can't. I believe they are hoping for the same reaction from the media that occurred after the Tet Offensive. We won the military battle then but lost the media one.

"Even if IFOR defeats the Serb military force, they hope the bloodshed will cause the people of the countries that contribute troops to IFOR to demand their soldiers be pulled out." She stared across the conference table. "There are many that agree with Mr. Hancock's assessment that the Balkans are not worth the lives of American soldiers."

"And the reaction is going to depend on how much blood the Serbs draw," the director noted. "The President is going to ask me for an intelligence estimate on that. The Pentagon will have theirs—what's ours?"

"Given the current military balance in the area," Gereg said, "I think the President should commit to enforcing the Dayton Accord. I don't think the Serbs can do significant damage."

" 'Significant damage'?" Hancock returned her stare across the conference table. "How many deaths do you consider significant damage? A hundred? A thousand?"

"What's the purpose of military force if it isn't going to be used?" Gereg asked. "Clausewitz said that war is an extension of politics. The politicians have tried to resolve this mess in the Balkans for a long time. Now the stakes have been raised."

"Clausewitz?" Hancock shook his head. "He was outdated half a century ago. The face of war and politics has changed dramatically since Clausewitz."

"Hancock?" the director asked. "Your final word?"

"There's one thing that bothers me," Hancock said.

"What's that?"

"It's why the Serbs are doing this now. What's changed? They started this war during the Gulf War, hoping to achieve their goals while the world was preoccupied. They weren't successful then. Why are they choosing to act now when NATO can focus force against them? Why do they think they'll be successful now?"

"Why is that a worry?" the director asked.

"Because I think Ms. Gereg's analysts are missing something," Hancock said. "I'd like permission to prepare a CDA strike team and stage it in Sarajevo."

While the director considered that request, Hancock stared once more across the table at Gereg. Her forehead was slightly furrowed, trying to figure out what angle he was playing.

"I'll ask the President tomorrow, but I'll recommend we do that," the director said. "Let's move on to other business."

Chapter Fourteen

The C-141 touched down at Rhein-Main Air Base, the U.S. military's air base adjunct to Frankfurt International Airport, German's largest airfield. Thorpe waited patiently as the plane taxied, glancing out the small, round window to his right. Known as the gateway to Germany, Rhein-Main was the primary port of call for U.S. personnel stationed in Europe.

During the Berlin airlift, Rhein-Main had been the center for most of the aircraft departing for that beleaguered city, loaded with the supplies that kept it running from 1948 into 1949. Despite the fall of the Berlin Wall, there were still over one hundred thousand American troops stationed in Germany, along with their dependents. The troops' mission had shifted from protecting Western Europe from the now-defunct Warsaw Pact, to trying to provide stabilization in an area of the world that had been thrust unprepared into a capitalistic society. The new domino theory was not one that worried about communism spreading from country to country, but rather economic destabilization spreading like a virus from country to country and damaging the world economy.

Thorpe knew that anyone who thought the Gulf War had been about freedom was naive. There had been no great deployment to Somalia after the bodies of U.S. soldiers were dragged through the streets. But threatening to cut off the flow of oil had led to the greatest U.S. deployment since the Vietnam buildup.

In fact, being a soldier and studying the history of war, he knew that almost every war was based on economics—hell, the Japanese had bombed Pearl Harbor only after the U.S. had imposed an economic blockade on the island kingdom, just one of many examples of the mighty dollar leading to bullets.

Thorpe saw the monument at the side of the airfield built to commemorate the Berlin airlift. Even that had been about economics and war had only been averted when the West had been able to keep West Berlin alive economically.

Thorpe followed Kinsley to the main terminal to check in. He smiled as he saw a tall, thin man sporting a faded green beret waiting inside the terminal. The man walked through the crowd, people stepping out of his way, making a beeline for Thorpe.

"Major Thorpe." The man held out a callused hand.

"Master Sergeant King," Thorpe read the man's name tag and gripped the other's hand. "How the hell are you? Dan Dublowski sends his greetings."

"Yeah, I talked to him on the phone yesterday," King said. He jerked a thumb over his shoulder. "I've got transport—how much gear you got?"

"Just the ruck."

"Wait a second." Colonel Kinsley stepped between the two men. "What's going on?

"I've got orders to escort Major Thorpe, ma'am," King said.

"Escort him where?" Kinsley demanded.

"I'm not at liberty to discuss that, ma'am."

"Orders from who?"

The edge of King's mouth twitched as he fought back a smile. "General Schaeffer, ma'am."

"Major Thorpe!" Kinsley spun from the NCO to face him. "What is going on?"

Thorpe shrugged. "Don't know, ma'am, but as you've told me, orders are orders."

"Major, I don't—"

Thorpe leaned close so King couldn't hear. "Ma'am, I'm a reservist. There isn't much you can do to me. And I'm going into a hornet's nest. All you could do was get yourself involved in something I don't think you want to be involved in. So my advice is steer clear and let it go."

Thorpe didn't wait for a response. He shouldered his ruck and followed King without a backward glance.

∽✤∾

Lieutenant Colonel Lisa Parker disembarked a plane at Fayetteville Airport at approximately the same moment that Thorpe met Master Sergeant King: midafternoon in North Carolina to the late evening of Germany.

The small airfield that serviced Fayetteville was used to military personnel coming in TDY—temporary duty. Parker quickly had her rent-a-car keys in hand and strode out into the lot, looking for the assigned vehicle.

She drove out of the lot and toward post, taking All-American Freeway most of the way, bypassing the numerous strip joints, tattoo parlors and pawnshops on Bragg Boulevard. The freeway ended on post and she headed for Moon Hall to check in.

Those following her had used two different cars to mask their surveillance and already knew what room she would be assigned. The two cars parked in the lot across the street from Moon Hall, the men inside masked by tinted windows.

∽✤∾

Takamura stopped at the Class VI store for a six-pack of beer on his way home. Then he headed west across Fort Bragg. He knew the military police usually staked out Chicken Plank Road, which he was on, trying to nail speeders.

Takamura pulled one of the cold cans out and popped the top, feeling a strange thrill at the illicit act. He wasn't completely foolish, though, keeping his speed exactly at the posted limit as other cars pulled out and passed him every so often.

His eyes shifted between the rearview mirror, to make sure the MPs didn't sneak up behind him, and the road ahead, searching for speed traps. Every time he was sure he was clear, he would take a quick, furtive sip of beer.

By the time he got to his trailer he'd gone through two beers, was buzzed, and felt more alive than he had since his high school prom and his date had allowed him to feel inside the top of her dress. Despite working at Special Operations Command for two years, the most exciting thing he had done was requisition some reservist experts for an element of Delta Force deployed overseas one time. He'd had no idea why they needed the experts, even though he'd checked the news diligently for weeks afterward looking for any sign.

He'd called Dublowski at the Delta Force Ranch during duty hours. Talking to the sergeant major had made what he was doing real, and necessitated the trip to the Class VI store and the beer for Takamura to keep going. Takamura turned on his computer before he turned on the lights in his trailer. The large-screen TV came alive with the images of the operating system loading. Takamura opened his third beer as he put the rest in the refrigerator.

He sat down in his recliner and put the keyboard on his lap. He adjusted the headset until the pointer was aligned with his straightforward gaze.

"Time to rock and roll," Takamura said out loud. He opened the arm of the chair and pulled out a remote. He pointed it at the stereo system resting on racks on the wall of the trailer and punched buttons. The CD player whirred and the music blasted out of the speakers: Pink Floyd's *Dark Side of the Moon*, heavy programming music for Takamura.

The list he had given Thorpe had contained over three hundred names. He pulled the profile Thorpe had given him. It was short and to the point:

Male
18–28
White
Higher-than-average IQ

Only four parameters, but Takamura knew they were more than enough to winnow the field down considerably. He began working the program to do exactly that as the music vibrated the walls of the trailer. He got up and retrieved another beer halfway through.

He paused in his programming and brought up the six photos. He lined the right side of the screen with the girls' visages. Terri Dublowski was the second one from the top.

Then he brought up the other missing girls from the military posts in the United States and put them on the left side. He took a sip of his beer and almost spit it out. Suddenly it didn't taste as good. Takamura blinked and shook his head, trying to clear it.

He forced himself to continue on the program. When it was done, he accessed the DOD database, sneaking his way in like he had the previous time. The green bar glowed at the top of the screen as the program began sifting through the records. The beer sat ignored on the arm of the chair.

Forty-two soldiers fit the profile and the assignment progression.

A large number, but better than before. He downloaded the names onto a disk.

Takamura's hand reached for the beer, but paused. He stared at the screen. He was missing something. Dangling at the edge of his programmer's mind. A link that hadn't been made.

He thought of the program he had used to initially get the names. The lines of programming, the flow.

Then he had it, or at least the beginning of it. He'd had an instructor once who had beaten into them that they always had to check their program by reversing the parameters.

Takamura pulled the keyboard closer to him on his lap. He aimed the pointer with his head.

"Access," he ordered. The program he had written appeared. "Oh, yeah," Takamura whispered to himself. His fingers typed as he moved the pointer with his head to the appropriate places.

He paused as he thought he heard something. He waited, fingers poised for several seconds. But there was no repeat of whatever it was, if it had been anything. He continued working.

When done, he ran the altered program. The green bar was

steady as it worked. This one was finished much more quickly than the first time, given that the numbers involved were much fewer. After a minute there were several names listed.

"Jesus," Takamura whispered. He picked up his phone and dialed the number from a card in his pocket.

"Dublowski." The voice on the other sounded wide awake, even though it was early in the morning.

"Sergeant Major, this is Specialist Takamura. Major Thorpe told me to call you if anything came up."

"Well?" Dublowski demanded.

"I've got something here. Something we didn't think of."

"What is it?"

"I'll bring it to you in the morning. Where should I meet you?"

"Main gate to the Ranch. You know where the Ranch is, right?"

"Yes, sergeant major."

"See you there at oh-eight-thirty."

The phone went dead. Takamura felt the blood rushing in his temples. "Download screen," he ordered, saving this data on the disk alongside what he had downloaded earlier.

He looked at the screen. "Enlarge," he ordered. The data doubled in size. He sat back in his chair and stared at it, thinking hard.

"Now, laddie, don't you think we know what you're doing?"

Takamura jumped, dumping his keyboard to the floor as he spun about. A man was silhouetted against the door of the trailer, but all Takamura's eyes could focus on was the glint of light from the large-screen TV reflected on the barrel of the gun in the man's hand.

"What do you want?" Takamura stammered.

"I find it interesting," the man said, his Irish accent almost musical. "Most people ask who I am before they ask what I want. But you're the straight-to-business type. That's good."

The man stepped forward. He was tall, about six feet, and slender. His face was covered with a large black beard that had streaks of gray in it. He wore small rimless glasses that were tinted a red color. Takamura couldn't see his eyes through the lenses. What he could see was that the barrel of the gun was locked on to him without the slightest tremor.

The man moved to a point where he could see the screen. "Ah, laddie, you turn over enough rocks sooner or later, you find a snake. Not a very healthful pursuit."

"Who the hell are you?

"Ah, too late," the man said. "I didn't answer your first question; what makes you think I'll answer the second?"

Takamura turned toward the big-screen TV. "Lights," he said.

"What was that?"

"Off."

The trailer went dark. Takamura dove to his left as the room was briefly lit by the muzzle flash of the Irishman's gun. There was no sound of the gun going off, only the metallic noise of the slide going back as a new bullet was loaded.

Takamura hit the small button on his central processing unit by instinct and the disk popped out. Takamura slid it into his pocket, then scrambled across the floor, putting the couch between him and the other man. Another strobe of light and a bullet punched through the couch, just inches behind Takamura. He could hear the sound of the bullet going through the cloth.

Takamura's fingers ripped aside a rug and grasped the handle for the bottom storm exit to the trailer. He pulled up the hatch and slid underneath as a third burst of light indicated another bullet being fired.

"Laddie, don't make it hard!"

The voice was muffled as Takamura scrambled through the mud underneath the trailer. He pushed aside the wood lattice and rolled free, pulling the keys out of his pocket as he did so. He jumped into his car and slid the keys in the ignition.

The sound of the engine starting brought the Irishman out the door of the trailer, gun firing. A round shattered the windshield, showering Takamura with safety glass. He ducked down and floored the gas pedal. The BMW's wheels spun in the dirt, then caught. He turned the wheel hard right and the car spun around the small parking area.

Takamura peeked over the edge of the dashboard and

steered down the drive. Another bullet smashed the rear window. As he got closer to the paved road, Takamura eased himself up higher in the seat. He glanced in the rearview mirror, but there was nothing to be seen.

With one hand on the wheel, he used the other to flip open the screen on the laptop and turn it on. The small screen lit the inside of the car as it booted up. Takamura pulled the disk out of his pocket and slid it in the slot on the side while still maintaining control with the other hand.

Takamura looked over his shoulder, half expecting to see lights from a trailing vehicle, but there was only the blackness of a deserted North Carolina road in the middle of the night. He eased up slightly on the accelerator so he could concentrate on what he was doing.

He leaned over and pulled his cell phone out of the glove compartment. He punched in the number for his office's fax/data line. As the phone rang, he plugged a cord from the cell phone to the laptop.

He looked once more in the rearview mirror. Darkness. "Goddamn, I got away," Takamura whispered to himself. Then he repeated it, screaming the curse at the top of his lungs in exhilaration.

There was the hiss in the cell phone as he was connected with the office computer. Takamura was reaching for the enter key on the laptop when the car was slammed forward, his head snapping back against the headrest. He grabbed the steering wheel with both hands as he fought for control of the car. His right tires dropped as the car went onto the narrow shoulder. Straining hard, Takamura managed to get back on the road.

He looked in the rearview mirror. There was a darker shadow behind him, another car, with its lights off. It raced up and slammed into his rear bumper again. Takamura was prepared this time and managed to stay on the road.

The car came racing up alongside. Takamura risked a glance. A man was driving, but there was something wrong with his outline. That was all Takamura managed to register as the other car slammed into his left side panel. Takamura shot his right hand out and hit the enter key as the BMW went off the road, flying across a ditch and stopping abruptly as it slammed into a hundred-year-old oak tree.

Takamura, unbuckled, went through the already shattered windshield, breaking both legs in the process as they were snapped against the top of the dashboard. His head hit the tree above the crumpled hood of the car, his neck snapping, killing him instantly.

On the road, the other car, a red Mustang, came to a halt. The Irishman stepped out. His upper face was covered with the bulk of a set of night-vision goggles. He carefully climbed down, across the drainage ditch, then up to the wreckage of the BMW. He noted Takamura's smashed body lying on the hood, the cant of the neck leaving no doubt as to his condition.

The Irishman looked in the open window. Through the greenish image the goggles gave him, he saw the glow of the laptop screen, still functioning, as a bright light. He reached in and pulled the laptop out from under the dash. Battered but functional. He pushed the small button on the side, ejecting the disk and pocketing it. He turned and headed back to his car, his voice softly humming an Irish ditty.

Chapter Fifteen

"Major Thorpe, Major Rotzinger." Master Sergeant King made the introductions in German.

Thorpe took the other's man hand, feeling the rough skin and the strong grip. Rotzinger was short, under five-six, but built like a tank, with immensely broad shoulders and a barrel chest. The German nodded his head at Thorpe, but didn't say anything as they sat down.

They were seated in a quiet *gausthaus* outside of the main gate for Seventh Army Headquarters in Stuttgart. King had driven Thorpe directly here from the airport and they'd waited over two hours for the other man to appear, an indication of the German's unhappiness about the meeting. Rotzinger was wearing tan slacks with a black T-shirt under a sports jacket. The coat was well tailored, as Thorpe could barely make out the bulge under the left armpit where Rotzinger's gun was concealed.

He knew GSG-9 members carried the Heckler & Koch P7, a rather radical pistol. The cocking mechanism, which was usually a slide in most pistol, was a lever along the front of the grip, which meant a firer could draw the gun and cock it with the trigger hand. Rotzinger's eyes had the shaded look of someone who had fired his weapon at live targets.

"It is good to meet you, Major," Thorpe said in German.

"It is not good for me," Rotzinger said in perfect English.

"Pleasantries are over," King said with a worried smile.

Rotzinger shifted his hard gaze to the master sergeant. "I owe you and I owe Sergeant Major Dublowski. That is why I am here. Let us get this over with."

"What can you tell me about the names you were given?" Thorpe asked.

Rotzinger splayed large hands on the top of the table and he seemed interested in only his fingernails. "They were American family members. Under the jurisdiction of your Criminal Investigation Division."

"Who disappeared in German jurisdiction," Thorpe said.

"Many people disappear," Rotzinger said. "Many Germans disappear."

"They were girls," Thorpe said. "Do you have children, Major?"

"I am not here to play emotional heartstring games," Rotzinger said.

"Why the hell are you here, then?" Thorpe leaned forward, getting close to the German. "You're a policeman, aren't you?"

"You know where I work," Rotzinger said. "I am not a flatfoot or whatever you call your regular police."

Thorpe knew he meant that GSG-9, part of Germany's border police, was a special unit designed specifically for antiterrorism work after the disaster at the 1972 Munich Olympics. They were Germany's equivalent of the army's Delta Force and the FBI's Hostage Rescue Team.

"You started as a cop," Thorpe said.

"The girls disappeared," Rotzinger said with a shrug. "It was investigated. Nothing turned up."

"One of those girls is the daughter of a friend of mine." Thorpe held himself back with a great effort. "Dan Dublowski's daughter."

"Do you know the problems we have here?" Rotzinger asked. "Everyone thinks it is so great now that the Berlin Wall is down. More than the Berlin Wall came down. We had to take in the East. With most of their police, their military now out of work. And their criminals still working. More terrain to cover. More border. Plus being that much closer to the scum in the other Eastern Bloc countries. It is a terrible mess."

Thorpe bore the outburst with strained patience. "Anything, *anything* you could tell me to help find her would be greatly appreciated."

"I know nothing that can help you," Rotzinger stood. "Good day, gentlemen."

"Asshole," Thorpe muttered at the broad back of the German as he left the bar.

King was also watching. "Something's wrong."

"What's that?"

"Rotzinger is a hard-core guy. No bullshit. And he owes me and Dan big-time. I think he *does* know something."

"I don't get it," Thorpe said. "Why wouldn't he tell us if he did?"

"Your guess is as good as mine." King stood. "Let's get you checked in on post. Let me get hold of him on my own and see if I can't get something out of him."

As they left the bar, neither man noticed the surveillance team parked across the street. The team was concealed inside a delivery van, using a camera built into the rack on the top to observe.

Thorpe and King also didn't notice the small man at the bar who had entered just after them and watched them covertly the entire time. The small man, though, did notice the van parked outside and he waited until the van left before leaving the bar himself.

∽✕∾

Parker opened the door and was greeted by the vision of Sergeant Major Dublowski in civilian clothes. It was four in the morning and the pounding on the door to her BOQ room had gone on for a while before she'd roused herself.

"Dan!" She hadn't seen him in a long time, since the debriefings for the Omega Missile incident. He'd aged more than the time that had passed. "What's going on?"

"Colonel," Dublowski nodded. "It's Takamura."

"Thorpe's friend?"

"He's dead. I got a call from a buddy in the county sheriff's office. They found my phone number on the body. They're out at the accident scene right now and we can make it before they remove the body if we hurry."

Parker was still trying to process the first sentence. "Dead?"

"Yes." Dublowski looked at his watch. "We need to get moving."

Parker went to the closet and stepped inside the crowded space. She began dressing as she spoke. "What happened?"

"His car hit a tree."

"An accident?"

"He wasn't wearing a seat belt and he appears to have been drinking."

"Shit," Parker muttered. "He was supposed to be running the list using the profile I brought, not out partying."

"He wasn't out partying," Dublowski said in a sharp tone that drew Parker up short as she reached for her jacket. "He called me an hour ago. Said he'd uncovered something. We were supposed to meet outside the Ranch this morning and he was going to give me it, whatever it is. I don't think he just hopped up, jumped in his car, and ran into a tree just for the hell of it."

Parker zipped up a jacket. "Let's go."

The drive was made in the numb silence that two people awakened in the middle of the night to tragedy sink into. They arrived at the scene of the accident a half hour after leaving the BOQ.

"He must have been coming back to the main post." Dublowski spoke the first words in that time as they pulled up and were bathed in the flashing lights from the various emergency vehicles.

Dublowski led the way, greeting his man in the sheriff's office with a cup of hot coffee he'd purchased on the way there. "What do you have, Sam?"

Sam eyed Parker distrustfully. His black face was deeply creased from his years patrolling the county, one of the drug byways in the I-95 corridor. His once-dark hair was now stark white and cut tight against his skull under his Sam Browne hat.

"She's all right," Dublowski said. "I'll vouch for her. She's from the Pentagon."

Sam pulled up the lid on the coffee and took a sip as he considered that. He nodded his head toward the smashed car. "Head-on with a stationary object. The car lost. Not good for the occupant, particularly without a seat belt. On the site cause of death is a broken neck. Coroner will have to confirm that, plus do a tox screen. They're going to pull the body now." He led the way toward the car.

Parker had seen death before, and she'd never met Takamura, but the young man splattered against the tree, his broken body on the crumpled hood of his car, caused her to pause before following.

"You can smell the beer," Sam continued. "Couple of empties in the car. Besides being tanked up, he might have been trying to do too many things at once."

"What do you mean?" Dublowski asked.

Sam walked around the front of the car. He pointed at Takamura's left hand. A cell phone was gripped in the dead fingers. A cord was attached to it.

"There's something else," Sam said.

"What's that?" Dublowski asked.

The sheriff pointed to the left side of the BMW. "Paint marks. I think someone might have helped your friend off the road. Unless, of course, he's been driving around with the side of his car all dented up. We also got some bumper work in the rear that looks like someone hit the car from behind. Green car, looks like."

"Any idea who?" Dublowski asked.

"No. Like I said, we're not sure how this happened tonight."

"Can I?" Parker asked, pointing at the phone.

Sam nodded. "We got all we need. You can look at it, but I need it back."

She tried to pry the phone out of Takamura's hand, but the fingers wouldn't budge.

"Here." Dublowski offered her a Leatherman, open to the pliers.

"Jesus," Parker muttered.

"I'll do it," Dublowski said. He used the pliers to pry back the dead fingers one by one until he could remove the phone. "What's the cord?" he asked as he worked.

"It's an adapter for a computer. So you can send from a laptop over the cell phone with a modem."

He handed the phone to her. She pushed some buttons. "Here's the last number he called. Less than an hour ago."

Dublowski looked. "It's on post."

Parker wrote it down.

"Was there a laptop in the car?" Dublowski asked.

Sam shook his head. "Nope."

Parker pulled out her own cell phone and dialed the number. She pulled the phone away from her ear when she heard the static hissing in it. "It's a modem."

"First thing we do"—Dublowski was staring at Takamura's body—"we find what that modem is connected to."

"Where did he live?" she asked.

Sam took a deep drink of coffee, then crushed the Styrofoam cup. "Well, that's another thing. We got his address from his wallet. He lived outside Aberdeen on State Road 211. Just so happens the Aberdeen Fire Department responded to a call at the same address thirty minutes ago. Last I heard, a trailer there burned to the ground."

Parker glanced at Dublowski.

"Mind me telling what's going on?" Sam added.

"If I had a clue, I'd tell you," Dublowski said.

"He had your number in his pocket, Dan. Don't bullshit me. I think we have a homicide here."

Dublowski sighed. "I'm telling you the truth, Sam. I don't know. But if he was killed and his trailer was burned down, then this is bigger than you or I and I don't think you're going to find the killer."

Sam nodded slowly. "Government shit."

"I don't know," Dublowski said. "But it's deep." He turned to Parker. "Let's go."

The two of them slowly walked to his car. They got in and Dublowski started the engine.

"What the hell is all this about?" Parker broke the silence as they left the scene of the accident behind.

"I don't know." Dublowski's jaw was working. "All he was

doing was checking on people, looking for whoever killed my daughter. And he must have hit a live wire. Maybe it's a wire connected to her, maybe it ain't. But he's dead and I'm gonna make someone pay for that."

"You said this might be connected to the government back there," Parker said. "What did you mean by that?"

"I didn't say that; Sam did."

"But you did nothing to contradict him."

"You'd be surprised at the shit that goes on," Dublowski said cryptically.

"Actually," Parker said, "no, I wouldn't. I was in the Omega Missile launch control center, remember?"

Dublowski pounded a meaty fist into the dashboard, startling her. "What's wrong?" she asked.

"Takamura was just a kid. It shouldn't . . ." Dublowski just shook his head. The rest of the trip was made in silence.

Chapter Sixteen

There's a lot of drugs, sex, you name it, they do it." The driver of the car pointed out the window to a shadowy group gathered on a street corner. "Dealers. I've seen dependent girls—and boys—selling themselves to get money to buy drugs."

The car's wipers made loud squeaks every time they swept across the dirty windshield. Thorpe shifted his gaze from the exterior of the car to the driver. Morty Lorsen was the next point of contact that Master Sergeant King had directed him to after Major Rotzinger had turned out to be a bust. Morty was a wizened old man, so short he could barely see over the steering wheel, a thin fringe of white hair framing his wrinkled and age-spotted head.

King had told Thorpe that Lorsen was a retired master sergeant who had settled in Germany, his last duty station. Married to a German woman, he had spent almost half his adult life in Germany and knew the ins and outs of Stuttgart as well as any American. He spoke fluent German with a Bronx accent, a mixture Thorpe found most interesting.

"One of the girls I'm looking for didn't do drugs and she wouldn't have been standing on a street corner trying to sell herself," Thorpe said.

Lorsen gave him a sideways glance. "Says who? Her parents?"

"I knew her."

"We don't ever know kids," Lorsen said. "Even our own."

"Listen, I—"

"I've lived a lot longer than you," Lorsen interrupted. "I thought I knew things and every day I learn I don't know things." He tapped the side of his skull with a gnarled finger. "You listen to Morty, sonny boy. I know things."

"Do you know what happened to Terri Dublowski and the other girls?"

Lorsen turned a corner and drove down a narrow alley. He stopped the car, then leaned back in the worn upholstery. "Listen, my friend. I will ask around. But you might not like the answers you get."

Thorpe pulled out several bills and placed them on the seat between them. "I just want an answer."

Lorsen glanced at the money. "We Americans think we can buy everything."

"I was told you worked as a private investigator."

Lorsen pocketed the money. "I do. And I'm an American. You think you know so much, who were the guys watching your meet with Rotzinger?"

"How do you know about that?" Thorpe asked.

"Because *I* was watching you meet with Rotzinger," Lorsen said. "And there was other surveillance there. Lots of people around here watching each other."

"Who do—" Thorpe stopped as his phone rang. He pulled it out. "Thorpe."

"Mike, it's Parker."

He could tell by her voice that something was wrong. "What happened?"

"Takamura's dead."

Thorpe sank down into the car seat. "What happened?"

"His car hit a tree. The police think it might be a homicide. His trailer was burned down also."

"Jesus," Thorpe said. "What have we got into?"

"I don't know. He called Dan just before he was killed. Said he found something. We're going to check on it."

"Be careful," Thorpe said.

"You can count on that."

"Give me a call the second you find out what it was."

"I'll do that. You be careful too."

The phone went dead and Thorpe sat back in the seat, deep in thought.

"Bad news?" Morty asked.

"Yes."

"Care to share it?"

"No."

"Come with me." Lorsen got out of the car, pulling his old green raincoat tight around his frail body and grabbing a paper bag from the back seat. Thorpe followed as Lorsen slipped into an alleyway. The brick buildings on either side were three stories high and the alley barely wide enough to allow a car to pass if it weren't for the dumpsters and cans scattered throughout.

Lorsen was walking quickly, glancing neither to the right or left. Thorpe caught movement out of the corner of his eye and his hand was on the butt of the 9mm pistol Dublowski had given him.

"Leave it alone," Lorsen said.

A girl was on her knees, giving a blow job to a man, the two of them crammed between a dumpster and the brick wall. The man was watching Thorpe torn between pleasure and wariness, the girl concentrating on the job in front of her. She looked to be no more than fifteen, but it was hard to see in the dim shadows. The man was obviously over fifty.

Thorpe followed Lorsen to a narrow opening on the left side. Lorsen stepped in, motioning for Thorpe to follow. They went down a narrow space between two buildings, less than three feet wide. Lorsen suddenly disappeared to the right. Thorpe stepped up and saw that an entrance had been hewn out of the rock. He could barely see Lorsen inside. Hand firmly on the pistol grip, he stepped inside.

"Who the fuck are you?" a voice growled in English to the left.

"Easy." Lorsen was holding the paper bag out to the owner of the voice, a black teenager with a shaved head. The kid took the bag, looked in it, then tucked it under his arm.

"What else you got, old man?"

Thorpe heard the crinkle of money exchanging hands.

"What do you want?" the kid asked.

Lorsen tapped Thorpe. "Show him the pictures."

As Thorpe pulled the pictures of the missing girls out of his pocket, his eyes were adjusting to the room they were in. It was about forty feet wide, by thirty long. Several thick beams rose from the floor to support the ceiling. There were other people inside, dim forms, most lying about on ratty mattresses, one or two moving about. The only light came from one boarded-up window high on the far wall and several candles. There was a dank smell of decay in the air.

Lorsen took the pictures out of Thorpe's hand and gave them to the black kid. He squinted, looking through them quickly. "Yeah, and?"

"Have you seen any of these girls?" Lorsen asked.

"What's it to you?"

"Is Crew here?" Lorsen asked.

"Yo, Crew!" the boy yelled.

Another figure came out of the shadows, a white boy, slightly smaller than his friend, his arms heavily tattooed. His face was drawn, dark circles under the eyes. "What's going on, Cutter?"

"Yo, Crew, these dudes looking for these girls." Cutter handed the pictures to Crew.

Crew nodded at Lorsen. "Old man. How you been?"

"I've had some better days, young man. Some worse ones too. You?"

"Living." Crew laughed. "Just living. But that's something, ain't it?" His body shook and Thorpe could see a sheen of sweat on his bare arms, even though it was chilly.

"We—" Thorpe began, but Lorsen nudged him to be quiet.

"One of those girls is the daughter of a friend of ours," Lorsen said. "We want to make sure she's all right."

Crew looked down at the pictures in his hands. "There's five girls here."

"They're all missing."

"Maybe they don't want to be found, old man. Not everyone wants to be rescued."

"Maybe," Lorsen agreed. "We just want to make sure she's all right."

"You're full of crap," Crew said.

Lorsen laughed. "No, I'm not." He held out another couple of bills, the money Thorpe had given him. "Those girls are missing. We want to find them. It would be worth your time to help us."

Crew shook his head. "Well, it don't matter, 'cause I don't know any of them." He tossed the pictures at Lorsen. They tumbled to the ground around the old man's feet. Thorpe turned as he sensed someone behind him. The girl who had been in the alley squeezed past, not saying a word. She disappeared into the shadows.

Lorsen sighed. "Maybe you could ask the others here for me?"

"Listen—" Thorpe edged forward. Lorsen put an arm out and stopped him.

"Who the hell are you?" Cutter's right hand was hidden inside his Dallas Cowboys jacket.

"He's my friend," Lorsen said.

"You got too many friends, old man." Crew stepped forward. Thorpe pulled his pistol out of the holster, keeping it hidden inside his jacket.

"A person can never have too many friends," Lorsen said. "Listen, we think these girls might be dead. That there's somebody killing them. And this person will kill again."

"I don't give a damn about—" Cutter began, but Crew put a hand across his friend's chest.

"Hold on, bro. Let's listen to the man. He's always been square with me."

"Whoever is doing this," Lorsen continued, "will kill again. Maybe one of your girls here."

"Hey, Marcy!" Crew yelled, his voice echoing off the brick. When there was no response, he yelled again. "Marcy, get your butt over here."

A slight figure came out of the shadows. A girl, her face thin and drawn. "Yeah, what do you want?"

"Check out those pictures." Crew pointed at the ground.

Lorsen beat Marcy to it, scooping them up, then handing them to her. "Do you know any of these girls?"

Marcy thumbed through, pausing at one of them. "That's Mary."

"Mary Gibbons?" Thorpe asked, remembering the names that went with the photos.

"Yeah."

"Do you know where she is?" Lorsen asked.

"She's been gone for a while," Marcy said. "I ain't seen her in weeks."

"Do you know where she went?" Lorsen pressed.

Marcy giggled. "To a party. She went to a party."

"What party?" Lorsen asked.

"With the Jewel Man."

"Oh, fuck," Cutter said. He pushed Crew. "See, man? See what you getting us into? You don't want to fuck with the Jewel Man."

"Who is the Jewel Man?" Lorsen asked, but he was ignored as Crew shoved Cutter back.

"Hey, man, that dude is weird," Crew said. He tapped the photos. "He could be doing these girls, man. Doing 'em bad."

"I don't want nothing to do with this." Cutter turned and walked away.

"Who is the Jewel Man?" Lorsen asked once more.

"Some crazy dude," Crew said. "I only seen him a couple of times. He always got drugs and money, but he's only interested in girls."

"Jesus." Marcy was looking at the pictures more closely. The giggle was gone. "All these girls are missing?"

"Yes," Lorsen said.

"I knew the dude was screwy," she said. "He's asked me to party a couple of times, but you can look in his eyes and tell he's weird. Freaky." She tapped the side of her head. "Some weird shit going on in there."

"Who is he?" Lorsen's voice was patient.

Marcy was still looking at the pictures. "Hey, these other girls look like Mary. Except this one." She held up Terri Dublowski's picture. "That's like weird, isn't it?"

"Have you seen her?" Thorpe tapped Terri's picture.

Marcy shook her head. "No."

"Who is the Jewel Man?" Lorsen asked once more.

"I don't know," Marcy said. "Wears rings on every finger. Lots of jewels." She giggled. "Guess that's why he's called that. He's not too big. Speaks with a weird accent. Dark-skinned like an eye-talian or Greek or something. Got weird eyes. Blue. Like really strange. Always looking around."

"Where can we find him?" Thorpe asked.

"He just shows up," Crew said. "Don't hang out nowhere I know of. Like she said, he's bad."

"Sometimes he got another guy with him," Marcy volunteered. "Big guy. He's, like, even scarier."

"A second man?" Thorpe asked.

"When's the last time you saw either of them?" Lorsen asked.

"The small guy," Marcy said, "a couple of weeks ago. At a rave."

"A rave?" Thorpe asked.

"A party," Lorsen explained. "The location changes all the time. Techno music."

Marcy nodded. "Yeah. Haven't seen him since then."

"Could this Jewel Man and his friend be soldiers from post?" Thorpe asked.

"Maybe," Cutter shrugged. "Their hair is short. They act like soldiers, but I don't know. There's something different about them. The way they speak. And they got drugs and money."

Lorsen pulled some cards out, handing one to Crew and one to Marcy. "You see either of those guys—the Jewel Man or his buddy—you give me a call right away. I'll make it worth your time." He nudged Thorpe. "Let's go."

They retraced their steps to the small alley. Just before they entered the larger alley, Lorsen put his hand out, stopping Thorpe.

"Let me ask you something."

"Yes?" Thorpe waited.

"These kids you're looking for. You know they're probably dead?"

Thorpe nodded.

Lorsen ran a hand through his thinning white hair. "Those kids we just talked to . . ."

"Yeah?"

"They're alive. It might not be much of a life, but it's all they have. It isn't up to you or me to judge them. You were ready to pull your gun on them, weren't you?"

Thorpe didn't answer.

"They've had that all their life—people threatening them."

"What was in the bag?" Thorpe asked.

"Needles. I got a buddy at the post hospital who gets them for me. Crew—you saw the way he was shaking? He's got AIDS. A lot of the other ones do too. Heroin is real big now. That place is not exactly the cleanest and they tend to share needles. And sex."

Lorsen jabbed a finger in Thorpe's chest. "It isn't up to you or me to get them killed. So if you catch up with this Jewel Man, you better make sure you make a clean sweep of things. Because he might come back here asking questions and I don't think he'll be as nice as we were. Do I make myself clear?"

Thorpe looked down the narrow alley, taking in the garbage, the used needles and condoms. "Yeah, I hear you."

"No," Lorsen said, "you only hear half of what I'm saying." He pulled the pictures out of his pocket. "You know one of these girls. The others are strangers. Would you be here if you didn't know one of them? Would you give a shit about these girls you don't know?"

To that, Thorpe didn't have an answer.

❧

The sergeant major had checked the post's reverse directory and learned that the number Takamura had called was in the G-1 section in SOCOM's headquarters building. Parker and Dublowski were both on the access roster for SOCOM headquarters, so while most of Fort Bragg was out doing physical training they entered the building, flashing their ID cards at the security guards. There was no one in the G-1 section and they split up, checking the phone lines until they found Takamura's desk.

"This is it," Parker said, sitting down in front of the computer that took up most of the space on top of the desk. She noted the little pewter *Star Trek* figure on the desk next to the monitor. She turned the computer on and they both waited as

it booted up. Getting the main screen, she accessed the fax/
E-mail program.

"Here it is." She pointed at the screen. "Incoming E-mail
early this morning. Same time as the call from Takamura's
cell phone."

"What is it?" Dublowski demanded.

"It's not that easy," Parker said. She typed in several commands, each one ending in a beep and ACCESSED DENIED. "I
can't get into it without Takamura's password."

"It's a goddamn army computer," Dublowski growled. "It
can't be that hard to beat."

"Well, it's harder than I can handle." Parker sat back in the
chair and checked her watch. "And this place is going to start
filling up with people in half an hour."

"I know someone who can get in there," Dublowski said.

"Can you get him here in the next twenty minutes?"

"No," Dublowski said, "but I can bring this to him." He
knelt down and pulled the CPU for the computer out from
under the desk. He pulled out his Leatherman and cut the lines
in the back and tucked it under one arm. "Let's go."

∾×∾

"How long before you can deliver what you promised?" The
Russian was flawless, the accent strange.

The colonel eyed the stack of bills piled on the table in
front of him. "I did not expect you back so soon."

"I do not care what you expected." The man pointed at the
money, jeweled rings flashing. "This is what you asked for."

"It will take some time. I was not prepared."

"Why not?"

The colonel laughed. "There are so many pretenders in the
world. Men pretending to be something they're not."

"I am for real."

"I know that now."

"The only reason I am here," the Jewel Man said, "is because your German contact was legitimate."

"I heard you tested the product," the colonel said. "I assume
it was to your satisfaction?"

"It worked," the Jewel Man allowed.

"Of course it worked," the colonel said. "It was used in Afghanistan. The test wasn't necessary."

"It was for me."

"What do you plan to do with the material?"

"That is not your concern."

"It could be."

"Just get me the material."

"Many people have spies watching many places," the colonel said. "It could be dangerous. It was dangerous to set up the German meeting. And expensive. You could have just come here in the first place."

"That would have been foolish," the Jewel Man said. "What's done is done. Just get the material."

"It will cost more than we agreed on."

The Jewel Man sighed. "You have been paid."

"Transfer another two million in American dollars to my account."

"I will pay," the Jewel Man said, "but do not ask for more. How large will the package be?"

"Not very large. A little bit goes a long way. For what you said you wanted, about six briefcases."

"How long will it take you to get that amount of material?"

"It will take me at least two days."

The Jewel Man looked out the grimy window of the hotel. He shook his head. "Two days in this pigsty?"

"I could perhaps arrange some company for you?" the colonel was stuffing the bills into a black sack. "Chernovsty is not such a bad place. I have been stationed at worse. Especially when I was in the Soviet army."

"I am sure you have seen worse," the man said. "I will survive without your company. You may go now."

Anger flashed in the Ukrainian colonel's eyes, but the weight of the black sack in his hand forestalled his words. He turned on the worn heel of his boots and left the room.

Alone, the Jewel Man pulled a chair to the window and stared out at the street. He pulled the titanium case out of his pocket and began flicking it through his fingers as he thought.

Chapter Seventeen

The Delta Force Ranch sprawled over a large part of the Fort Bragg Reservation. It was surrounded by a wire-topped link fence with a patrol road on the inside. The compound contained not only the buildings housing the various elements of the force, but numerous training areas, including several live-fire ranges, a live-fire building, along with the fuselage of a Boeing 707 and a full-sized train for the troopers to practice their skills on.

Delta Force had earned its name from its official designation of Special Forces Operational Detachment Delta. Traditional Special Forces groups consisted of an Alpha Detachment (A-team), Bravo Detachment (B-Team, or company headquarters) and Charlie Detachment (C-Team, or battalion headquarters). When Colonel Charlie Beckwith formed a new unit in 1977 specifically designed to fight terrorism, he called it the SFOD-D, or Delta Force.

Beckwith had spent a tour of duty with British SAS, Special Air Service, and upon his return to the United States, realized his own army had no unit quite like the SAS, even though one was needed. Contrary to the common image of Special Forces, Green Berets were not specifically trained to be commandos or counterterrorist specialists, but rather were primarily designed to be teachers—force multipliers who could train other country's peoples to fight for themselves, whether it be in the guerrilla mode or counterguerrilla as they had in Vietnam.

Colonel Parker knew all about the history of Special Forces and the formation and mission of Delta Force from her time in air force Special Operations, which had often worked with their army counterparts. Her ID card and top-secret clearance, along with Sergeant Major Dublowski's presence, got her through the gate to the Ranch.

Inside the fence she picked up the altered atmosphere immediately. The men walking around looked different from the norm—it was something she had noted before when around Special Operators. They carried themselves with more confidence, but they weren't cocky. They were men who had volunteered for a dangerous assignment, gone through the training that had weeded out the wannabes and left only those capable of doing a hard job and doing it well.

Dublowski drove up to a low sand-colored building with a red tile roof. He carried the hard drive they had taken from Takamura's office with him as they walked to the door and entered.

"We got a specialist for just about everything," Dublowski explained as they went down a long corridor. "Locksmiths, weapons, surveillance, aircraft, vehicles, you name it. Our computer guy is supposed to be real good." He kicked his foot against a door and pushed into the room beyond.

"Hey, Simpkins!" Dublowski called out.

A mountain of a man looked up from a table where he was peering through a large magnifying glass. His shaved scalp reflected the powerful light he had angled just in front of him. White teeth shone as his ebony face split in a wide smile.

"Dublowski, my man. How they hanging?" Simpkins spotted Parker and the rank on her collar and he straightened slightly, nodding toward her. "Ma'am."

"Colonel Parker, meet Chief Warrant Officer Simpkins, our local computer nerd."

"Chief." Parker's hand disappeared inside Simpkin's massive paw. "You don't look like any nerd I've ever seen."

"Most of the guys here think if you can add two plus two, you're a math genius," Simpkins said. He picked up what he had been working on. A small black box, about four inches long by a two inches wide and an inch high. On each corner, tiny metal spikes poked out. "Cute, heh? This is Freddie One." Simpkins put the box down on the table, then he went to a computer at another table.

Dublowski held up the CPU and started to say something, but Simpkins hushed him with a large finger. "Watch this."

He entered something into the keyboard. The box began "walking" on the metal spikes, each one rotating slightly forward, planting, then pulling the box forward. "Look here." Simpkins pointed at the screen.

An image of the tabletop Freddie was on was displayed—from Freddie's low-level point of view.

"I can also get audio," Simpkins said. "Range about a half a mile."

"It's not moving very fast," Dublowski noted.

Simpkins laughed. "You rather that goes into a hostage situation to take a look or *you* poke your head in?"

"Won't the terrorists see it and stomp it?" Dublowski asked.

"Not if it's nighttime. Or we send Freddie in an air duct. Or we keep him under cover. Freddie can even carry a very small payload."

" 'Small' being the operative," Dublowski said.

"I'm working on one a little bigger, Freddie Two." Simpkins sounded hurt.

"Okay, okay." Dublowski tapped the side of the CPU.

Simpkins reluctantly turned from the computer screen. "What you got there?"

"We need to get something out of this," Dublowski said.

Simpkins grabbed the unit and walked across the room. With one arm he cleared a spot on a table. He looked at the back of the CPU, then across at Dublowski, holding up the severed cables. "You're supposed to unscrew these."

"I was in a hurry."

"This has a government ID below the serial number," Simpkins said as he began removing the connections. "Am I going to get in trouble for working on this?"

"Not if no one finds out," Dublowski said.

Simpkins laughed as he tossed the cut cables into the trash and began connecting new ones. He plugged the CPU in and turned it on, pulling a seventeen-inch monitor close and laying a keyboard across his large thighs.

The screen came alive as the CPU booted. "Whose is this?" Simpkins asked as he typed in a few commands.

"A guy who works in SOCOM G-1," Dublowski said.

"He's done some modifications." Simpkins put his chin in his hand as he stared at the screen for several moments, then he began typing. "Anything in particular I'm looking for?"

"An E-mail was sent to this machine last night, about two in the morning," Parker said. "It was transmitted from a laptop via a cell phone to the modem. We need to know what that E-mail was."

After a few moments, Simpkins sat back in the chair. "I can find the message. But I can't open it. It was sent to a locked file. I need the code word to open that file."

"Can't you break in?" Dublowski asked. "I thought that was what you were here for."

"I can break in," Simpkins said, "but whoever devised the lock booby-trapped it. You're lucky you brought this to me. Someone of inferior intelligence and expertise would have tried cracking the lock and the file would have been wiped clean."

"Well, with your superior intelligence, is there a way you can get us in?"

"Get me the code word and I'll get you in," Simpkins said. "I don't suppose you can ask whoever set this up what the password is?"

"He's dead," Dublowski said.

"That rules that out." Simpkins drummed his fingers on the edge of the desk, staring at the jumble of code on the screen.

"Takamura had to have known we would try to get this information," Parker said. "There has to be a way in."

"Takamura?" Simpkins asked.

"The man who sent the message and whose computer this is," Parker said.

"He was army?" Simpkins said. When Parker nodded, he spun on his chair and shoved himself away from the desk toward another computer. He quickly went to work. "I'm accessing his personnel records."

"Won't you get in trouble for that?" Parker asked. "I was told you could get traced back. We don't want anyone to know what we're doing."

Simpkins jabbed a thumb at Dublowski. "Contrary to what my friend there thinks, I am pretty good with a computer. Not only that, but here in the Ranch we have the highest access available on the Department of Defense system. We can also access State Department, NSA, CIA, just about everybody. There's some places they don't want us peeking at, but overall we have pretty good access. No questions asked."

He tapped the screen. "Here we go. James Takamura. He's still alive according to this record."

"He was killed in a car crash early this morning," Dublowski said.

"Right after he sent an E-mail to this computer via a cell phone from his laptop?" Simpkins didn't wait for the answer. He scooted back over to Takamura's CPU. "Read me his date of birth."

Parker sat down and read out the data.

"Not it," Simpkins said. "Mother's maiden name."

Parker read that and Simpkins entered it in the password block.

"Nope." Together they went through every piece of information that Simpkins could think might be used as a password. While he was doing that, Dublowski made coffee and stood by the pot until it was full. Then he poured mugs for everyone. Finally Simpkins had exhausted all possibilities.

The warrant officer leaned back in his chair. Then he cocked his head, looking at the stickers on the side of the computer. "This guy one of those *Star Trek* nuts?"

"I don't know," Parker said. "I guess so from those. He had a little figure of the *Enterprise* on his desk."

Simpkins began chuckling, a low rumble from deep inside his chest. "I don't believe it." He typed in a word. The screen changed. "I'm in!"

"What was the password?" Parker asked.

" 'Computer,' " Simpkins said.

"What?" Dublowski asked.

"He used the word 'computer' as his password. In *Star*

Trek, when they want to access the computer, they just call out, 'Computer,' " Simpkins explained. "It's so obvious no one would think of it unless they watched *Star Trek.*"

"Sort of the purloined letter technique," Parker said.

"What's that?" Dublowski asked.

"Hiding a stolen letter in a mailbox," Parker explained as she looked over Simpkins's shoulder.

"This is the E-mail," Simpkins said. "It's a file this guy Takamura lifted from personnel records, but the personnel code is funny. Not active. Not family members. I've seen this before." He paused in his typing. "Oh, yeah. Foreign students."

"What?" Dublowski and Parker said at the same time.

Simpkins tapped the screen. "These are foreign student files. You know. Guys from other countries who come here to go through the Q-Course or the School of the Americas at Benning. Any kind of training. We even get some guys here once in a while. We have an exchange program with the Brits—send one of our guys over to go through their selection course every year and then serve a year with an SAS troop and they send one of their guys over.

"Your guy Takamura has pulled two records from the database. Looks like he got them by cross-referencing some sort of criteria with the foreign student database. Location and characteristics of the people." Simpkins hit the enter key. Dublowski and Parker leaned over Simpkins's shoulders and watched as two faces appeared on the screen.

"And there they are," Simpkins said.

❧

Hancock's desk was no longer the clear surface he liked to have at the end of the day. Files covered the top. He was writing on a legal pad, jotting notes, when there was a buzz.

He opened the left top drawer and pulled out the secure phone, a slim black handset that he tucked under his left ear as he leaned back in his seat. "Yes?"

"This is Ferguson. Dublowski and Parker are together now. Someone in Thorpe's office was killed. A specialist named

Takamura. State police think it was a homicide. Parker and Dublowski went out to the accident site."

"And?"

"They got Takamura's office computer and took it to the Delta Force Ranch."

"What else?" Hancock asked. Ferguson was the CIA representative to Special Operations Command at Fort Bragg. As such, Hancock knew, his primary job was to constantly deny request by the army people for intelligence while trying to cram CIA agents in the various schools run by SOCOM. His other job, maybe even more important, was to keep an eye on the Green Beanies and make sure they didn't use too much of their initiative.

"Takamura's laptop was not found in the ruins of his trailer—he usually kept it in his car. His body was found with a cell phone in hand and a data cord that could hook to the modem of his cell phone. I've pulled the phone records—he called his office modem just before his accident. I think he sent some files to the office computer via the cell phone."

"And of course you found all this out *after* Dublowski and Parker had figured it out," Hancock said.

There was no reply. Hancock stared up at the ceiling, then returned his gaze to the chess sets on the right side of his desk. "Anything else?"

"I've got an inquiry from the state police in reference to Takamura's killing. They want to know if we know anything."

"Do we?" Hancock asked.

"Not that I know of." There was a pause. "Do we?"

"Anything else?" Hancock asked once more.

"I think they're one step ahead of us," Ferguson said.

Hancock laughed. "You don't even know where I'm going, my good man, so how could you even suppose they might be one step ahead?"

"Well, it's just—"

"Oh, no," Hancock cut him off. "Quite the contrary. Them thinking they're one step ahead means they're three steps behind."

"What do you want me to do?"

"Nothing right now. I'll call you."

Hancock hung up the phone. There was another buzz and his secretary's voice echoed out of a speaker built into the desk. "The D/O is here to see you, sir."

"Send her in," Hancock said as he cleared his desktop with a swipe of his arm into an empty drawer.

The double doors whished open on pneumatic arms. Kim Gereg strode in. She walked to one of the chairs in front of his desk. Instead of immediately sitting in it, she pulled it to the side where the chess sets were located and put it down just outside the rings of light reflecting down on them. She sat down, in as much shadow as Hancock was at his desk.

"What can I do for you?" Hancock asked.

"One of my men died yesterday in a car accident," Gereg said.

"I saw it in the morning brief," Hancock said. "Most unfortunate."

"Yes," Gereg said. A long silence played out before she spoke again. "You were very qualified in your support of stronger intervention in the Balkans."

"We either need to shit or get off the pot," Hancock said. "If you'd pardon my French."

"You don't care which?"

"Not particularly. I don't think that part of the world is in our strategic interests."

"World War I started in that part of the world," Gereg noted.

"World War III won't."

"You sound sure of that."

"Nothing is certain. But I do see certain parallels between this situation and the quagmire in Vietnam and I would prefer not to repeat history."

"I didn't know you cared so much," Gereg said.

Hancock smiled, not taking the bait.

"That was Adviser Lane's view, wasn't it?"

"It was."

She turned and looked at the wall of photos.

A long silence played out.

"I've gone through Welwood's files," Gereg finally said.

"Welwood?" Hancock asked.

A twitch of a smile touched the ends of Gereg's mouth. "My man who died yesterday."

"Ah, yes."

"He was doing some checking on a couple of operations. One code-named Romulus and one code-named Remus."

Again Hancock waited, not offering anything to Gereg.

"Have you heard of these operations?" Gereg asked.

"How should I know anything? They were obviously something run by your department," Hancock said. "After all, it was in your man's files. Why are you coming to me?"

"I've never heard of either of these operations and they're clearly connected, given the code names."

"You expect me to believe you've never heard of an operation run by your own department? What would the director think of that?"

Gereg stared at him for several seconds, then stood. "Thank you for your time. I know how busy you are."

"No more busy than you are," Hancock said to her back.

❧

"Can you get to a secure modem?" Parker's voice sounded faint in the SATPhone.

"Hold on," Thorpe said. He turned to Master Sergeant King. "Is there a secure modem here?"

King nodded and wrote on a slip of paper. "Here's the E-mail address." He pointed across the office. "It's for that computer there." They were in the G-3 shop of Special Operations Command, Europe. Morty Lorsen had dropped Thorpe off in front of the building an hour ago and Parker had just called.

Thorpe read the address to her. "What do you have?"

"We recovered the last thing Takamura pulled up on the computer," Parker said.

"What is it?"

"Best you see for yourself, then give me a call back. It's being sent right now."

"All right." Thorpe hung up, then followed King over to the computer. It was evening in Germany and the room was deserted except for the two of them.

"We got it," King said. "Here it is."

Two faces appeared on the screen line by line. "Who the hell are you?" Thorpe whispered. Both men had dark skin and straight black hair. Their eyes were identical—deep blue with a steady gaze into the camera. The combination of eyes and skin color was disconcerting.

Names appeared below each: Jawhar Matin and Akil Matin. And that was it.

Thorpe punched in Parker's SATphone number. "Who are they?" he demanded as soon as she answered. "Are there two killers?"

"As near as we can tell, the last thing Takamura did was a search for foreign students at the posts where the girls disappeared. He came up with these two."

"Foreign? What country are they from?"

"Saudi Arabia."

"With a name like Matin?"

"Jawhar there was at Fort Rucker when two girls disappeared. His brother, meanwhile, was at Fort Benning going through Ranger School at the time one girl disappeared there."

"You don't have any time at Ranger School to go kill anyone," Thorpe said. Thorpe remembered his own Ranger School experience quite vividly. He also remembered there were several foreign officers in his class. The same with his Special Forces qualification course.

"Ranger students get a twelve-hour break between each phase," Parker noted.

"And you're usually too tired to do anything other than eat and sleep."

"And maybe have your brother visit you," Parker said.

"What about Germany? Were either of them around Stuttgart? Who the hell exactly are these guys? Where are they from?" Thorpe was trying to assimilate this information.

"Their training files are sealed," Parker said. "This was all Takamura was able to get. Other than the names and those stateside assignments, we don't know anything."

"So it's a long shot they're who we're looking for?" Thorpe closed his eyes, remembering the little round man who he had gotten involved in this. "Anything further on what happened to Takamura?"

"He was run off the road. Dan thinks he was murdered. The last thing he did was send those two pictures and names by modem from his laptop in his car to his computer in the office. His trailer was burned to the ground early this morning also."

Thorpe opened his eyes and stared at the screen. "Let me talk to Dan."

Dublowski's low growl came over the phone. "Hey, Mike. You see the two sons-a-bitches."

"I see them. Was Takamura killed?"

"Yes."

"Who did it?"

"We have no idea, but whoever it was tried to make a clean sweep of things. I'll keep in contact with my man at police headquarters but I think they're going to come up with zip."

"Could these guys have done it? Are either of these guys I'm looking at in the States?"

"I don't know," Dublowski said. "Even if one of them is, the reaction was too damn fast. Takamura had just come up with this and called me and whoever killed him was on top of him within the hour."

"So someone was watching him."

"Right."

"Which means there's a good chance someone is watching you and Parker," Thorpe added.

"Right again. We're on the Ranch right now, so we're safe for the moment."

"I wouldn't bet my life on it," Thorpe said.

"Let's not go too far with a conspiracy here," Dublowski said.

"I don't think you can ever go too far with a conspiracy," Thorpe replied. "These two guys can't be this on top of things by themselves."

"I don't know what the fuck is going on," Dublowski said, "but we'll get to the bottom of this."

"At least I have something to work with on this end," Thorpe said. He told Dublowski about what he had learned from the kids Lorsen had taken him to. "Maybe one of these guys is this Jewel Man."

"Terri wouldn't have gotten within fifty feet of no drug dealer," Dublowski growled. "Or gone to any party with scumbags like these two."

"We don't know what happened yet." Thorpe remembered what Lorsen had said about kids but knew better than to mention that to the sergeant major. "Does Parker think these guys are the ones?" Thorpe asked. "Her profile said one killer."

"They're brothers," Dublowski said. "Maybe one kills and the other doesn't know." There was a long pause. "All we have are the pictures and the names. We need more."

Thorpe considered the situation. "If this one guy—Akil Matin—went through Ranger School, there's a chance he might have attended one of the schools at the JFK Center there at Bragg. The Q-Course or maybe one of the specialty schools."

"I can check on that," Dublowski said.

"Okay. Let me talk to Parker."

As soon as she got the phone, Parker began speaking. "Mike, if these guys are involved in any way, we have to run it up the flagpole. Bring in the people who are supposed to take care—"

"Takamura was killed," Thorpe cut her off, knowing where she was going. "Remember when we waited for the air police to help us get into the launch control center for Omega Missile? They almost all got killed and we ended up having to do it ourselves."

"Mike—"

"No!" Thorpe's yell drew King's attention from the other side of the room. Thorpe leaned forward, lowering his voice. "Listen, Lisa, Takamura was killed because I got him involved. Dan's daughter is missing. The other girls. If we pass the buck on this, there's a good chance more people are going to die. We have to do it ourselves."

"Are you sure that's the reason?" Parker asked.

"Everyone with the questions," Thorpe muttered. "Hey, something big is going on here. Takamura getting killed so quickly after coming up with these guys' names is very strange."

"Strange?" Parker repeated.

"Keep your eyes open there," Thorpe said. "Maybe our guy is right there at Bragg."

"All right."

"Listen, I've got to go. I got some checking to do here. I'll talk to your shortly."

He pressed the off button on the phone, then turned to King. "Who could we talk to, to find out if those two fellows have ever been around here?"

King laughed. "Morty, of course."

"Let's go."

Chapter Eighteen

Jawhar had walked back and forth in front of the gray-streaked window of his room for hours, his expensive boots wearing a path in the thin, worn rug. The titanium vial repeatedly made its trip through his fingers, hitting against the bulky rings he wore.

The colonel wanted more money. That wasn't unexpected.

He felt a pull, an emotional hook embedded in his mind, demanding that he leave the room and seek out a woman. Akil should have been the one to do this, Jawhar knew. Akil was always business when business was at hand. Akil only "played" when there was no business to attend to. When he was bored.

For Jawhar it was different. He could never escape the pull. He felt trapped inside the room, the dingy walls closing in on him. He turned on his heel and quickly walked to the door, threw it open and strode down the corridor.

The old elevator made so much noise taking him down that Jawhar regretted getting on it and not taking the stairs. However, it made it to the bottom safely. He pulled the steel gate aside and walked into the lobby. There was the sound of drinking, muted music, coming from a hallway to the left. Jawhar followed the sound, feeling a flush run up his neck.

The bar was dark, not for ambience but rather frugality. A few dim lights left most of the room in dark shadows. A radio sputtered out some unidentifiable music amid the clink of

glasses and conversation. The smell of cheap Russian ciga-
rettes filled the air.

Jawhar walked to the bar and took a stool. He had been in
this type of place before and he knew the choices for drink
would be limited.

"Yes?" The bartender, an old, portly man, asked in Russian.

"Budweiser," Jawhar did not particularly care for the American beer, but he knew it would be far better to drink than
anything local. Hard liquor might have the right label but
would most likely be filled with some local swill.

"Such a beer travels a long way to get here—" the old man
began, but Jawhar cut him off by dropping several bills on the
bar. Three American twenties. The old man had them scooped
up before they even settled. The beer appeared quickly.

Almost as quickly, a dark-haired woman claimed the seat
next to him, barely beating out another woman, a younger
blond. Jawhar ignored her for the time being. Something
brushed against Jawhar's left leg and he turned.

"Hello." The woman was rubbing her hand up his thigh.

"Leave me," Jawhar said the words flatly.

"Oh, come on, baby, don't—" she never finished the sentence as Jawhar pressed his thumb into the forearm that was
rubbing him, squeezing down on the pressure point just as
Akil had taught him. Her eyes widened and she quickly va-
cated the seat with a curse.

The seat remained empty for a minute. Finally, the pull was
too strong. Jawhar turned and made eye contact with the
young blond. She hesitatingly came forward and claimed the
seat.

"How are you? I'm Katrina."

Jawhar stared at her, his eyes narrowing. If she'd been an
animal in the wild she would have read the look he was giving
her for what it was—nature's way of saying "predator." Unfortunately for her, she was an animal of civilization.

"Are you looking for some fun? A good time?"

"Perhaps."

He took a long drag from his beer, polishing it off. The
bartender was good; he was there in a second. Jawhar nodded
at the incline to the man's head. He needed another. The bar-

tender raised his eyebrows and gestured at Katrina's glass. Jawhar shrugged and threw down several more American bills.

"Are you staying here?"

Jawhar looked her over more carefully. "Yes. Are you?"

"I could be."

Jawhar could see the shadows in her eyes. She was experienced, but not as experienced as someone her age would be if she had been doing it since she was able. The free-market economy had changed many things in the past few years.

"You have very nice eyes," she said.

"Are you a student?" Jawhar guessed.

She nodded. "I was. I hope to go back to school soon."

"What did you study?"

She slid the drink closer. "Psychology. Real interesting stuff, don't you think?"

Jawhar shrugged. "I don't know."

She sucked in the cherry from the drink, toyed with it on the end of her tongue and winked. "I can be very understanding because of my studies." She swallowed the cherry.

Jawhar looked at her blankly for a second and then relaxed. Katrina didn't seem too perturbed by his lack of verbal repartee. "You are visiting our city?"

Jawhar nodded. "Just here for business."

"What kind of business?"

Jawhar smiled. "Contract work for the government."

She licked around the rim of her glass for a second and then put it down. "Sounds exciting. What kind of contracts? You're not with the KGB or anything like that, are you?"

"No."

"Going to be in town long?"

"No. Where are you from?"

She gestured vaguely. "North. A long way north. Where it gets very cold at night when you sleep alone."

Jawhar noted that she'd gestured in the wrong direction. North was behind them. That was the problem with too many people. They didn't know where they came from.

She'd finished her drink. He could tell she didn't know what exactly to do next, as he was still toying with his beer.

"Tell me about yourself." He looked at her intently and

smiled. "You seem to be a very fascinating woman."

She gave him a look of such genuine happiness that he was surprised for a second. "I would love to talk to you. Let's go somewhere else. By the way, you never told me your name."

Jawhar stood up and put his hand to her waist to guide her out, his rings glittering in the bar light. "Jewel, my name is Jewel."

She smiled. "A most interesting name."

They didn't speak as they left the bar and went toward the elevator. She started to speak when the elevator gate closed, and continued all the way to his room. "I want to be a psychiatrist. I wanted to be a surgeon, but my grades weren't good enough and I was not a man. Unfortunately, I've always been just smart enough to get in the door. Not quite smart enough to get what I wanted. It didn't help being a woman."

Jawhar unlocked the door to his room and ushered her in.

"Psychology is most fascinating, though," Katrina continued. "I enjoyed my studies."

"And you are here to pay your way through school?" Jawhar asked.

"Times are difficult," Katrina said with the resignation Jawhar had heard from many in the former Eastern Bloc.

"I do not believe in psychology," Jawhar said as he pulled out his titanium case and began unscrewing the lid. He had had it carefully cleaned after Bosnia so it could go back to its original use. "Seems like they spend an awful lot of time looking backward instead of dealing with life now."

Katrina paused in the doorway to the bathroom. "But the source of our discontent and our madness is in our past. Until you can get to the source and understand it, you'll always be lost." The door swung shut.

Jawhar took a deep sniff of cocaine from the case. The hook in his brain was pounding now, a throbbing thing with a life of its own. A psychology student? He found that most amusing and ironic.

Katrina came back out. She flipped open the small refrigerator in the room. "Beer?" It was local stuff. Almost as bad as drinking piss water, in Jawhar's opinion.

Jawhar accepted the can and popped the top. "I have something you might like." He held up the titanium case.

"What is it?" she asked.

"Cocaine. Have you ever tried it?"

"Once."

"Did you like it?"

She nodded.

He poured a line on the table next to his chair. She came over and knelt, nose to the cheap wood. She snorted, then stood and went back to the bed.

He settled into the chair near the window and Katrina sat cross-legged on the bed, fluffing the pillows up to get comfortable. She looked at him quizzically, as if wondering why he wasn't joining her on the bed, but she didn't push it.

She blinked. The first wave hit her brain. "Judging from what you said before I went into the bathroom, you seem to be one of those people who believe that looking into the past is a waste of time."

Jawhar waved his hands. "I prefer to expend my energy on the present."

"But sometimes the energy you expend on the present is wasted energy if you aren't expending it in the right areas because you don't understand your past."

Jawhar sipped his beer and considered her. The understanding prostitute working on a degree in psychology. She thought she knew so much. "It is all bullshit."

Katrina leaned forward, her pupils dilated now. "What happened to you that was so terrible that you don't want to remember it?"

Jawhar closed his eyes. All of a sudden he was tired. The cushions of the chair enveloped him, dragging him down. "Nothing happened to me."

Katrina leaned back on the pillows. "I'm willing to listen. I'll be gone tomorrow, so you won't have to worry. I don't even know your last name. Tell me your dark secret."

"My mother was a bitch," Jawhar said.

"Why is the mother always blamed?" Katrina wondered. "I think it is more the father's fault in most cases."

"Oh, I blame him too," Jawhar said. "His time is coming."

"His time?"

Jawhar opened his eyes and looked at her closely. "You want to know something?"

"Yes?"

"I've killed."

Katrina blinked. "What?"

Jawhar smiled coldly. "I said I've killed."

She looked at the door briefly and then back at him. "Anyone I know?"

Jawhar took a sip of his beer. "The first time was in Kuwait. You remember, don't you? The great oil war?"

She seemed to relax slightly. "You were there?"

Jawhar nodded.

"Who did you kill?"

"A woman."

Katrina leaned forward on the bed. "A woman? Why?"

"She was in the wrong place at the wrong time," Jawhar lied. "She had to die."

"Did you feel bad about it?"

Jawhar stood. "No." He was now next to the bed, looking down on her. Her eyes were wide as she looked up. He knew what she was feeling as the cocaine rushed through her system.

"How did you kill her?"

"With a knife. I cut her throat." Jawhar sat on the bed behind her and put his hands on her shoulders.

"But you did it because it was war. Right?"

"Oh, yes," Jawhar whispered. He reached down and cupped her breasts. She rolled back against him.

"What did it feel like?" she whispered.

"I felt like a god. I felt like I had the ultimate power. I felt like I was in control for once." He pulled and her blouse parted, buttons spilling on the bed and floor. He picked her up and threw her back on the bed, her head on the pillows. She looked up at him with a glazed look—no resistance. She wanted it. He could feel it.

"I want to play a game," he said. He pulled out a wad of bills and threw them on the bed next to her. She looked at the bills, then back up at him. It was more money than she could make in a year working the bar downstairs.

"What kind of game?"

"A fun game. It will very much be worth your time."

He saw her struggling to think. He pulled more bills out. She nodded, then closed her eyes.

Jawhar used the remains of her blouse on her left wrist, tying it to the bedpost. Her bra unfastened in the front and he used it to fix the right wrist. She was writhing now, struggling against the bonds. Jawhar looked about. A shirt was lying on the dresser. He went and got it. Returning to the bed, he knelt on top of her, his groin pressing up against her large breasts. She looked at him as he rolled the cloth. The last vision she had of him was his smile as he placed the cloth over her eyes. He lifted her head and tied it. Then he got off her and stepped back from the bed. She was still playfully struggling against the bonds.

Jawhar reached down and removed the knife he always carried strapped behind his back. The blade was long and curved and very sharp. He went back to the bed. Using one hand, he unbuttoned her skirt down the side and laid it open. Her cheap black panties beckoned.

Jawhar placed the point of the knife under the waistband. Feeling the knife, Katrina froze. "What are you doing?"

Jawhar didn't say a word. The sharpened blade slid through the material. Jawhar pushed his free hand down on her mound. She was wet. He pressed hard and she writhed under his ministrations. Jawhar played with her for a few minutes until she was arching off the bed—then he stopped.

He went back to the dresser. Another piece of cloth. He went back to the bed. Wadding her panties up, he held them in one hand. He looked down on her for a long minute. He reached down and played with her for a few seconds. She opened her mouth to gasp with the pleasure and he rammed the panties in. She jerked up and he quickly wound the cloth around and sealed them in place. He ignored her muffled protests.

Jawhar removed his clothes slowly. She was kicking now. The pleasure was gone. This was serious. He knew she knew that. But it was too late. He grabbed her ankles and spread her legs. She was strong, but he was stronger. He pinned the legs down and pressed his body on hers. His cock slid in effortlessly—she was still wet from the beginning.

Jawhar pushed his head up next to hers and whispered as he fucked. "The one in Kuwait was the first. She was a prisoner. A local woman who had cooperated with the Iraqis. Or so her neighbors said. Who knows if that was the truth? She was given to me to interrogate. That's when I learned about being in control."

Jawhar took a moment to catch his breath. Katrina was arching up to keep him going, the cocaine and his low voice bringing her back to thinking this was indeed a game.

"It was so easy. If I had known how easy it was, so many things would have been different for my brother and I. Remember I said she was the first? Well, there were others." Jawhar could feel the pressure in his balls build. "All over the world." Katrina's moans reached a crescendo. Barely enough to make it to the door of the room, never mind summon help.

"They all really wanted to die. They all deserved to die. Just like you." Katrina was crying now, her muffled sobs dying in her throat and her tears staining the blindfold.

Jawhar almost paused then because a vision of another woman crossed his mind. Then he felt himself coming. He shuddered and thrust deeper. He felt himself pour out into her.

After a minute Jawhar lay still. He pulled out and stepped back. Katrina wasn't moving. Maybe she was hoping he'd leave now or just let her go. Jawhar blinked, shaking off the effect of the sex, cocaine and beer. They were all the same.

Jawhar scooped up the knife from where he had laid it on the nightstand. He dressed quickly and put the knife in its sheath. Katrina remained frozen throughout.

He considered the room. He knelt down next to Katrina's head. "Did your psychology help you? Did you understand me?"

Jawhar removed the blindfold and she blinked, trying to adjust to the light. He levered his right forearm across her neck, slowly applying pressure. Her eyes bulged and her legs drummed against the mattress. Jawhar put all his weight behind that arm. Her eyes were terrified, a animal caught by a predator. Jawhar released the pressure and he could hear the wheeze of air as she desperately tried to get oxygen around her gag.

Getting off the bed, Jawhar took the beer can and crushed it, throwing it in the trash. He got another out of the refrigerator and sat in the chair by the window.

His SATPhone rang. He wanted to ignore it, but he knew better. He pulled it out of the coat pocket and punched the on button.

"Yes?" He knew it could only be one person, his brother Akil.

"Have you met the colonel yet?"

"Yes. He is getting what we want."

"How soon?"

"Two or three days. He wants more money."

"How much?"

"Two million, American."

"I'll tell the old man."

"He'll pay," Jawhar said. Two million was nothing to their father.

"Be careful. We've received whispers from the West that the colonel is not to be trusted."

"I don't trust him." Jawhar's eyes were on the bed. He could see the rise and fall of Katrina's naked chest.

"Our Western contact says the colonel has already made plans to go to Colombia."

"Before or after he completes his end of the bargain?"

"Let us hope afterwards. Perhaps it is good he wants more money," Akil said.

"I believe he will come back for the additional money. He said he will return in two days."

"I will come to your location in two days to bring the money and to make sure the colonel delivers."

"Good," Jawhar said.

"I will see you then." The phone went dead.

Jawhar pulled the knife out and played with the razor-sharp edge as he considered Katrina. At least he would not be bored while he waited.

Chapter Nineteen

"YOU think these are your guys?" Morty Lorsen pulled out a pair of rimless glasses and looked at the two downloaded images.

"Yes." Thorpe was in the passenger seat, Master Sergeant King cramped in the back of Lorsen's old car. "We think they're from the Middle East," he added. "Saudi Arabia."

"Odd names for Saudis," Lorsen noted. "I got just the guy for us to see." He threw the old BMW into gear and pulled into traffic.

"Who?" Thorpe asked.

"You'll see," Lorsen said.

They wove through the narrow streets of the old part of Stuttgart, several times almost colliding with a car coming the opposite way. With a squeal of breaks badly needing servicing, Lorsen spun the wheel and came to a halt in a narrow alley that barely allowed them to open the doors on the driver's side. Thorpe slid across the seat and followed Lorsen out, King getting out of the back.

"Do you know every back alley in Stuttgart?" Thorpe asked, trying to see into the darkness ahead.

"Not every." Lorsen was already walking and Thorpe and King hurried to catch up.

Thorpe stopped as Lorsen suddenly disappeared to the right. "Come on, come on," the old man's voice echoed back.

Thorpe turned the corner and saw Lorsen standing in front

of a steel door. Above the door a video camera was staring at them, the little red light on the top letting them know they were being observed.

Lorsen was looking up at the camera and waving. "Me they know. You they'll be wondering about."

"Who?" Thorpe asked once more.

"You'll see. If they ever open this door." Lorsen waved his hands in front of the camera. "Let's go, let's go."

Thorpe was surprised when the door quietly opened, swinging back so smoothly he had no doubt it was being done mechanically. There was no one inside the small, white-painted foyer that beckoned. A wooden door was on the other end ten feet farther in. Another camera was above that door.

Lorsen ushered Thorpe and King in, the steel door swinging shut behind them with a solid thud.

"Are you armed?" Lorsen asked.

"Yeah," Thorpe answered.

"Put your weapons here." Lorsen pulled out a snub-nosed revolver and placed it on a small shelf.

Thorpe placed the 9mm pistol he had been given by Dublowski on the shelf, while King deposited a Beretta.

"One way mirror," Lorsen jerked his thumb at the large pane of reflective glass to their left.

"Who's watching us?" Thorpe asked. He felt naked without his weapon and the elaborate security measures did nothing to ease that feeling.

"Mossad," Lorsen finally informed him.

Thorpe had suspected as much. If anyone would have tabs on Middle Eastern personnel, it was the Israeli security agency.

The wooden door swung open. A tall, thin man waited. His face was drawn, the bones tight under the skin. He had short dark hair, a generous portion of it turning gray. His eyes were deep-set and a very dark brown, almost black.

"My old friend Mr. Lorsen." The man waved them inside. "With friends. At least I assume they are friends, although they came to my door armed."

"Everyone comes to your door armed," Lorsen said. "It's a calling card of the trade."

The man led them down a corridor into a small room with a table and several chairs. The walls were an off-green color that had seen better days. A fan revolved very slowly above their heads.

The man perched himself on the edge of the table. Lorsen sank down gratefully into one of the chairs. Thorpe and King remained standing.

"This is Major Thorpe and Master Sergeant King," Lorsen said by way of introduction. "Can I tell them your name?" he asked the man who let them in.

The man nodded.

Lorsen gave a small bow. "And this, my friends, is Esdras. At least that's the name he is currently using with me. Whether it is his first or last name, I know not and care not to know."

Esdras smiled. "Always a joker, old man." The smile disappeared. "What do you want?"

Thorpe pulled the printout of the two pictures and names out of his pocket and placed it on the table. Esdras picked it up. His face grew even more taut, if that was possible.

"How do you know these men?"

"They attended some military schooling in the States," Thorpe said. "James and Alex Matin. Our records indicate they are officers in the Saudi Arabian army."

Esdras tossed the paper back onto the desk. "What about them?"

"We feel they might have a role to play in the disappearance of several American military dependent girls in this area," Lorsen said.

"That is not my concern," Esdras said.

"The Samson option," Thorpe said, catching everyone in the room off guard.

Esdras's head snapped around. "Mr. Lorsen, please take Sergeant King into the corridor." His eyes remained focused on Thorpe.

Lorsen and King left the room, the door swinging shut behind them.

"The Samson option is fiction," Esdras said.

"It is now," Thorpe agreed. "But a year ago it was fact. I suggest you call your superiors and tell them my name. And the name Colonel Parker. And you might want to mention the Omega Missile."

Esdras turned and left Thorpe alone in the room. The second hand on the plain clock on the wall slowly made its way around as he waited. After five minutes the door opened once more and Esdras came back in. He took a seat on one side of the table and Thorpe sat across from him.

"I am informed that the State of Israel owes you a great deal of gratitude," Esdras spoke without inflection, "and that I am to extend to you and Colonel Parker any courtesy short of compromising my nation's security."

Considering he and Parker had stopped a nuclear missile just seconds from making Tel Aviv a fused-glass parking lot, Thorpe thought that was most kind of the State of Israel.

"Tell me about them." Thorpe stabbed his finger at the pictures. "Jawhar and Akil. You have a file on them?"

"I have our file on them being copied," Esdras said, "but I am fully up to date, as they are on our Level A list."

"Level A?"

"People who are considered real threats to Israeli security and interests." Esdras picked up the pictures. "Jawhar Matin, a.k.a. the Jewel Man, and his brother Akil."

"Why is Jawhar called the Jewel Man?" Thorpe asked.

"He wears a ring on every finger. His hands are probably worth a half million dollars, given all the jewels on those rings."

"Does Akil have a nickname?" Thorpe asked.

"He doesn't need one," Esdras said. "He's a killer. Most of his training comes courtesy of your United States. But the instinct, the cold blood and lack of conscience, that he was born with. Their father is Prince Hakim Yasin. Have you ever heard that name?"

Thorpe shook his head.

"Hakid is one of the top three oilmen in Saudi Arabia. So rich you don't even bother putting numbers against his name. More powerful than most countries. Which explains why these two pigs"—Esdras indicated the pictures—"are on our Level A list yet are still breathing."

"They both went to some military schooling in America,"

Thorpe said. "At Fort Rucker and Fort Benning."

Esdras nodded. "Jawhar is a helicopter pilot—trained at your aviation center at Fort Rucker. Akil is the commando. A graduate of your Ranger School at Fort Benning and Special Forces school at Fort Bragg. They are both colonels in the Saudi army, but they report only to their father.

"They are twins. Not identical, as you can see. Akil is the elder, born two minutes before his brother, Jawhar."

"But they're known by the name Matin, not Yasin," Thorpe noted.

Esdras nodded. "That is so. They are Hakim's eldest sons but not his heirs. Their surname is Matin, which in Arabic, Abd al Matin, means 'servant of the strong.' Which is why they are in the army and not in the oil business."

"Why aren't they his heirs?"

"Because of their mother." The door Esdras had gone through opened. A young woman handed him a file without looking at Thorpe and just as quickly departed. Esdras flipped open the file as he answered Thorpe's last question.

"Their mother was neither Yasin's wife nor Arab. Either one of those facts would have been enough to rule them out—both, well, it's surprising Hakim didn't kill them at birth. It would have been better for many people if he had.

"Here." Esdras slid a pair of color photos across. "Note their eyes, which you can't really see in your black and white image."

Both men had surprisingly blue eyes in their dark faces. Thorpe looked up from the photos.

"Their mother was American."

"Who was she?" Thorpe asked. "And how did she hook up with Yasin?"

Esdras rubbed his chin as he searched for words. "You might not technically call her a prostitute. I suppose that would be too harsh a term. But do you know anything about what goes on inside these rich Saudi families?"

Thorpe shook his head.

"Well, you do know that women do not exactly hold the greatest place in that society. The wives are veiled in public and strictly quarantined in private. The men, however are very much free to do what they wish and those with the money do exactly what they desire. Those that are not strict believers in the word of the Koran, that is.

"There is a very strong trade in women—almost a slave trade—except the women are usually paid off quite well for a year or so of, shall we say, work? If they are beautiful and any good at what they do, I understand the current payoff after a year's service is easily in the mid-six figures, U.S. money.

"Jawhar and Akil's mother was one such woman. Their father was apparently very fond of her. Normally if such a woman becomes pregnant, there is no question about it—an abortion is immediate. But Hakim Yasin is a strange man. Rather paranoid, actually, with good reason. Our theory is that he allowed this woman—Naomi Matherson was her name, by the way—to give birth once he found out that not only were they twins, but they were to be boys.

"He apparently felt that such boys could be raised to be loyal to him—Arabs are very big about blood ties and all that good stuff. Who knows? He couldn't raise them or even keep them in his immediate household—that would be a disgrace and embarrassment to his household and his wife. So he let their mother raise them."

Esdras turned a page in the file. "We don't have the complete story here, but she appears to have been—shall we say a 'bitch'? Because he sent her away to raise the boys, she could no longer enjoy the life she had had in his palaces. And because he wanted the whole thing low-key, she could not live a public life wherever she set up home. And because she had the boys, she was tied to him forever. So she ended up with the worst of both worlds. They spent most of their youth on the continent here, at some of the best boarding schools. But Yasin insisted she stay close by wherever they were and do nothing that could cause a scandal. He had men watching her all the time. She hated it. A prison without walls. After all, a woman who would end up in her situation is not the type who would enjoy sitting at home sipping tea and packing the boys' lunches, eh?

"She took it out on the boys every chance she could." Esdras looked up from the file. "Abused, treated like the bastards they were, et cetera, et cetera. Not that I—or you, for that matter—give a shit, given what they are now. You can blame the process, but you also have to deal with the end result.

"When they turned fourteen, their mother tried to kill both of them and then kill herself. She succeeded in the latter, but unfortunately failed in the former. I hate incompetence, don't you?" Esdras did not wait for an answer.

Thorpe was growing a bit anxious with this lengthy discourse. He still had no idea if they had killed Terri Dublowski and Takamura. However, he knew that Esdras, like all in covert operations, felt that a complete briefing was critical to understanding a situation. There was also the possibility that Esdras would have no idea if the twins had had anything to do with Terri or the other girls.

"After their mother's death, their father brought them back to Saudi Arabia, but they were the bastards, so they were not treated well there either. He sent them into the military when they turned seventeen and there they have been ever since. Have you ever been on a UN operation?" Esdras asked in an abrupt change.

Thorpe nodded.

"Have you ever seen any Saudi troops? Even during Desert Storm, which was a UN operation?"

"Not in action," Thorpe said. "I heard they committed troops to Desert Storm, but I never saw them."

"Correct. Saudi Arabia's contribution to that and other UN operations consists primarily of money, which they have plenty of. They did send some troops to Kuwait, but they did little during the offensive.

"Of course, they don't want to give all that money and not have someone on the ground to see how things are going. Enter Jawhar and Akil. They travel around, with Jawhar piloting their own plane and helicopter. Visit UN forces around the world. Report back to their father on how his money is being spent. Not that Hakim gives a damn about the UN, but he does give a damn about political leverage, and he can use the UN for his own means."

"Could the twins be involved in the disappearance of American dependent girls from around this area?" Thorpe finally asked.

Esdras spread his hands. "It is possible. They do come to this area every so often to coordinate with your Seventh Army, which is headquartered here and is the higher headquarters for American forces deployed on the IFOR."

"I know it's possible," Thorpe pressed, "but"—he leaned forward—"you were told to cooperate."

Esdras sighed. "We know they kill. That they are sociopaths. Your intelligence people know they kill. All the intelligence agencies have a folder on these two. Who they've killed—how many they've killed . . ." He shrugged. "That we don't know, and to be honest, it has not been anyone's priority."

"No one's priority," Thorpe said. "How can—"

"Jawhar and Akil are agents of their father and their government. Our concern has always been their actions in the international arena."

"Great," Thorpe said.

"Jawhar was actually arrested once. In England. On suspicion of killing a seventeen-year-old girl. Three years ago. Not only did he have diplomatic immunity, his father wields a mighty economic lever. Jawhar was out of the country within forty-eight hours. He is banned from ever going back there—officially, at least."

"So he can get away with murder?"

"Yes. Jawhar seems to have a particular fetish for killing young women."

"Jesus Christ," Thorpe exclaimed, now knowing in his gut that Jawhar was their man. "And you guys just sit back and watch?"

"Would you prefer we kill Jawhar and start a war?"

"That's bullshit and you know it," Thorpe said.

"Maybe not start a war, but, for example, have Saudi Arabia pull the six hundred million dollars it has allocated to the IFOR in the Balkans? That is what concerns those who give me my orders and your intelligence people their orders. And why these two scum are virtually untouchable. I do not like it, but . . ."

"But you're just following orders, right?"

Esdras's lips drew into a thin line. "I am instructed to give you information, but please do not——"

"Tell you the truth?" Thorpe interjected. He leaned across the table until he was less than a foot from Esdras. "It's bullshit and you know it. You yourself said they were sociopaths. Doing whatever the hell they want, whenever they want, because their daddy pays money to the UN?"

"You are not so naive," Esdras shot back. "You Americans have a saying for it: Money talks."

"Yeah, that's right," Thorpe said, "but only to those who listen to that kind of talk." He sat back down and gripped the arms of his chair.

"What do you want from me?" Esdras asked.

"Where are Jawhar and Akil now?" If either of them were still in the States, Thorpe knew he had to get word to Parker and Dublowski. That would help explain what had happened to Takamura, at least.

"I don't know." He held up a hand to stop Thorpe's next words. "I sent a request to my headquarters for the latest information. The reply should be coming back any minute."

Thorpe forced himself to lean back and release the arms of the chair. "When Jawhar——" he began, but the door opened once more and the woman handed a sheet of paper to Esdras.

He read it, then looked up. "Akil and Jawhar are assigned to IFOR headquarters in Sarajevo. At the moment, Akil is listed as being back in Saudi Arabia."

"Not the States?"

Esdras raised an eyebrow. "No."

"When will he return to Sarajevo?"

"In three days."

"And Jawhar?"

"Jawhar is in the Ukraine. Chernovsty, to be exact."

"What's he doing there?"

"I don't have that information."

"How long will he be there?"

"We don't know."

"Can I take that file with me?" Thorpe asked.

"No."

"Do you know exactly where in Chernovsty Jawhar is?"

"Yes. He's staying at this hotel." Esdras slid a piece of paper across to Thorpe, who pocketed it.

"Do you have an agent in Chernovsty?"

"Yes."

"Can I contact him?"

"I'll check on that. I will get you the contact information through Mr. Lorsen." Esdras stood. "I believe that completes our business."

Thorpe didn't stand. "I don't think so."

"There's nothing more I can give you that—"

"What I was going to ask you before," Thorpe said. "When Jawhar and Akil came to Stuttgart."

"Yes?"

"If they are on your Level A list as you say, then you had to have put surveillance on them." Thorpe stood. "You know what they were doing here. You know whether they killed my friend's daughter. And I'm not leaving until you tell me the truth."

Esdras rubbed his forehead, then he walked over to a cabinet. "A drink?"

"No."

"Well, I'll have one." Esdras poured himself a shot. He threw it down with one quick practiced motion, then poured himself another, before sitting back down at the table.

"You are correct. We try to keep them under surveillance when they come into our area of operations."

Thorpe waited.

"I have been at this assignment for seven years," Esdras said. "It is an important one. Of course the Germans know we are here. We allow them some intelligence access in our own country. It is the way the game is played. A balancing act."

"Just like the Samson option and Red Flyer," Thorpe said.

Esdras nodded. "And Operation Delilah. I pretended not to know, but I knew about the Samson option. And your Red Flyer team placing their fake nuclear bomb outside of our storage site in the Negev Desert. Part of the game." Esdras wagged a finger. "But your Omega Missile getting launched— that was not part of the game."

"Omega Missile was launched by the man who designed it to stop the game-playing," Thorpe said.

"It didn't work."

"No," Thorpe agreed, "it didn't."

"Because people will be people and governments will be governments." Esdras threw the shot glass to his lips and emptied it. He got up and walked to the cabinet and poured one more.

"I drink too much," he said. "I know my superiors know. But what can they do?" He shrugged. "There are only so many people who can do this job. When they feel I am no longer an asset, they will put me out to pasture like they did the generation before me. Old men with crazy stories no one will believe. No one wants to believe." He sat down. "Do you know what our priority here is? Not espionage. No. We are here to watch the skinheads. 'Never again' is the cry. So we watch idiot youths run around and kick foreigners to death.

"Those youths are not the danger. They have little power. It is the people with power who would use the skinheads for their own means we have to fear. But people with real power—like Hakim Yasin—make governments do as they want, so we do nothing. All a game. A pawn cannot defeat a more powerful piece."

"It can if it gets close enough," Thorpe said. "You—" Thorpe began, but Esdras wasn't done.

"The Man Who Waits. Do you know who he was?"

"The man who sat on top of your nuke in Washington?"

"Yes. He was a friend of mine. We served together in a counterterrorist unit before the Mossad."

"The 269th of the Parachute Infantry Brigade?"

Esdras gave a wan smile. "See? There are no secrets."

"No, there aren't. You know what Jawhar and Akil did here." Thorpe said it as a fact, not as a question.

Esdras's eyes were unfocused, staring off into the distance. His fingers played with the shot glass. "I saw them in action once. The brothers. And did nothing. They killed a boy and a girl. After Jawhar raped her, of course. Watched them through my night-vision scope. The crosshairs of my rifle centered on

Jawhar's head. It would have been so easy, but I had my instructions. Watch only."

Esdras looked over at Thorpe. "Do you judge me for that? I was following them. They made a meet with some people before and after the killing. Black market weapons people. We were able to give the information to the Germans and then closed down those weapons people and save many lives. So maybe it was the greater good?" Esdras didn't sound like he believed that much.

Thorpe tapped the picture of Terri. "Was this the girl you saw killed?"

"No."

"Do you know if they killed my friend's daughter? Terri Dublowski?"

Esdras ran a hand along the side of his face. "The two I saw killed were the only ones we know of for sure. I have heard rumors that Jawhar has taken some girls."

"Taken?"

"As I said earlier, there is almost a slave trade going on in certain Middle Eastern countries concerning women. While many know of those who are well paid to be there, there are also those who are not asked to come, but rather taken there, held prisoner and not paid, and who never come back. Especially if you are talking about underage girls."

"She might be alive?" The possibility had never occurred to Thorpe.

"They are only rumors," Esdras warned.

Thorpe remembered what the kids in the room had said about the Jewel Man. "Where would he take them?"

"I don't know. Somewhere back in Saudi Arabia, but the Yasin family has so many palaces and houses . . ." Esdras shrugged.

"Find out where."

Esdras nodded. "I'll try."

"The black marketers that Akil and Jawhar met," Thorpe said.

"Yes?"

"Why would the brothers meet with such people? They would have access to all the weaponry they want through legitimate means in their own country, wouldn't they?"

"That is a fair assumption," Esdras said.

"You don't know why they made the meet?" Thorpe was astounded. "I thought you said you shut down the black marketers. You must have interrogated them."

"I didn't shut them down," Esdras said. "We are in Germany, after all. We passed the information on to the Germans. GSG-9 took them down."

Thorpe felt like he was pulling teeth. "And what did *they* come up with in interrogation?"

"I don't know."

"You don't know? Bullshit. You're the one who talked about balance. They would have given you that information in exchange for giving up the targets."

"You would think they would have," Esdras agreed, "but they didn't."

"What are they up to?"

"I don't know."

Thorpe stood.

Esdras stood also. "What are you going to do?"

"I'm going to find Jawhar. And you're going to help me."

Chapter Twenty

The field training center for Special Forces was in the center of the Camp Mackall Training Area, a sprawling military reservation on the west side of Fort Bragg, separated from the post by a narrow strip of civilian land. It wasn't far from where Takamura's trailer had been, and Colonel Parker and Sergeant Major Dublowski had passed the site of the specialist's fatal car accident on their way to Mackall.

They had not spoken since leaving Bragg, each lost in private thoughts, considering the information that Thorpe had called and given them. Parker had had to restrain Dublowski from jumping on the next thing flying to Germany when he heard there was a possibility his daughter was still alive.

"If neither Akil or Jawhar are here in the States, then who killed Takamura?" Parker finally broke the silence, trying to get Dublowski into the here and now.

"Thorpe said they were dealing with arms dealers," Dublowski said. "Some of those people have a long reach."

"But how could Takamura have even gained their attention?"

"I don't know?"

Another long silence ensued. As they got farther from Fort Bragg, Parker felt impelled to talk. "Why did Special Forces put their training area so far off post?"

"Huh? Oh, to get away from the bullshit of the regular army people on Bragg. Mackall is our own little world out here.

Used to be pretty primitive—the main camp, that is—until they did some building a couple of years back. When I went through the Q-Course, we lived in poncho hooches. Now they got all the comforts of home.

"Delta trains a lot at Mackall too. We use the old airfield there for various operations. The Rangers also use it to practice airfield seizure. Lots of Special Ops people go through Camp Rowe."

"Camp Rowe?"

"Used to be called Camp Mackall, but they renamed the main compound after Colonel Nick Rowe. He started up the SERE—survival, evasion, resistance and escape—school for Special Operations. He had a lot of firsthand knowledge he thought it was important to pass on. He'd been a prisoner of the Viet Cong for five years before escaping. He was a pretty remarkable guy."

They had just passed a sign telling them they were back on a military reservation after traveling through the North Carolina countryside for half an hour.

"You keep saying 'was.' What happened to him?"

"Assassinated in the Philippines in 1989. Supposedly by communists."

"Supposedly?"

Dublowski sighed. "That's the official version." He reached a three-way intersection and turned right on a narrow dirt road with tall pines on either side.

"And the unofficial version?"

"Long story," Dublowski said. "The short version of the long story is that Rowe was helping investigate some people— our people, CIA and SF—for drug smuggling out of Colombia in the late seventies and early eighties. The Noriega connection. Quite a few people who were involved in that whole mess had accidents or were killed. Too many for it to be a coincidence. Someone was covering their tracks and they did it well."

"Jesus," Parker whispered.

"Yeah. Of course it just might have been a hit by the communists. Who knows? I sure don't." A fenced compound came up on their left. "There's the obstacle course." Dublowski pointed out the window. "It runs under this road in a tunnel they got to crawl through. That at least hasn't changed much since I went through."

They drove around and reached the main gate for the camp. Two helicopters were parked across the street in an open field, a group of students clustered around them. Dublowski drove through the gate and parked.

"This way," he said, leading her toward one of the many metal-sided, one-story buildings that filled the camp. The sign on the door said it was the camp headquarters.

Dublowski walked straight through a small office area, ignoring the various people working there, and straight to a door marked CAMP SERGEANT MAJOR.

"Don't you know how to knock?" a voice bellowed.

Parker looked over Dublowski's shoulder. A small wiry man was sitting behind a very large desk. He jumped to his feet and came around the desk, walking with a limp. He began pumping Dublowski's hand as soon as he reached him. "Goddamn, Dan. Long time no see."

"Good to see you, Pete." Dublowski turned. "Pete Kilgore, this is Colonel Parker. She wears a blue suit when she's on official business."

Kilgore nodded. "Ma'am." He took in her civilian attire, and Dublowksi's comment and mood, and sat back down behind his desk. "What brings you out this way?"

"I need information on a student," Dublowski said.

"You could have got that from the Puzzle Palace," Kilgore said, referring to the Special Warfare Center and school headquarters at Bragg.

"I could have got paperwork from SWC," Dublowski said. "But someone might have wanted to know why I was asking, and I also want some firsthand feedback on this guy."

"So this really ain't official?"

"No," Dublowski said. "I need a favor."

"Well, I owe you a few," Kilgore granted. "But giving out info on students—man, you have no idea what it's like out here. We get guys actually bringing lawsuits against the school when we kick them out. Saying we weren't fair.

"I remember when an instructor could look at the way a

guy tied a knot putting up his poncho hooch and tell him to pack his shit and walk the forty miles back to Bragg. And he wasn't booting him because of the knot, but because the instructor knew the guy wouldn't make it on a team. Now you got to have a whole freaking file and consult a guy a half dozen times and document it and all sorts of crud to even begin the process of separation."

"The person I'm interested in is a foreign student," Dublowski said. "Came through here about two years ago. You were out here then, right?"

"Yeah, been here almost five years now," Kilgore said. He reached down and thumped something under the desk. "Ever since they chopped the old hoofer off. I can still ruck with the students, though. Makes 'em feel pretty small, to have a one-legged old man walking out in front."

"This guy I want to know about was a Saudi," Dublowski said, cutting into Kilgore's ramble.

The smile left Kilgore's face. "A Saudi? Two years ago?"

"Name of Akil Matin." Parker spoke for the first time.

"I remember him," Kilgore said. "Son-of-a-bitch. He was a hard ass. Lots of foreign students, especially from certain countries, they just want to punch their ticket and go home, expending minimal effort in the meanwhile. Once they figure out we ain't gonna fail them, that is." Kilgore looked at Parker. "Long time ago we used to grade foreigners just like U.S. students. Flunk 'em out if they weren't up to snuff. Then we failed a couple of guys from a certain African country. When those guys got home—swack—their heads got chopped off for disgracing their country. State Department didn't think that made for too good diplomacy so the official, unofficial policy is to not fail the foreigners.

"But this Matin guy, he didn't need no help. That was one tough hombre." Kilgore shook his head. "Why do you want to know about him?"

"I think he might have killed my daughter," Dublowski said. "Or, if she isn't dead, he's holding her somewhere."

"Holy fuck," Kilgore exclaimed. "You're shitting me." One look at Dublowski's face, though, and he knew this wasn't a joke. "What can I do to help?"

"I'm going to go after Matin," Dublowski said. "One way or another, he and I are meeting. Anything you can tell me will help."

"Damn," Kilgore said. "Be careful. He dislocated a guy's elbow in the pits during hand-to-hand training. Got him in an elbow lock and pushed it. Everyone could hear it go. I'd have kicked the SOB out, but he was a foreign student. He's good with his hands. Good shot too. But mean. And he didn't play well with others, to put it nicely. Not a team man at all. A loner."

"Did you ever meet his brother, Jawhar Matin? Chopper pilot?" Parker asked.

"No."

"Any idea where his home is?" Dublowski asked. "Where he might hole up?"

"No, but we got another Saudi officer here right now," Kilgore said. "Want to talk to him? He might know something about this Matin fellow."

Dublowski had already turned for the door. "Yes."

They walked out of the headquarters building and followed Kilgore across the compound to the east side, where a sixty-foot wooden tower was set in a small clearing. A line of men waited to climb the stairs to the top, where instructors were hooking in students to ropes and sending them over the side to rappel down.

"Where's al Arif?" Kilgore asked one of the men wearing a green beret who was supervising the men holding the ropes at the bottom on belay.

"Over at the east LZ for STABO," the instructor answered.

"This way." Kilgore could move amazingly fast for a man with an artificial leg.

They walked along a narrow path through the pine trees. Parker could hear the sound of a helicopter coming closer. They came to a field where a group of students and a couple of instructors were clustered. Dublowski nudged her and pointed up. A Blackhawk helicopter was coming in from the west. Parker squinted, trying to see what was dangling on a rope fifty feet below the chopper.

She stopped as she realized there were four men, arms

linked, at the end of the rope. The chopper came to a hover high overhead, then slowly descended, the men coming closer to the ground. They touched down and quickly unhooked from the rope. They ran clear as the chopper came in and landed.

Parker returned her attention to the ground. Dublowski was standing next to one of the Green Beret instructors, talking to him. Parker walked over.

"There's al Arif." Dublowski pointed at a man wearing lighter, sand-and-brown-patterned camouflage among the green-camouflaged Americans. He walked through the students and tapped the Saudi on the shoulder. "I'd like to speak to you."

"Yes?" al Arif looked from Dublowski to Parker and back.

"About Akil and Jawhar Matin."

There was a slight hesitation that Dublowski caught before the other man answered. "I do not know those names."

"Akil and Jawhar Matin—Hakim Yasin's bastards," Dublowski amplified.

"Oh, no," al Arif's head was on a string, jerking back and forth. He stepped back. "I will not talk about them."

Dublowski tapped him on the shoulder. "We're going for a ride together."

"What?" Parker asked, but Dublowski was already walking forward, pulling al Arif with him. He grabbed a small FM radio from one of the instructors, clipping it onto his belt, running the wires up inside his shirt and putting the headset on, the boom mike in front of his lips and the earpiece in.

He picked up a STABO harness and strapped it on, pulling the green nylon straps tight. It went around his chest, with two straps through his legs and over his shoulders. Arif was having a harness put on, assisted by one of the instructors. The blades of the Blackhawk were still turning, the crew chief making sure the rope was free of any snags.

Dublowski gave the crew chief a thumbs up and the Blackhawk lifted off, the rope pulling up below it. Dublowski walked to the end of the rope and clipped the snap link to the front of his rig. He gestured for al Arif—who was looking a bit confused to be singled out to go next—to come closer. He snapped Arif in.

"Clear," Dublowski said into the mike.

"Lifting." The pilot's voice was a crackle in his left ear.

Dublowski smiled at al Arif, who was looking up with wide eyes at the chopper fifty feet overhead. "Relax and enjoy the ride," Dublowski advised him. He reached down, fingers running along al Arif's harness. "Here, let me adjust this for you."

"I do not want to do this!" al Arif cried out.

"Too late." Dublowski felt the harness tighten around his body, then his feet leave the ground. Al Arif's body was pulled up against his. He heard a whine of pain from the other man as the leg strap he had "adjusted" tightened against al Arif's testicles, the man's body weight adding to the force.

Dublowski reached with one hand and grabbed the Saudi by the neck, while with the other he pulled the strap back into proper position. "I think you want to talk to me now, don't you?"

Tears were coming out of al Arif's eyes. The Blackhawk began moving horizontally and they were pulled along, flying a hundred feet above the treetops.

"What's going on down there?" the pilot asked over the radio.

"Just fly," Dublowski growled into the mike. He tightened his grip on al Arif's neck. "Jawhar and Akil Matin. Talk to me."

Al Arif started to shake his head, then realized he better not. He gasped the words out with each tortured breath. "I cannot speak of them. It would be dangerous."

"This is dangerous," Dublowski said. "This is dangerous *now*. You can worry about the Matin brothers later or me now. Your choice." He released his grip on al Arif's neck and reached down to the snap link connecting the other man's harness to the rope. He turned the locking screw until it was free.

Al Arif tried to fight Dublowski, but the Green Beret blocked the smaller man's efforts. He pressed the snap link gate in. "Long way down," Dublowski said.

Al Arif's eyes were wide open, staring down at the pine trees rushing by below his dangling feet. "Please!"

"What the hell are you doing down there?" The pilot's voice was worried.

Dublowski looked up. He could see the crew chief leaning out of the cargo bay, watching them.

"Just fly the helicopter," he said into the mike. "Tell me about Jawhar and Akil," he said to Arif, shaking the smaller man's harness.

"They are very powerful. Their father is very, very powerful." Al Arif looked down at the open gate. "Please, close it!"

Dublowski let it snap shut, but he didn't screw the lock down. "More."

The Blackhawk was banking, turning back toward the landing zone.

"They are army like me, but they are more than army. They work for the secret police."

"Do they kidnap girls?"

"I don't know."

The chopper was slowing as they approached the LZ.

Dublowski pushed on the snap link once more, opening the gate. "Do they kidnap girls?"

Al Arif's head bobbed anxiously. "I have heard rumors."

"Where do they take them?"

"I—" Al Arif thought better of what he was about to say. "I have heard only rumors. A place. A secret place. Called Nabi Ulmalhamah. I do not know where it is. I swear on Allah!"

The tops of the tall pine trees were fifty feet below them. Dublowski could see the large open area where the airfield was off to the northeast.

"What are they up to?" Dublowski lifted the Saudi up, free of the snap link, his legs dangling.

"I do not understand!" al Arif whined.

Dublowski felt something wet on his leg. He looked down—al Arif had wet himself.

"They met with some arms dealers in Germany. Why?"

"I do not know! I swear. What Prince Yasin does, no one knows except him."

The chopper was lowering them straight down. Dublowski

let go of al Arif. The other man yelped, his eyes closed. The harness clicked into the snap link. Their feet touched down. He unhooked as Sergeant Major Kilgore and Colonel Parker came rushing up.

"What the hell was that?" Kilgore demanded. "The pilot's been having a fit over the radio."

Dublowski pulled free of the rope. Al Arif collapsed on unsteady legs, an instructor unhooking his harness from the rope. The Blackhawk sidled over and landed about sixty feet away. The pilot was out the door and striding over to them.

"Who the hell do you think you are?" the pilot pulled off his helmet and demanded of Dublowski.

"Whoa!" Parker yelled as Dublowski pulled a pistol out from under his shirt and pulled the slide back. She stepped between the sergeant major and the pilot. "Why don't we all calm down a little here?"

"Don't get in my face," Dublowski yelled at the pilot.

"Who the fuck—"

"Enough!" Parker yelled, pulling her ID card out and shoving it in the pilot's face. "I will take care of this man. Is that clear?"

The pilot saw the rank on the ID card, but his face was still flushed. "He could have killed that man—" He pointed at al Arif. "When we're in the air, every person attached to that helicopter is my responsibility, ma'am."

"I understand that," Parker said. "And as I said, I will take care of this man. He's under my command."

"Let's all just chill out here," Kilgore said. "We're just training. The sergeant major was just introducing our allied friends to a form of interrogation."

The pilot shook his head and walked away. Parker grabbed Dublowski by the arm and pulled him in the opposite direction. "What the hell was that?" she demanded.

"Our friend was reluctant to talk," Dublowski said. "I helped him open up."

"You're a flaming asshole," Kilgore said with a laugh. "Surprised your little friend didn't shit in his pants."

"Can you keep him away from a phone?" Dublowski asked as they passed the rappelling tower.

"Hell, yeah," Kilgore said. "Al Arif's entire class is going to the field for two weeks. Ain't no phones out there in the woods."

"Thanks," Dublowski said. "I owe you."

They walked though the compound to Dublowski's truck.

"Anything else you need, give me a call," Kilgore called out as they climbed in.

Dublowski started the car and drove out the gate.

"Stop the car," Parker said as they turned onto the dirt road.

"What?"

"Stop the car."

Dublowski braked and they stopped in the shade of the pine trees. "What's up?"

Parker turned in her seat until she faced the sergeant major. "Are you going to be under control?"

"I was—"

"You could have killed that man and he wasn't the enemy," Parker said.

"I just—"

"Are you going to be under control?" Parker spit the words out flatly and harshly. "I understand your concern for your daughter, but I'm not going to have the cure be worse than the disease here. I've been there before and I'm not going there again. Is that clear?"

Dublowski stared at her for several seconds, a muscle on the side of his face jumping. Then he nodded. "Clear."

Chapter Twenty-one

The Ukrainian colonel came to an abrupt halt three feet inside the door as he caught sight of the bed.

"What is that?"

Jawhar pushed the door shut behind the colonel and put an arm around his shoulder, pulling him farther into the room. He smiled. "I call it art."

"It's a woman," the colonel said.

"Yes. My friend Katrina. She has kept me occupied while I waited for you."

"Is she alive?"

Jawhar let go of the colonel and looked at the bed. "Yes."

The bed was soaked with blood from the body. Long slices crisscrossed Katrina's body. Some were still slowly oozing blood, others had scabbed over already.

"What is that?" The colonel pointed at a bag attached to a coat hanger looped over the top stanchion of the headboard. A tube ran from the bag to the woman's neck.

"Plasma. I wouldn't want her to bleed out on me," Jawhar said. "It cost me quite a bit on the black market, but fortunately everything is for sale here." He took a step closer to the bed. "As I cut, I replace what comes out. This can go on for a very long time."

The Ukranian colonel was a hard man, but his face was white.

Jawhar held out his knife. "Would you like to contribute to my work in progress?"

"No." The colonel cocked his head as he heard a faint mewling noise.

"Her screams." Jawhar held up a glass from the nightstand. There was something floating in it. "Her tongue. I removed it first to keep working conditions tolerable and the neighbors from investigating."

The colonel stepped back. "But the police—"

"Oh, come, now," Jawhar said. "You know as well as I do that the police will not care about some prostitute. Besides, I will be long gone before she is found, will I not?"

"But I am associated with this room." The colonel couldn't take his eyes off the woman on the bed.

"Certainly this is very minor compared to what you are doing for me," Jawhar said. "I wouldn't think you'd be hanging around after we conclude our deal. I understand South America. Colombia, to be exact?"

"But we have yet—"

Jawhar put down the glass holding her tongue. "You do not have it?"

"It takes time."

"You've had time."

"I must get you out of here," the colonel said. "We have to be more secure. There are spies everywhere. Have you wired the additional money?"

"I would be a fool to pay you again and have yet to receive anything in return," Jawhar said. "And you would be a fool if you came here without checking your account and knowing that the money has not been wired."

"We must leave now. I will take you to a safe place."

Jawhar stared at the colonel for several seconds, then reluctantly nodded. "All right. Give me a few minutes to pack, then I will join you downstairs."

The colonel paused at the door. "The girl—"

"Do not concern yourself," Jawhar pushed the door shut in his face. Then he turned toward the bed. He leaned over and smiled into the girl's pain-filled eyes as he removed the IV from her neck. "Pleasant dreams," he whispered.

Chapter Twenty-two

Terri had listened, but other than the food being brought, she didn't hear Mary being returned to her cell. Every time she woke from a fitful sleep, she went to her door and called out for the girl. Her voice echoed down the corridor in vain. The other girls had stopped talking or answering—in fear of the same fate that had befallen Mary.

Leslie and Cathy were still in their cells and they hadn't been taken out again. A doctor had come to see them, checking the wound on their sides, removing the stitches, all without saying a word. Both girls had no idea what had been done to them. But Leslie confirmed there was something hard under her skin, in her right side.

Terri had taken to sitting with her back pressed into the farthest corner of her cell, knees tight up against her chest, eyes focused on the door. She held on to one thing—her dad would come for her. She knew that as firmly as she could feel the concrete against her back.

Chapter Twenty-three

Hancock unfolded his napkin and laid it across his lap. He waited as the waiter poured a cup of coffee for him and the man seated across the table.

"Gereg's having me surveilled," Hancock said as soon as the waiter moved away.

The other man laughed. "Ah, the Man with One Red Shoe strikes again," he said, referring to the Tom Hanks comedy about the CIA. "Shall we stand in the middle of a lawn with the sprinklers on to have a private conversation?"

"Laser resonators could pick up such a conversation," Hancock noted.

"Ah, Karl, you are always so serious."

"It's my nature," Hancock acknowledged. Of course, the man across from him had much more reason at the moment to be serious. William Hill, the former national security adviser to the President, was currently under sixteen different indictments and a special prosecutor had been assigned to the case by the Justice Department. The only reason the media wasn't having a field day with the story was that everything involved was classified and the investigation was being done very quietly.

"I should have listened to you about Kilten," Hill said, the smile disappearing from his face.

"To a certain extent Kilten was predictable," Hancock said. "His plan was elaborate and worked well as far as he could take it before he was killed by McKenzie."

"It's not over yet," Hill said.

"No, it's not. No game is over until checkmate or one side resigns."

Hill's eyes shifted around the restaurant, even though they both knew they would not be able to spot their surveillance and that every word they were saying was being picked up and recorded.

"So how's your game?" Hill asked.

"Quite good."

"The latest match?"

"Progressing quite well. As usual, when a game develops, the board needs a little thinning, but I'm taking care of that. Cleaning up loose ends that are no longer needed, that sort of thing."

Hill leaned forward. "I'm trusting you this time."

"And well you should. Here come's our breakfast."

❧

"I still think we should go to the authorities," Parker said.

"What authorities?" Dublowski asked. They were driving on post, heading back to the Delta Ranch after a trip to the BOQ so Parker could pick up her gear. Dublowski had recommended she stay in the guest quarters on the Ranch for security reasons.

Dublowski made a right turn. "Who has authority in this case? You were there at the oil rig. You're the counterterrorist POC at the Pentagon. You know SEAL Team Six has an anti-pirating mission and has actually conducted several live operations in that field around the world. Because there is no authority on the high seas. Here we are, at the end of the twentieth century, and we still have pirates running around the oceans.

"This is the same thing. Once people cross international boundaries with their crimes, who's responsible for catching them if their own country protects them? Who's responsible when crimes are committed in places where the local government doesn't care?"

"Mike's going into a foreign country all alone—what's he going to be able to do?"

Dublowski was watching the rearview mirror. "He'll do whatever he can." He turned left off the paved road onto a one-lane dirt road.

"Where are we going?" Parker asked.

"Anzio Drop Zone."

"Why?"

"So we can nail the asshole who's following us."

Parker looked back over the bed of the pickup. "I don't see anyone."

"He's holding back." The road came out of the trees and a vast expanse of open space lay in front of them, the far tree line over a mile and a half away. To the left it was clear as far as they could see along the rolling terrain. The ground was sandy, with clumps of waist-high grass here and there.

"But when we don't come back down the road in a minute, he's going to have to have to come forward." Dublowski hit the accelerator and the rear tires kicked up a plume of sand as he raced across the drop zone. A flash of light glinted in the rearview mirror. "He's at the edge of the woods," Dublowski said.

"I see him," Parker said. "White Ford Explorer. He's holding in the tree line."

Dublowski kept them heading across the DZ toward the far tree line. "Let me know when he follows."

"He's coming," Parker said as the Explorer left the cover of the trees.

Dublowski spun the wheel hard and they skidded around to face back the way they had come. He gunned the engine and they were headed straight for the Explorer.

"You're under control, right?" Parker tightened her seat belt.

"Oh, yeah, I'm under control," Dublowski assured her. The driver of the Explorer slowed, uncertain. Dublowski accelerated further.

"Jesus, Dan!" Parker exclaimed as the gap between the two vehicles narrowed, dropping under a hundred meters.

The Explorer stopped, then began going in reverse. The

driver spun his wheel, turning, trying to point in the opposite direction, but the sand slowed him down.

"Dan!" Parker screamed as they closed within twenty meters of the Explorer. At the last moment, less than ten meters from the other truck, Dublowski slammed on the brakes. The pickup slid through the sand, the front bumper slamming into the side of the Explorer. Dublowski threw his door open and leapt out, pistol in hand.

He used the Explorer's bumper as a step and jumped up onto the hood of the truck, weapon pointed at the windshield.

"Get out!" he yelled.

When the driver hesitated, Dublowski fired a shot into the windshield, cracking it.

"Get out!"

The passenger door swung open and a man scooted out, hands held over his head. "Take it easy!"

"Fuck you, take it easy." Dublowski had the muzzle trained right between the man's eyes. "I know you. You're the Clowns in Action rep here. Ferguson. Why are you following us?"

"Lower the gun."

"Fuck you," Dublowski repeated. He jumped off the hood of the Explorer, landing five feet in front of Ferguson.

"Your vocabulary needs—" Ferguson's retort ended abruptly as Dublowski stepped forward and smacked him a sharp blow in the nose with the barrel of the pistol.

"Jesus!" Ferguson's hands dropped to try to stem the flow of blood that gushed forth. "You broke it!"

"That ain't all I'm gonna break." Dublowski shoved Ferguson, tumbling him to the ground. The sergeant major put his foot in the CIA man's chest. "Why are you following us?"

"Why the hell do you think? Orders."

"From who?"

"My boss."

"A name."

"The D/BO, director of Operations."

"Kim Gereg?" Parker asked.

Ferguson nodded, immediately wincing in pain as blood sprayed the ground around him.

"Why would she want us followed?" Parker asked.

"Shit, I don't know." Ferguson tried to sit and Dublowski shoved him back down.

"What do you know about Takamura getting killed?" Dublowski demanded.

"Who?"

Dublowski leaned over. He pressed the tip of the muzzle against Ferugson's nose, bringing a yelp of pain.

"Don't play stupid. You know everything that goes down in this part of the country. That's your job."

"I know that some GI named Takamura was killed. I requested a copy of the state police report. Other than that, I don't know anything."

Dublowski shook his head. "You're lying."

"What are you going to do?" Ferguson sat up. "Shoot me?"

"Yes." Dublowski leveled the 9mm pistol at Ferguson's head and his finger wrapped around the trigger.

"Dan!" Parker yelled.

Dublowski pulled the trigger. The round cracked past Ferguson's head into the sandy ground.

"I find out you're holding out on me, I swear, I won't miss next time." Dublowski put the pistol back in the holster hidden under his BDU shirt. "Let's go," he said to Parker.

∽⌒∾

Getting to the Ukraine had turned out to be not as hard as Thorpe had thought it would be. He'd hopped a IFOR flight from Stuttgart to Croatia, where—as a result of a phone call Master Sergeant King had made—a member of the First Battalion, Tenth Special Forces Group had been waiting with a HUMMV. They drove to the northeast corner of Serbia, where Thorpe crossed the border into Romania, paying off the border police not to inspect his bags or check his passport. He then took several trains across Romania to the border with the Ukraine, where it was once again a case of bribing corrupt border guards.

Ten years ago the journey would have practically been impossible under the various countries' communist regimes, but under the present economic situation, border guards lived more

off their bribes than off their intermittent salary. The infrastructure of these countries had broken down so severely,
Thorpe was surprised there even were any border guards.

Chernovsty was only thirty kilometers from the Romanian
border and Thorpe arrived less than ten hours after leaving
Germany. Studying the map of the town on the train had
shown him that the hotel the Mossad said Jawhar staying in
was within walking distance of the train station.

Without hesitating, he left the station and strode through
the streets of Chernovsty. It was a dark and dreary town, a
film of black from the nearby coal plant covering even the
brightest of colors. There were few cars in the streets and the
market stalls held scant goods.

Thorpe paused as he turned a corner. The hotel was down
the block and across the street. He stared at it for a minute,
then walked directly toward the front door. He put his hand
into the pocket of the raincoat he was wearing, wrapping his
fingers around the pistol grip of the 9mm automatic. There
was a round in the chamber and it was double-action, so he
was as prepared as he could be. He pulled open the front door
and walked into the dim lobby.

He noted the man behind the front desk eyeing him. The
hair on the back of his neck tingled as he noted the man's
attitude—he was very nervous about something.

As he walked toward the desk, Thorpe caught movement
out of the corner of his eye. His finger slipped through the
trigger guard and curled around the thin sliver of metal. A
tough-looking man with a scar running down the left side of
his face was approaching Thorpe. Behind that man, two others
were spreading out on his flanks.

"Easy, my friend." The man's voice was a harsh whisper.
"Esdras told me to greet you," he added as he got closer.

Thorpe kept his finger on the trigger. "You have surveillance on Jawhar?"

"We've been waiting for you." The man lightly touched
Thorpe's right arm at the elbow. "Relax. We do not need an
incident here in the lobby."

Thorpe allowed himself to be led toward the staircase to

the left of the gated elevator. As they took the first couple of stairs, the man began speaking.

"My name is Mikael. We have been waiting for you."

"Is Jawhar up here?"

"There is something you must see," Mikael said.

Thorpe didn't appreciate his questions being ignored, but with Mikael next to him and the two other men right behind them on the stairs, he wasn't in the best position to complain.

"This way." Mikael pushed open the door to the second-floor hallway. One of the Mossad agents waited at the door as they walked down the corridor. Thorpe began to pull the pistol out of his pocket, but Mikael squeezed his elbow. "You will not need that."

They halted in front of a door. The second Mossad man faced down the corridor toward the fire exit while Mikael slid a pass key into the lock. He swung the door open. "This was Jawhar's room."

"Was?" Thorpe repeated. Mikael stepped into the room, Thorpe followed and he immediately grimaced as he smelled a foul odor.

"Jesus!" Thorpe exclaimed, seeing the body on the bed. For a second he thought it might be Terri, but then he noted that the hair was blond. The bed underneath the body was crimson from blood. Thorpe had never seen that much from one person.

As if knowing what he was thinking, Mikael pointed a long finger at an IV tube hung on the headboard. "As he cut her, he replaced more of the blood to keep her alive." The finger shifted. "He cut out her tongue to keep her from screaming."

"Where is he now?"

Mikael nodded toward the door. "Let's get out of here. He won't be back."

~⚬~

"Nabi Ulmalhamah." Dublowski repeated the words exactly as al Arif had shouted them.

"The Prophet of War," the man on the other side of the table promptly translated.

"What?" Parker asked. They were in the Delta Force cafeteria, Dublowski having pigeonholed the Force's Middle Eastern intelligence officer, Major Aguirre.

"The Prophet of War," Aguirre repeated. "That's a literal translation of those words."

"It's a place," Dublowski insisted.

"It might well be," Aguirre agreed.

"Have you ever heard of it?" Dublowski asked.

Aguirre leaned back in the plastic chair and contemplated his mug of coffee. "Dan, you—"

"No speeches," Dublowski cut the officer off. "I've heard all the speeches I want to hear. Have you ever heard of a place called Nabi Ulmalhamah?"

Aguirre shifted in the seat, uncomfortable. "I've heard of it. But," he added quickly, forestalling Dublowski's next words, "I don't know exactly where it is. I know it's one of Prince Hakim Yasin's palaces. A palace to an Arab can mean just about anything from a one-bedroom apartment to a real palace. Given that we're talking about Yasin, I would tend to lean toward the latter. He's got dozens of palaces all around Saudi Arabia. He's got a chateau in Switzerland. Even a brownstone in New York City."

"I thought you were our Middle East expert," Dublowski said.

"I am," Aguirre said. "We do the best we can."

"Well, what the hell've you been doing?"

"I've spent the last two months setting up our forward deployed strike team in Israel." Aguirre leaned forward. "You find this place and if your daughter is there, we can bring the wrath of God down on their heads with what we got over there now, I assure you that."

"Who would know where it is?" Parker asked.

"If anyone, the CIA."

"Fuck!" Dublowski exclaimed. "The damn CIA's been dogging this thing from the get-go. We're not going to get any help from there."

"Maybe we will," Parker said.

"How?" Dublowski asked. "I don't think Ferguson is going to volunteer to help."

"Not after what you did," Parker agreed, "but I know some-one I can ask. Kim Gereg, the head of Operations."

"Shit," Dublowski said. "Ferguson said he was following us on Gereg's orders."

Parker looked at the old sergeant major. "Did it ever occur to you that Ferguson might have lied about that to keep us from going to Gereg?"

❧

"Where is Jawhar?"

"The local army barracks," Mikael answered. They were seated in the back of a battered van, a curtain pulled across separating them from the two guards in the front seats. The van had been parked in an alley two blocks away from the hotel. As soon as they got in, it began moving.

"What is he doing?" Thorpe asked.

Mikael leaned back, crossing his long legs. He pulled a small baggie out of his pocket and some rolling papers. "Cig-arette? It is always best here to roll your own, as you Amer-icans say, or else pay top dollar for black market—even then, there are those who repackage cheap Russian versions in American packs and cartons. You would be amazed at the scams—is that the right word?—that some of these people come up with."

Thorpe shook his head at the offer. He waited impatiently as Mikael rolled a thin cigarette and lit it. The Israeli agent took a deep drag, then tapped the ash onto the floor. "What is Jawhar doing? What he and his brother have always done. Stirring up trouble. He has met twice with a Colonel Kostenka. Who is—was—assigned to the research and development sec-tion at the Chemical Troops classified training center at Leon-idovka." Mikael took another drag. "You know about VX, correct?"

Thorpe nodded. VX was, along with sarin, one of the two most deadliest chemical weapons.

"The Russians have long had VX," Mikael said. "They used it in Afghanistan. It is the only major new chemical weapon devised since the end of World War II, actually. Or was. As you know from your military training, there are many disadvantages to the use of chemical weapons. Many have tried to make better chemicals to get around those disadvantages."

Mikael was looking at the ceiling of the van. "Your CIA has a term called 'breaking the ice.' What they mean by that is that anytime something new is done, it breaks the ice and makes it easier for others to do it. When that cult used sarin in the subway in Tokyo, the ice for the use of chemical weapons by terrorists was broken.

"The Russians also broke the ice, so to speak, several years ago when they developed a new form of chemical weapon. They call it VZ. Fast-acting, it kills within five seconds in the same manner as VX, by breaking down the nervous system. More importantly, it also dissipates within twenty seconds, which makes it much safer to use, with less likelihood of friendly casualties. Also, it must be inhaled. You can smear it on your skin and no problem. One sniff, though, and you are dead."

"Why are you telling me this?" Thorpe asked.

"Because Jawhar is here to pick up a rather large amount of VZ. Large in terms of effect—small in terms of actual material."

Thorpe rubbed the side of his face, feeling the stubble of a beard. He was tired and the adrenaline rush of anticipating a confrontation with Jawhar was wearing off.

"To what end?" Thorpe asked.

"We're not certain of that," Mikael said.

The van came to a halt. One of the men in the front stuck his head through the gap in the curtain and said something in Russian.

"We're here," Mikael said. He uncrossed his legs and knelt, pulling a footlocker close.

"Here?"

"Outside the army barracks," Mikael said. He opened the lid on the locker. AK-74s and other weaponry were inside. He pulled an assault rifle out along with several thirty-round clips. He handed them forward. Then he did the same with a second rifle.

"What are you doing?" Thorpe asked as Mikael grabbed a

third rifle and inserted a thirty-round magazine in the well.

"We have had this place under surveillance ever since we became aware of the contact between Jawhar and Colonel Kostenka. Besides this van, we have six other men in two other vehicles nearby.

"The State of Israel frowns upon chemical or biological agents falling into the hands of those we consider our enemies. We don't really care what Jawhar has planned for the VZ." He pulled back the charging handle on the AK-74 and let it slam forward. "We're going to stop this exchange. When Jawhar leaves the barracks, we attack. Great plan, eh?"

Chapter Twenty-four

Dublowski watched the plane take off, then turned and scanned the small group of people in the Fayetteville Airport. Parker was on her way back to D.C. to try and arrange a meeting with Kim Gereg, the chief of Operations for the CIA. Dublowski didn't think much of the plan, but Parker was still a colonel and he was a sergeant major, so there wasn't much he could do to dissuade her.

He went to the closest pay phone and took out his wallet. A card was tucked into the deepest fold in the worn leather and he retrieved it. He used a calling card, then dialed the number. It was answered on the second ring.

"Giles."

"Sir, it's Dublowski."

"What did you do this time, Dan?"

Dublowski almost smiled. "Sir, we got some problems here and need some help."

"We?"

"Mike Thorpe and I."

"Thorpe's in Europe. Stuttgart, last I heard."

Dublowski wasn't surprised that Giles knew that. The old boy network in Special Operations was very efficient. "Right now he's actually in the Ukraine," Dublowski said.

"What are you guys screwing up now?" Giles asked.

Dublowski gave the retired colonel a thumbnail sketch of the most recent events, all the while watching the terminal to see if anyone was watching back. When he finally rattled to a close, there were a few seconds of silence before Giles said anything.

"I'll be at Bragg tonight."

"Yes, sir," Dublowski acknowledged, feeling a small measure of relief.

"Out here." The phone went dead.

Dublowski walked out of the terminal to his truck and got in. He drove out of the parking lot and toward post, keeping an eye on his rearview mirror. He hadn't spotted Ferguson since the confrontation at Anzio Drop Zone, but that didn't mean there wasn't some other CIA dink following.

As he drove, Dublowski pulled out a metal briefcase and flipped open the lid. A small laptop computer was inside, courtesy of Chief Warrant Officer Simpkins. Dublowski turned the laptop on and did as Simpkins had instructed him.

The screen cleared, then a series of concentric circles appeared in the center. Across the bottom a bar line indicated the receiver attached to the computer was racing through the spectrum of radio frequencies.

The bar froze on a frequency and a dot blipped exactly in the center of the circles. Dublowski nodded to himself.

He drove through the main post onto Chicken Plank Road and headed west, across the training areas that made up the bulk of Fort Bragg. He passed the spot where Takamura had been killed; there was nothing to indicate the fatal accident except the bark scraped from the tree where the car had hit. The dot still remained in the exact center of the computer screen, which didn't surprise Dublowski in the least because the dot indicated a bug planted somewhere in his truck.

He passed Camp Rowe, continuing to the old, abandoned airfield. He drove across the pitted tarmac onto the dirt, continuing into the tree line. He parked in a small clearing surrounded by pine trees. He pulled a FAMAS from under the seat. The French-made automatic weapon was unique in that the magazine went behind the trigger, thus shortening the overall length to less than thirty inches. A laser sight was screwed onto the long carrying handle on the top. Dublowski pulled the charging handle back, loading a round in the chamber.

He exited the truck and walked out of the clearing into the woods to the west. He walked along the tree line until he found a spot that suited him, with a clear field of fire encompassing both the truck and the one road leading in. He lay down on his stomach, resting the forward guard of the FAMAS on a small log in front of him.

✦

"Do you know where Nabi Ulmalhamah is?" Thorpe asked.

Mikael had a set of binoculars on a tripod, mounted just inside the small window in the rear of the fan. He was seated on a stool behind the glasses, eyes fixed on the compound. They had been waiting now for over an hour and Thorpe could tell that the Mossad men were ready to wait however long was necessary. They had several coolers full of food and drink, even a small chemical potty in the back.

"No."

"Anything on Jawhar kidnapping young girls?"

Mikael kept his eyes to the glasses. "No, although it wouldn't surprise me after seeing what he did in that motel room. This is the first time Jawhar has been here, so it is the first time I have had any sort of contact."

"How did you get on to Jawhar and this colonel?" Thorpe asked.

"Intelligence from headquarters," Mikael said. "How they got their information, they didn't bother to share with me."

"But if you didn't uncover this," Thorpe wondered, "who did?"

"I don't know," Mikael said, "but the hit team in the other vans was sent to me six days ago."

"Six days?" Esdras had said nothing about a hit team or a nerve agent weapons deal. He'd also said that the Germans had given them no information on the takedown of the arms dealer in Germany.

Mikael pulled back from the glasses. "Is there something I should be aware of?"

"If you don't know, I don't know," Thorpe said, "but something strange is going on with this entire situation."

∽✵∾

Hancock stood alone, the late afternoon sun casting a long shadow across the perfectly cut grass. His shadow merged with that of the tombstone in front of him.

He assumed he was being watched. He always assumed that everything he did as well as everything he said outside the confines of his secure office was seen and heard. And even inside his office he often wondered and played it as safe as he could. When the scale had to tip between pursuing the country's best interests and one's own career's best interests, there were many inside the Agency who tipped it toward the latter.

Hancock always preferred to make the two synonymous as much as possible. What was good for the country would be good for him. That attitude had allowed him to survive and prosper for many years in the labyrinth of the CIA. He had never acted out of emotion, but always cold logic after careful evaluation of the facts. At least until now.

He looked down at the letters etched in the stone:

JAMES HANCOCK
1969–1998

Just the name and the dates of a life cut short. Cut short by bullets fired from American guns during a mission supporting American goals. The irony of his brother's death was not lost on Hancock, but what was important to him were two things. One was the hand that had actually fired the gun that had killed his brother on that beach in Lebanon. The second—and more important—was the person who should have made sure that hand wasn't in the wrong place at the wrong time.

Hancock didn't believe in coincidences. He understand the concept that two things that affected each other could actually be unrelated, but he had long ago learned he couldn't afford the luxury of believing they weren't related. The Special Operations Nuclear Emergency Support Team was on that beach in Lebanon for a reason, of that Hancock had been convinced from the first moment the operation his CDA team was running was interdicted. And there was only one reason Thorpe and McKenzie had been there—Kim Gereg, the CIA liaison to SO/NEST, had sent them there. She'd played her hand and in the long run it had worked out quite well for her.

But the game wasn't over yet. Hancock turned from the headstone and strode across the grass toward his waiting car.

Dublowski turned his head and stopped breathing as he listened for a repeat of the sound. He held his lungs for thirty seconds, then slowly exhaled. He'd been in the same position for two hours, not moving, all his senses tuned to the forest around him. The sun was very low on the horizon, dusk settling in, the tops of the pine trees highlighted with the last rays of light.

Whoever had planted the bug in his truck had not come rushing up as he had hoped. That ruled out Ferguson. Dublowski seriously doubted the CIA man had the self-discipline to hold back more than two minutes despite the broken nose.

The hair on the back of Dublowski's neck rose, a feeling he'd had before. He rolled, pulling the FAMAS around, settling the stock into his shoulder, finger curled around the trigger. The muzzle swept back and forth as his eyes scanned the darkening forest behind him for any movement. Nothing.

But Dublowski *knew* there was someone out there. He had not expected for it to take this long and regretted not bringing night-vision equipment. With his back against the log, he checked out the woods in small arcs, taking in every little detail he could make out, the muzzle of the FAMAS staying synchronized with his eyes.

There was the noise again. A stick cracking to the right. Dublowski turned slightly, lining up the weapon. A figure was moving through the woods thirty meters away, the outline of a rifle visible in his hands.

Dublowski sighted in on the man, his finger tensing on the trigger. A second silhouette appeared behind the first, causing

Dublowski to pause. A line of men passed by, moving stealthily through the woods, a patrol of Special Forces students from nearby Camp Rowe.

Dublowski waited until the patrol disappeared into the dim woods, then he stood, stretching out his back. He headed back to his truck in the clearing. The toes on his left boot hit a tree root and he stumbled, saving his life as the bullet cutting across the top of his head parting his thinning hair, slicing the skin.

Dublowski continued the fall, turning it into a forward roll, tucking the FAMAS into his stomach. He came up to his knees firing, sending a spray of bullets into the forest, uncertain where the round had come from, as there had been no sound of a weapon firing.

Two seconds later, as the bolt slammed home on an empty chamber, he dove to the left, pulling a fresh magazine out of the cargo pocket of his fatigue pants. The woods still echoed with the sound of his firing as he slammed the fresh magazine home.

His body was tensed, expecting a bullet at any moment. His eyes darted back and forth, hoping he'd spot the muzzle flash and survive long enough to return fire.

Nothing.

He heard voices, men moving through the forest. The training patrol was returning, investigating. Dublowski lowered his weapon and reached up. His fingers probed the tear in his scalp. Another inch lower and his brains would have been splattered all over the forest floor.

"Son-of-a-bitch," Dublowski muttered as he looked at his blood-covered hand.

Chapter Twenty-five

"That's Akil in the right front of the lead vehicle." Mikael offered the binoculars to Thorpe. "We can get two for the price of one."

Thorpe adjusted the focus. Three Land Rovers were pulling up to the gate of the army compound. Each had four men inside. He could see the occupants in the glow of the large lights highlighting the gate. Dawn was still a couple of hours away.

"He's brought some muscle," Thorpe noted.

Their van was parked on a dirt road on the side of a hill overlooking the entrance to the Ukrainian army camp. The other two vans carrying the rest of Mikael's team were hidden on the other side of the hill, awaiting orders.

"What's the plan?" Thorpe asked as the two Land Rovers pulled up to a large building. Thorpe watched through the binoculars as Akil jumped out, arms gesturing, giving orders.

The door to the building opened and two men walked out to greet Akil.

"Jawhar is on the left," Mikael said. "Colonel Kostenka on the right."

Thorpe adjusted the focus and zeroed in on Jawhar's face. Even at this distance, over two thousands meters, the blue eyes showed clearly through the lens. Thorpe remembered the girl on the bed in the hotel room in town. Jawhar was smiling as he greeted his brother with a hug.

"I need him alive," Thorpe said.

"Our priority is to stop the VZ transfer," Mikael said.

"He's holding the daughter of a friend of mine captive," Thorpe reminded Mikael.

"What is one life against thousands?" Mikael asked. He lowered the boom mike on the headset he wore and rattled off some orders in Hebrew. Then he sat on the floor of the van and pulled out a map. "The plan? Here." His finger stabbed a point on the map. "They will drive from the compound to the airfield where Jawhar left his plane. We will ambush them here on the road. I've already sent the other two vans to the site. Both will block the road in front. We will be following and block from the rear. We will kill everyone—*everyone*," he emphasized to Thorpe. "We will rig the VZ with timed charges on thermite grenades. The heat will destroy the agent as we make our escape along this route." His finger traced a winding road through the hills.

"Our emergency rally point is here, five kilometers from the kill zone," Mikael continued. "There are two cars there, money, petrol, weapons. From there we will go to an extraction pick-up zone—here—to meet a helicopter to take us home. Anything goes wrong, you head directly to the extraction point. Questions?"

"If there is any way we capture either Akil or Jawhar—" Thorpe began, but Mikael sliced a hand down in front of his face, cutting him off.

"We kill everyone. We can take no chances. Your friend's daughter is not here. Even if you capture one of the brothers, which would be difficult, and he tells you where Nabi Ul-malhamah is—which he wouldn't—it still is not here. And it is not as important as the VZ."

One of the men in the front called back to them in Hebrew. Mikael hopped to his feet and looked through the binoculars. "They're loading."

Thorpe pressed up against the eyepieces of the second set of binoculars. The men were coming out of the building.

"The metal briefcases," Mikael said. "That's the VZ."

Thorpe counted six briefcases, two going into each Land

Rover. Colonel Kostenka stood on the steps of the building as the convoy headed for the gate.

"There is enough in each of those cases to kill tens of thousands," Mikael said. "We must account for every single case. Do you understand?"

Thorpe nodded.

"Let's go," Mikael ordered. He pulled aside the curtain between them and the front of the van.

The drive down the hill to the road was harrowing, as the driver kept the lights of the van off. Thorpe knew the driver could see clearly, as he was wearing night-vision goggles, but not having a set himself, it was eerie to hurtle through the darkness as such high speeds. They reached the paved road and turned in the direction the convoy had gone.

"Eight miles to the kill zone," Mikael informed Thorpe.

The van rushed through the night. All Thorpe had was the impression of the blacker road flashing, trees on either side corralling them in. Thorpe felt like he was hurtling down a dark tunnel, out of control, his fate being decided for him. It was a feeling he'd had before on military operations, but never before so strongly.

A flash of red appeared ahead.

"Easy," Mikael was leaning forward next to the driver. "That's the last vehicle in the convoy."

The van slowed slightly. They kept far enough back to keep the tailights in sight every so often as they hit a straight stretch of road.

"How far?" Mikael asked the driver.

"Another mile."

Thorpe gripped the AK-74 tightly.

"Shit!" Mikael exclaimed as the brake lights glared on the Land Rover.

The van slowed as the driver tried to maintain the distance. The lights suddenly disappeared.

"Speed up!" Mikael ordered.

"No!" the driver exclaimed. "They've stopped! Two hundred meters ahead."

Thorpe looked at Mikael. He knew a decision had to be made now.

"Have they seen us?" Mikael asked the driver, who had slowed them to a crawl.

"I don't know. The Land Rover is just—"

The question was answered more directly as a string of green tracers ripped through the darkness just above the van, then getting the range and smashing into the windshield. A round blew the top of the driver's head off, spraying Thorpe and Mikael with blood and brain.

Thorpe dove to the floor as tracers cut through above him, punching out the back of the van. He felt Mikael next to him.

The van was still moving, the driver's dead foot resting on the gas pedal, bringing them closer to the ambush. The van drifted right as more bullets sprayed it, killing the man in the right front as he tried to bring his weapon up. The van rolled off the road and the front end smashed into a tree, bringing it to an abrupt halt.

Thorpe rolled with the impact, sliding up against the front seats, Mikael on top of him. The Mossad agent slid off, reaching up and pulling open the side door and rolling out of the van, Thorpe following. The firing had stopped, a still silence disconcerting after the gunfire.

They ran into the cover of the trees, halting twenty meters from the van, weapons at the ready. Thorpe heard the sound of an engine starting. The Land Rover was leaving. He ran forward to the road. Mikael sprinted past him, peered in the van, saw the other two men were dead, then looked up the road.

"Come on!" Mikael grabbed him by the arm and they ran after the truck. "They'll hit the ambush in less than a mile."

The Land Rover was gone. Thorpe ran after Mikael, the AK-74 in his right hand. His boots slammed into the pavement as he settled into a fast pace, his lungs gasping for air.

"Shit!" Mikael exclaimed as two explosions reverberated back to them. "Come on!" he urged, running even faster.

Thorpe forced himself to pick up the pace. There was a glow ahead. Gunfire echoed. Thorpe knew from the sound they weren't too far.

They rounded a bend in the road and saw the firefight. The lead Land Rover was on fire, flames shooting up a hundred feet into the night sky. The second one sat in the middle of the road, men hiding behind the doors, returning fire at the two vans blocking the road.

The third Land Rover was backing up. Straight toward Thorpe and Mikael. The driver spun the wheel expertly and the Land Rover was now pointed toward them. Mikael threw his AK-74 to his shoulder and fired a long burst. The bullets hit the windshield in an explosion of glass.

Brakes screeched. Thorpe had the stock of the AK tight in his shoulder. The Land Rover's headlights were blinding him. He fired a quick three-round burst, then another, taking out both lights. Silhouetted against the burning first truck he saw the back doors of the truck swing open.

Someone was firing back, hiding behind the right door. Thorpe recognized the profile—Akil. Another burst of green tracers from the Saudi's weapon lanced out. Jawhar was firing from behind the left door.

Thorpe heard Mikael grunt and out of the corner of his eye saw the Mossad agent stagger back a few steps. Thorpe returned fire at the muzzle flash. Green tracers cracked by his left ear and Thorpe dove to the pavement, rolling twice and firing again from the prone position.

Thorpe looked to the right. Mikael was on his knees, trying to bring the AK up to fire again. Akil was sighting in on the Israeli. Thorpe rolled and grabbed Mikael, dragging him off the side of the road into the drainage ditch. A line of bullets snapped by overhead.

"Stop them." Mikael was looking down at his chest in amazement, watching the blood flow out of three bullet holes. "Stop them," he repeated.

Thorpe started to poke his head up to take a look, but bullets tore up the edge of the road inches away and he ducked down. He heard a door on one of the vehicles slam. The firing from the front was dying down.

"Stop them!" Mikael was on his knees, staggering to his feet, bringing his weapon up. Thorpe reached for him when a line of bullets smashed into the Mossad man's chest, blasting him backward and causing Thorpe to dive for cover once more.

The Land Rover roared by, Akil spraying a full magazine out the window, then it was gone. Thorpe had his back against the side of the ditch nearest the road. Mikael was lying at his feet, empty eyes staring up into the dark sky.

Chapter Twenty-six

Dublowski didn't wince as the medic sewed up his scalp. He looked up as the door to the infirmary opened and Colonel Giles walked in, accompanied by the Delta Force commander, Colonel Patten.

"What the hell is going on?" was Giles's way of greeting Dublowski. The sergeant major had returned to the Ranch after talking his way out of being held by the Special Forces patrol at Camp Rowe. Upon arriving at the Ranch, he'd gone to the infirmary to get his head looked at.

"Sir." Dublowski started to nod at the retired colonel and only succeeded in ripping the last stitch out. The medic cursed at him and slapped him on the back of the head in the best tradition of Special Forces medicine, and replaced the stitch.

"Colonel Giles has filled me in on what he knows," Colonel Patten said. "Which isn't too damn much. Who the hell shot at you out at Mackall?"

Dublowski almost shook his head and caught himself at the last moment. "Don't know, sir. Whoever it was, was good. Patient. I think that it was the same person who killed Warrant Officer Takamura."

Colonel Patten sat down. He was a tall, thin man, similar in build to Giles. He'd earned his combat infantry badge as a young lieutenant in Vietnam in 1973 and had served in Special Operations units for over twenty-five years. He'd been a seasoned captain in Delta at the Desert One fiasco and a Special

Forces group commander during Desert Storm.

Patten was well respected by the men who served under him not only because of his background but also because he had made it very clear when taking over Delta that this was his last assignment in the army. He had no desire to go anywhere else or be promoted, and because of that, his focus was men and mission and not career, a rather unusual find in the modern army.

"I don't understand what's going on," Patten said.

"I don't either, sir," Dublowski said. "But I expect to hear from both Major Thorpe and Colonel Parker soon, and hopefully they'll have more information."

Giles turned to Patten. "I'm going to go to D.C. and give Parker a hand. If she's trying to deal with Langley, she may be in over her head."

Patten nodded. "Keep in touch."

~⋈~

Thorpe looked around the emergency rally point and the faces he saw reflected the failure he felt.

"They knew we were there," Aaron said. He was the leader of the first two vans and the assault team that had been brought in from Israeli for this mission. With the death of Mikael, Aaron was in charge of the survivors. Four of the eight men had been killed, their bodies stacked in the only surviving van.

"We destroyed two of the Land Rovers," one of the commandos noted.

"And one got away," Aaron shot back. "With two briefcases of VZ *and* our primary human targets, Akil and Jawhar." He looked at Thorpe. "They got away past *you*."

Thorpe said nothing, knowing there was nothing he could say. It was true. Akil and Jawhar had driven past him, and Mikael had died right next to Thorpe. He knew, in the Israelis' eyes, he should have died before allowing the last Land Rover to escape. And in his own eyes, with time to reflect, he realized he would feel the same way.

"What now?" one of the men asked.

Aaron spit. "The scum are in Romania, probably already

on board their aircraft. They are beyond our reach." He glanced at Thorpe, then away. "Akil and Jawhar and the VZ are someone else's problem now. Our exfiltration helicopter will be here in twenty minutes. Get the bodies ready and rig the van for destruction. We're going home."

∽✕∾

It was only seven in the morning, but Parker had already made a half dozen phone calls from a secure line in a friend's office in the Pentagon. She'd also received a call from Thorpe on his secure SATPhone that had made her mission all the more imperative.

She'd left the Pentagon via the freight entrance, walked several blocks away along the Potomac and then hailed a cab to get to her present location.

Right now she was close to CIA headquarters at a strip mall, outside a local coffee shop. A blue, late-model BMW with tinted windows pulled up to the coffee shop. A tall woman got out and quickly walked inside.

Parker crossed the lot. She stood next to the driver's door of the BMW. The door to the shop opened and Kim Gereg walked out, a cup of coffee in her hand. It had taken four of those calls for Parker to find out about this habit of the chief of Operations.

Gereg saw Parker but didn't break her stride. "Excuse me," the C/O said as she unlocked her doors with a remote entry.

"Ma'am." Parker held out her military ID.

Gereg halted. She looked at the ID and then at Parker. "What can I do for you, Colonel Parker?"

"We need to talk."

"Reference?"

"Two suitcases of VZ that just left the Ukraine in the hands of two terrorists."

Gereg stared at Parker for a few seconds, then peeled back the lid of her coffee. She nodded toward the car. "Get in. You've got my attention."

∽✕∾

Hancock walked in the door and headed directly for a black leather chair in the rear of the operations center for his CDA section. The center was shaped like a smaller version of NASA's launch center, with rows of people with computer consoles arrayed below Hancock, all facing a large screen that took up most of the front wall.

"Are we tracking?" Hancock asked as he settled into the chair.

His operations officer, Dilken, sat directly below Hancock. He wore a headset through which all reports were sent and had four computer screens arrayed around his seat.

"Yes, sir. An hour ago we had a flight take off out of Radanti whose configuration matches Jawhar's plane. Heading is southwest toward Budapest. Touchdown is estimated in five minutes. We think they'll switch over to Jawhar's helicopter, which is currently hangared there, to continue on to Bosnia to make the delivery of the VZ to the Serb patrol. Satellite imagery confirms the Serb patrol is closing on the meet point."

"Our team?" Hancock asked.

"Ready to go wheels up at Sarajevo. They need authorization to go soon if they're going to be able to interdict the meet."

"Tell them to go," Hancock said. He leaned back in the leather, enjoying the unique pleasure of watching a complex plan pull together.

Dilken relayed the order, then left his desk and approached Hancock.

"What?" Hancock's good feeling was gone. He knew the look on his assistant's face and he also knew that Dilken was the only one clued in to the entire situation.

"Dublowski is still alive. He's holed up in the Ranch."

Hancock considered that. "A problem, but not a fatal one. That loose end can be cleared up later." He leaned forward. "And Thorpe?" They had taken satellite surveillance of the ambush site in the Ukraine. Given that Hancock had had Akil tipped off about the probability of a Mossad ambush through a cut-out, they had been surprised that the two Saudis had barely made it out alive.

"The Mossad team was pulled just after dawn local time.

Thorpe made a call on his secure SATPhone prior to that to Colonel Parker."

"Shit!" Hancock exclaimed, a sign of extreme agitation. "Where is he now?"

"He's heading back to Israel with the Israeli team."

"And Parker?"

"She went into the Pentagon this morning as usual. Surveillance hasn't seen her leave. No calls on her phone."

"She's not just sitting there doing nothing," Hancock said.

"Maybe she's waiting for Thorpe," Dilken said. "We . . ." he paused and put a hand on the side of his headset. "Satellite has picked up Jawhar's chopper heading southeast."

"Get our team wheels up," Hancock ordered. "We take care of this, the rest will fall into place."

❧

"VZ?" Colonel Patten looked older than his years.

"Yes, sir." Dublowski had just gotten off the SATPhone with Parker.

"Destination?" Patten asked.

"Romania, as an intermediate stage, then God knows where," Dublowski said.

"And the CIA is on top of this?" Patten asked, his voice indicating what he thought of that.

"Colonel Parker is with the chief of Operations as we speak," Dublowski said. "But, sir—" Dublowski began, but Patten raised a hand.

"I know what you're going to say." Patten gave a weary smile. "Fucking Clowns In Action are more likely to screw things up than solve anything, but this is their province, not ours. However," he continued, forestalling another outburst from Dublowski, "it doesn't hurt to be prepared. I've got a forward-deployed reaction team in Israel. I'm putting them on alert. I'll also get some air support—Combat Talon, Blackhawk, Apaches—our usual air package—lined up just in case."

Dublowski's scalp was sewn. He stood up. "Sir, request permission to—"

"No!" Patten cut the sergeant major off. "You've gotten in enough hot water as is. Besides, by the time you got over there, anything that's going to have happened will have happened. You stay here and stay out of trouble. If you're capable of that."

∽◦∾

Thorpe placed his pistol on the worn wooden tabletop. "They knew they were going to get ambushed."

"Put that away," Major Rotzinger growled.

They were seated in a windowless room somewhere on the outskirts of Tel Aviv. Thorpe had no idea exactly where he was, as they'd been hustled off the helicopter the moment they landed into the back of a truck that had no windows, and driven to this spot.

He'd been surprised to see Rotzinger waiting inside the room; not so surprised to see Esdras seated in the corner. A man who had introduced himself as Yaron was seated at the end of the table, Aaron, the senior surviving member of the ambush team, to his right. Yaron was an old man, with a wrinkled, bald head covered with spots, and the tiredest-looking eyes Thorpe had ever seen. He'd pursed his lips at Thorpe's statement and appeared to be deep in thought.

Esdras was the only one who hadn't reacted to the weapon or Thorpe's announcement. He was seated across from Thorpe, regarding him quietly with his dark eyes.

"I've got no more time for people bullshitting me," Thorpe said. "We—we, Thorpe emphasized, staring first at Rotzinger, then Esdras, "have a common problem. In the form of two briefcases full of VZ nerve agent in the hands of a couple of guys who I think you know more about than you've told me."

"You were looking for a young girl last time I saw you," Rotzinger said. "Now you come to us with this crazy story?"

"Karl." Esdras turned to look at the German. "We lost four men last night trying to stop the shipment. We got two-thirds of it, but we needed to do a one-hundred-percent interdiction."

"The two brothers are being tracked," Rotzinger said. "They—and the VZ—will be contained and sterilized."

"How the hell do you know that?" Thorpe demanded.

Rotzinger's bushy eyebrows contracted. "You came to my country asking questions. You sit here with a gun on the table threatening me? And you want information? You want help? You are a fool."

Thorpe met his gaze squarely. "You never took down the arms brokers that Jawhar and Akil met, did you?"

Rotzinger's eyes shifted to Esdras for the briefest of moments, then back to Thorpe.

"They were intermediaries," Rotzinger said. "Representing some Russian military officers. Taking them out would only have slowed things down, not stopped them. This way everything is wrapped up tight—people, weapons, both ends. A great coup."

"Which way are you talking about?" Thorpe demanded. "Who's going to stop Jawhar and Akil now?"

Rotzinger turned to Yaron, who finally spoke. "Your own people are taking care of things now."

"What people?" Thorpe demanded.

"The CIA is on top of this," Yaron said quietly.

"The CIA?" Thorpe repeated.

A quick smile flittered across Yaron's face and was quickly gone. "You do not trust your own government?"

"No, I don't," Thorpe said.

"Interesting," Yaron said. He pointed a finger at Aaron. "Were you set up?"

Aaron nodded. "Yes, sir. I think the brothers knew someone would be attacking them."

Yaron steepled his fingers and tapped his thumbs together for a few seconds. "Then there must be either a leak or a traitor working somewhere. Sounds like a double-cross. Perhaps even a triple. Who knows these days?" He stood. "I would ask you gentlemen to remain here for a short period of time while we see what develops."

Rotzinger stood also. "I came here as a courtesy from my government to yours. I don't have—"

"Sit down." Yaron's voice was like a whip, causing Rotzinger to step back. "You have not been honest with us. I am wondering what other lies and deceptions play a role in this.

I assure you I will find out, and when I do, there will be a reckoning."

◦◦◦

Parker and Gereg were in the latter's office. It had taken Parker only ten minutes to get the chief of Operations up to speed before they were heading to Langley and directly to Gereg's office. Along the way, Parker had called Dublowski, updated him on what Thorpe had told her, and then continued talking to Gereg, telling her all she had learned from Thorpe, along with the information about the missing girls.

"I don't understand how the girls are connected to this," Gereg said as she sat down at her desk. She pushed a button and a panel slid back, revealing photos on a large screen recessed into the wall.

"Through these two Saudis—Jawhar and Akil."

Gereg shook her head. "I know that, but Dublowski's daughter getting grabbed? Seems to be too much of a coincidence." She reached into a drawer and pulled out a file folder and threw it on the desk. "That's what I've been able to gather on the two brothers. They've been kidnapping girls for a while. Some they kill, some they take back home."

"You've known—"

Gereg held up her hand, cutting Parker off. "No, I haven't known diddly about this. I just got this report from the Israelis. A comrade of mine in Tel Aviv is very concerned about Saudi terrorists having two briefcases of VZ nerve gas."

Parker opened the folder. Her eyes widened. "Who's this?" She held up a photo.

"Their mother."

Parker pulled a printout from her briefcase. "Look at these girls. They're the ones we know are missing in Germany."

Gereg glanced over. "They look like a younger version of the mother. Petite and blond." She tapped the rest of the file. "According to this, the boys hated their mother and their father. Maybe they're taking out their hatred against Mom on these girls."

"Maybe," Parker agreed, but something about that didn't

sit quite right with her. She looked at the photo once more. "Except for Terri Dublowski," Parker noted. "She doesn't look like the others."

Gereg nodded. "That's interesting, isn't it? Almost like someone wanted Dublowski involved—and through him, you and Thorpe. And through you," she added with a twist of her mouth, "me." She typed into her computer. "Let me check on something." A couple of seconds later, she had her answer. "The request to put Thorpe back on active duty went through the office of the reserves in the Pentagon, but it originated here. Someone here wanted Thorpe on active duty."

"Hill is no longer national security adviser," Parker said. "He would—"

"There's someone who was Lane's protégé." Gereg was still typing on her keyboard.

"Who?"

"That's who." Gereg pointed at the screen. "That's an intercept from the Direct Action operations center. We spend more time, resources and energy spying on each other here than on foreign countries. The CDA, chief of Direct Action, is a man named Hancock. His brother was one of the CIA men killed in Lebanon by Thorpe and McKenzie. I have no doubt that Hancock blames me for the SO/NEST team being on that beach, even though he never informed me of the operation. And he definitely blames Thorpe for his brother's death.

"Hancock was in line to be the director until Operation Delilah, which he was running for Hill, blew up in his face. He's a very dangerous man."

There was action on the screen that diverted Parker's attention as she tried to assimilate everything Gereg had just told her. "What are they doing?"

"Hancock has a Direct Action Team—DAT—on call in Sarajevo. He made a point of asking the director a couple of days ago to do just that."

"Then he knew something was going to happen?" Parker asked.

Gereg laughed without any humor, a low rumble from deep in her throat. "Knew something? He doesn't just know things, he sets things up. Cut through everything that's going on, and somewhere back there, you'll find the long reach of Mr. Hancock and behind that, Mr. Hill. Our old friend is still out there pulling strings."

"Can the Direct Action Team stop the VZ?"

"I hope that's what Hancock has planned. Even Hancock wouldn't go so far as to let nerve gas get loose." She paused. "At least I don't think he would."

"What can we do?"

"For now? Just watch. This hand has already been dealt."

Chapter Twenty-seven

Terri woke to the sound of shouting and boots tramping down the corridor. Doors slammed open, the steel thudding against concrete. A girl screamed and Terri ran over to the door and pressed against it, listening. A man was yelling in a language she had never heard before.

Terri fell into the hallway as her door was suddenly jerked open. A boot swung and hit her in the ribs, knocking the air out of her lungs. She scuttled away from the boot as it swung once more at her. Several men in light-colored camouflage had the other girls in the corridor. The man who had just kicked Terri reached down and grabbed her by the neck, hauling her to her feet.

She kicked him and earned a throttling in retaliation. Terri gasped for air as the man's hand tightened down, cutting off the flow of air to her lungs. With bulging eyes she stared into his dark-skinned face.

She realized she was going to die; that this was the last minute of her life. She kicked with weakening legs, feeling them strike his body, but there was no loosening of the hand around her neck.

She didn't want to die. That was the only thought that resonated through her mind. Her vision was fading, the sounds becoming muted.

A man's voice rose above the commotion, screaming something in the strange tongue.

The hand released and Terri collapsed to the floor, gasping for breath. She felt the boot kick her once, twice, a third time, but she didn't react; she was so grateful to feel the oxygen in her lungs, to know she wasn't going to die.

She looked up. A tall man was striding down the corridor, yelling at the men in camouflage. This man wore a dark green uniform, with numerous badges on it and gold epaulets. She could see guards kicking the other girls, all of whom were on the floor like she was.

With a kick to get her attention, the guard who had choked her gestured for her to stand up. Terri got to her feet and the guard threw her back into her cell, slamming the door shut.

Terri sank down onto the floor, back against the door. She was hyperventilating, and with great effort she forced herself to stop. She got the breathing under control—barely—and curled up in a ball on the floor, sobbing. She could hear the other girls crying and for once she didn't call out to comfort them. She barely had the strength for herself.

Chapter Twenty-eight

Kiril positioned the SAM-9 missile with a field of fire covering the abandoned railroad tracks. Then he deployed the rest of his men around the embankment with all the hard-earned knowledge he'd gained fighting for the last decade.

He'd already plotted the route they would take south to Sarajevo. IFOR was building up forces around the city, preparing for an offensive against the Serbs. Over twenty thousand NATO troops were now camped within a twenty-mile radius of the city. The thought of what the VZ gas, released from a hill overlooking the city, would do to both the soldiers and citizenry of Sarajevo did not weigh heavily on Kiril's conscience. He had seen too much over the years. He simply wanted it to be over and he knew this was the only way.

He pulled back the worn sleeve of his fatigues and checked the watch strapped to his wrist. The crystal was chipped and cracked, but he could make out the hands beneath—another hour and the Saudi brothers would be here.

Two HH-60 Nighthawk helicopters were lifting off from the U.S.S. *Nimitz,* blades chopping through the salty air. Sailors watched, wondering who the black-uniformed men on board were. Since arriving on the ship four days ago, the men had stayed to themselves, totally ignoring crew members, test-firing exotic weapons off the edge of the flight deck and generally acting—in the words of one chief petty officer—like "bad asses."

An Apache gunship followed the two Nighthawks and the three aircraft headed due east—toward "Indian" country, as the pilots who overflew the Balkans called that airspace.

∽↺∾

In his operations center, Hancock was watching a red dot moving westward across the outline of Romania projected on the screen. A green dot was moving eastward out of the Adriatic on the same latitude.

"Do we have satellite confirmation that we're tracking Jawhar's helicopter?" Hancock asked Dilken.

"Yes, sir. We got a Keyhole look from the KH-14 satellite at the airport it took off from and confirmed that is Jawhar's Bell Jet Ranger. Projecting its course puts it directly on line for the same spot where it went before to meet the Serbs— just north of the Sava River."

"Time to target?" Hancock asked.

"Forty-two minutes for Jawhar. Our team will be there five minutes before that and hold to the west, awaiting your order for final interdiction."

Hancock tapped a well-manicured finger against his upper lip. "I want to get them all on the ground."

"Yes, sir."

Hancock picked up the phone built into the right armrest of the chair and punched in number one. The line bypassed the director's secretary.

"What is it?" The director's tone was abrupt. Hancock had no idea what he had interrupted, but he knew now was the time to cross the Rubicon.

"Sir, we have a developing situation you should be aware of. I'm in the operations center."

"Give me an idea." The director sounded irritated.

"We're tracking two briefcase loads of VZ nerve gas in a helicopter owned by personnel known to affiliate with terrorists. It's heading toward Bosnia, where we believe it's going to be given to the Serbs."

"I'll be there in a minute."

Hancock put the phone down. He leaned back in his seat and stared up at the dots moving on the screen.

ཀྵ

"He's made his move," Gereg said. "He must be pretty confident to bring in the director."

Parker was still trying to process what Gereg had told her. "If the brothers kidnapped Terri Dublowski to draw her father in and then Thorpe and I, then that means they're working with Hancock. Especially if he's the one who had Thorpe brought back on active duty." She shook her head. "I can't believe all that."

"Why not?" Gereg didn't seem in the least surprised by that assumption. "Hancock could have arranged it with the brothers through a cut-out. There are quite a few people in the covert world who exist simply to pass information from one group to another. Groups that never want it known they are talking to each other. It is a rather lucrative business for some."

"Akil and Jawhar might not even know who requested they snatch Terri or why. Most likely it was a trade. They got something they wanted in exchange for kidnapping Terri Dublowski.

"And," she continued, "my report from Tel Aviv says that the brothers were forewarned of the Mossad attempt to interdict the VZ. I'm not the only one who has a contact in Israel."

"Are you saying Hancock tipped off Jawhar and Akil about the ambush?"

"It wouldn't surprise me. He wants the glory for himself. It's the way things work in the covert world."

"But Hancock is betraying the brothers now," Parker noted.

" 'Betrayal' is a strong word," Gereg said. "It indicates loyalty in the first place, something I would say our friend Mr. Hancock has never had with anyone or anything except his own interests."

Gereg pointed at the screen. The two dots were closing on

a spot along the border between Bosnia and Croatia. "He uses everything for his own purposes. If his DAT team takes down these people and the VZ, he'll be a hero. Plus he'll solve several other problems at the same time. He's already tied *me* to these brothers and set it up so that I get blamed for tipping Jawhar and Akil off about the Mossad ambush in the Ukraine." She proceeded to tell Parker of the death of Welwood.

"It's a lose-lose situation," Gereg said. "Which is the position Hancock likes to put those he views as enemies in." She pointed at the screen. "We have to hope his DAT team succeeds in stopping the nerve gas, but if they do, then he succeeds."

"He gets away with kidnapping and killing?"

"It isn't the first time and it won't be the last," Gereg said. "Don't you think now that he was behind Takamura's murder? Takamura was killed when he got too close to identifying Jawhar and Akil too quickly."

"If Hancock set all this up, then that makes sense. But who did he use to kill Takamura?"

Gereg frowned. "He wouldn't have used one of his people for that. Not in the States. That would be going too far, even for him."

"Who would he use, then?" Parker pressed.

Gereg stretched out her long legs and leaned back in her chair. "I've been asking myself the same question ever since Welwood was killed in what the police are labeling a traffic accident last week."

"Takamura's was made to look like an accident!" Parker said.

Gereg nodded. "I know. There are a lot of players who would do such a job either for money or an exchange of favors." She pulled another file out of her desk. "Here's my choice. He's used the car accident method several times before on other jobs we know of overseas."

Parker picked it up and opened it. "James O'Callaghan?"

"IRA, but he's been known to freelance to keep his traveling options open."

"Meaning?"

"Meaning he likes to be able to come and go as he wants,

and to do that, he needs someone like Hancock pulling some strings in the background."

"Jesus!" Parker exclaimed. "You people are in bed with terrorists everywhere!"

"Not *this* person." Gereg uncrossed her legs and sat up straight. "This is a nasty business, but I always try to do the right thing, the right way. A lot of people around here don't like that, and—" she stopped as her phone buzzed and she picked it up. She listened for a few seconds, then put it down. "The director's joined Hancock in the CDA operations center. He's making his play."

"Where is Nabi Ulmalhamah?" Thorpe demanded.

They were waiting on Yaron. Rotzinger was seated at one end of the table, appearing even more unhappy than his usual dour look.

"We have been checking on that," Esdras said. "All we have managed to come up with is confirmation that it is one of Prince Yasin's palaces. We don't have a location."

The door opened and a young man came in. He leaned over and whispered in Esdras's ear, then left without looking at either of the other men in the room.

Esdras looked at Thorpe. "Your people have launched three helicopters to interdict Jawhar and Akil. Also, your Delta Force team here in town has gone on alert."

"I don't understand," Thorpe said. "Why a team here in Tel Aviv?"

Esdras shrugged. "Who knows?"

Thorpe stood. "Can you hook me up with them?"

Esdras waved at him to sit down. "They can do nothing staging out of here without our permission. Let us see what develops before we go off, as you Americans, say, half-cocked."

Kiril heard the helicopter long before it flew by, barely twenty feet above the rail line. It was the same type as last time. A Bell Jet Ranger with IFOR markings. He climbed up the embankment as the helicopter banked a quarter mile away and headed back.

Kiril frowned as the chopper gained altitude.

∽◊∾

Four miles away, the two Nighthawks and one Apache were hiding below the tree line, hovering just above the Sava River. They were linked by SATCOM to an IFOR AWACS surveillance plane, circling two hundred miles to the south.

The AWACS had the entire area "painted" with radar, as well as having its own uplink to a KH-14 reconnaissance satellite that was feeding it live images of the area. The location of the Jet Ranger was being updated every tenth of a second with an accuracy of within two meters.

Those in the waiting helicopters had no doubt they could run down the Jet Ranger easily. Their orders, however, were to wait until the meet was made and the VZ transferred, then to bag the whole lot.

On board the Apache, the gunner armed his missiles, while on the Nighthawks, the men dressed in black locked and loaded their weapons.

∽◊∾

"Hold in place," Kiril ordered into his radio, keeping his men under cover in the swamp. The Jet Ranger was now overhead, a hundred feet up.

Kiril looked up into the rotor wash. He was growing weary of these games. There was plenty of room for the helicopter to land where it had before.

A spasm rippled down his throat. His nose burned. His hand grabbed for his radio mike as he realized he was already as good as dead.

His fingers squeezed the send button, but no words came out of his mouth, only the gagging reflex as his lungs refused to work. He felt pain rip up his spine and he staggered back two steps, then dropped to his knees. His head was still angled up, staring at the chopper overhead, but everything was moving in slow motion now. He could even see each blade turning, so slowly, it seemed.

Kiril pitched face forward into the gravel between the rail lines, dead. The SAM-9 man managed to arm his missile before he too was hit by the VZ. He died, desperately trying to pull the trigger and failing as his nerves seized up faster than his mind could issue the order. Kiril's entire patrol was dead within thirty seconds.

❧

"Chopper is still airborne," the voice of the radar operator on board the AWACS repeated.

"What are they doing?" The Director had taken over Hancock's chair, relegating the CDA chief to a position standing next to him.

"Probably checking the area out," Hancock answered.

"Sir!" Dilken's alert was unnecessary, as they could all see the red dot moving east.

"Did it land at all?" the director asked.

"No, sir," Dilken answered.

"They might have done an airdrop of the VZ to the Serbs," Hancock said, but he knew as the words left his mouth that they were ridiculous. Only a complete buffoon would do such a thing to such a deadly cargo, when they could just as easily land the helicopter to off-load. He caught Dilken's attention. "Tell the DAT to go!"

Dilken relayed the order.

❧

"What the hell is going on?" Parker demanded.

Gereg was watching the action on the display and listening to the orders being given with growing alarm. "I think it's not developing exactly the way Hancock planned."

❧

As the Apache and one of the Nighthawks raced off to the east, running down the Jet Ranger, the remaining Nighthawk halted above the place where the other chopper had hovered. The body of a man was clearly visible on the tracks below.

"I've got more bodies in the swamp." The copilot had a pair of thermal goggles on and he was scanning the area.

"Oh, shit," the senior man in the rear of the helicopter muttered. "Suit up!" he ordered. He keyed his radio. "We've got bodies here. Looks like a bio or chem weapon was used."

❧

The director turned the seat slightly and stared at Hancock. "What's going on? I thought you said this was to be a transfer of VZ."

"It was." A nerve twitched on Hancock's left temple. "We've got it under control."

"Under control?" The director stared at Hancock. "If that report is right, VZ was just used!"

"The Apache will take out the chopper and the Nighthawk with it will secure the VZ. My other team will clear the site," Hancock said. "We can keep a lid on this."

"You'd better," the director warned.

❧

One the blue-suited men peered through the plastic face mask at the display of the machine in his hand. The reading, along with the nature of the bodies, left no doubt about what had happened here. He had only seen this in a training lab at the army's Chemical Warfare Center on Johnston Atoll. And then the bodies had been monkeys.

"It's VZ!" he reported over the FM radio to the commander in the chopper hovering above. Two ropes, one from each side of the helicopter, dangled to the ground, where a half dozen men in environmental suits were combing the area.

"How hot?"

"We're clear now," the man reported. "VZ has a time on target of less than a minute."

"Stay suited and sealed," the commander warned.

"No shit," the man on the ground muttered as he dug the plastic toe into one of the bodies, noting the obvious signs of a painful death on the man's face. He pulled a small plastic container off his combat vest and sprinkled the powder inside over the body, covering it from head to toe. Then he pulled a thermite grenade off his vest, pulled the pin, and dropped it onto the body. With a hiss, the grenade began burning, igniting the powder, consuming flesh.

Twenty miles to the east, the Apache was closing on the Bell Jet Ranger, the Nighthawk right behind. The Apache pilot slid his finger over to the transmit button on his radio and the signal was relayed through the AWACS to Langley.

"We have visual on the target," he reported.

"Put it down," Hancock ordered.

The gunner, seated in front of the pilot, had several options with which he could follow out that order. Slaved to his helmet, the 30mm chain gun under the nose of the helicopter followed each movement of his head. He also had Hellfire missiles loaded in pods under the short, stubby wings that he could lock on target, fire, then forget about as they tracked whatever they had locked on to.

A small flip-down sight was over the gunner's left eye on which his firing data was displayed along with the crosshairs for target designation. He put the center over the rear of the Jet Ranger, his finger curling around the trigger for the 30mm cannon.

The gunner pulled back and the Apache vibrated from the recoil of the gun located just below the nose of the craft. A string of rounds crossed the distance between the two helicopters and ripped into the rear of the Jet Ranger.

"Target is down," the pilot reported as the Jet Ranger nosed over and smashed into the ground. A fireball consumed the wreckage and the Apache and Nighthawk came to a hover two hundred feet overhead.

✦

Gereg turned off the computer feed from the Direct Action operations center. "He did it."

"What can we do?" Parker asked.

"The only thing we can do is throw ourselves on the mercy of the director," Gereg said. "With no proof, it isn't the recommended course of action." She shrugged. "But if we do nothing, you can be sure Hancock has more cards to play and I'd rather upset his timetable than let him play them when and where he wants."

She pointed at the folder. "If Mr. O'Callaghan is involved, he is the one who took a shot at Sergeant Major Dublowski at Camp Mackall. You can be sure that Hancock won't leave any loose ends."

"He's killed people," Parker said.

"We have no proof of that," Gereg reminded her. "I don't trust Hancock and *I'm* not even sure he's behind any of what has happened."

"I'm not going to sit by and do nothing," Parker said.

Chapter Twenty-nine

The magnesium burned hot, keeping the Nighthawk team from getting close to the remains of the Jet Ranger for over thirty minutes, even though they used fire extinguishers to put out most of the flames.

Working his way between the still-smoldering wreckage, the team leader approached the remains of the Jet Ranger's cabin. There were two bodies smashed up against the instrument panel, dark green flight helmets partially melted, flight suits charred black.

Using the tip of his MP-5 submachine gun, the team leader pried back the helmet on one of the bodies. The face revealed was battered and burned, but still recognizable. The team leader stared at it for a few seconds, then did the same to the second body.

There was no doubt.

He looked at his men poking through the wreckage. "Got the briefcases?"

He got their answer, then signaled for the Nighthawk to pick up the search team.

Chapter Thirty

The director steepled his fingers under his chin. "That's a pretty strong accusation you're making."

Gereg towered over the other three people arranged around the chair the director still occupied and she didn't react to the comment he directed at her.

"There are girls missing," Parker stepped in. "Girls kidnapped by the men that were just killed. They're the priority."

"Whatever Mr. Jawhar and Mr. Akil have been up to," Hancock said, "they no longer are a threat. My team has taken care of that."

"Very convenient," Parker snapped.

"Listen, Colonel—" Hancock began, but he was interrupted by a loud curse coming from the front of the operations center.

Dilken came rushing up. "It's not them. In the chopper. It's not Jawhar and Akil. And the VZ cases aren't there. Just a small dispenser."

There were a few seconds of silence as everyone digested that information.

"Looks like things haven't worked like you planned," Parker said, breaking the silence. "You've been double-crossed."

"We have to find the VZ." Gereg turned to Dilken. "Get the KH-14 and AWACS to backtrack to the airport that chopper took off from. Trace every flight that's taken off from there."

"Yes, ma'am."

"Wait a second—" Hancock began, but the director's sharp voice cut him off.

"Enough. Gereg, you're in charge. Mr. Hancock, you are relieved of your position until further notice." The director slapped his hand on the arm of the chair. "Find that nerve gas, Ms. Gereg. I have to inform the President."

There was always a Boeing E-3A Sentry AWACS on duty over the Balkans. A new model based on the 767 airframe was entering the system, but the current plane on duty was the venerable one based on the Boeing 707 airframe, painted dull gray with a thirty-foot-diameter radome piggybacked on top.

Using the radar inside the dome, the crew inside could paint an accurate picture of the sky for two hundred miles in every direction. Ever since the U.S. Secretary of Commerce had been killed in bad weather visiting the region, the workload for the AWACS had gone up considerably. The plane was the air traffic controller for all NATO flights in the region, from aircraft bringing in supplies to Sarajevo's main airport, to helicopters conducting local reconnaissance.

Coordinating with a KH-14 spy satellite, Lieutenant Jack Boorstin had tracked the helicopter thought to contain the two Saudis at the request of the CIA. Now, at the CIA's request, Boorstin was doing another search, backtracking through the tapes, to see if any other aircraft had taken off from the same airfield as the helicopter.

It took less than a minute and a half. Boorstin keyed his mike and his message was relayed back to the Direct Action operations center at Langley.

"I've got a fixed-wing aircraft that took off from Budapest twenty minutes after the chopper," Boorstin reported.

A new voice came over the radio. "This is Kim Gereg, Central Intelligence Agency director of Operations. Where is that aircraft headed?"

Boorstin reached up with a stylus and traced the path the craft had followed, south across Romania, over Bulgaria and Turkey to its current location over the Mediterranean just southwest of Cyprus, heading southeast. "Middle East some-where. Maybe Egypt. If it continues past there, then it will be over the Red Sea, which gives us the Sudan or Saudi Arabia as options."

❧

"They're going home with the VZ." Gereg was watching the electronic screen where a new red dot had just appeared over the Mediterranean. Parker felt helpless watching the symbol move across the screen. Hancock had left the operations center shortly after the director, and neither Gereg nor Parker had the time or the inclination right now to find out where he had gone.

"We could contact the Israelis," Dilkin suggested. "They could scramble some jets and take the plane down."

"How fast is the plane moving?" Parker asked.

Dilkin relayed that question to Boorstin.

"It's a jet—got to be, at that speed—maybe a Lear," Boorstin's voice came over the speaker. "It's making about four hundred miles an hour."

"Jawhar's personnel jet is Learjet 35A," Dilkin added. "It's flagged as a Saudi air force jet."

Parker knew what that meant. "We shoot it down, we're committing an act of war."

Gereg nodded. "*And* we might make the same mistake. What if they aren't on board that plane either? And even more important than making sure we get Jawhar and Akil is making sure we get the VZ. We've got to be one hundred percent certain we've interdicted the nerve gas."

"There's only one way to do that," Parker said.

Gereg nodded. "I'll inform the director once we have an option. He'll have to get sanction for us to do anything." She claimed Hancock's seat. "What about the DAT?"

"Still on the ground," Dilken said. "They'd have to reboard their choppers, head out to the *Nimitz* and then take a flight from there to the Italian mainland to get a flight capable of transporting them and their gear to wherever the plane is go-ing."

Gereg swiveled to face Colonel Giles. "What about your Delta Force team in Tel Aviv?"

"They should be ready to go wheels up," Giles said. He glanced at his watch. "If that plane is making for a landing in somewhere in Saudi, it will do so just after dark. Our people— already closer—can be overhead as they land. Perfect time for a strike."

"U.S. Military forces assaulting an objective inside of Saudi Arabia?" Dilkin was aghast. At least he appeared to be. Parker wondered how much allegiance he still owed to Hancock.

"Thorpe is in Tel Aviv," Parker said. "We need to get him up to speed on what is going on."

"Do it," Gereg ordered. "Have him hook up with the Delta Force team."

"That will clue in the Mossad!" Dilken objected.

"Get the Delta team in the air," Gereg ordered. "At least the director will be able to give the President an option."

◦◦◦◦

Thorpe turned off his SATPhone and turned to stare at Rotzinger. "You were in on it with Hancock, weren't you?"

"What are—" Rotzinger began, but Thorpe cut him off.

"The mission to interdict the VZ failed. It's believed that the two brothers and the VZ are on a Learjet currently over the Mediterranean, heading for Saudi Arabia."

"That cannot be!" Rotzinger protested.

"But it is," Thorpe said. "It appears Jawhar and Akil are not playing their parts the way they were scripted. The Delta Force forward element will go airborne in twenty minutes. We're going to track the jet to its landing field and then interdict there."

"You can not cross Prince Yasin," Rotzinger said. "He is too powerful."

"It's not Yasin we're going after," Thorpe said. "It's his two bastards. And I think they've already crossed him also."

The door to the room opened and Yaron walked in. He took the seat at the end of the table, steepled his fingers.

He waved a hand as Thorpe began to speak. "I know of

the failure to interdict and the Learjet." He pointed a long finger at Rotzinger. "If I find out that you were part of the betrayal of my team in the Ukraine—" Yaron abruptly turned to Thorpe. "I have a car waiting to take you to the airfield. Please make sure you succeed or else we will have to take extreme action."

Chapter Thirty-one

Dublowski prowled about the Delta Force Ranch like a caged bear, thinking about the information Parker had relayed. Finally, he went into the electronics shack. He found Chief Warrant Office Simpkins working over the innards of a computer.

Dublowski told the warrant officer what he wanted to do and, as he'd hoped, Simkins had just the thing.

Two metal suitcases in hand, Dublowski left the Ranch in his pickup truck.

✎

Thorpe felt in his element for the first time since he'd put his uniform back on. The throbbing roar of turboprop engines from the nearby combat Talon filled his ears. The smell of JP-4 fuel burning was a familiar one that brought back memories of being at many other airfields preparing to deploy.

The twenty men of the Delta forward element wore black fatigues with no markings. They were loading their gear onto the plane, MP-5 submachine guns slung over their backs.

Thorpe walked up to the man directing the loading. "You in charge?"

The soldier, a tall black man with a completely shaved head, checked Thorpe out, taking in the SOCOM patch on the shoulder, the Special Forces branch insignia on the collar, the combat infantry, scuba and master airborne patches on his chest, and lastly the name tag.

"No, sir. I'm Master Sergeant Grant. Major Dotson is in charge." Grant pointed to a younger white man standing near the back ramp of the plane.

Thorpe walked over. "Major Dotson."

"Yeah?" Dotson looked over Thorpe in the same manner as Grant. "So you're Thorpe. Heard you screwed the pooch in the Ukraine and we've got to close this out."

"I'll be coming with you," Thorpe said.

"Great," Dotson muttered. "What am I, a cruise ship director?"

"The Israelis lost four men 'screwing the pooch,' as you say," Thorpe said. "We stopped two-thirds of the shipment. I would like to be there to help finish the job."

Dotson sighed. "All right. See Grant to get some gear. Make sure you're sterile. Last thing we want is to leave a body that can be identified as American on Saudi soil."

Thorpe noticed something he had never seen before on a combat Talon—two pods bolted to the body of the plane, just forward of the wheel wells.

"What's that?"

Dotson followed his pointing finger. "Hummingbirds. Mixture of high-explosive and diversionary loads."

Thorpe almost laughed. It had come full circle from the rig in the Gulf of Mexico to here. He hoped their assault went better than the previous one.

∼✺∽

"They're staying over Egyptian soil," Parker noted.

"They're not stupid enough to even get close to Israeli airspace," Gereg said. "What's the status on Delta?" she asked Giles.

"They'll be wheels up in two minutes."

"What else do we have on call?" Gereg asked.

Dilken ticked off the firepower. "The U.S.S. *John C. Stennis* just finished transiting the Red Sea en route to relieving the *Lincoln* in the Persian Gulf." Dilken hit a key and the small image of an aircraft carrier's silhouette appeared in the Gulf of Aden, just out of the Red Sea. "It has a full complement of combat aircraft along with its battle group, armed with cruise missiles."

"Scramble some air support to be on station farther north in the Red Sea."

"Yes, ma'am."

Everyone turned as the back door to the ops center opened and the director walked in. He went directly to Gereg. "We have National Command Authority Sanction for this mission. However, we must avoid escalation to direct conflict with Saudi troops."

"That might be hard to do, sir," Gereg noted.

"I don't care how hard it is, you make sure we don't start World War III here or piss off the number-one oil-producing country in the world."

◆◆◆

Terri had made her decision and when she heard the door clang open at the end of the corridor, she quickly padded across her cell to a position to the right of her cell door. She heard another door open, a yell from Leslie as she was dragged out of her cell. Then Cathy's door opening. Both girls were dragged away and still Terri waited, pressed against the hard concrete, her eyes on the door, her ears listening for any movement.

Two men were speaking in a foreign tongue; they laughed; then heavy boots walked away, the door at the end of the corridor slamming shut. Then a lone set of boots came down the corridor.

She heard the key in the lock, then the door swung wide, covering her behind it. A man in sand-colored camouflage stepped in, pistol leading.

Terri pounced, grabbing the arm holding the gun and biting down just above the wrist, her teeth tearing through flesh and bringing a yelp of pain from the man. The gun hit the ground with a clank.

The soldier turned toward her, but she was already moving,

pushing off the wall with all her strength, knee leading directly into his groin. A gargled yell came out of the man's throat, but Terri continued as her father had taught her, slamming the knee twice more into his groin. Then she swung her left elbow, hitting him in the face, snapping his head against the door.

The soldier staggered as Terri dropped to her knees, hands grabbing, wrapping around the butt of the pistol. She brought it up, business end pointing at the soldier's face. He was still moaning, hands over his groin.

Terri's finger curled over the edge of the trigger. She realized that the sound would bring others. She pushed forward, shoving the barrel into the man's ample stomach, and pulled the trigger, the flesh muffling the sound.

The man's eyes went wide, both in disbelief that a woman would shoot him and from the pain. Terri stepped back. She pulled back the slide—the pressure against the man's body having kept it from working properly after the first shot—and put another bullet in the chamber.

The man dropped to his knees, hands over his stomach, blood flowing over them. Terri waited, watching.

❧

"This is the route we will take to the Red Sea." Major Dotson ran his finger along the map.

Glancing out the window to the left, Thorpe could see rocky outcroppings along a ridge at a height equal to that at which they were flying. The combat Talon was less than eighty feet above the ground, the plane bobbing and weaving to follow the contour of the earth along a canyon.

Dotson's finger had traced a route across southern Israel, where the country grew narrower and narrower until just a tiny part of it touched the Gulf of Aqaba between Egypt and Jordan.

"We go feet wet," Dotson continued. "The pilots will put us just about on the wave tops through the Gulf of Aqaba until we touch the Red Sea. Then we have to see exactly where our target goes."

"Won't we get picked up by Saudi radar when we go by Aqaba?" Thorpe asked.

"The Israelis run training flights along this route every day," Dotson answered. "The flights stay at least twelve miles from each shore, in international airspace. We'll get picked up, but the Saudis will assume we are just another training flight." The officer shrugged. "One aircraft—a transport plane, at that—flying alone will not raise much interest."

The Talon was indeed a transport plane, but probably the most sophisticated one in the world. Built on the classic C-130 Hercules transport airframe that has been in service around the world since the late 1950s, the combat Talon was updated in every area. Four powerful turboprop engines pulled it through the air at 340 miles per hour. A large bulbous protrusion under the nose held sophisticated imaging equipment that allowed the pilots to fly low-level even in the worst conditions.

The twenty men of the Delta team were crowded into the rear half of the cargo hold, with about enough space to hold three cars end to end. The front half of the hold was blocked from them by heavy black curtains. Behind those curtains were the stations for the electronic warfare specialists who manned the equipment that helped them evade, confuse and, if need be, jam enemy radar.

Ungainly and slow, the Talon was often mocked by other pilots, especially those who flew jets, but the aircraft had proved its worth time and time again. Talon crews pointed to the fact that a Talon had once penetrated the U.S.S. *United States'* battle group unnoticed to within fifty meters of the massive carrier.

"Where's the Lear?" Thorpe asked.

Dotson tapped the map. "AWACS has it here, south of us, just going feet wet off the coast of Egypt over the Red Sea."

"And when they land?" Thorpe asked. "What's our plan?"

"Plan?" Dotson repeated. "We just got alerted. We have no idea what the objective will look like. They could land at the international airport at Medina or Mecca, in which case, presidential sanction or not, I don't think we really can do much."

Thorpe shook his head. "I think they're heading for Nabi

Ulmalhamah, wherever the hell that is. I don't think they'd try to bring VZ in through an airport. They'll land at a private strip."

"I hope so," Dotson said. "We can go in a couple of ways—we've got HALO and HAHO gear—although it might take some convincing to get the pilots to go that high. More likely we'll go out LAQO."

Thorpe had never heard of that one. He knew about HALO—high altitude, low opening—and HAHO—high altitude, high opening—parachuting and he agreed that the pilots would never take them up to altitude to try that infiltration technique. "What's LAQO?"

"Low altitude, quick opening," Dotson said. He pointed to the back ramp, where a pallet of gear was tied down. "We got special chutes. You step off the ramp at two hundred feet altitude, they open within a second with three main canopies. Slow you enough so you don't die when you hit the ground."

That didn't sound very encouraging to Thorpe, but he'd jumped as low as four hundred feet with a regular canopy.

"The only problem is that there is no reserve," Dotson continued. "Your chute don't work, you won't have time to deploy a reserve."

"So you plan on simply jumping right on top of the target?" Thorpe asked. "That is the plan?"

"It's the start of a plan," Dotson said. "We'll use a couple of Hummingbird cruise missiles to give us a couple of seconds' advantage when we need it."

"I wouldn't be too sure of that advantage," Thorpe muttered, his words unheard in the roar of the engines. One thing he had learned in the army was it was easier to critique something than do it. His critique of the Delta/SEAL assault on the oil rig in the Gulf was hanging over their head now, as they were in a similar situation and essentially coming up with the same plan and Thorpe had no advice to offer on how to make it any better.

❧

"Still over the Red Sea, passing Al Wajh now," Dilken reported. "And descending," he added, which caused a stir of interest.

"Toward where?" Gereg asked.

Dilken hit some keys on the computer in front of him. The map on the display changed scales, focusing on the west coast of Saudi Arabia, northwest of Mecca. "Somewhere along the coast here."

Parker could see that the Talon was less than sixty miles behind the Lear. There were other symbols moving on the screen.

"We've got a flight of F-14 Tomcats closing from the south," Dilken added.

"If they jump in," Parker asked, "how are they getting out?"

"Already thought of that," Colonel Giles said. He pointed to the left side of the screen. "We've got the multinational peacekeeping force in the Sinai scrambling two of their Blackhawks."

"That's a long trip," Parker noted.

"It's the best we can do," Giles said. "They know the situation and it's part of their job."

∾⚬∾

The sky outside the Talon was growing dark, the sun a glow on the western horizon over Africa. The Red Sea below was a dark, flat surface, barely fifteen feet below the belly of the plane. In the cockpit, the pilots were watching their low-light-level television monitor in conjunction with their various radar readouts to fly the plane. Their major concern, given they were over water, was running into a ship.

In the rear of the plane, Thorpe was rigging his gear. He had a combat vest with extra ammunition and grenades. A pistol was strapped to his right thigh, a double-edged Fairburn on his left. An MP-5 submachine gun with a silencer was strapped to his right side under his armpit for the jump.

Master Sergeant Grant tapped Thorpe on the shoulder, yelling to be heard above the rumble of the engines. "Here's your chute." He held up an OD colored pack with a harness attached. The harness was the same Thorpe was used to for regular static line jumping and he quickly strapped it on. Then Grant showed him what was different as he tapped a small plastic pod on the upper part of the left vertical chest strap.

"No static line. That's your drogue. Remember how you warn jumpers to make sure their reserve doesn't deploy in the plane?"

Thorpe nodded.

"Well, you get to the edge of the ramp and pull this." He touched the red handle on the outside of the pod. "It deploys the drogue and—whoosh—you're out of the plane and then the drogue deploys the three main chutes." Grant smiled. "At least that's the theory." He turned to get his own gear ready.

"The Lear is under two thousand feet and still descending," Dilken reported. He pointed with the laser. "Glide path says they'll touch down here."

The red dot highlighted a small, triangular-shaped island just off the shore of the Saudi Arabian mainland.

"Give me imagery on that island," Gereg ordered.

"Coming up live from the KH-14," Dilken said. The screen cleared, then a black and white image appeared. A runway next to a compound, a large building set inside a wall. A dock with a large yacht and a smaller powerboat tied up was about two hundred meters away from the palace on the Red Sea side of the island. Eight hundred meters of water separated the island from the mainland.

"Nabi Ulmalhamah," Parker said.

"How come we never saw this?" Gereg asked.

"The runway is clear under thermal imaging," Dilken said, "but we never picked it up on regular imaging because it's painted to match the surrounding terrain." He shrugged. "It's not in a strategic location, so there never was a request to do thermal imaging."

"Aside the Red Sea shipping lane?" Gereg retorted. "The Red Sea is part of the Suez Canal choke point. The channel is as narrow in most places as the canal. Shut the channel, you shut the canal."

"There was no—" Dilken began, then stopped as Gereg glared at him.

"I think you knew exactly where Nabi Ulmalhamah was, didn't you?"

"Ma'am—" Dilken began, but she cut him off again.

"Do your job now, that's all that counts. Is that clear?"

Dilken swallowed and nodded. "Yes, ma'am."

"Do you have any intelligence on the compound that we can forward to the Delta team?" Parker asked.

Dilken shook his head. "This is the first time I've seen this."

"Forward the imagery we're seeing to the Talon," Gereg ordered.

√

Thorpe and the others crowded around Major Dotson, staring at the imagery just brought back to them by an air force officer from the forward half of the cargo bay.

"We've got to jump fast," Dotson yelled. "The plane will be over this island in six seconds."

Thorpe knew it would be very difficult to get twenty men out of the plane in that short a time.

Dotson grabbed the air force officer's shoulder. "I want an HE hummingbird in the wall, here and here." He tapped a spot on either side, on both wings of the palace. "I want a flash-bang Hummingbird to be launched at the same time. The HE to go off exactly one minute after we jump, the flash-bang five seconds after that. Can you do that?"

The officer nodded.

"I also want an HE hummingbird on top of the Lear at that time." Dotson turned to the men in black. "We'll have one minute on the ground. Those of you who land outside the compound, wait for the Hummingbirds to blow gaps in the wall. Those on the inside, try to get into the palace. When the wall blows, shut down your goggles for the flash-bang and keep your ear plugs in. Take them out right after.

"They're going to hear the 130 go by overhead, so we won't have that much surprise, and every second will count. Everyone stay up on the FM frequency. Kill everything that moves."

"Hold on!" Thorpe yelled. "There's some girls being held captive there."

Dotson glanced at Thorpe, then back to his men. "Priority one is to secure the VZ. Priority two is to kill Jawhar and Akil. If you see some girls, grab them and bring them out."

"What about exfil?" Grant asked.

"North end of the island is our exfil PZ. Only problem is our choppers won't be there for two hours after drop. Let's hope we secure the island and the enemy's help doesn't show before then."

❧

The Lear's tires touched the runway; the plane bounced very slightly, then settled down, racing down the concrete. Thrusters reversed and it slowed a quarter mile short of the end of the runway. The plane turned and taxied for the hangar to the left front of the palace.

The palace contained over twenty thousand square feet. A central three-story-high main structure made up the bulk of it, with two one-story wings coming off on either side. The entire compound was surrounded by a ten-foot-high reinforced concrete wall topped with razor wire. Several guards were awaiting the plane as it came to a halt and the door opened, extending stairs down to the ground.

Akil bounded off, a metal briefcase in each hand, Jawhar right behind.

"Is everything ready?" Jawhar demanded.

The head guard nodded. "Yes."

Without another word they strode through the gate.

Chapter Thirty-two

Dublowski checked the readout as he drove down Chicken Plank Road—the glowing dot was still centered, which meant the bug was still working. He glanced in his rearview mirror. Nothing there. Yet.

❧

Terri reached out with her toe and nudged the body. There was no response. The man's eyes were open and unfocused, his chest still. A pool of blood surrounded him. She took the extra magazines from the pouch on his belt along with the ring of keys and turned to the door of her cell.

She took several deep breaths, then edged out of the door.

❧

"One minute!" Master Sergeant Grant's yell was grabbed by the wind swirling in the open back ramp of the Talon and swept away, but every man's eyes were focused on the single black finger he held up in the air and knew what it meant. Everyone hit the timer on their watch, set for two minutes, the time the HE hummingbirds would hit the wall.

The light above Grant's head glowed red. Behind the plane, the surface of the Red Sea looked like a flat, unbroken, black piece of glass.

They crowded forward on the ramp, Thorpe in the middle of the group. He slid the night-vision goggles down over his eyes and turned them on. Everything now showed up in a brightly lit green world.

"Get ready!" Grant yelled.

Thorpe put his hand on the rip cord for the drogue.

The light flashed green, a searchlight in the goggles. "Go!" Grant screamed and then he was gone. In a flash the men began disappearing off the ramp. Thorpe pulled the cord, the drogue popped out and then he was pulled off the ramp in an instant.

He was immediately jerked upright as the three canopies were pulled out of the backpack by the drogue and opened. Thorpe barely had time to glance up and make sure he had good canopies before he looked down, seeing the top of the palace level with him and then the large pool in the back directly below.

He hit water, submerged. His boots touched the bottom of the pool and he pushed up, surfacing underneath one of the canopies. The night-vision goggles shorted out and he was blinded. He ripped the goggles off, then fought with the canopy as it settled down around him, trying to pull him under.

Thorpe drew his knife and sliced through the nylon. He kicked toward the edge of the pool.

It was very quiet after the sound of the plane and with the earplugs in. Thorpe pulled himself over the edge of the pool, started to stand, then fell over as some of the lines to the canopy were caught on his vest. He used the knife to cut the cords.

A light went on near the low wing of the house to his left. Two men came running out, yelling in Arabic. Thorpe fired a sustained burst, killing both, the only sound the working of the bolt and the expended brass tinkling onto the patio. He saw another abandoned parachute to his right, just inside the wall. A man dressed in black was moving parallel to Thorpe, toward the door the two men had just come out of.

Thorpe ran forward in the same direction. There was a rattle of automatic weapons fire from a watchtower on top of the wall near the main gate to the left. The team'd had the element of surprise for about forty seconds.

The Delta trooper hit the wall on the right of door, putting his back against it. Thorpe hit on the left.

Thorpe dimly heard a beep. He threw his arm across his eyes.

The first wave of hummingbird missiles hit. Two into the compound wall, hitting square on and blasting chunks of concrete into the air, leaving two gaping holes. The third hit the body of the Learjet. The secondary explosion from the refueling truck next to the jet lit the night sky with a tremendous fireball.

The Delta troopers who'd landed outside the wall poured through, breaking into assault teams as they'd been trained.

Thorpe kept his arm over his eyes through those explosions. Five seconds later a hummingbird flew over the compound scattering sixty flash-bang grenades. The cacophony of sound and searing light totally overloaded the senses of all the guards outside.

Thorpe pulled his arm away, looked across at the Delta solider, who whipped off his night vision goggles. The Delta man pointed at his own chest with one finger, then at Thorpe with two. Thorpe nodded, holding his MP-5 at the ready.

The Delta man dashed into the doorway, across to the left. Thorpe followed to the right.

"Who is it?" Jawhar demanded.

Akil was staring at the video screens that showed the outside of the palace. He could see parachutes draped here and there, dark-suited men closing on the building, his guards blinded, deafened and overwhelmed. The attackers moved with the precision of expert soldiers.

"Probably Israelis," Akil said. He could see that the Lear had been destroyed.

"They wouldn't dare!" Jawhar protested. The rattle of automatic gunfire came down the corridor. They were in a large room, about forty feet square. The two girls were locked down on gurneys; the doctor was nervously glancing up. Akil waved his gun in the man's direction and he continued with his delicate task.

Akil pulled out his cell phone and punched in a code, then he flipped it shut. "Help will be here from Father in forty minutes," he said.

The firing was getting closer.

"Forty minutes?" Jawhar had his titanium case out, running it nervously through his fingers. "They will be in here in a minute!"

"While you were away playing, I prepared for this," Akil said. "The vault is finished downstairs. We lock ourselves in, no one can get to us before help arrives. Are you done?" he demanded of the doctor.

"Yes."

"This way." Akil led them toward a set of double doors.

∞∞∞

"The NSA has picked up a SATPhone transmission from Nabi Ulmalhamah," Dilken reported.

"How far out are the Blackhawks?" Gereg asked.

"An hour and twenty minutes," Dilken answered.

"Too far," Parker said. "They're going to get caught on the island."

"The F-14s?" Gereg asked.

"They're circling over the Red Sea, five minutes' flight time away," Dilken said.

"You can't send those F-14s in," the director said.

"We can't abandon those men," Gereg responded.

∞∞∞

Thorpe fired a quick burst to suppress anyone who might be down the corridor. He moved into the corridor, muzzle of his weapon leading the way—the corridor was empty. Thorpe glanced at the Delta trooper who was with him. The man shrugged, then held up a finger for Thorpe to follow him down the short corridor. The few remaining guards were giving way quickly, withdrawing faster than the Delta men could clear their way in.

"Mask up!" Major Dotson ordered over the radio. Thorpe knew he was fearful that they were being drawn into a trap. He pulled the mask out and slipped it over his head, tightening the straps down. He covered the inlet and sucked in a breath. The mask compressed around his face, letting him know he had a good seal. He continued on his way.

∽✕∾

Lieutenant Boorstin was watching his screens carefully. The AWACS rotodome was picking up everything in the air throughout the region. He had the combat Talon clear of the target area and heading back to Israel by the same route. The four F-14 Tomcats were holding in a very tight pattern over the Red Sea, burning fuel.

A new grouping of dots appeared on the screen. Boorstin adjusted the reading, but he already had a very good idea what he was looking at.

He keyed the radio linking him to Langley. "Ops, this is AWACS Eye. We've got four helicopters airborne out of the Saudi air force field at Al Wajh."

"This is Gereg. How long until they reach Nabi Ulmalha-mah?"

The dots were moving and Boorstin made a quick calculation. "Approximately thirty minutes."

∽✕∾

The key opened the door and Terri slid through. A long concrete passageway beckoned. Halfway down, about thirty feet away, she could see an opening to the right where the stairs came down. A large steel door was at the other end, sixty feet away.

She padded down the hallway. She had heard the loud explosions and gunfire, but that had stopped about thirty seconds ago. She had no idea what was going on and she refused to allow herself to believe that rescue was here.

She heard the thud of boots on stairs and brought the pistol up. The man with all the rings stepped into the corridor, turning toward the steel door and away from her.

Terri didn't hesitate. She dashed forward and jammed the gun hard against the side of Jawhar's head.

"I'll kill him!" she screamed at the group of men still on the stairs, most of them caught with their weapons pointed up the stairs.

※

As Thorpe turned the next corridor, he saw Major Dotson in the main hallway of the east wing, the officer rattling off orders, coordinating the movement of his elements toward the center of the palace. Thorpe fell in behind the eight troopers with Dotson, willing to let the experts take the lead.

But it appeared the battle was over, as they encountered no more resistance. They closed on the center of the palace from both wings, the troops in the west wing also reporting no opposition.

Both groups reached the large center room on the first floor at the same time.

"The stairs." Dotson waved his men forward toward a double-wide door beyond which a set of stairs headed down.

※

"You will not shoot," Akil had his submachine gun centered on Terri's forehead.

She dug the barrel of the gun deeper into Jawhar's temple. "I will. You know I will. Just as you shot Patricia, I'll shoot your brother down."

Akil's eyes shifted between his brother and the girl. "Listen—"

A burst of bullets from above blew one of the guards down the stairs.

"Stop it!" Akil screamed. "Stop shooting! We have the girls!"

❧

"Hold your fire!" Thorpe shoved his way in front of the Delta Troopers. "Hold your fire!"

He stood in the middle of the stairs. A small cluster of guards, holding the two girls, was grouped behind Akil. Thorpe couldn't see who Akil was pointing his weapon at. He edged down another step, braving the muzzles of the guards' guns, sensing the weapons from the Delta men behind him.

He saw Terri holding the pistol on Jawhar.

❧

Dublowski caught a glimpse of the car in his rearview mirror. Dark green, just like the paint scrapings on Takamura's car. The other driver was good, but three turns left no doubt the man was following.

❧

"Clock's ticking!" Dotson muttered. "We take them down now, we get the VZ, we get the bad guys. We get the hell out of here."

Thorpe could see the two metal briefcases being held by the guard closest to Akil. "And kill three girls."

"There's no—" Dotson began, but Thorpe waved him to be silent. He slowly bent over and placed his submachine gun on the step at his feet.

"We can work this out," he shouted.

Akil's eyes were shifting back and forth from his brother to Thorpe. "I do not think so."

"She'll kill your brother," Thorpe said.

Akil nodded, ever so slightly. "Yes. I know she will. She was the best of them. But if she does, she dies. If you shoot at us, you will all die."

"I don't think so, buddy boy," Dotson growled, the small red dot from the laser sight on his MP-5 centered right be-tween Akil's eyes.

"All the VZ is not in the cases," Akil said. He turned away from Terri very slowly, so as to not precipitate any untoward action. His gun now pointed at the two girls.

"Where is it?" Thorpe asked.

Akil nodded toward the girls. "In them."

"*In them*?" Thorpe repeated.

"Yes," Akil said, "and if I shoot them, it will set off a small charge rigged against the container which is just below their left lungs. The charge will explode, sending VZ into the air. Everyone here will die. No one wins." He barked an order in Arabic and a guard reached out and lifted the left side of Leslie's smock. Thorpe and all the Delta men could see the long scar on her side.

"You're full of shit," Master Sergeant Grant muttered.

"No," Akil said, "they are full of nerve agent. Injected with a needle by our good doctor directly into the canister," Akil said. "Didn't he?" he asked Leslie.

She nodded. "He put something inside of us a while back." She was speaking quickly, taking quick, shallow breaths in between, as if afraid even that act would set off the device. "We could feel it. I can still feel it inside me. And the doctor took something out of those cases and used a needle to put it into us. Into the thing, whatever it is."

❧

Dublowski went over a rise in the road. The trailing car was out of sight, as it had been most of the time. He twisted the wheel and skidded off onto a dirt trail on the right side. He flipped open the lid to the other case Simpkins had given him and turned a knob on.

Simpkins had prepared the program. It took over the frequency of the bug secreted in Dublowski's truck and projected the same signal. Except with diminishing power, as if the truck were still going down the road.

Dublowski jumped out of the truck, a small backpack over his shoulder. He walked to the side of the road, a thick tree hiding him. He heard a car's engine and an old Mustang came racing over the rise. He caught a glimpse of the driver—the glasses, beard—just as Parker had described O'Callaghan.

Dublowski stepped forward as the Mustang came by. O'Callaghan's head swiveled, staring wide-eyed in surprise at Dublowski standing at the side of the road as his foot reached for the brake.

Dublowski tossed the backpack onto the trunk of the Mustang, the powerful magnet clinging to the metal. The tires on the Mustang locked as the car skidded, trying to slow from sixty miles an hour.

The bomb inside the backpack exploded, blowing through the trunk and igniting the gas tank in a ferocious secondary explosion as the car was still sliding.

Dublowski shielded his eyes as the fireball consumed the car and O'Callaghan.

"Once too often." Dublowski spit, then turned for his truck. He paused suddenly, his head cocked as if he heard something. "Ah, Terri," he whispered, his eyes looking to the dark eastern sky.

⚭

"What kind of deal?" Thorpe asked.

"We give you the girls, we go into the bunker"—Akil nodded his head toward the large steel door at the end of the corridor—"and you leave. There is no other solution other than all of us dying."

"We can't make deals with this scum," Dotson hissed.

"We have to have the VZ," Thorpe said.

"She lets my brother go now," Akil bargained.

"Don't trust them!" Terri yelled.

"All right," Thorpe said to A.K.I.

"You don't have the authority to—" Dotson began, but Thorpe cut him off.

"Trust me."

Terri pressed the gun tighter against Jawhar's head, bringing a yelp of pain. "I'm not letting him go! You can't!"

"Terri, you know me," Thorpe called to the girl. "Do what I say. It's what your dad would do."

"My dad wouldn't let them get away."

"We have to get the nerve gas," Thorpe said. "Thousands of lives are at stake."

Terri was shaking her head, tears flowing down her cheeks. "No. No. You can't let them get away with it."

"Put the VZ down and let the girls go," Thorpe said.

Akil barked an order in Arabic and the two cases of VZ were placed on the floor. "You get the girls when my brother is freed and we are in the vault."

Master Sergeant Grant edged close to Thorpe. "We don't have time for this bullshit. A reaction force will be here soon."

Thorpe ignored everyone but Akil and Terri. "Move down the corridor," he instructed Akil.

The Saudi and his men backed up, keeping Leslie and Cathy between them and the Delta men who moved into the corridor. Terri and Jawhar were now also directly between the two groups. Thorpe, empty hands outstretched, took one cautious step after the other, closing the distance between himself and Terri and her prisoner.

He reached the two. Blood from the torn skin under the muzzle was mixing with the sweat that dripped down the side of Jawhar's face. Thorpe remembered the body in the hotel in the Ukraine. He forced himself to focus.

"Terri." Thorpe kept his voice low. "Terri, you need to trust me."

She was still crying, her head shaking, but the gun hadn't wavered. "You don't know what he's done!"

"I have a very good idea," Thorpe said. "Trust me on this. Please, Terri."

She dropped her hand and Thorpe stepped forward and caught her, keeping her from hitting the floor. Jawhar smiled at Thorpe, then quickly strode down the hall and joined his brother. Thorpe could feel Terri's body shaking as he held her tight.

Akil slid a key into a panel on the side of the door. With a rumble, the massive steel panels slid open. Akil barked at his men, hustling them through until he and Jawhar along with the other two girls were in the corridor.

"We will meet again," Akil called as he pushed his brother

through the door, then stepped through himself, the heavy steel sliding shut.

"No, we won't," Thorpe whispered as the Delta men rushed forward, securing the VZ and the two girls.

"We need to get the hell out of here," Dotson yelled.

Thorpe checked his watch and shook his head. "You heard the report. The Saudi choppers will be here in five minutes, the Blackhawks in forty-five."

"So what do you recommend?" Dotson will still upset about the brothers escaping. "Stand here with our thumb up our ass while they sit in that vault?"

"No," Thorpe said. "I have a plan."

"Saudi choppers are three minutes out," Dilken reported.

"This is going to be a mess," Gereg muttered. She raised her voice so the director could hear her. "Sir, I recommend we let the F-14s take out those choppers now."

"Negative," the director replied.

"Damn it, sir!" Parker slammed her fist into a desktop. "You can't do things halfway. Either we go all the way or we shouldn't have gone in at all."

"I am working within the boundaries of the sanction I was granted," the director said. "We will not, I repeat, not, engage Saudi armed forces in combat."

"What happens when they engage our people?" Parker asked.

To that the director had no answer.

"You can clear a homicide with this, Sammy," Dublowski said.

The sheriff stared at the wreck, the metal still hot. "It just exploded?"

Dublowski nodded.

"And you just happened to be driving by?"

Dublowski nodded once more.

"And you say when I run this guy's prints—or more likely his dental records, since it don't look like there'll be much left to take prints from—that this guy will come up as wanted IRA terrorist?"

Dublowski's head bobbed for the third time.

"*And,*" Sammy continued, "this guy killed that Takamura fellow and the paint from this car will match the paint on his car?"

"Roger that," Dublowski said.

Sammy tucked his thumbs in his equipment belt and regarded Dublowski for several seconds from under the brim of his Sam Browne hat. "Spontaneous combustion, eh?"

"That's what it looked like to me," Dublowski said.

"Then why is there what appears to be a downward forced explosion on the trunk?"

"Don't know," Dublowski said.

"This guy was bad?" Sammy asked.

"Very."

Sammy nodded. "Okay. I'm ruling it an accident. Get out of here."

❧

"Have your men stand down," Thorpe told Major Dotson.

The Delta commander was staring at the flight of helicopters rapidly approaching the island from the mainland. Two Cobra gunships were in the lead. "We're not surrendering to these people," Dotson said.

"I'm not asking you to surrender. I just want to talk to the man in charge of those helicopters."

The Cobras—American craft sold to the Saudi military—did a flyby over the compound while the troop-carrying transports settled down on the sand outside the front gate. Dozens of men ran out of the large aircraft, weapons at the ready.

Thorpe walked forward unarmed, hands raised. He strode out the main gate between the guns of the Delta men behind and the Saudis in front.

"I need to speak to Prince Hakim Yasin," Thorpe yelled.

The Saudis had paused in a half circle around the gate, guns pointed. The Cobras flew by overhead once more, then turned and hovered a hundred meters back, the nose guns pointing right at Thorpe.

A man in camouflage walked forward. Thorpe could see the insignia on his collar—a colonel in the Saudi army. "Who are you?" He spoke with a strong English accent.

"I am an American officer," Thorpe said. "I need to speak to Prince Hakim Yasin."

"What are you doing on Saudi soil without permission?" the colonel demanded.

"I will explain that to Prince Yasin."

"No, you will explain it to me." The colonel looked past Thorpe, seeing the black-uniformed Delta men deployed along the wall of the compound. "What of Prince Yasin's sons?"

"They are safe," Thorpe said, "in the vault under the palace."

"You have not answered my question about why you are on Saudi soil," the colonel said.

"We came here to recover some VZ nerve gas and some American citizens kidnapped by Prince Yasin's sons," Thorpe said.

The colonel's eyes flickered past Thorpe, then back to him. "There are—"

"I don't have time to stand here and argue," Thorpe said. "I have something Prince Yasin needs to see."

The colonel snapped a command and held his hand out. A man came running up with a cell phone. The colonel pressed a button, then turned his back to Thorpe. All Thorpe could hear was some rapid speaking in Arabic muted by the sound of the Cobras hovering.

The colonel flipped the phone shut and turned back toward Thorpe. "What is it you wish to show Prince Yasin?"

"For his eyes only," Thorpe said.

"You are not in a position to ignore my question," the colonel said.

Both men turned to the north as another helicopter appeared. This one was painted black and very sleek, the wheels retracted into the body. Thorpe recognized the make—an Aerospatiale SA 365 Panther—with the tail rotor enclosed in the vertical fin at the rear, the trademark of that make.

"Prince Yasin, I assume," Thorpe said to the colonel as the landing gear on the helicopter quickly deployed and the aircraft settled down fifty feet away, the blades blowing sand, forcing Thorpe to put his hand over his eyes. The chopper lifted, and by the time Thorpe was able to see again, a tall man wearing a well-cut business suit was striding toward him.

"What is your name?" Prince Yasin demanded. He had dark features with piercing black eyes. There was no gray in his hair and it was difficult to determine how old he was.

"My name is Thorpe."

"You have something to show me?"

"American citizens your sons kidnapped from Germany," Thorpe said.

"There are diplomatic ways this could have been resolved," Yasin said. "An assault by American forces on Saudi Arabian soil will bring the severest of consequences."

"I don't think so," Thorpe said. He turned toward the gate. "Bring them out," he called out to Major Dotson.

Master Sergeant Grant and another Delta trooper appeared at the gate, helping support Cathy and Leslie.

"What is this?" Yasin demanded.

"Look familiar?" Thorpe said.

Yasin's dark eyes were fixed on the girls. "I don't understand."

"Akil and Jawhar did not deliver the VZ nerve gas to the Serbs as was arranged. As you arranged. They killed the Serbs who were supposed to get it and brought it here.

"Did you also arrange for them to be killed by the CIA reaction force? Was that your plan? Or did you really want the Serbs to get the gas?" Thorpe shrugged. "I don't know what your plan was, but I know now what Jawhar and Akil's was."

He pointed at the two girls. "They look like Jawhar and Akil's mother, don't they?" Thorpe didn't wait for an answer. "Your mistress. They put nerve agent inside of them in a dispenser. With an explosive charge. They were going to send them to you. Probably as a gift. And then kill you and all those around you."

Thorpe knew Yasin was one of the richest men in the world and he held that position because of his intelligence and cunning. The prince didn't argue with what Thorpe had just said, but rather stood there regarding the girls for several more seconds. A small muscle jumped on the left side of his cheek, his only reaction. He nodded. "You may leave," he said to Thorpe.

Chapter Thirty-three

"They're on the Blackhawks heading back." Dilken seemed surprised by the news.

"Do they have the VZ?" the director asked.

"Yes, sir."

"What about the girls?" Parker asked.

"They recovered three hostages," Dilken said. He glanced down at his notepad. "Catherine Walker, Leslie Marker and Terri Dublowski."

Parker sank down into a seat, feeling the tension drain from her body for the first time in days. She picked up a phone and dialed the number for the Ranch to let Dublowski know the good news.

❧

Thorpe sat next to Terri Dublowski, an arm around the young girl's shoulder, his fatigue jacket over the smock. He could feel her trembling.

She looked up. "You shouldn't have let them go. They killed the other girls. They'll do it again."

"I don't think they'll be killing anyone else," Thorpe said.

❧

Prince Yasin stood in front of the vault door. He watched as welders sealed the seam. He had designed the room himself and knew this was the only way out. When the welders were done, he dismissed them.

He looked at the door one last time, then turned and left.

Epilogue

"Favors being owed are the oil that keeps the machinery of international relations working." Former National Security Adviser Hill poured himself a shot of bourbon, then raised the bottle with a questioning look toward former CIA Director of Operations Hancock.

Hancock declined. They were in a cabana on the west coast of Costa Rica with a magnificent view of the Pacific Ocean crashing on a pristine beach less than fifty feet from the double doors opening to the deck. Jungle surrounded them, and guards from the Costa Rican army, supplemented by mercenaries, patrolled the perimeter. The cabana was luxurious, with every modern comfort money could buy and import.

"They'll seek to extradite us," Hancock noted as Hill sat in a large wicker chair across from him.

"They have to find us first," Hill said. "That will take them a year or two. By then we'll move on. I have many people owing me favors—as do you."

"Prince Yasin is looking for us also," Hancock said.

"We did Yasin a favor by showing him the true nature of his bastard sons," Hill said.

Unnoticed by either man—and the security guards—a small, crablike object crept out of the ocean on metal legs. With a body less than four inches in size, it walked across the beach toward the open double doors.

"It was bad luck, really," Hill continued.

Hancock shook his head. "No. Jawhar and Akil had their own agenda and I should have foreseen that. It cost us everything."

"Not everything," Hill said. "Who knows? With a new administration coming into office—and there is no doubt the pendulum will swing the other way with the next election—we may very well be able to go back to Washington and reclaim our old jobs."

Hancock was listening to his mentor, but he was distracted by a very slight clicking noise. He looked about, then saw the mechanical creature stalking in through the doorway, the metal legs making the noise against the hardwood floor.

"What is that?" Hancock stood up.

Hill turned. A small optical wire on the top turned in their direction, like an crustacean's eye. It fixed on the two men.

Hill pulled his cell phone out of his pocket and was punching in for the head of security when a small canister about two inches long by one in diameter popped out of the top of the device. The canister rolled onto the floor with a hissing noise.

"What the hell—" Hancock leaned forward to look at the canister when he felt his throat seize up.

❧❧

Dublowski watched the VZ kill Hill and Hancock. Certain they were dead, he hit the self-destruct on Freddie Two, and the image on the small TV screen in the cabin of the rented boat went black.

Dublowski climbed up the short ladder to the boat's bridge. He engaged the engine and headed north from his position three miles off the coast of Costa Rica. In two days he was meeting his wife and daughter in San Diego for a week of vacation and he wanted to make sure he made it in time. He knew Simpkins would be happy to know Freddie worked.

❧❧

Parker knew the driver was checking her out, but more out of curiosity than male lust. That was a relief, given he was over sixty and looked like life had not been too kind to him.

"How much farther?" she asked as they turned another narrow street in Stuttgart.

"You sound like my grandkids," Morty Lorsen groused good-naturedly. He pulled the car into an alley and stopped. "We're here."

Parker got out of the car and looked around with some concern.

Lorsen saw her expression and laughed. "Yeah, this is it. Looked worse a month ago, if you can believe that. Our friend, he has . . ." Morty shook his head. "Well, you must see. Come on, come on."

They walked down the alley and then turned right through a narrow doorway. Morty opened the door and extended his right hand, inviting her in.

Parker walked through and blinked. Bright lights illuminated the center of the large room where several teenagers were gathered at a table while a tall, thin man was speaking in a low voice, pointing to a computer.

"That's Esdras," Lorsen said. "He's teaching them basic computer skills. And here . . ."—Lorsen led Parker around a thick concrete pillar to another section of the room—"is your friend Mr. Thorpe."

Thorpe had a roller in his hands and was perched precariously on a ladder. The ceiling above his head was half painted and Thorpe was covered with white spots. He saw Parker and smiled. "Hey." He climbed down.

A thin young man with tattoos all over the parts of his body that were visible poked Thorpe in the arm. "Hey, man, no breaks. You said it!"

"I've got to talk to the lady, Crew," Thorpe said.

The young man doubled over coughing, then straightened with a weak grin. "Yeah, well, I want to see this done."

"We'll get it done," Thorpe promised. "Maybe you should take a break too."

"Nah." Crew dipped his roller in the paint.

Thorpe walked over to Parker. "How go things back in the States?"

"Things are good. Dublowski sends his regards and his thanks for the hundredth time."

Thorpe nodded.

"Hill and Hancock are dead," Parker added.

"How?"

"According to Gereg, someone infiltrated some VZ gas into where they were in Costa Rica."

"Interesting," was Thorpe's only comment on that.

"That seems to close everything out," Parker said.

"You think so?"

"Are all the world's problems solved?" Parker asked rhetorically. "Of course not. But a couple of them are."

"Jawhar and Akil haven't been spotted, have they?"

Parker shook her head. "Not a peep."

"I think Daddy took care of them," Thorpe said.

"We've kept an eye on Nabi Ulmalhamah," Parker said. "Nothing since Yasin left. No one's gone in there or out. Looks abandoned."

Thorpe sat down in an old chair that the stuffing was coming out of in several places. Parker settled down on a battered couch.

"There's something else," she said hesitatingly.

"What?"

"The German link who set up Jawhar and Akil with the Russian military. We've received word from the Israelis that—"

Thorpe held up his hand, then pointed. "See that wall?"

A splash of colors covered the concrete. The pattern caught the eye and held it, as the mind tried to make sense of the swirling images.

"It's beautiful," Parker said.

"Crew did that," Thorpe said. "He created something."

Parker opened her mouth to speak, then paused.

Thorpe leaned forward. "We're creating something here. A place for these kids to be safe. Because there will be more Jawhars. And Akils. And Hancocks. And Hills. All of them. I don't care about who the German intermediaries were and what they're doing now." He stabbed a finger at the floor. "As long as they don't come here. Nabi Ulmalhamah was the last mission. The Omega Sanction, to use CIA terminology. I'm done destroying."

Thorpe stood up. "We've got an extra brush if you want to help."

Parker nodded. "Sounds like a plan."

TURN THE PAGE FOR AN EXCERPT FROM
COLIN HARRISON'S EXCITING NEW NOVEL,

Afterburn—

AVAILABLE SOON IN HARDCOVER FROM
FARRAR, STRAUS & GIROUX . . .

CHINA CLUB,

HONG KONG

September 7, 1999

HE WOULD SURVIVE. Yes, Charlie promised himself, he'd survive *this*, too—his ninth formal Chinese banquet in as many evenings, yet another bowl of shark-fin soup being passed to him by the endless waiters in red uniforms, who stood obsequiously against the silk wallpaper pretending not to hear the self-satisfied ravings of those they served. Except for his fellow *gweil*—British Petroleum's Asia man, a mischievous German from Lufthansa, and two young American executives from Kodak and Citigroup—the other dozen men at the huge mahogany table were all Chinese. Mostly in their fifties, the men represented the big corporate players—Bank of Asia, Hong Kong Telecom, China Motors—and each, Charlie noted, had arrived at the age of cleverness. Of course, at fifty-eight he himself was old enough that no one should be able to guess what he was thinking unless he wanted them to, even Ellie. In his call to her that morning—it being evening in New York City—he'd tried not to sound too worried about their daughter Julia. "It's all going to be *fine*, sweetie," he'd promised, gazing out at the choppy haze of Hong Kong's harbor, where the heavy traffic of tankers and freighters pressed China's claim—everything from photocopiers to baseball caps flowing out into the world, everything from oil refineries to contact lenses flowing in. "She'll get pregnant, I'm sure," he'd told Ellie. But he wasn't sure. No, not at all. In fact, it looked as if it was going to be easier for him to build his electronics factory in Shanghai than for his daughter to hatch a baby.

"We gather in friendship," announced the Chinese host, Mr. Ming, the vice-chairman of the Bank of Asia. Having agreed to lend Charlie fifty-two million U.S. dollars to build his Shanghai factory, Mr. Ming in no way could be described as a friend; the relationship was one of overlord and indentured. But Charlie smiled along with the others as the banker stood and presented in high British English an analysis of southeastern China's economy that was so shallow, optimistic, and full of euphemism that no one, especially the central ministries in Beijing, might object. The Chinese executives nodded politely as Mr. Ming spoke, touching their napkins to their lips, smiling vaguely. Of course, they nursed secret worries—worries that corresponded to whether they were entrepreneurs (who had built shipping lines or real-estate empires or garment factories) or the managers of institutional power (who controlled billions of dollars not their own). And yet, Charlie decided, the men were finally more like one another than unlike; each long ago had learned to sell high (1997) and buy low (1998), and had passed the threshold of unspendable wealth, such riches conforming them in their behaviors; each owned more houses or paintings or Rolls-Royces than could be admired or used at once. Each played golf or tennis passably well; each possessed a forty-million-dollar yacht or a forty-million-dollar home atop Victoria's Peak, or a forty-million-dollar wife. Each had a slender young Filipino or Russian or Czech mistress tucked away in one of Hong Kong's luxury apartment buildings—licking her lips if requested—or was betting against the Hong Kong dollar while insisting on its firmness—any of the costly mischief in which rich men indulge.

The men at the table, in fact, as much as any men, sat as money incarnate, particularly the American dollar, the

euro, and the Japanese yen—all simultaneously, and all
hedged against fluctuations of the others. But although the
men were money, money was not them; money assumed
any shape or color or politics, it could be fire or stone or
dream, it could summon armies or bind atoms, and, indif-
ferent to the sufferings of the mortal soul, it could leave or
arrive at any time. And on this exact night, Charlie thought,
setting his ivory chopsticks neatly upon the lacquered plate,
he could see that although money had assumed the shapes
of the men in the room, it existed in differing densities and
volumes and brightnesses. Whereas Charlie was a man of
perhaps thirty or thirty-three million dollars of wealth, that
sum amounted to shoe-shine change in the present company. No, sir, money, in *that* room, in *that* moment, was
understood as inconsequential in sums less than one hundred million dollars, and of political importance only when
five times more. Money, in fact, found its greatest com-
pression and gravity in the form of the tiny man sitting
silently across from Charlie—Sir Henry Lai, the Oxford-
educated Chinese gambling mogul, owner of a fleet of jet-
foil ferries, a dozen hotels, and most of the casinos of Macao and Vietnam. Worth billions—and billions more.

But, Charlie wondered, perhaps he was wrong. He could
think of one shape that money had not *yet* assumed, although quite a bit of it had been spent, perhaps a hundred
thousand dollars in all. Money animated the dapper Chinese
businessman across from him, but could it arrive in the
world as Charlie's own grandchild? This was the question
he feared most, this was the question that had eaten at him
and at Ellie for years now, and which would soon be answered: In a few hours, Julia would tell them once and
forever if she was capable of having a baby.

She had suffered through cycle upon cycle of disap-
pointment—hundreds of shots of fertility drugs followed
by the needle-recovery of the eggs, the inspection of the
eggs, the selection of the eggs, the insemination of the eggs,
the implantation of the eggs, the anticipation of the eggs.

She'd been trying for seven years. Now Julia, a woman of only thirty-five, a little gray already salting her hair, was due to get the final word. At 11:00 a.m. Manhattan time, she'd sit in her law office and be told the results of this, the last in-vitro attempt. Her *ninth*. Three more than the doctor preferred to do. Seven more than the insurance company would pay for. Good news would be that one of the reinserted fertilized eggs had decided to cling to the wall of Julia's uterus. Bad news: There was no chance of conception; egg donorship or adoption must now be considered. And if *that* was the news, well then, that was really goddamn something. It would mean not just that his only daughter was heartbroken, but that, genetically speaking, he, Charlie Ravich, was finished, that his own fishy little spermatozoa—one of which, wiggling into Ellie's egg a generation prior, had become his daughter—had run aground, that he'd come to the end of the line; that, in a sense, he was already dead.

And now, as if mocking his very thoughts, came the fish, twenty pounds of it, head still on, its eyes cooked out and replaced with flowered radishes, its mouth agape in macabre broiled amusement. Charlie looked at his plate. He always lost weight in China, undone by the soy and oils and crusted skin of birds, the rich liverish stink of turtle meat. All that duck tongue and pig ear and fish lip. Expensive as hell, every meal. And carrying with it the odor of doom.

Then the conversation turned, as it also did so often in Shanghai and Beijing, to the question of America's mistreatment of the Chinese. "What I do not understand are the American senators," Sir Henry Lai was saying in his softly refined voice. "They say they *understand* that we only want for China to be China." Every syllable was flawless English, but of course Lai also spoke Mandarin and Cantonese. Sir Henry Lai was reported to be in serious talks with Gaming Technologies, the huge American gambling and hotel conglomerate that clutched big pieces of Las Vegas, the Mississippi casino towns, and Atlantic City. Did

Sir Henry know when China would allow Western-style casinos to be built within its borders? Certainly he knew the right officials in Beijing, and perhaps this was reason enough that GT's stock price had ballooned up seventy percent in the last three months as Sir Henry's interest in the company had become known. Lai smiled benignly. Then frowned. "These senators say that all they want is for international trade to progress without interruption, and then they go back to Congress and raise their fists and call China all kinds of names. Is this not true?"

The others nodded sagely, apparently giving consideration, but not ignoring whatever delicacy remained pinched in their chopsticks.

"Wait, I have an answer to that," announced the young fellow from Citigroup. "Mr. Lai, I trust we may speak frankly here. You need to remember that the American senators are full of—excuse my language—full of shit. When they're standing up on the Senate floor saying all of this stuff, this means nothing, *absolutely* nothing!"

"Ah, this is very difficult for the Chinese people to understand." Sir Henry scowled. "In China we believe our leaders. So we become scared when we see American senators complaining about China."

"You're being coy with us, Mr. Lai," interrupted Charlie, looking up with a smile, "for we—or some of us—know that you have visited the United States dozens of times and have met many U.S. senators personally." Not to mention a few Third World dictators. He paused, while amusement passed into Lai's dark eyes. "Nonetheless," Charlie continued, looking about the table, "for the others who have not enjoyed Mr. Lai's deep friendships with American politicians, I would have to say my colleague here is right. The speeches in the American Senate are pure grandstanding. They're made for the American public—"

"The *bloodthirsty* American public, you mean!" interrupted the Citigroup man, who, Charlie suddenly understood, had drunk too much. "Those old guys up there know most voters can't find China on a globe. That's no joke. It's shocking, the American ignorance of China."

"We shall have to educate your people," Sir Henry Lai offered diplomatically, apparently not wishing the stridency of the conversation to continue. He gave a polite, cold-blooded laugh.

"But it is, yes, my understanding that the Americans could sink the Chinese Navy in several days?" barked the German from Lufthansa.

"That may be true," answered Charlie, "but sooner or later the American people are going to recognize the hemispheric primacy of China, that—"

"Wait, wait!" Lai interrupted good-naturedly. "You agree with our German friend about the Chinese Navy?"

The question was a direct appeal to the nationalism of the other Chinese around the table.

"Can the U.S. Air Force destroy the Chinese Navy in a matter of days?" repeated Charlie. "Yes. Absolutely yes."

Sir Henry Lai smiled. "You are knowledgeable about these topics, Mr."—he glanced down at the business cards arrayed in front of his plate—"Mr. Ravich. Of the Teknetrix Corporation, I see. What do you know about war, Mr. Ravich?" he asked. "Please, tell me. I am curious."

The Chinese billionaire stared at him with eyebrows lifted, face a smug, florid mask, and if Charlie had been younger or genuinely insulted, he might have recalled aloud his war years before becoming a businessman, but he understood that generally it was to one's advantage not to appear to have an advantage. And anyway, the conversation was merely a form of sport: Lai didn't give a good goddamn about the Chinese Navy, which he probably despised; what he cared about was whether or not he should soon spend eight hundred million dollars on GT stock—play the corporation that played the players.

But Lai pressed. "What do you know about this?"

"Just what I read in the papers," Charlie replied with humility.

"See? There! I tell you!" Lai eased back in his silk suit, running a fat little palm over his thinning hair." This is a very dangerous problem, my friends. People say many things about China and America, but they have no direct knowledge, no real—"

Mercifully, the boys in red uniforms and brass buttons began setting down spoons and bringing around coffee. Charlie excused himself and headed for the gentlemen's restroom. Please, God, he thought, it's a small favor, really. One egg clinging to a warm pink wall. He and Ellie should have had another child, should have at least tried, after Ben. Ellie had been forty-two. Too much grief at the time, too late now.

In the men's room, a sarcophagus of black and silver marble, he nodded at the wizened Chinese attendant, who stood up with alert servility. Charlie chose the second stall and locked the heavy marble door behind him. The door and walls extended in smooth veined slabs from the floor to within a foot of the ceiling. The photo-electric eye over the toilet sensed his movement and the bowl flushed prematurely. He was developing an old man's interest in his bowels. He shat then, with the private pleasure of it. He was starting to smell Chinese to himself. Happened on every trip to the East.

And then, as he finished, he heard the old attendant greeting another man in Cantonese.

"Evening, sir."

"Yes."

The stall door next to Charlie's opened, shut, was locked. The man was breathing as if he had hurried. Then came some loud coughing, an oddly tiny splash, and the muffled silky sound of the man slumping heavily against the wall he shared with Charlie.

"Sir?" The attendant knocked on Charlie's door. "You open door?"

Charlie buckled his pants and slid the lock free. The old man's face loomed close, eyes large, breath stinking.

"Not me!" Charlie said. "The next one!"

"No have key! Climb!" The old attendant pushed past Charlie, stepped up on the toilet seat, and stretched high against the glassy marble. His bony hands pawed the stone uselessly. Now the man in the adjacent stall was moaning in Chinese, begging for help. Charlie pulled the attendant down and stood on the toilet seat himself. With his arms outstretched he could reach the top of the wall, and he sucked in a breath and hoisted himself. Grimacing, he pulled himself up high enough so that his nose touched the top edge of the wall. But before being able to look over, he fell back.

"Go!" he ordered the attendant. "Get help, get a key!"

The man in the stall groaned, his respiration a song of pain. Charlie stepped up on the seat again, this time jumping exactly at the moment he pulled with his arms, and then *yes*, he was up, right up there, hooking one leg over the wall, his head just high enough to peer down and see Sir Henry Lai slumped on the floor, his face a rictus of purpled flesh, his pants around his ankles, a piss stain spreading across his silk boxers. His hands clutched weakly at his tie, the veins of his neck swollen like blue pencils. His eyes, not squeezed shut but open, stared up at the underside of the spotless toilet bowl, into which, Charlie could see from above, a small silver pillbox had fallen, top open, the white pills inside of it scattered and sunk and melting away.

"Hang on," breathed Charlie. "They're coming. Hang on." He tried to pull himself through the opening between the wall and ceiling, but it was no good; he could get his head through but not his shoulders or torso. Now Sir Henry Lai coughed rhythmically, as if uttering some last strange code—"Haa-cah . . . Haaa! Haaa!"—and convulsed, his eyes peering in pained wonderment straight into Charlie's, then widening as his mouth filled with a reddish soup of undigested shrimp and pigeon and turtle that surged up over his lips and ran down both of his cheeks before draining back into his windpipe. He was too far gone to cough the vomit out of his lungs, and the tension in his hands eased—he was dying of a heart attack and asphyxiation at the same moment.

The attendant hurried back in with Sir Henry's bodyguard. They pounded on the stall door with something, cracking the marble. The beautiful veined stone broke away in pieces, some falling on Sir Henry Lai's shoes. Charlie looked back at his face. Henry Lai was dead.

The men stepped into the stall and Charlie knew he was of no further use. He dropped back to the floor, picked up his jacket, and walked out of the men's restroom, expecting a commotion outside. A waiter sailed past; the assembled businessmen didn't know what had happened.

Mr. Ming watched him enter.

"I must leave you," Charlie said graciously. "I'm very sorry. My daughter is due to call me tonight with important news."

"Good news, I trust."

The only news bankers liked. "Perhaps. She's going to tell me if she is pregnant."

"I hope you are blessed." Mr. Ming smiled, teeth white as Ellie's estrogen pills.

Charlie nodded warmly. "We're going to build a terrific factory, too. Should be on-line by the end of the year."

"We are scheduled for lunch in about two weeks in New York?"

"Absolutely," said Charlie. Every minute now was important.

Mr. Ming bent closer, his voice softening. "And you will tell me then about the quad-port transformer you are developing?"

His secret new datacom switch, which would smoke the competition? No. "Yes." Charlie smiled. "Sure deal."

"Excellent," pronounced Mr. Ming. "Have a good flight."

The stairs to the lobby spiraled along backlit cabinets of

jade dragons and coral boats and who cared what else. Don't run, Charlie told himself, don't appear to be in a hurry. In London, seven hours behind Hong Kong, the stock market was still open. He pointed to his coat for the attendant then nodded at the first taxi waiting outside.

"FCC," he told the driver.

"Foreign Correspondents' Club?"

"Right away."

It was the only place open at night in Hong Kong where he knew he could get access to a Bloomberg box—that magical electronic screen that displayed every stock and bond price in every market around the globe. He pulled out his cell phone and called his broker in London.

"Jane, this is Charlie Ravich," he said when she answered. "I want to set up a huge put play. Drop everything."

"This is not like you."

"This is not like anything. Sell all my Microsoft now at the market price, sell all the Ford, the Merck, all the Lucent. Market orders all of them. Please, right now, before London closes."

"All right now, for the tape, you are requesting we sell eight thousand shares of—"

"Yes, yes, I agree," he blurted.

Jane was off the line, getting another broker to carry out the orders. "Zoom-de-doom," she said when she returned. "Let it rip."

"This is going to add up to about one-point-oh-seven million," he said. "I'm buying puts on Gaming Technologies, the gambling company. It's American but trades in London."

"Yes." Now her voice held interest. "*Yes.*"

"How many puts of GT can I buy with that?"

She was shouting orders to her clerks. "Wait . . ." she said. "Yes? Very good. I have your account on my screen . . ." He heard keys clicking. "We have . . . one million seventy thousand, U.S., plus change. Now then, Gaming Technologies is selling at sixty-six even a share—"

"How many puts can I buy with one-point-oh-seven?"

"Oh, I would say a huge number, Charlie."

"How many?"

"About . . . one-point-six million shares."

"That's huge."

"You want to protect that bet?" she asked.

"No."

"If you say so."

"Buy the puts, Jane."

"I am, Charlie, *please*. The price is stable. Yes, take this one . . ." she was saying to a clerk. "Give me puts on GT at market, immediately. Yes. One-point-six million at the money. *Yes*. At the money. The line was silent a moment. "You sure, Charlie?"

"This is a bullet to the moon, Jane."

"Biggest bet of your life, Charlie?"

"Oh, Jane, not even close."

Outside his cab a silky red Rolls glided past. "Got it?" he asked.

"Not quite. You going to tell me the play, Charlie?"

"When it goes through, Jane."

"We'll get the order back in a minute or two."

Die on the shitter, Charlie thought. Could happen to anyone. Happened to Elvis Presley, matter of fact.

"Charlie?"

"Yes."

"We have your puts. One-point-six million, GT, at the price of sixty-six." He heard the keys clicking.

"*Now* tell me?" Jane pleaded.

"I will," Charlie said. "Just give me the confirmation for the tape."

While she repeated the price and the volume of the order, he looked out the window to see how close the taxi was to the FCC. He'd first visited the club in 1970, when it was full of drunken television and newspaper journalists, CIA people, Army intelligence, retired British admirals who had gone native and crazy Texans provisioning the war; since then, the rest of Hong Kong had been built up and torn down and built up all over again, but the FCC still stood, tucked away on a side street.

"I just want to get my times right," Charlie told Jane when she was done. "It's now a few minutes after 9:00 p.m. on Tuesday in Hong Kong. What time are you in London?"

"Just after 2:00 p.m."

"London markets are open about an hour more?"

"Yes," Jane said.

"New York starts trading in half an hour."

"Yes."

"I need you to stay in your office and handle New York for me."

She sighed. "I'm due to pick up my son from school."

"Need a car, a new car?"

"Everybody needs a new car."

"Just stay there a few more hours, Jane. You can pick out a Mercedes tomorrow morning and charge it to my account."

"You're a charmer, Charlie."

"I'm serious. Charge my account."

"Okay, will you *please* tell me?"

Of course he would, but because he needed to get the news moving. "Sir Henry Lai just died. Maybe fifteen minutes ago."

"Sir Henry Lai . . ."

"The Macao gambling billionaire who was in deep talks with GT—"

"Yes! Yes!" Jane cried. "Are you sure?"

"Yes."

"It's not just a rumor?"

"Jane, you don't trust old Charlie Ravich?"

"It's dropping! Oh! Down to sixty-four," she cried. "There it goes! There go ninety thousand shares! Somebody else got the word out! Sixty-three and a—Charlie, oh Jesus, you beat it by maybe a minute."

He told her he'd call again shortly and stepped out of the cab into the club, a place so informal that the clerk just gave him a nod; people strode in all day long to have drinks in the main bar. Inside sat several dozen men and women drinking and smoking, many of them American and British journalists, others small-time local businessmen who long ago had slid into alcoholism, burned out, boiled over, or given up.

He ordered a whiskey and sat down in front of the Bloomberg box, fiddling with it until he found the correct menu for real-time London equities. He was up millions and the New York Stock Exchange had not even opened yet. Ha! The big American shareholders of GT, or, more particularly, their analysts and advisers and market watchers, most of them punks in their thirties, were still tying their shoes and kissing the mirror and soon—very soon!—they'd be saying hello to the receptionist sitting down at their screens. Minutes away! When they found out that Sir Henry Lai had died in the China Club in Hong Kong at 8:45 p.m. Hong Kong time, they would assume, Charlie hoped, that because Lai ran an Asian-style, family-owned corporation, and because as its patriarch he dominated its governance, any possible deal with GT was off, indefinitely. They would then reconsider the price of GT, still absurdly stratospheric and dump it fast. Maybe. He ordered another drink, then called Jane.

"GT is down five points," she told him. "New York is about to open."

"But I don't see *panic* yet. Where's the volume selling?"

"You're not going to see it here, not with New York opening. I'll be sitting right here."

"Excellent, Jane. Thank you."

"Not at all. Call me when you're ready to close it out."

He hung up, looked into the screen. The real-time price of GT was hovering at fifty-nine dollars a share. No notice had moved over the information services yet. Not Bloomberg, not Reuters.

He went back to the bar, pushed his way past a couple of journalists.

"Another?" the bartender asked.

"Yes, sir. A double," he answered loudly. "I just got very bad news."

"Sorry to hear that." The bartender did not look up.

"Yes." Charlie nodded solemnly. "Sir Henry Lai died tonight, heart attack at the China Club. A terrible thing." He slid one hundred Hong Kong dollars across the bar. Several of the journalists peered at him.

"Pardon me," asked one, a tall Englishman with a riot of red hair. "Did I hear you say Sir Henry Lai has *died*?"

Charlie nodded. "Not an hour ago. I just happened to be standing there, at the China Club." He tasted his drink. "Please excuse me."

He returned to the Bloomberg screen. The Englishman, he noticed, had slipped away to a pay phone in the corner. The New York Stock Exchange, casino to the world, had been open a minute. He waited. Three, four, five minutes. And then, finally, came what he'd been waiting for, Sir Henry Lai's epitaph: GT's price began shrinking as its volume exploded—half a million shares, price fifty-eight, fifty-six, two million shares, fifty-five and a half. He watched. Four million shares now. The stock would bottom and bounce. He'd wait until the volume slowed. At fifty-five and a quarter he pulled his phone out of his pocket and called Jane. At fifty-five and seven-eighths he bought back the shares he'd sold at sixty-six, for a profit of a bit more than ten dollars a share. Major money. Sixteen million before taxes. Big money. Real money. Elvis money.

IT WAS ALMOST ELEVEN when he arrived back at his hotel. The Sikh doorman, a vestige from the days of the British Empire, nodded a greeting. Inside the immense lobby a piano player pushed along a little tune that made Charlie feel mournful, and he sat down in one of the deep chairs that faced the harbor. So much ship traffic, hundreds of barges and freighters and, farther out, the supertankers. To the east sprawled the new airport—they had filled in the ocean there, hiring half of all the world's deep-water dredging equipment to do it. History in all this. He was looking at ships moving across the dark waters, but he might as well be looking at the twenty-first century itself, looking at his own countrymen who could not find factory jobs. The poor fucks had no idea what was coming at them, not a clue. China was a juggernaut, an immense, seething mass. It was building aircraft carriers, it was buying Taiwan. It shrugged off turmoil in Western stock markets. Currency fluctuations, inflation, deflation, volatility—none of these things compared to the fact that China had eight hundred and fifty million people under the age of thirty-five. They wanted everything Americans now took for granted, including the right to piss on the shoes of any other country in the world.

But ha! There might be some consolation! He pushed back in the seat, slipped on his half-frame glasses, and did the math on a hotel napkin. After commissions and taxes, his evening's activities had netted him close to eight million dollars—a sum grotesque not so much for its size but for the speed and ease with which he had seized it—two phone calls!—and, most of all, for its mockery of human toil. Well, it was a grotesque world now. He'd done nothing but understand what the theorists called a market inefficiency and what everyone else knew as inside information. If he was a ghoul, wrenching dollars from Sir Henry Lai's vomit-filled mouth, then at least the money would go to good use. He'd put all of it in a bypass trust for Julia's child. The funds could pay for clothes and school and pediatrician's bills and whatever else. It could pay for a *life*. He remembered his father buying used car tires from the garage of the Minnesota Highway Patrol for a dollar-fifty. No such thing as steel-belted radials in 1956. You cross borders of time, and if people don't come with you, you lose them and they you. Now it was an age when a fifty-eight-year-old American executive could net eight million bucks by watching a man choke to death. His father would never have understood it, and he suspected that Ellie couldn't, either. Not really. There was something in her head lately. Maybe it was because of Julia, but maybe not. She bought expensive vegetables she let rot in the refrigerator, she took Charlie's blood-pressure pills by mistake, she left the phone off the hook. He wanted to be patient with her but could not. She drove him nuts.

HE SAT IN THE HOTEL LOBBY for an hour more, reading every article in the *International Herald Tribune*. Finally, at midnight, he decided not to wait for Julia's call and pulled his phone from his pocket and dialed her Manhattan office.

"Tell me, sweetie," he said once he got past the secretary.

"Oh, Daddy . . ."

"Yes?"

A pause. And then she cried.

"Okay, now," he breathed, closing his eyes. "Okay."

She gathered herself. "All right. I'm fine. It's okay. You don't have to have children to have a fulfilling life. I can handle this.

"Tell me what they said."

"They said I'll probably never have my own children, they think the odds are—all I know is that I'll never hold my *own* baby, never, just something I'll never, ever do."

"Oh, sweetie."

"We really thought it was going to work. You know? I've had a lot of faith with this thing. They have these new egg-handling techniques, makes them glue to the walls of the uterus."

They were both silent a moment.

"I mean, you kind of expect that *technology* will work,"

Julia went on, her voice thoughtful. They can clone human beings—they can do all of these things and they can't—" She stopped.

The day had piled up on him, and he was trying to remember all that Julia had explained to him about eggs and tubes and hormone levels. "Sweetie," he tried, "the problem is not exactly the eggs?"

"My eggs are pretty lousy, *also*. You're wondering if we could put *my* egg in another woman, right?"

"No, not—well, maybe yes," he sighed.

"They don't think it would work. The eggs aren't that viable."

"And your tubes—"

She gave a bitter laugh. "I'm *barren*, Daddy. I can't make good eggs, and I can't hatch eggs, mine or anyone else's."

He watched the lights of a tanker slide along the oily water outside. "I know it's too early to start discussing adoption, but—"

"He doesn't want to do it. At least he says he won't," she sobbed.

"Wait, sweetie," Charlie responded, hearing her despair, "Brian is just—Adopting a child is—"

"No, no, *no*, Daddy, Brian doesn't *want* a little Guatemalan baby or a Lithuanian baby or anybody else's baby but his own. It's about his own goddamn *penis*. If it doesn't come out of *his* penis, then it's no good."

Her husband's view made sense to him, but he couldn't say that now. "Julia, I'm sure Brian—"

"I *would* have adopted a little baby a year ago, two years ago! But I put up with all this shit, all these hormones and needles in my butt and doctors pushing things up me, *for him*. And now those *years* are—Oh, I'm sorry, Daddy, I have a client. I'll talk to you when you come back. I'm very—I have a lot of calls here. Bye."

He listened to the satellite crackle in the phone, then the announcement in Chinese to hang up. His flight was at eight the next morning, New York seventeen hours away, and as always, he wanted to get home, and yet didn't, for as soon as he arrived, he would miss China. The place got to him, like a recurrent dream, or a fever—forced possibilities into his mind, whispered ideas he didn't want to hear. Like the eight million. It was perfectly legal yet also a kind of contraband. If he wanted, Ellie would never see the money; She had long since ceased to be interested in his financial gamesmanship, so long as there was enough money for Belgian chocolates for the elevator man at Christmas, fresh flowers twice a week, and the farmhouse in Tuscany. But like a flash of unexpected lightning, the new money illuminated certain questions begging for years at the edge of his consciousness. He had been rich for a long time, but now he was rich enough to fuck with fate. Had he been waiting for this moment? Yes, waiting until he knew about Julia, waiting until he was certain.

He called Martha Wainwright, his personal lawyer. "Martha, I've finally decided to do it," he said when she answered.

"Oh, Christ, Charlie, don't tell me that."

"Yes. Fact, I just made a little extra money in a stock deal. Makes the whole thing that much easier."

"Don't do it, Charlie."

"I just got the word from my daughter, Martha. If she could have children, it would be a different story."

"This is bullshit, Charlie. Male bullshit."

"Is that your legal opinion or your political one?"

"I'm going to argue with you when you get back," she warned.

"Fine—I expect that. For now, please just put the ad in the magazines and get all the documents ready."

"I think you are a complete jerk for doing this."

"We understand things differently, Martha."

"Yes, because *you* are addicted to testosterone."

"Most men are, Martha. That's what makes us such assholes."

"You having erection problems, Charlie? Is *that* what this is about?"

"You got the wrong guy, Martha. My dick is like an old dog."

"How's that? Sleeps all the time?"

"Slow but dependable," he lied. "Comes when you call it."

She sighed. "Why don't you just let me hire a couple of strippers to sit on your face? That'd be *infinitely* cheaper."

"That's not what this is about, Martha."

"Oh, Charlie."

"I'm serious, I really am."

"Ellie will be terribly hurt."

"She doesn't need to know."

"She'll find out, believe me. They always do." Martha's voice was distraught. "She'll find out you're advertising for a woman to have your baby, and then she'll just flip out, Charlie."

"Not if you do your job well."

"You really this afraid of death?"

"Not death, Martha, oblivion. Oblivion is the thing that really kills me."

"You're better than this, Charlie."

"The ad, just put in the ad."

He hung up. In a few days the notice would sneak into the back pages of New York's weeklies, a discreet little box in the personals, specifying the arrangement he sought and the benefits he offered. Martha would begin screening the applications. He'd see who responded. You never knew who was out there.

HE SAT QUIETLY THEN, a saddened but prosperous American executive in a good suit, his gray hair neatly barbered, and followed the ships out on the water. One of the hotel's Eurasian prostitutes, watched him from across the lobby as she sipped a watered-down drink. Perhaps sensing a certain opportune grief in the stillness of his posture, she slipped over the marble floor and bent close to ask softly if he would like some company, but he shook his head no—although not, she would see, without a bit of lonely gratitude, not without a quick hungered glance of his eyes into hers—and he continued to sit calmly, with that stillness to him. Noticing this, one would have thought not that in one evening he had watched a man die, or made millions, or lied to his banker, or worried that his flesh might never go forward, but that he was privately toasting what was left of the century, wondering what revelation it might yet bring.